TRAIN MAN

Also by P. T. Deutermann

TRAIN MAN

P. T. DEUTERMANN

ST. MARTIN'S PRESS ☒ NEW YORK

Deu

Library of Congress Cataloging-in-Publication Data
Deutermann, Peter T.
        Train man / P.T. Deutermann.—1st ed.
            p.   cm.
        ISBN 0-312-20375-6
        I. Title.
    PS3554.E887T72   1999
    813'.54—dc21   99–23846
                                                    CIP

First Edition: October 1999

10 9 8 7 6 5 4 3 2 1

To the memory of the brave men who constructed
the magnificent iron and steel railroad bridges
over the Mississippi River during the past century.
They were amazing feats of civil engineering then,
as they would be today if we had to replicate them.

Acknowledgments

I am indebted to Simmons-Boardman Books, Inc., and John Armstrong, for permission to use material from *The Railroad, What It Is, What It Does*, which I found to be the best all-around reference for the layman on railroad operations. Also to Harold A. Ladd, author of the definitive *U.S. Railroad Traffic Atlas*, for permission to extract definitions relating to railroad terms. I also consulted Ronald Kessler's excellent book, *The FBI*, for insights on Bureau organization and argot, which were very useful preparation for talking to people within the Bureau itself. I'm particularly indebted to Don Schwartz, Scott Curley, Bob Lauby, Neal Schiff, and the FBI Public Information Office, for technical advice on government law enforcement organization and other matters. In some cases I have taken considerable dramatic liberties with their inputs, and I have deliberately blurred the technical details relating to some of the bridges and to explosives and demolition techniques. Other omissions and/or errors are, of course, all mine. The characters in this book are entirely fictitious; any resemblance to persons living or dead is purely coincidental. And finally, my thanks to George Witte and Carol Edwards, editors extraordinary, and to Nick Ellison for some truly outstanding representation work.

TRAIN MAN

THE RIVER was boundless and almost invisible in the darkness. He could sense the power of the late-spring rains in the current as a sizzle of foam surfaced a pungent stink of alluvial mud. He was letting the current carry him down toward the bridge. He was running the Missouri side to ensure that no one in the fish camp on the Illinois side could hear the boat. He watched for the lights of barge traffic but saw only the occasional wink from a channel buoy glimmering across the wide river. The spectral structure of the bridge loomed ahead, its black steel trusses nearly invisible.

He shifted his weight in the small boat, pulling the coil of damp rope closer as the small outboard muttered behind him at idle speed. He fingered the steel points of the grapnel hook and touched the bulky backpack with his left hand. To his far left, a faint yellow aurora silhouetted the bluffs where line signal lights pointed their message of caution eastward into Illinois. He scanned the top of the bluffs for signs of life. There was a public housing project next to the tracks up there in the village of Thebes, and he wanted to make sure no one was up and about on the rail line. As the bridge took shape, he reached back and shoved the engine tiller to starboard, twisting the throttle handle slightly to bring him back out into the middle of the river. He wanted to be on line with the western channel pier tower, which was gaining definition now in the darkness. The tower was one of two massive concrete and steel structures supporting the center span across the main channel. It loomed nearly one hundred feet over the river.

The sounds of the swollen river began to echo off the steel girders up above as he neared the bridge. His hand tightened on the tiller and then he switched the engine into reverse and again advanced the throttle. The aluminum boat responded at once, its head falling off slightly to starboard as the prop bit in, until he was nearly stationary on the river, hovering in the black current a few yards upstream of the base of the pier tower. He could see the iron ladder hanging down now, its side rails throwing up two light gray bow waves in the muscular spring current. He reduced the rpm, letting the boat drift down to bump against the ladder. He held that position for an instant and then let go of the tiller, leaned forward, and hooked on the grapnel even as the stern of the boat began its swing out into the current, coming around rapidly as he scrambled to secure the rope to the front seat. The boat fetched up against the base of the pier tower with a muffled metallic bump, bow into the current now, facing upriver. With the engine at idle, he sat back, craning his neck to look straight up.

He was directly under the western end of the center span. The river sound was louder here, the noise of the eddies and ripples echoing off the underside of the bridge. For one vertiginous moment, the tower looked like the bow of an enormous ship rushing at him through the current. He looked over to the west bank, dark and shapeless, hidden behind three more pier towers between his mooring and the shore. He checked the rope again and then pressed the light button on his watch. Early. Good. But time to go.

He crouched in the boat, steadying himself against the sudden tilt, and hefted the backpack onto his knees. He checked the mooring rope again and then swung the heavy backpack slowly onto his back, struggling to keep his balance while he secured it. He put on leather gloves and reached for the ladder, testing it, feeling the scabrous paint rubbing off on his leather gloves, and then hoisted himself up onto the rusty rungs in one smooth motion. He steadied himself on the first rung, getting his balance, getting the feel of the pack, and then began to climb. The ladder swayed a little under his weight; some of the bolts holding it to the con-crete pier had rusted away. It was an old bridge.

Forty rungs later, he reached the first steel platform and pushed his head through the open trapdoor through which the ladder was suspended. He was puffing a little, but his heart was still beating faster more from excitement than fatigue. The pack caught momentarily on the edge of the trapdoor, but he turned sideways and squeezed through. Once on the grating of the platform, he rested, sitting with his knees up, his head forward to balance the pack. He could really hear the river up here, an incessant slushing noise echoing off all the concrete and the steel facets around him. He checked his watch again and then sat there for another minute until his breathing returned to normal. Time to go, he told himself again.

He heaved himself up off the grating and made his way around to the other side of the platform, to the second ladder. Climbing purposefully now in the darkness, he climbed the final thirty feet up to the main girders supporting the track-bed structure. The ladder continued up the side of the trussed arch. He stepped off the ladder and then swung the pack off his back, laying it down carefully on the grating, making sure it was not going to roll off the edge. Leaving the pack, he walked ten feet along the platform toward the junction of the arched truss and the main horizontal girders of the center span. He found the short ladder and climbed down to the ledge under the track bed where the truss pins were. He knelt down and felt along the steel in the darkness, running his gloved hands over silver dollar–size rivet heads until he found the pins.

He reached into his vest pocket and removed a slim black metal flashlight, pointed it down into the space between the pin housing and the truss girders, and switched it on. He saw the cavity he was looking for. It matched the plans. He switched off the light and climbed back up the ladder. From where he stood on the catwalk, the shining steel of the westbound track was level with his face. He reached forward and hefted himself up to the track level until he was standing astride the westbound tracks. He faced west and experienced the premonitory tingle of dread everyone feels when standing on a railroad track, the gleaming rails pregnant with the possibility that a train might loom out of the darkness, or was coming up even now, unseen, from behind. He stepped across the tracks and hopped down onto the pine-board catwalk between the track beds. The planks reeked of creosote and engine oil, and he was surprised at their flimsiness. The river below remained invisible, but as the cool wet air rose between his legs, he visualized the hundred or so feet of space between his perch on the catwalk and the swirling surface below. He clambered back over the tracks and swung down to the outside catwalk to study the structure.

The center span track-bed support truss was attached to a pier tower at each end; it was nearly two hundred feet long. The overhead truss arch was constructed of a heavy steel vertical lattice on the upstream and downstream sides of the bridge, woven together with a lateral truss structure across the top. At the base end of each truss, well below the track bed, were two massive steel boxes, one on each side of the tracks. Each box had a twelve-inch-diameter hole drilled horizontally through the center. Passing through the hole was the main truss pin, a foot in diameter and five feet long. The pin ends penetrated the box on either side and were secured in a saddle mounting, which, in turn, was bolted to the concrete ledge on the pier tower itself. The descending side girders of the arch were supported entirely by these pins.

Each saddle mounting was nestled in a concrete cavity cast into the inside face of the pier tower. The entire structure looked as solid as Gibraltar, but he knew that the truss could actually flex on its pins, expanding and contracting in broiling summer heat and icy winter air, and also when the weight of a train deflected the center span. These massive river bridges were alive, and, while they looked solid, they were flexing all the time, in infinitesimally small degrees, reacting to the stresses of temperature, winds, and loads. Even the pins themselves were free to rotate in fractions of degrees.

He returned for the backpack and dragged it down to the pin structure on the upstream side of the bridge. He opened the pack and carefully lifted out the two coffee cans packed on top of the contents, setting them gingerly down on the main horizontal girder. He dug back into the pack, first extracting two pieces of wooden dowel, each a foot long and one inch in diameter, and then brought out six limp plastic bags of black powder, stacking them in a mound. Holding the flashlight in his teeth, he leaned into the cavity and began to pack the three-pound bags into the space between the inner face of the concrete cavity and the inside face of the pin. After he had placed two bags, he set one of the wooden dowels upright between them. Moving faster now, he set the remaining four bags, pushing and tamping them until they fit snugly around the inside face of the dinner plate sized pin, with the dowel protruding a few inches at the top. The stack completely covered the round face of the pin, with no space between it and the concrete.

He picked up the backpack, clambered across the track beds to the opposite side of the bridge, and repeated the arrangements, again packing the bags between the pin and the concrete cavity's inside face. When he

4

was finished, he checked his watch. If the operating schedule was holding, he had just under thirty minutes. Enough time, he thought. Just enough.

He climbed back to the upstream side of the tracks, picked up one of the coffee cans, and returned to the downstream side of the bridge. With the flashlight again in his teeth, he removed the plastic lid, discarding it into the darkness, and then removed a quarter stick of dynamite and one blasting cap from a nest of torn rags in the can. He unwrapped the wax paper at one end of the quarter stick and gently pushed the blasting cap into the center hole until only its silvery top and two hanks of bell wire stuck out. Leaning over the powder stack, he wiggled the dowel, raising it carefully so as not to disturb the stack. He threw the dowel into the river below and then slid the quarter stick into the hole, fitting it snugly into the stack until only the wires were visible.

He reached into another vest pocket and pulled out two coils of bell wire and a roll of electrical friction tape. He twisted the bared conductor from one of the coils together with one of the blasting cap's wires and then put the coil down on the concrete. He repeated the procedure with the second coil of bell wire, then pitched the coffee can off the bridge. Some of the rag fragments drifted up between his feet momentarily in the updraft.

Standing up, he tied the two lengths of bell wire together in a loose knot and wrapped the married wires around a section of the truss base. He taped the bare connections, picked up the empty backpack, and then began threading the two lengths of bell wire under the eastbound track bed, across the catwalk, then under the westbound track bed, reaching down under the rails as he made his way back across to the upstream side.

Ignoring the black emptiness beneath his feet, he set the two coils of wire down, being careful not to let them touch each other. He then opened the second can and set the north-side powder stack's trigger, once again discarding the dowel and the second can into the river. When he was finished, he took one of the bell-wire coils from the south-side stack and connected it to one of the wires coming from the blasting cap in the north-side stack. He reached into another vest pocket and removed what looked like a regular-size plastic flashlight, except that its light lens and back cap had been removed. There was a single wire sticking out from either end of the flashlight case. He placed the flashlight on top of the stack. He removed a small plastic box the size of a cigarette pack from his vest.

He knelt down and taped the truncated flashlight on top of the stack with some friction tape. He frowned as he realized that the plastic bags of black powder had already begun to accumulate dew, causing the tape to slip. He then connected the second wire from the blasting cap to the single wire coming out of one end of the flashlight case. He grasped the small plastic box in his left hand and pulled a thin springy wire out of the box to a length of six inches, letting it hang down out of his hand. He pressed a button on the face of the box. A half-inch-wide lighted window appeared, much like the dial on an electronic watch. Digital lettering in the dial read PRESS ONCE FOR TEST. He pressed the button again. The box emitted a tiny beep. The lettering now read PRESS TWICE FOR SET. Still holding the light in his teeth, he attached the remaining wire from the flashlight case to a terminal on the end of the plastic box, then attached the box to the steel saddle mounting right next to the stack of powder bags. A magnet on the box case held it securely and also established a ground. He then connected the end of the second wire from the south-side stack to the second terminal on the box and taped the bare connections.

He leaned back and removed the flashlight from his teeth, exhaling forcefully, suddenly aware that he had been holding his breath. He looked at his watch again. Twenty minutes until train time. Now for the Detacord. He retrieved the backpack and extracted a coil of what looked like television coaxial cable, except that it was denser than coax and felt more like solidified putty. He taped off one end of the Detacord to a section of the truss and then walked west down the catwalk toward the center of the next inboard span, unreeling the cable and pressing it flat against the wood planks of the catwalk until he had sixty feet straightened out on the catwalk. Then he went back to the start point and pulled it back in toward him. When he had the end in his hands, he got down on his hands and knees and began stuffing the cable into a crack between the top of the massive side I beam and the steel frame of the deck, pushing it up and behind the nest of utility cables already there. When it was all in place, he taped off the far end and went back to the explosives stack. He inserted the end into the powder stack, slipping it between the black powder bags until he felt the end physically touch the quarter stick. Then he stood up.

Reflexively, he looked over his shoulder to the west, but there was still only the darkness, broken by a faint halo of lights on another distant signal tower. He thought about going up to the track bed and placing his ear against a steel rail to see if he could really hear a train coming from a long way off, then decided against it. He stretched, his knees cracking in the silence. The gentle breeze cooled the perspiration on his face. He took a deep breath; up here, the bridge smelled of old steel, rust, diesel engine grease, and sunbaked creosote. He almost thought he could hear the bridge creaking in the darkness as the river tugged relentlessly at its concrete feet.

He went back down to the truss pins, closed his eyes, and reviewed the connections in his mind. The circuit was correct. The placement was correct. Another image slid into his mind, that of a dismembered and burned-out car, mangled almost beyond recognition, surrounded by several yellow body sheets around it covering . . . He swallowed hard, opened his eyes quickly, and took another deep breath.

That's why you're here, he told himself. That's what this is all about. So do it. Do it now.

He leaned into the pin-mounting cavity, felt for the box, and pressed the button. Once. *Beep.* Twice. *Beep.* The little box emitted three beeps in quick succession, and the words RECEIVER SET appeared in the window. He nodded, picked up the empty backpack, put the tape and the red penlight into it, and slipped it over his shoulders. Moving quickly, he retraced his climb back down the side of the pier tower to the boat. The motor was still idling quietly, burbling oily two-stroke smoke at the back of the boat. He looked over in the direction of where the fish camp should be, but all was still darkness there.

He dropped into the boat, settled himself on the seat, and advanced the throttle. When the tension came off the rope, he jerked the grapnel hook off the iron rung of the ladder. The boat's head fell off immediately in the current, and he was swept diagonally across the center channel, moving out from under the bridge as the current carried him downriver. He pointed the boat directly back upstream and gave it more power, turning left slightly to hug the west bank again, keeping away from the darkened trailers three hundred yards across the river. A minute later, he passed back beneath the bridge and then headed upstream, opening the distance from the bridge slowly as the small motor fought the powerful current. The banks on either side remained completely dark except for the glow of streetlights up in the village of Thebes on the right-hand bluffs.

Once he had the boat steadied on course, he extracted the transmitter box from his inside vest pocket. It was warm in his hands. He pulled a spring-wire antenna out of its side and then held the box in one hand as he continued to steer the little boat upriver. He felt for the slide button on its face and pushed the slide up until it hit a detent. A tiny red light came on. He looked at his watch and then cut back out into the center of the river, keeping one eye on the bridge behind him.

The train came out of the western darkness when he had gone about a third of a mile upstream from the bridge. At first, he was able to see only the loom of its wobbling approach light in the mist above the high banks, then the main headlight as the big diesels rumbled into view, a three-pack multiple unit strung together. The lead engine appeared to be pursuing the long yellow beam of its main headlight as a powerful drumming noise slowly overcame all the river noises.

He throttled down to idle and let the boat take its own head while he twisted around on the seat, holding the transmitter box now in both hands. His mouth was dry and his heart was beating rapidly again. Twelve years he'd been planning for this night. Twelve lonely, painful years, made bearable only by his plan for revenge. He watched the train come pounding out onto the bridge, past the first pier, the second, the third, the steel latticework flaring into sharp relief as the engine set passed each tower. The train seemed to slow down the farther it went out onto the bridge, but he knew that was just an optical illusion. The three big engines passed the fourth, main channel pier on the Missouri side and drove out onto the center span.

Still he waited. The engines thundered powerfully across the center span, the clicking and clacking noise of the individual cars audible now above the rumble of the diesels. The engine set passed through the first channel pier tower on the Illinois side, and then the next pier. He mentally counted one more second and then pushed the slide button on the transmitter all the way up against its spring tension.

A bright red glare appeared below the track level on the western channel pier tower, followed by two nearly simultaneous and shockingly powerful thumps. A flash of what looked like yellow-red lightning shot back toward the Missouri side underneath the bridge deck, momentarily transfixing the underside of the train in a photoflash. For a microsecond, he could even make out some of the letters on the sides of the boxcars. Then, almost in slow motion, the western end of the center span sagged and collapsed into the river with a great roaring crash. The eastern end remained attached for several seconds before it, too, pulled away from its tower and crashed down under the weight of the train. The boxcars and flatcars that were still west of the center spilled off the edge of the span into the river in neat succession, one after another, like huge steel lemmings, never faltering in their speed, each succeeding car pulled over the edge by the one in front. He stared as the cars thundered down off the bridge into the maelstrom below, bouncing first off the canted remains of the center span and then disappearing into the thrashing black water. Some of the tank cars came boiling back up on the surface for an instant before rolling over and disappearing again, carried off into the darkness by the swift current.

After thirty seconds, a pile of wreckage began to emerge from the river. It took almost another minute for the remainder of the train to make the plunge, with the last cars smashing directly onto the pile, then slipping and banging sideways into the water on either side, some remaining intact while others ruptured and spilled their contents out into the black river. Three or four cars from the east span had also gone into the river, but by now the front end of the train had disappeared around a curve on the east bank side. A vast cloud of smoke and mist was enveloping what was left of the bridge as echoes of the crash reverberated off the high banks.

He watched in awe as the destruction piled up, the booming and crashing of the cars getting louder and louder, until he realized that he had been drifting rapidly back toward the unfolding calamity. He hit the throttle then, going wide open to avoid being swept down into the steaming pile of wreckage. A silvery tank car surfaced right behind him in a great boiling uproar like some enraged steel hippo, its relief valves noisily venting acrid chemical vapors until it rolled over and submerged again into the roiling water.

He jerked the boat's head around and accelerated back upriver into the darkness, subconsciously aware that there were lights coming on now in the campers and trailers down at the fish camp. The noise of the wreck still seemed to be echoing along the high bluffs on the Illinois side, so he wasn't worried about his engine noise now, only about getting away. There was a sustained roaring noise behind him as another tank car's pressure-relief valve let go, assaulting the night air with a howl of venting product.

After rounding the first bend upstream, he could see all the way upriver to the old Cape Girardeau highway bridge six miles upstream, backlit by the lights of the barge port. He kept the boat going wide open, her bow aimed into the center of the channel. Now that he was around the bend, the only sound he could hear was the night wind whistling in his ears above the rattling buzz of the outboard. He glanced back over his shoulder, where an ominous glow was beginning to show through the tangled trees along the bend.

That's one, he thought, squinting against the wind in his face. He had expected to feel some exhilaration, some sense of victory, but he felt nothing at all. He remained dead inside, all of his emotions ground to powder long ago. He had achieved his first objective, nothing more, nothing less. After twelve years, the planning was over. He was now simply a force of nature. One down, he thought. Five to go.

2

MAJ. TOM MATTHEWS scanned the inside of the refrigerator, looking for something besides a cold beer. He was the Anniston Army Weapons Depot's command duty officer, which meant he had to refrain from his usual evening libation. He spied one can of Coke at the back and was reaching for it when the phone rang. His wife answered it in the other room and called him. She said it was Depot Operations. He looked at his watch. Dinnertime, he thought. Of course. He picked up on the kitchen phone.

"CDO," he said.

"Major, this is base ops. We've got a weird one."

"Is there any other kind, Sergeant?" Matthews said. "So—speak."

"We got an emergency call from an Air Force C-one thirty. Pilot says they got smoke in the cockpit, possible electrical fire on board. They're calling for clearance to make an emergency divert to our field."

"The big strip has been closed for years, Sergeant." Matthews said, glancing out the window. It was almost sundown. "The only operational part is the helipad. There aren't any landing lights outside of the pad. I don't think you can even see the lines anymore."

"Uh, sir? This guy is kind of excited. He isn't really asking for permission. Said they're inbound, ETA about eight minutes."

"Holy shit!" Matthews said, straightening up. "All right: Call the post fire department; tell them roll. On the double! I'll go directly to the airfield. And alert the med response team."

"Yes, sir!"

Matthews hung up and ran to get the duty truck's keys, his portable radio, and his wallet. A minute later, he was wheeling out of the post housing area in the Army pickup truck assigned to the depot's duty officer. He flipped on the radio and checked in with operations, which confirmed that the C-130 had declared an in-flight emergency and was headed directly into the Anniston field on a straight-in approach from the east. The base fire trucks were on their way to the landing strip. The chief was requesting instructions as to where to position.

"Hell, I don't know," Matthews said, running a stop sign and turning left onto the road that led back into the interior of the depot. "Which way is the plane coming in?"

"They say they're east of here, Major. They report they have our TACAN locked up and will come straight in." The sergeant was obviously getting excited.

Matthews turned onto the perimeter road that led past the weapons storage areas and accelerated. He was trying to remember how long the abandoned strip was. He was pretty sure it was oriented east-west, with the helipad area at the east end.

"Tell them to position the trucks down toward the western end of the field. If they crash, that's where the wreckage will end up. You notified the CO?"

"We've paged him, but we haven't had a callback yet."

Matthews acknowledged as he made another turn, this time onto a gravel road that ran along the north security perimeter of the weapons storage areas. He accelerated, fishtailing the truck a little. High double barbed-wire fences stretched into the forest on his left, crowned with coils of razor wire that glinted in his headlights. Except for the helipad, the Anniston landing strip had no lights, no tower, no nothing, he thought. The last time he'd been out here, the concrete had been growing weeds. He called operations again. "Sergeant, page the CO again. And call these guys; make sure they know this is an *abandoned* field. As in no facilities and weeds on the runway."

"Roger, sir."

He put the radio down and pushed the truck up to fifty. A C-130 was a turboprop job, so they ought not to need miles and miles of concrete to get it down and stopped, even if they were Air Force. But any successful landing depended on the plane's control systems working. Even a minor electrical fire could compromise everything. There was dust hanging above the road ahead, caused by the fire trucks, he hoped. Good. Then the sergeant came back to him.

"Major, pilot says they can't divert anywhere else; it has to be a military field, and things are turning to shit up there. He's estimating four minutes to touchdown, and he's requesting a full security perimeter on the field, and a decon team."

Matthews took his foot off the accelerator. "A *decon* team? What the hell's with that?"

"Sir, don't know. Guy's not talking right now. I kinda think they got their hands full, you know what I mean?"

Matthews acknowledged. He saw the final turn up ahead. The airfield was to the right, behind a wall of pine trees. The dust cloud from the fire trucks was heavier in his headlights. He slowed some more while he tried to figure out what to do. The Anniston Army Weapons Depot was a chemical weapons storage facility. A call for a decontamination team raised very specific implications, none of which were good.

"Okay," he replied with diminishing confidence. "Call away the CERT. And then get on to Fort McClellan and get an MP detachment over here. Emergency deployment, both units. And keep paging Colonel Anderson."

The sergeant acknowledged as Matthews made the final turn through a corridor of pines. The road opened onto a concrete apron area that surrounded a control tower whose doors and windows had been boarded up long ago. A single base fire department Suburban was caught in his headlights. He could see flashing emergency lights congregated down at the western end of the field as he drove up. He slammed on the brakes, grabbed his portable radio, and got out to talk to the fire chief, who was dressed out in full gear and holding a portable radio in gloved hands.

"I'm Major Matthews, the CDO," Matthews said. "They tell you what we got going here?"

"Just that we might have a possible plane crash," the chief said. He was a civilian, heavyset, in his fifties, and looking worried. The word CHIEF was emblazoned in Day-Glo letters on his fire hat. "I've got one foam-capable unit and two pumpers down at the far end. I've called for two more pumpers from the county. Somebody better call the main gate so they can get in. Maybe escort 'em back here?"

"Right," Matthews said. "I'll take care of that. This is a C-one thirty. Medium-big transport. Can your people deal with a big plane crash?"

"No, sir," the chief said bluntly. "But we're all they're gonna have."

Matthews nodded and scanned the darkened eastern skies. There was no sign of the approaching plane. He called ops and told them about the additional fire-fighting units coming to the base. The dispatcher reported that the depot's Chemical Emergency Response Team was on the way to the field and that McClellan had a dozen MP's MOPPing up and on the way.

"MOPPing up?"

"Yes, sir. I told them we were deploying our CERT. I figured the guard force ought to be dressed out if the CERT was needed."

Matthews swore to himself. He should have thought of that. The CERT was a specially configured detachment that came in to contain and decontaminate in the event of an accidental chemical weapons release. Of course the guards needed to have their chem suits and hoods with them. The sergeant was playing heads-up ball, and he told him so. He wondered what the hell was on this C-130.

"There, Major," the fire chief said, pointing into the eastern sky. Matthews looked up, and then back down, closer to the horizon formed by the tops of the dark pines at the eastern end of the runway. The winking red lights of an approaching aircraft were just visible in the distance. Almost as if the aircraft had seen them looking, its white landing lights blazed on. They couldn't hear it yet, though. Matthews shook his head and tried to think of what else he should be doing. The fire chief was closing up his suit and checking his air tank.

"Tell your people this is a cargo plane," Matthews said. "The only people on board will be up at the nose, so concentrate their rescue efforts there."

The chief nodded and began talking into his collar microphone. Matthews walked out closer to the edge of the actual runway. The headlights from his truck revealed that the concrete slabs were indeed overgrown with weeds. He wished they had time to go out there and sweep off any debris or objects, but those white lights were getting a lot closer and he could now hear the rumble of the four turboprop engines. He called ops and told them to hustle up with that CERT, that they had the aircraft in sight. The sergeant reported that he had lost comms with the aircraft.

Why me? Matthews thought, staring at the approaching aircraft. He really wished that Colonel Anderson were here. This was shaping up to be a lot bigger incident than he wanted to deal with.

The chief had climbed into his Suburban and was headed slowly down the left edge of the runway, emergency flashers going, as the big plane descended. Matthews held his breath when it appeared almost to clip the tops of the pine trees, and then it was swooping down in a roar, looking much too big for the narrow ribbon of old concrete suddenly illuminated in the harsh white landing lights. A moment before touchdown, Matthews saw in the glare of reflected light that the transport's landing gear was barely visible. He reflexively yelled a warning, but his shout was overwhelmed by the engine noise.

The pilot flew it directly onto the concrete. A horrendous screech of tortured metal erupted from the runway as the aircraft crunched down and was enveloped in a fiery trail of sparks and smoke. It hit hard enough that the near wing flexed dangerously down toward the concrete. One of the propellers spun right off its engine and went clattering diagonally across the runway right past Matthews, who didn't have time even to flinch. Then the plane was flashing down the strip, its roaring engines drowning out all thought as the remaining props were reversed. He instinctively threw up his hands at the fireworks display screaming past him, the sound of grinding and tearing metal battering his ears. The transport made a slow pirouette to the right while continuing to slide down the runway at a cocked angle, the noise beginning to diminish now.

But to Matthews's horror, its speed was not diminishing, and he realized an instant before it happened that the plane was going to take out one, if not two, of the fire trucks. They had positioned themselves in the middle of the end of the runway, instead of on the sides. The nose of the transport rammed one of the water-pumper trucks square amidships in a thumping crash that was audible above the screech of belly metal. A huge cloud of water was punched into the air by the crash as the truck went rolling like a toy into the pine woods at the end of the runway. The plane's right wing clipped the top of the other pumper, shredding the top-mounted ladders into toothpicks. Only the large foam-capable truck avoided being hit as the plane ground to a stop fifty yards off the runway in a deadly clatter of snapping pine trees.

Matthews ran for his truck as the plane disappeared in a cloud of dust and smoke at the edge of the woods. He shouted over his radio that the plane was down and had made a belly landing, and that they needed as many ambulances as they could get out here ASAP. As he got in the truck, he saw headlights approaching from the main base area. He sped right down the centerline of the runway, dodging chunks of metal and some smoking tires, following the black smear of the plane's track down the remaining three thousand feet of concrete. He hit the brakes hard when he realized he was about to drive right into the wreck. Ahead, the remaining fire truck was spewing a carpet of heavy viscous foam all along the smoking underbelly of the transport. He could not see the truck that had been hit, but the crew of the other one was running for the woods behind the aircraft. He could smell aviation fuel through the open windows as he skidded to a stop and turned the truck sideways, but so far, thank God, there was no fire. The stink of scorched metal assaulted his nose as he got out.

His portable radio went off. It was the CERT leader calling, requesting instructions. He looked back up the runway and saw the lights of four Humvee vehicles speeding in his direction. He directed them to hold on the north side of the landing strip and to send their medic forward on the double. He wanted to keep them generally upwind of whatever the hell was in that plane. Which reminded him: He did not have any chemical-defense protective clothing in this truck for himself, not even a mask.

The foam truck was illuminating the front end of the transport with spotlights, and Matthews could see firemen gathering around the smashed nose. He got back in the truck and followed the last of the CERT vehicles over to the north side of the strip, where he got out to talk to the team leader. Behind them, the second fire truck, minus its ladders, had approached and was now spraying water on the wreckage of the aircraft's nose. Matthews wanted to go over and help, but first he had to attend to the CERT. The team's leader, a Chemical Corps captain wearing a full chem suit but still carrying his hood, approached, saluted, and asked what was going down. The team's medic went sprinting toward the front of the aircraft, carrying two medical bags.

Matthews told the captain what he knew, which wasn't very much. "For some reason, they asked for a decon team, but then we lost comms," he said. "The plane hit one of the fire trucks. I've gotta get over there and find out how many casualties we have. You guys deploy, but stay upwind."

The captain acknowledged, and Matthews skirted the fuel-soaked foam and went toward the front of the aircraft. He got a sick feeling in his stomach when he saw the nose, which had been smashed in almost back to the wing root. He could see in the light from the fire truck's spotlights that a single human leg was sticking out of a tangle of conduits, wiring, and insulation on the left side of the aircraft. The fire truck that had lost its ladder was still in motion, a crewman spraying the top of the fuselage with a high-velocity mist of water. The other fire truck was completely upside down in a nest of shattered pine trees, with all of its wheels missing. He was surprised that none of the firefighters was tending to the overturned truck, until he realized that there were a lot of firemen working the plane. With a wave of relief, he realized they must have seen the plane coming and bailed out in time. The damaged pumper was creeping in right up against the nose of the transport. The CERT medic had scrambled up on top of the truck, poised to clamber onto the smashed nose. The fire chief was out of his Suburban, standing to one side, and directing the operation on his radio.

There was still a lot of smoke in the air, and fumes from the foam and JP-5 aviation fuel made it difficult to breathe. Except for the collision with the fire trucks, Matthews realized, it looked like they'd dodged a big bullet. The lake of aviation fuel seeping out from under the foam blanket was already saturating the deep gash of red clay and was beginning to pool behind and under the aircraft. The CERT captain reported that he was ordering his vehicles to get farther away from the fuel, and then the foam truck came back around and laid down some more of its noxious product.

Matthews went back to his truck and drove slowly around to the left side of the aircraft, being careful to stay out of the foam. He saw two county water trucks behind him and what looked like the base ambulance coming down the runway now in a blaze of lights and sirens. He got as close as he dared to the foam area, then got out. He radioed to the approaching rescue units to hold two hundred feet from the aircraft due to spilled fuel, but to send forward paramedics. Then he went over to the damaged fire truck, where several firemen were wrestling the remaining ladder off its side. They positioned it up against the less damaged side of the transport's nose and three firemen scrambled up to help the CERT medic look for survivors in the wreckage of the nose.

Matthews called into operations and told them to cancel the call for all available ambulances until they knew more about casualties. The chief brought over one of the firemen, who appeared to be staggering in shock. His face was white and he was talking a mile a minute, yammering on about how they'd just gotten out in time, how the wing had gone right over their heads, and about "the noise, man, the goddamned noise." The chief handed the man over to the base EMTs who had come hustling up from the Anniston ambulance.

"What've we got here, Chief?" Matthews asked, looking at the smoking aircraft fifty feet away.

"My people're okay," the chief said. "Although I don't know how in the hell they got out of that truck in time." He nodded up at the white leg sticking out of the wreckage. "Looks like at least one fatality."

The chief's handheld radio went off and he put it to his ear, listened for a moment, and nodded. "They've got one guy alive up there in the right seat, or what's left of it. The left-seat one is dead, and they think there's another guy at the back of the cockpit; no status on him. They're gonna have to cut their way in."

"Those county guys may have some Jaws," Matthews said, and the chief went to see. Matthews called operations and reported the casualty count, then waited for the knot of men struggling up on the fuselage to break their way into the aircraft. There were now just enough people up there that they were going to be getting in one another's way in a minute. He tried to think of what else he should be doing, but first they had to get the people out of there, especially if there were some survivors. The risk of a big fire was apparently past them, for which he thanked God.

Thirty minutes later, the rescue crew had broken into the main hatch and retrieved one crewman—"Make that crew*woman*," they reported. She was conscious, banged up, but apparently not seriously injured. The right-seat pilot was another story: serious abdominal injuries and both legs crushed under the remains of the console. The left-seat one was confirmed dead; apparently no other personnel on board. The crewwoman was asking to speak to the base CDO before they transported her. Insisting on it, as a matter of fact.

Matthews relayed all of this information to operations and then went to the nearest ambulance, where they were hooking the young woman up to an IV. More rescue people were climbing up to the area of the nose, and the fire truck had one of its big spotlights pointed at the right side. As he approached the ambulance, Matthews noticed that the foam blanket was creeping toward them. He told the driver of the ambulance to watch that foam, and then he pushed through the small crowd to the back of the ambulance. A white-faced woman who looked much too young even to be in the service was trying to talk. There was a nasty gash along the right side of her head, just below where her helmet would have been. Her green flight suit was stained with blood. She looked at him blankly as he bent near, and then she focused on his face. Behind him, one of the fire rescue crew blasted a CO_2 bottle into an engine turbine inlet; the sudden noise made everyone jump. Matthews identified himself as the CDO.

"Okay," she said. She asked the medics to step back so she could talk to Matthews. They looked at her for a moment, and then at Matthews. He shrugged and nodded his head. They moved away, out of earshot. She looked around to make sure she could not be overheard. He bent down to listen. She was plain-faced, with short black hair and frightened eyes. "As soon they get it stabilized, Major, back 'em out," she said. "Keep everyone out of the cargo compartment. Then we need a security perimeter set up a thousand feet away from the bird."

"We?" he asked. "What were you guys carrying in that thing?"

"This is a Special Operations Command aircraft, Major," she said immediately, as if she'd expected the question. "Is the base CO available?"

Matthews looked around. He couldn't see all that well in the glare of spotlights and headlights, but there was still no sign of Colonel Anderson. He told her they'd paged him. She nodded.

"Okay, sir," she said. "Him we can tell. This is Anniston, right? The chemical weapons depot? You've got a decon team here?"

"They're right over there. But they need to know what the hell they're facing."

She took a deep breath and then appeared to regret it. He started to call over the medics, but she grasped his arm. "I'm okay, Major. Scared shitless when we landed without wheels, maybe, but, hey, we're down and there was no fire. Are the pilot—?"

"They're working on the pilots right now. Look, I don't mean to be hassling you, Sergeant, but we have to know *something* about what we might have to clean up. What kind of agent or toxic—it drives what materials my guys'll need to preposition."

She hesitated. "If I tell you, then you, your people, and all these EMT people are going to have be locked down on base until the Pentagon decides what's going to happen next."

Matthews's portable radio squawked at him. "Hang on a minute," he said, and replied to the operations dispatcher.

"Colonel Anderson is inbound to your location."

Thank God, he thought as he acknowledged. He told the sergeant that the base CO was coming and that in the meantime he would go set up the security perimeter. He then gestured for the EMTs to come back over. The sergeant thanked him as he walked away.

Matthews gave the CERT leader deployment instructions and then went to meet the MP detachment trucks that were coming down the runway. The fire chief had sent the county units home now that the fire danger was apparently over. Matthews instructed the sergeant heading up the MP detachment to set up a basic security perimeter, and then he went to meet Colonel Anderson, who showed up driving his private car down the runway.

Col. Henry Anderson (Chemical Corps), U.S. Army, commanding officer of the Anniston Depot, was a tall, scholarly-looking officer. His often dry, precise demeanor belied a caring personality and a healthy quotient of skepticism toward the various bureaucracies with which the huge Anniston Depot had to contend. He took good care of his people, and they tended to take good care of him in return. The colonel, dressed in uniform, got out of the car, surveyed the huge transport squatting just off the end of the runway in a puddle of foam and aviation fuel, and shook his head. Matthews was very glad to see him. He saluted and briefed him on what had happened so far.

"Okay, Tom," Anderson said finally. "You and your people did well. I'm very sorry about the pilots. Now let's find out why the crew chief wants a decon team and all these guards."

"She wouldn't tell me anything, Colonel," Matthews said. "She said she would talk to you."

The EMTs had the sergeant stabilized in the back of the ambulance. When they saw the colonel coming, they said something to her and then backed away again. Matthews waited out of earshot with the EMTs while the colonel conferred with the crew chief. They told him the second pilot had just died. Matthews swore softly. An operational airfield's fire crew would have known not to park their trucks on the runway. He felt bad that he had not thought of it in time. He checked on the radio to make sure the security perimeter was getting set up, then checked in with ops to find out what reports had gone up the line about the incident. When he saw Colonel Anderson coming back out to the runway, he hurried to meet him.

"Okay, Tom," Anderson said. "Tell your CERT leader that the team is to stand down but remain in place. The team can relax MOPP except for three men, who are to be fully suited up at all times."

"Yes, sir," Matthews said. "But what's the toxic?"

Anderson hesitated. "What's in that aircraft is close-hold, need to know, Tom. Right now, I want you to put the CERT leader in charge here as on-scene commander; then mosey these fire-fighting people along as soon as possible."

Matthews reported the news about the second pilot. The colonel nodded sadly. "Ordinarily, with two people dead, we'd have to initiate a JAG-MAN investigation," he said. "But right now, what I want is to get their remains extracted as soon as possible, and then I want all these civilians out of here."

"Yes, sir, but—"

"All I can tell you now is that we need more security forces deployed out here just as soon as the fire department civilians are gone. I also want everyone to know where the wind is coming from at all times, and to be ready to get upwind of that aircraft on command."

Colonel Anderson gave Matthews a moment to let the significance of knowing where the prevailing wind was coming from sink in. "The Special Operations Command is sending in some technical people," the colonel continued. "They'll be arriving by helicopter in a few hours."

Matthews was baffled. What the hell was in that aircraft that required everyone nearby to have full protective gear ready *and* to know where the wind was coming from? It couldn't be chemical, and there were no more biological weapons. That left—nukes? On a C-130? Not likely. The damaged fire truck started up and began to back away from the aircraft.

"Get a landing signal team set up for the SOC helo," the colonel said. "It's probably going to be one of those big fifty-threes."

"Yes, sir," Matthews said, and hurried off to carry out the colonel's orders.

"Oh, and Tom?" Anderson called after him. "Tell ops to hold any further reports to the Army Operations Center until I personally release them. No matter how much noise Washington makes."

Whatever you say, boss, Matthews thought. He was very relieved that the colonel was on station and in charge.

Matthews was in the base operations center at midnight, wrapping up the incident summary report, when a call came through from Colonel

Anderson's office. There would be a meeting in Anderson's office in twenty minutes. Matthews, whose full-time job was depot operations officer, was to attend. He turned over the report-writing job to the assistant command duty officer, grabbed his portable radio, and went outside to get a breath of fresh air. The CO's office was within twenty minutes' brisk walking distance. He had been back at the ops center for several hours after the plane crash. The Army Operations Center in the Pentagon had been bombarding them with questions and requests for status reports when he returned to the ops center, but then all the noise had abruptly stopped. Colonel Anderson had apparently made a call.

The Special Operations Command team helicopter had arrived at 2200, touching down in the middle of the airfield. Matthews had been there, along with Colonel Anderson, one fire truck, and the base's helicopter-landing signal team. The huge CH-53 helicopter had nearly blown them all off the airfield with its eighty-mile-an-hour downwash. Colonel Anderson met the four-man team, then accompanied them down to the C-130. One of the CERT's Humvees was called in to move some equipment from the CH-53 down to the C-130. Matthews had been invited to remain outside of the security perimeter when the team went through. In the darkness, he had not been able to see who the team members were, or what the equipment was. Maybe he was now going to get the chance to find out.

The meeting was being held in the colonel's secure conference room on the second floor of the depot's headquarters building. Matthews was surprised to see MPs stationed around the hallway, and even more surprised when asked to show ID to get into the colonel's office complex, a place he went to routinely in the course of his duties as operations officer. He grabbed a cup of coffee before going into the conference room.

Once inside, he was surprised to see that Maj. Carl Hill, the depot's transportation officer, was at the table. Hill was a rail-logistics expert assigned to Anniston to oversee railroad operations. He and Matthews had served together for three years at the depot. Hill raised his coffee mug at Matthews in an early-morning *salud* and asked him what was going on.

"Beats me," Matthews said. "You heard about the plane crash?"

"Yeah, everybody heard. I understand the CERT went out there. But who's that in there with the boss?"

"Don't know," Matthews said, taking a place at the junior end of the conference table. "There's a team out on the field from the Special Operations Command, so it's probably their boss. How's twenty-seven thirteen coming?"

Hill rolled his eyes. Train 2713SP was the culmination of a special project that had been Hill's personal tar baby for more than two years. With the signature of the international Chemical Weapons Convention, each of the Army's chemical weapons depots had begun the process of destroying America's chemical weapons arsenal. One by-product of this extremely complex process was a huge number of bomb and rocket casings, from which all the toxic materials had been extracted. Although empty, the casings were being treated as being highly contaminated, and each of the depots was shipping its accumulated casings by special Army trains to the Army's large-scale chemical weapons destruction facility at Tooele, Utah.

"Same old, same old," Hill said. "Still putting out grass fires concerning the route. Although I think we're just about done, thank God. The train is all here, except for the engines. We'll begin the final consist build-out in two days." He looked at his watch. "I can't imagine what the hell they want me here for, though."

Matthews was beginning to get an idea about that when the colonel's inner office door opened and Anderson came in. With him was another colonel, wearing Desert Storm-style fatigues. He was a large man, not tall, but extremely broad, with severely short buzz-cut gray hair and a scowling froglike face. The black-lettered name label on his fatigues read Mehle. Matthews was surprised to see that Colonel Mehle was wearing a sidearm. Colonel Anderson introduced his two staff officers to Mehle, who simply nodded back at them. Mr. Personality, Matthews thought to himself. They all sat down.

"Gents," Anderson began, addressing Matthews and Hill, "Colonel Mehle is from the Special Operations Command. That was an SOC aircraft that crash-landed on our field tonight. What he's going to tell you is classified top secret. You two will be the only two staff officers in the loop here at Anniston besides me, and I'm sorry to inform you that we're all confined to the base until this matter is, um, resolved. Is that understood?"

Mehle leaned forward. He seemed to be uncomfortable in his chair. "*Confined* means that you are physically not to leave the base and you are not to have any communications with anyone outside the base until further notice," he said. His voice was rough and raspy, and Matthews thought he detected a faint Germanic accent. Hill spoke up.

"Colonel, I'm in the process of assembling a special weapons train. I have to talk to the environmental protection agencies of every state along the projected route just about daily, and also the railroad operations people."

Mehle frowned at him. "Your train is what we are here to talk about, Major." He looked over at Anderson. "Colonel?"

"Right. Carl, Tom, the C-one thirty that crash-landed here tonight was carrying—is carrying—four nuclear weapons."

Matthews nodded to himself. Nukes. He'd been right. Although nukes on a C-130 was rather unusual, now that he thought about it.

"Not American weapons," Mehle interrupted. "Russian warheads. Specifically, four Russian submarine torpedoes with nuclear warheads."

"Son of a bitch," Hill exclaimed. "Where in the hell did we get—"

"That is not for you to know, Major. And I would strongly discourage speculation."

"The problem," Anderson said quickly, "is that the crash damaged the weapons. The cargo compartment of that C-one thirty is now a hot zone. That's why we have the CERT there, and the guard force."

"Tritium leak?" Matthews asked, prompting a surprised look from Mehle. Matthews had been a nuclear weapons handling and safety officer at a previous command several years ago, in preparation for which the Army had sent him to a four-week nuclear weapons safety course.

"Yes, we think so," Mehle said grudgingly. "Although these weapons were leakers right from the beginning. But low-level. Now we have unacceptable radiation levels."

"Where were you taking these weapons?"

"To the INEL," Mehle said. "That's the Idaho National Engineering Laboratory, near Idaho Falls. They were going there for analysis, and then for entombment."

Hill had figured it out. He began to shake his head. "Now wait just a minute, Colonel Mehle," he began, but Anderson cut him off.

"No, Carl, go into the receive mode. This decision has come down from the highest levels of the Army staff in Washington. It's far too dangerous now to put those things on an aircraft. Your train was going to Utah. Now it's going to Idaho."

"But, sir, we've worked for two years to get clearance for twenty-seven thirteen. We've been up front with every agency involved—the state people, the federal people, the railroads. You know they'd never clear us if they got wind of this."

"They *will not* 'get wind' of this, Major," Mehle said forcefully. Colonel Anderson was clearly uncomfortable.

"Carl, and you, too, Tom: Colonel Mehle's people think the torpedo warhead casings were cracked in the crash landing. The radiation problem could get a lot worse than it is right now. We need to get those things out of here. Off this base, if you get my drift."

"You have special containment railroad cars already here at Anniston," Mehle said, still glaring at Hill. "We will need four of them, one per weapon. We are flying in lead-lined containers and environmental-control packages."

"Our instructions are to embed these weapons in twenty-seven thirteen," Anderson said. "Once they're in their proper containments, they'll represent no greater threat than the rest of what's going on that train."

"Colonel, I respectfully disagree," Hill said. "The stuff we're shipping is not contaminated with chemical weapons—just the binary constituents. They are, admittedly, toxic, but we're talking residual chemical contamination, not nerve gas. He's talking about actual atomic weapons. Russian weapons, for God's sake—who knows what level of safety those things have?"

Colonel Anderson sighed. He was not used to doing business this way. Matthews could tell he was sympathetic to what Carl was saying, but, having served for almost twenty years in the Army, Matthews could also detect the signs of an Army steamroller in motion here. Anderson looked at the wall clock. It was almost one in the morning.

"Gentlemen. We have our orders. Colonel Mehle's people will prepare the weapons. Tom, set up a plan to move them from the C-one thirty to double-lock assembly in Building Nine. Carl, figure out what you have to do to free up four heavy units to contain the weapons; then work up an integration plan."

"Including security en route," Mehle interjected. "We will need a twenty-four-hour guard force on board, and continuous secure communications capability."

Hill looked from Mehle to Anderson. "Yes, sir," he said finally. "I'll order up a command car for the train. And a bunk-room car for the guards. Colonel Mehle, you do understand this will be about a three-day trip, maybe longer?"

"My people will work on getting us priority," Mehle said.

"How will you do that, without telling the railroads why?" Matthews asked.

"That's my problem, Major. You attend to yours. Colonel Anderson, I think this meeting is over. You and I need to talk."

Anderson nodded and got up. He seemed reluctant to leave just like that, but Mehle was already moving toward Anderson's office. Matthews gave him a covert "we'll work it out" gesture, and then he was alone with Carl Hill.

"I can't believe they want to do this," Hill said softly. "It's taken us two—no, three years now to build trust and confidence with all those civilians on the outside about what we're doing. That the stuff we're shipping is toxic but essentially safe. That there are no actual weapons, just toxic constituents. And now—"

"Yeah, I know, Carl," Matthews said, getting up and gesturing for Hill to come with him, out of the conference room and away from Anderson's closed door. "But you and I both have families living here on base. The colonel's right: We need to get those damn things out of here, off this base, before a bad situation get's worse."

They walked down the hall, past the guards, and out into the night. Hill wasn't convinced.

"Okay," he said, "But suppose something happens en route? Never mind how we'd explain it—what the hell would we *do* about it?"

"It's not like they're going to go high-order or anything," Matthews said. "Not even the Russians keep the initiators with the weapons."

Hill stopped on the front steps. The headquarters compound was separated from the chemical operations side, whose windowless concrete buildings were a half a mile away. "That's not something you *know*, Tom. Fact is, we don't *know* anything about those weapons except what this Mehle chooses to tell us, and I sure as hell don't trust that guy. But I'll tell you one thing."

"What's that?"

"Don't care if I am just a major. I'm gonna want these orders in writing."

Matthews nodded thoughtfully in the darkness. In a way, such a request would be something of an insult to Colonel Anderson, but Carl was right. He was suddenly glad he was not the trainmaster for 2713. Not now. Not with nukes.

3

AT THE HEADQUARTERS of the Federal Bureau of Investigation on Ninth and Pennsylvania Avenue, Washington, D.C., Acting Assistant Director William Morrow Hanson was conscious that the shooting noise had subsided as he began his preparations on the indoor range. He concentrated on his prefire checks. He examined his Sig Sauer model P-228 pistol, put on hearing and eye protection, and then loaded two magazines.

He had deliberately chosen a qualification time in the middle of the morning on the headquarter's modified Practical Pistol Course range, but it never seemed to matter. The word got around that Hush Hamson was on the range, and people wanted to watch. It used to embarrass him, but now he just ignored the distraction and concentrated. He chambered and then holstered his weapon, pressed the range-request button on the pylon at the close-in position, and waited, hands at his side, long fingers flexing.

Seven yards away, in the semidarkened target area, a torso-shaped target swung around to face him. He drew and fired in one smooth motion. He reholstered the weapon and then repeated the draw-and-shoot procedure for five more rounds. When a yellow light came on at his pylon, he moved diagonally back to the fifteen-yard line and repeated the sequence against a new target. He did a timed reloading at the fifteen-yard line, then completed the sequence with six rounds at the twenty-five-yard position, and six more using his left hand. Then he did it all again with fresh targets.

He would never admit how much satisfaction he got out of a session on the PPC. Here there were no bureaucratic politics, politically correct sensitivities, or nuances of expression to worry about. Just that reflexive movement, the smooth draw-and-fire motion, the beautifully balanced weapon swinging out and locking up on the target as if it were an animate thing. Because his hands were large, he fired one-handed, standing in a slight off-center crouch, his left hand holding back his jacket while the right hand took care of business. There was no hesitation to aim or to squeeze one eye shut or to arrest his breathing. Just pull it and shoot it as the gun sight and the top centroid of the blob that was the target merged, everything and everyone around him frozen into a white-noise background, his mind's eye visualizing a laserlike white-hot vector of superheated air between the sight and the target's face each time the 9-mm pistol fired. The names Domingo, Herrera, Santos, and Belim whispering subliminally beneath the sounds of the gun firing. The rush that came when he chose which eye to put the round through and saw the paper wink to black. He could, by God, shoot.

After firing the modified PPC, he safed and checked his weapon and then put it down on the safety-line counter. He shook his arms out and took several deep breaths as he watched a small electronic counter box mounted above the safe line. Three quivering octal eights in an orange digital readout stared indifferently back at him. He removed his eye and ear protection. He was vaguely aware again of the people standing behind him. The box flickered and then registered 300. Perfect score. He ignored the murmuring behind him as a range-master's assistant snaked the paper targets back to the line. There were several other agents at headquarters who could pull a 300 score. What would cause the comments was the fact that the facial portion of each target had been reduced at eye level to a tattered blackened mask.

Hush picked up the magazines and carried the Sig, barrel high, the open slide visible, over to the cleaning station, where Morisson, the range-master, a buzz-cut ex-Marine, was waiting.

"Center of mass, Mr. Hanson?" the range-master murmured, eyeing the target sheets as Hush walked up. The next round of shooters, getting set up behind them on the PPC, were also examining the faceless target sheets.

Hush smiled but said nothing. He handed over his weapon so that the firearms maintenance people could clean and inspect it.

"Back in an hour, sir," Morisson said. As Hush walked away, the range-master put the fingers of each hand through the holes blasted into the targets' faces and held them up to the daylight like mail on a spindle.

Hush was intercepted by Special Agent Jimmy Watkins, who came walking rapidly across the foyer of the firing range in his direction, a yellow piece of Teletype paper in his hand. Watkins presented the piece of paper to Hush with an almost military flourish. He was the newest agent in IITF.

"Director needs to see you, sir," he announced, a little louder than necessary.

"Oh, goody," Hush said, scanning the message. A summons from the director's office was usually an occasion for trepidation. On the other hand, the subject line of the Teletype spoke of a bridge bombing. Put that together with a summons to the director's office and life might get interesting.

Hush and the younger agent strode across the range foyer toward the elevators, the younger man hustling to match Hush's long stride. Hush Hanson cut a Lincolnesque figure at just under six feet four inches. He walked in a sort of towering slouch, as if subconsciously aware that most doorways were going to give him a bare four inches of clearance. He had clear blue-gray eyes set under bushy salt-and-pepper eyebrows, and a long, lean, and somewhat morose face that was proportionate to his out-sized frame. His English ancestors would have recognized Norman features. His hair was long on top but short along the sides and back, in deference to the fact that it was beginning to go gray along the sides. His tailor-made dark suit was appropriately conservative for the FBI head-quarters. He wore a subdued silk tie on a white shirt, and highly polished size-twelve cordovan wing-tip shoes. Hoover would have approved.

Once in the executive elevator, Hush slipped on his reading glasses and read the Teletype. It was from Joseph Herlihy, the special agent in charge at the FBI Field Division Office in St. Louis, Missouri, reporting a major train accident on a bridge over the Mississippi River near a place called Cape Girardeau, Missouri. Hush vaguely remembered hearing something about a train wreck on CNN that morning, but he had not paid much attention. The interesting bit was what the SAC was reporting: The initial police investigation indicated that the bridge had not collapsed, as originally reported, but had been dropped with explosives. Hush frowned and took off the reading glasses.

"We have anything else on this?" he asked, waving the Teletype.

"No, sir," Watkins said, craning his neck to look Hush in the face. "The ops center sent us down that copy after the director's office called. I would surmise this will come to IITF?" Watkins, a sandy-haired, blue-eyed twenty-seven-year-old lawyer, had his notebook out, pen ready for instructions. Hush wondered if he had ever looked that young and inexperienced. Probably, he thought.

"Yes, I expect it will," was all he said. He stared down at the carpeted floor of the elevator as it rose to the seventh floor. He felt the usual butterflies in his stomach when summoned to the director's office. Hush Hanson has been assigned as the head of the FBI's Independent Investigations Task Force, abbreviated IITF, by the previous director following an extremely successful investigation, and simultaneously nominated for the Senior Executive Service rank of assistant director. The current FBI director, however, was keen on putting his own people in all the headquarters AD slots, and there had already been some sudden retirements, so several such appointments were still on hold. Hush was was one of these. He was serving in the IITF director's job as an *acting* AD at the civil service equivalent rank of GS-16, as were three other unit and section chiefs at headquarters.

The elevator doors opened onto the foyer of the executive suite. The director's office was at the north end of the main hallway, fronted by two glass doors and a receptionist's area. The executive suite also contained the offices of the deputy director, the chief of staff, some special assistants, two receptionists, the executive conference room, and a node of the headquarters main communications center. Hush could see several other of the more senior assistant directors standing around in the reception area, and one striking woman whom he felt he should recognize but whose name escaped him. Watkins took one look at the group of senior officers down the hall and prudently stepped back into the elevator as the door closed behind Hush.

Hush realized this was going to be an operational meeting: the assistant directors in charge over Criminal Investigation, Finance, Information Resources, National Security, the Inspection Division, Public and Congressional Affairs, and the Laboratory were present with their deputy assistant directors. The deputy director of the Bureau, whose name was George Wellesley, was standing right next to the glass doors. It was he who greeted Hush, who kept his face neutral as he walked up.

"Mr. Hanson," Wellesley said, looking up into Hush's face as he extended his hand.

"Good morning, Deputy Director," said Hush, shaking hands formally.

It was as if the two had never met. George Wellesley was a lean, dark-faced man who was two years younger than Hush. He had been an Air Force brigadier general in the highly politicized Military Doctrine Division of the Air Force headquarters staff before coming to the Bureau. The fact that he had not risen from the ranks within the Bureau made him impervious to the normal network of career allegiances and favors owed, as, no doubt, the director had intended when he brought him over from the Pentagon. Behind his back, his nickname within the Bureau was "Heinrich," as in Himmler, based partially on his facial resemblance to Hitler's notorious henchman, as well as on Wellesley's perceived bureaucratic role within the executive suite. The director called him George; Wellesley had warmly invited everyone else to address him as "sir" or, alternatively, "Deputy Director."

Wellesley looked at his watch and then at the group. "Gentlemen," he said. "And, ah, lady. Assistant Director Hanson and I will go in to see the director for a few minutes, and then we'll have the incident briefing in the executive conference room. This won't take too long."

Wellesley ushered Hush through the large mahogany door into the director's suite. The director was standing at a large library table covered with stacks of color-coded folders positioned all around it. His work habit was to attack each stack in turn, moving around the table throughout the day. The office was L-shaped and spacious, decorated more as a living room than as an office. In the long leg of the L, there was a second library table, with fewer folders, a large leather armchair with a communications console positioned alongside, a leather couch, side tables, bookshelves, and a formal fireplace at the end of the room. The short leg of the L contained a traditional desk and an executive chair. There were framed pictures of the President, the current Attorney General, and J. Edgar Hoover on the wall behind the desk.

The director gestured for his two visitors to sit down on the couch, which faced the armchair. The partially draped floor-to-ceiling windows behind them overlooked Pennsylvania Avenue, which disappeared in the morning smog into a perspective V pointing down toward the White House. Muted sounds of traffic below just penetrated the otherwise-quiet office, and the director's pen scratching was audible. All of the windows had small antieavesdropping wires attached.

"Just one second," he intoned as he finished with an executive summary paper, scrawling a comment across the bottom with a large red felt-tipped pen. No one else in the Bureau headquarters was permitted to use red ink.

"All right." He exhaled, closing the folder and coming over to settle into the leather armchair. He moved carefully, but with a grace belying his seventy years of age. "I gather someone's blown up a railroad bridge?"

"Yes, sir," replied the deputy director. "A rather big railroad bridge, over the Mississippi, complete with a freight train."

"We know for a fact that the bridge was deliberately sabotaged?" the director asked.

Hush squirmed a little on the couch; because of his height, he had to sit with his knees at a pronounced angle, almost like an adult attending a grade school teacher's conference. The couch, he noticed, was measurably lower than the director's chair. He folded his long hands together and listened carefully.

"Yes, sir," Wellesley replied. "Missouri and Illinois state police were first on the scene, followed by the railroad company's own police. Then the Union Pacific—they own the bridge—accident investigators. There's a Railroad Safety Office go team arriving from Washington this morning. The state police report that there are clear signs of explosives on the Missouri end of the center span. Since it was clearly not an accident, the RSO people may back out. Also, since the explosion was on the Missouri side, the Missouri State Highway Patrol CIB people have taken charge."

The director sighed. "Indeed," he said. "And I assume you recommend that IITF work this one?"

The previous director had constituted IITF to handle those large-scale investigations where several agencies of the government were likely to get involved. The current director had not as yet done anything to change this arrangement, although Hush was aware that some of the more senior assistant directors, especially Carswell, who was over National Security, wanted to carve up IITF in order to enlarge their own baronies. Hush was early-retirement eligible, and there had been some subtle probes in that direction over the past year. If the director went along with assignment of a major case to IITF, it would be considered a vote of confidence.

"Yes, sir," Wellesley was saying. "This apparently was a major train wreck, with nearly a hundred railroad cars in the river, tank cars, chemical spills—the works. ATF may disagree, but I definitely think we should run this one, and IITF gives us an interagency modality through which to run it. I also propose to put Acting AD Hanson in charge. Personally."

The director nodded, his patient expression suddenly giving Hush the feeling that the two of them might be walking through a script. "Well," the director said, "that's entirely within your prerogative, George. So why did you want to see me? Other than to confirm that we're getting on with it?"

Good question, Hush thought as he studied Wellesley's face. It was quite unusual, although not unheard of, for the Bureau to assign a head-quarters assistant director to handle a field case personally.

Wellesley put down his briefing folder. "Well, sir, I also want to solve an internal political problem."

"Yes?" The director still wasn't following. Neither was Hush.

"I want to assign Carolyn Lang—she's currently the assistant section chief in the office of Public and Congressional Affairs, as the number two on this case, working as task force deputy to Mr. Hanson."

Hush saw a flare of recognition in the director's hooded eyes and realized they had come to the heart of the matter. The director was looking over at him now with that zero parallax, eagle-eyed expression for which he was becoming famous in the Bureau. Headquarters people had some colorful descriptions for that look.

"How very interesting, George," the director murmured. "Are you annoyed with Mr. Hanson here?"

Wellesley smiled with his teeth and slowly shook his head. He let the import of what the director had just said grow on Hush, who had finally recognized Lang's name and made the connection with the woman in the anteroom outside.

"Why, no, sir, not at all," Wellesley said.

The director turned back to Wellesley. "Well, George, that's possibly a brilliant idea. Make her the number two on a high-profile investigation while letting her know she's on parade. If she screws this up, she's history. If she does well, we defang her with a promotion. I think I like it."

He turned to face Hush. "And, Mr. Hanson, I think you'll like it, too. Especially since I like it, as I'm sure you understand." The sounds of a traffic accident penetrated the room, and the director got up and walked over to look out of the windows overlooking Pennsylvania Avenue. "I presume you've recognized Carolyn Lang's name?" he said over his shoulder.

"Yes, sir, I've heard of Miss Lang," Hush said. The couch was beginning to feel confining. He was now more than ever convinced that the director and his deputy had preplanned this little scene.

"That's Ms. Lang to us mortals," the director said, still looking out the window. "You need to disregard the beautiful facade and think in terms of edged adjectives: *competent, lethal, ambitious, intelligent, cunning, ruthless.* She is a beautiful, professional woman who is intent on getting ahead and who purportedly has few scruples about taking prisoners along the way." He returned to his chair, giving Hush a moment to digest what he had just said. Wellesley studied his fingernails while the director spoke.

"Ms. Lang is not to be confused with anything so trivial as some kind of bra-burning feminazi," the director continued. "Although she has been known to brandish the sexual discrimination and harassment stick from time to time. But in point of fact, I think she's mostly ambitious. Both eyes firmly on the prize. Professionally focused." He treated Hush to another eagle-eye. "In other words, very much like us, Mr. Hanson."

Wellesley anticipated Hush's next question. "So why are we doing this?" he asked rhetorically. "Principally because there were some problems in her last tour out in the field. She was sent out to St. Louis to be the ASAC. Things didn't work out."

"If things didn't work out, why are we having this discussion?" Hush asked, being careful to address his question to Wellesley and not the director. He did not want to seem to be challenging the director, but it was the director who answered.

"Because we're not entirely sure what happened out there, and Himself Herlihy has chosen to be somewhat . . . reticent. The upshot was that another senior agent, who purportedly had been in line for the number-two slot there, retired abruptly amid some extremely disagreeable sexual harassment vapors."

Hush began to understand what was going on. Whatever had happened out in St. Louis, there was apparently just enough mud on the Bureau's skirts to require that Lang get another chance. Which meant that somewhere, somehow, she must have some senior top cover. It was also apparent that neither the director nor the deputy director was going to elaborate further.

"All right, I think I'm getting the picture," Hush said finally.

Wellesley's face brightened. "Good," he said. "That's settled, then."

"Not quite," the director said. He sat upright in his chair, his hands on his knees, looking very much like the Washington potentate that he was. Even with the height disparity between chair and couch, he had to look up to meet Hush's eyes. "Mr. Hanson, you are a temporary GS-Sixteen holding an assistant director's position. In an 'acting' capacity. *Ms.* Lang is a GS-Fifteen. As I said, she is an extremely competent investigator. She has been commended for her work in her specialty field of financial fraud. She displays a willingness to work as long and as hard as it takes to get the bad guys all the way to court, and to do so in a manner that not even all those creeping-Jesus liberals over at Main Justice can screw up the case."

Hush said nothing.

The director leaned forward in his chair. "I'm going to be completely up front with you, Mr. Hanson," he said. "When this case is over, one of you is going to get promoted to permanent SES level. The other of you will probably retire."

"And you will have the advantage of knowing what's at stake in your working relationship, won't you?" Wellesley added. They both looked at Hush expectantly. In other words, Hush thought, the woman is a problem. You have a choice: Do her in for us, and you get the permanent promotion. Or don't, and we'll give it to her. They were both still looking at him. He decided to say nothing, simply nodding instead.

"Now I know why they call you 'Hush,' " the director said with a complimentary smile. "There are many people in this building who could learn something from you, I suspect. I think we're done here, George, unless Mr. Hanson has any questions?"

"Just one," Hush said. "We're going to be awash in other government agencies with this one. As my deputy, Lang will have a key role in coordinating the interagency task force, both practically and politically. If she bungles that, am I allowed to pull her off?"

"You are allowed to *recommend* that she be pulled off," the director said. "To George here, who will of course consult with me. *We* will make any such determination, if it comes to that, as to when, and *if,* she has officially failed."

The director raised his eyebrows, nodded at both of them, and got up, signifying that the meeting was over. Hush and Wellesley stood. The director looked back over at them. "Frankly, Mr. Hanson, I don't think her *in*competence is going to be your problem. Good day, sir."

The deputy director touched Hush's elbow, easing him toward the door. "I've called a principals' meeting in the executive conference room," he told the director. "We'll get an overview of the case, after which, I'll announce the assignments."

"Fine, George," replied the director, who was already attacking the next stack of folders. Hush followed the deputy director out of the office, wondering what in the hell he had just gotten himself into.

They walked over into the conference room, where the other senior division managers were already seated. A briefer from the FBI operations center was waiting patiently at the podium. Wellesley took the director's empty chair, a small but effective expression of his own close-to-the-throne power. Hush walked in front of the backup row along the wall to his seat. In the director's conference room, only assistant directors in charge could sit at the table. Deputy ADICs and lesser mortals sat along the wall in what was known as "the backup row," ready to hand their bosses quick facts and figures should a question come up.

As he lowered himself carefully into the chair, Hush saw Senior Special Agent Lang sitting in the next-to-the-last chair in the backup row across the table from him. Her face was turned toward the front of the room, allowing him to study her surreptitiously. She appeared to be tallish, five nine, maybe even five ten, with a wide-shouldered, athletic figure and thick ash-blond hair. She had a clear complexion and was wearing no visible makeup. Her clothes were subdued and very businesslike: dark slacks, ivory blouse, a conservative blue blazer, low-heeled shoes, and no jewelry. She's very pretty, he thought, but not beautiful. Her expression, at least in profile, was much too severe. The room grew silent, and he, too, focused on the briefer.

"Go ahead," ordered the deputy director.

The lights dimmed and a video began to roll on the rear-projection screen. There were several audible "mnnhh's" and other expressions of dismay at the scene of the train wreck. The video had been shot in early-morning light from the Missouri side of the river and a few hundred yards upstream, then sent to Washington on the FBI's video teleconferencing net. The center span of the bridge was still partially attached to the eastern pier, on the Illinois side, although it had deformed during the collapse, with its western half mostly submerged under the small mountain of wrecked railcars sticking up out of the river. There were several people visible up on the western pier tower, standing among ribbons of yellow crime-scene tape fluttering through the heavy steel latticework. Two Army

Corps of Engineers fireboats were stationed on the downstream side, where smaller pusher boats were attempting to stream an oil-containment boom across the river.

"All right, this *is* a big deal," the deputy director said. "What facts do we have as of this hour?"

The briefer raised the lights as the video ended. He consulted his briefing notes.

"Sir, the incident occurred sometime around one-thirty this morning central time, based on the fact that the Union Pacific's railway operations center lost track continuity and communications across that bridge at about one-twenty-five. AT&T confirms loss of several long-haul trunk circuits at that same time. The train involved was a mixed freight, which means both boxcars and tank cars. There were eighty-eight cars and multiple engines. The bridge was apparently blown after the engines had crossed the center span. Eleven cars made it across behind the engines. Seventy-seven cars went into the river, as you saw on the video."

"No personnel casualties?" asked CID.

"No, sir. Union Pacific says that the only crew would have been in the engines; although they did say that there is always the chance of a hobo on one of the cars."

"There's no caboose anymore?" asked Information Resources. He was in charge of the FBI's world-famous criminal identification data banks. There were some small chuckles audible in the room.

"No, sir," replied the briefer with a straight face. "We asked the same question. Cabooses are unusual these days."

"Featherbedding ain't what it used to be," observed the Laboratory, to more laughter.

"How about toxic or hazardous materials in those tank cars?" National Security asked.

"Negative on toxics, but there were nineteen tank cars with flammable liquids, and, of those, sixteen went into the river. The Corps of Engineers is attempting to lay a containment boom, but this is the Mississippi we're talking about. The spring current is quite strong. There's probably going to be a major environmental impact out of this incident."

"So we'll have EPA in it," Wellesley said. "Wonderful. Now, what facts do we have on the cause?"

"Sir, the known *facts* are these: There is evidence of explosives residue present on the western center span pier tower, and that track continuity was lost at one-twenty-five."

"Opinions?"

"In the opinion of the senior Missouri State Patrol forensics investigator, the bridge was blown while the train was out on the bridge, dropping the center span and most of the train into the river. The perpetrators either set a timer or controlled the detonation remotely, possibly to let the engines get across."

"Evidence?"

"The shadow image of wiring burned onto the concrete in the vicinity of the explosive focus point."

"Any physical evidence of receivers or other electronics?"

"Not so far, sir, but they've got quite a mess out there, and they've just really begun to look."

"Okay, how about the explosives?"

"The initial indications from the field indicate Pyrodex."

"Pyrodex? What is that?"

The Laboratory director leaned forward to speak. He was a large, burly man, whose ruddy Irish face was topped by a shock of grayish red hair. He spoke with a loud voice.

"It's gunpowder. Actually, Pyrodex is a substitute for black powder. Used by cap-and-ball hobby shooters, and black-powder hunters. Acts like black powder, but it's cleaner and more stable and consistent in performance."

"But to blow a bridge?"

"Well, black powder used to be called 'blasting powder.' You want to shatter something, like a rock ledge or a coal seam, you use a *detonating* explosive, like dynamite. It all goes at once, gives you a maximum instantaneous hammer punch. But if you want to move or dislodge something large, like a big old stump, you'd use a *deflagrating* explosive, such as nitrocellulose or plain old black powder. *Deflagrating* means it burns very fast, but it doesn't go at the speed of heat like dynamite. You get an expanding and massive lifting force rather than an instantaneous hammer blow. Mind you, now, we're talking a differential of hundredths of a second here, but there is a difference."

"This is all speculation, of course," observed CID. "We'll need to get the residue into the lab before we know anything."

"Yeah, Bill, I understand that," replied the Laboratory. "But we were talking opinions. To me, this indicates somebody in this group knows what he's doing with explosives. Or maybe it's a matter of availability. To shatter a bridge structure of that size, you'd need a lot of dynamite. Not that easy to come by anymore. Pyrodex you can buy at the local gun shop. Hell, I think you can even mail-order it."

"Wouldn't it take a trash-can load of black powder to blow up something as big as that bridge?" asked CID.

"Depends on where he put it. But you could acquire quite a stockpile in an entirely legal manner, long as you had the time."

"Okay, back to the issue here," Wellesley said. "What's the impact of losing this bridge?"

"Sir, the Union Pacific owns that bridge. They haven't come in with that information yet."

"Union Pacific corporate headquarters said they would have a statement later this morning," offered Public Affairs. "But I get the impression that they're already running for cover."

"Why?"

"Think EPA, toxic spill, shippers' lawsuits, charges of lapsed security. They were referring me to their general counsel's office."

"All right, I guess that's enough for the incident overview," Wellesley interrupted, glancing at his watch. "CID, any ideas as to who or what we're dealing with here?"

The assistant director of the Criminal Investigation Division, a small, balding man who wore oversized gold-rimmed spectacles, rustled some papers on the table in front of him and then, to everyone's surprise, slowly shook his head.

"The short answer is," he replied, "we don't have a clue. A superficial scan of our intelligence database indicates this kind of sabotage does not fit the MOs of the known domestic subversive groups, the extreme militias, or even individuals, for that matter."

"Other sources?"

"We've asked National Security to liaise with our brethren across the river, of course, to see if foreign agents or operatives might be involved." He looked up at the people around the table. "But right now, I'm embarrassed to report that intelligence has nothing. Zilch, really. This incident is entirely out of profile."

The deputy director frowned. Hush knew why. CID's admission was totally out of character. The FBI's intelligence organization almost always had at least some information, or at least they made sure to give the impression that they did. The silence grew around the table.

"All right," said Wellesley. "I've spoken to the deputy AG at Main Justice. The Bureau's been given verbal authorization to head up this investigation. Now, then: I plan to assign it to the IITF Division."

The director of the National Security Division raised an immediate objection. "This is clearly a terrorist act," he said. "That's our bailiwick."

Wellesley shook his head. "The director agrees that this case will end up generating a rather large interagency task force. That's what we formed IITF to do."

The National Security director, a large, florid-faced man named J. Kenneth Carswell, threw down his pencil but said nothing more. Carswell had opposed the formation of IITF under the previous director, and took every opportunity to let people know he still felt IITF was a dumb idea. On the other hand, he and everyone else in the room had noted Wellesley's reference to the director. Wellesley chose to ignore him.

"Acting AD Hanson will run this personally," he said. There were murmurs around the table. "I understand it's been done before," Wellesley continued. "Oh, and Senior Special Agent Carolyn Lang will be detailed from PCA to act as the task force deputy."

Hush admired the smooth, almost nonchalant way Wellesley dropped that little bombshell. He saw Lang's head come up at the announcement, and observed some quick, covert glances shooting around the room, especially among the back-row staffers. The deputy director did not allow any time for further reaction.

"Mr. Hanson," Wellesley continued, "we'll leave it up to you as to where you set up shop, either out there or here in the building. I assume you'll want to get on-scene today?"

"Yes, I will," said Hush. He was aware that Carolyn Lang was looking over at him now, but he kept his eyes on the deputy director.

"Good. We'll excuse you and Ms. Lang, then. I'd like the other principals to stay behind for a few minutes. I have a couple of long-range budgeting issues to discuss."

The meeting paused while the senior aides filed out of the conference room. Hush and Carolyn Lang were last out. Hush thought he caught a faint smile from the deputy director as he held the door open for Lang. The two of them walked down the corridor and then stopped to wait for an elevator. The top of her head was about level with his chin.

"William Hanson," he said, offering his hand.

"Mary," she replied, taking his hand. "Typhoid Mary." There was a hint of amused challenge in her eyes as she cocked her head up at him.

"That one *f* or two?" Hush asked with a perfectly straight face.

She smiled then, and he released her hand. "Carolyn Lang, Mr. Hanson. Did you know about this before the deputy director announced it at the briefing?"

He could not tell how old she was, but her skin was flawless. She had either green or hazel eyes, and he had to force himself to quit staring at her. "By 'this,' I presume you mean your assignment as the task force deputy?" he said. "Yes."

"I see. Was my appointment the only reason you had a one-on-one with the director?"

Hush paused. Basically, she had asked an impertinent question: An AD's meeting with the director was none of her business. But then he thought again: Maybe not her business, but vitally important to her nonetheless. Still, he decided to hedge.

"Not exactly. Headquarters assistant directors rarely head up field operations. He informed me that you would be the task force deputy, but the bridge incident was the focus of our conversation."

The executive elevator arrived, and he turned to step in. She followed. Once in the elevator, he detected a faint hint of perfume as he slipped his card into the control panel and pushed the button for his floor. He found himself uncomfortable at beginning their working relationship with a lie.

"I see," she said again. "When Wellesley made the announcement, it occurred to me that this was going to be my chance to 'get well'."

"Does your career need repairing?" he asked. The elevator began to chime off the floors as they went up.

She gave him another smile and patted her hair. "You must not get around much, Mr. Hanson," she said. "I would have thought I was rather more notorious than that."

"A legend in your own mind, you mean?"

She laughed out loud. She was being totally disarming, and her demeanor did not square with what he had been told in the director's office.

He had expected multiple sharp edges and frosty, politically correct professionalism. The elevator doors opened, and Hush decided not to elaborate beyond what he had already said. He still felt a twinge of conscience about his answer to her initial question, but until he knew exactly what he was dealing with, he was going to operate in the "Hush" mode. He preceded her out of the elevator. She kept up with him as they walked down the corridor toward his office.

"I hope you're ready to travel," he said. "I want to get out to the scene right away, and I think you should be there, too."

"When?" she said, looking at her watch. He stopped in front of his office and looked at his own watch.

"I'll have my IITF deputy, Tyler Redford, see if the Air Force has anything available out of Andrews. He'll let you know departure time. I expect to be out there for maybe two days, and then we'll be coming back here. Right now, I'm going to have my people set up in one of the situation rooms in the ops center until I see where this thing's going. Have you ever worked on an interagency task force?"

"No, sir, I have not." There was no more banter. She was all business. She had a small notebook out and was taking notes. If his story about the meeting in the director's office was bothering her, she gave no sign of it now. He was pleased to hear her say "sir." He decided to cement that distinction.

"Do you mind if I call you Carolyn?" he asked.

"Not at all, Mr. Hanson."

Good, he thought. "Okay, the way it usually works is that I, as IITF director, designate a lead senior agent and a single deputy. The lead then decides who and what else they need as the case unfolds. That's more efficient than detailing a whole mob right from the start and then having people stand around. The ops center sets up the nucleus of a situation room until we determine the composition of the interagency task force."

"And my job, as deputy?"

"In a case like this, the Bureau is going to interact with other agencies of the government—lots of them, I suspect. I will depend on you to do a lot of the setup and liaison work. You're in Congressional Affairs now, aren't you?"

"Yes."

"Good," he said. "Then you'll know something about ego management. Like I said, we'll add Bureau assets as we get into the case." He glanced at her clothes, which, close-up, looked expensive. "We're going to be climbing around on a bombed-out bridge. I recommend you bring some outdoors gear. Any further questions for me?"

She gave him an appraising look. She has a very direct gaze, he thought. Still not beautiful, but no man would just walk by without a second look. And this one might just look back. He remembered who she was and quickly extinguished these thoughts.

"No, Mr. Hanson," she said. "I'll be ready to go when you are."

Hush nodded and went into his office, trying not to think about the director's warning.

Hush arrived on board the Air Force C-21 executive jet in his office suit and changed in the lavatory into khaki trousers, a long-sleeved khaki shirt with large hunting jacket pockets, and high-topped Army-style boots. In deference to the plane's air conditioning, he put on a dark blue windbreaker, which had the letters FBI embroidered across the back and arms in large letters. The jacket had a flashlight stuffed in one pocket and leather gloves jammed in the other. A small voice recorder made a rectangular bulge in one of his shirt pockets. As an assistant director, he was not required to carry his weapon, so he had left it behind in his office. He sat down and, being the senior person on board, strapped into the single large executive chair at the back of the cabin.

Carolyn Lang surprised him when she arrived. She showed up wearing a straight skirt, low heels, and a semitransparent blouse covered up by a buttoned blazer. She carried a small overnight bag and a single hanging bag, which she put in the aisle closet. Her blond hair was pulled back in a severe bun. As the port engine started, she nodded politely at him, then sat down in the chair facing his, crossing her legs carefully. A crewman came in to check that their seat belts were secured and then returned to the flight deck as the second engine spooled up. Hush wondered if she planned to climb around the bridge in that outfit.

They sat silently in their seats through takeoff from Andrews Air Force Base and the climb-out to cruising altitude for the flight to Missouri. Once the jet leveled off, the flight crewman showed them where refreshments were stowed in an icebox next to the magazine rack. Hush unstrapped and helped himself to a soft drink after offering one to Carolyn Lang. He returned to the executive chair and then eyed her for a moment.

"Why did you want to know if your assignment was the reason I had to go in to see the director?" he asked. Even with all the insulation, he had to speak up to make himself heard.

She looked down at the carpet for a moment before answering. "I've been in career limbo since coming back to headquarters from St. Louis," she said. "I've been expecting something but didn't know what. With Heinrich and the director involved, one never knows."

He cautioned himself to keep his eyes on her face. "I think you give yourself too much credit, Carolyn," he said. "The deputy director asked if I had any problems having a woman as my deputy, and I said no, as long as she was competent. He said you were very competent and that was that. What's the big deal?"

Lang looked at him speculatively. "Heinrich said that? I've made a lot of noise about equal opportunity since I've been in the Bureau, and I have the distinct impression that it has not been appreciated."

"Have you personally been discriminated against as a woman, Carolyn?"

"Not that I can prove, Mr. Hanson," she said. She was displaying almost none of the deference he was used to as an AD, even if he was just acting.

"Then I can understand if the powers that be don't appreciate the noise."

She raised her eyebrows. "Are you saying that there isn't discrimination against women in the Bureau?"

"I'm saying that no one elected *you* to represent the interests of women's equal opportunity in the Bureau. You can speak for yourself anytime, of course. If you've been discriminated against, or been the subject of harassment, sexual or otherwise, or the target of any other kind of abuse, you're entitled to make noise, be heard, and to receive satisfaction."

Lang's face colored slightly, but then that mask of reserve reset, and she nodded.

"Whatever the history," he said, "it needs to be left behind. This is a field operation now, and we'll both need to concentrate. To begin with, we're probably going to have some ruffled feathers at the St. Louis Field Division Office."

"Mr. Herlihy," she said, as if she had just realized in whose territory the bridge had been blown.

"That's right. And the state cops will probably bristle when we bring in some big-deal federal task force. Not to mention Carswell and his merry band, who want IITF to go away. We'll have a busy backfield, and not just with the case."

"I understand," she said, and then looked away.

He felt slightly disappointed with himself that their conversation had degenerated into a lecture. He had been something of a long, tall ugly duckling for his entire adult life, and good-looking women tended to put his guard up. He pulled out his briefcase and pretended to start on some paperwork. When she got up to get a magazine, he swung the high-backed chair to face aft, opened his zippered notebook folder, and extracted Lang's personnel file, which Wellesley's office had sent down before he left. She had openly referred to Wellesley as Heinrich, which, given the fact that she and Hush were not colleagues of long standing, was not a very politic thing to do.

Carolyn Brownell Lang, preBureau nickname "Colley." He thought for a moment: Colley. That name had probably fit when she was much younger, but not now. A little too much armor plating now for a Colley. He went back to the file. She had grown up in a Coast Guard family with two brothers in San Diego; attended UCSD, majoring in finance and business. Got her first job at a large bank in Los Angeles, worked there for three years, then went back to grad school for an MBA at UCLA's Anderson School. From there to a job working for the financial fraud division of the California attorney general's office in Los Angeles. At age twenty-eight she had applied to join the FBI. He paused and wondered why. He looked up her birth date and did the math: She would be almost forty-one now. Six years younger than he was. Didn't look it, either, damn her.

He kept going. Almost thirteen years in the Bureau. Initially, the conventional string of junior agent field assignments, with personnel evaluations well above average. She had done the obligatory stint in the Inspection Division early on, a move that signaled she wanted to get on the career path. He did detect a few carefully coded sentences in the verbal evaluations that hinted at a certain personal abrasiveness, a readiness to raise issues that the boss might have preferred to let lie. And yet there were also three commendations in her first seven years. After her last commendation, she had been posted to Washington. From that point forward, her assignment profile seemed to change. A series of eighteen-month assignments, culminating in the posting as the assistant special agent in charge, or ASAC, in the St. Louis office a year and a half ago. It looked almost as if someone in high places had been steering her through the gates to promotion. Or her boss could stand having her around for no more than a year and half before finding a way to move her on. That would fit with what Heinrich had been saying.

He closed his eyes. An ASAC job in a medium-sized field office at about the ten-year point. That would make her a hot runner, actually. Something didn't square here.

The special agent in charge, or SAC, in St. Louis was Joseph Michael Edward Herlihy, nicknamed "Himself." He was a large Irishman who had been known to voice strong opinions about having women as operational agents in any capacity other than as what the Langley spooks liked to call "honey traps." Anyone who had known Herlihy could have predicted that a woman like Carolyn Lang would inevitably develop a personality conflict with her boss, with an equally predictable outcome. The Bureau was very much like the military when it came to personality conflicts: The senior person ended up with the personality; the junior person ended up with the conflict. He wondered if she had been set up by Herlihy, except, as he recalled, it had been Herlihy's handpicked candidate to get the ASAC job who had been burned into early retirement. Still, he wondered what someone had been thinking when they sent Carolyn Lang to be Herlihy's ASAC.

He looked over her departure evaluation from Herlihy, but it gave few clues to what had actually happened. This meant the issue had been settled off-line to avoid formal proceedings. He remembered headquarters grapevine tales of a cloud of sexual harassment charges, first from Lang and then, surprisingly, a countercharge from Herlihy. The harassment issue did not involve overt leers and gropes, but, rather, centered on Lang's assertion that her male subordinates were undermining her authority. Herlihy maintained that Lang precipitated that reaction by exhibiting a hair-triggered sensitivity to supposed discrimination, all to the detriment of the office's mission. But then the three other female agents in the St. Louis office elected to run for cover rather than support Lang, which had the effect of isolating her. In the end, she had been transferred back on-staff at the Washington headquarters, then was sent to Public and Congressional Affairs. Wellesley had detailed someone else from the Washington headquarters to be ASAC at the St. Louis office.

He put the folder back into his notebook and closed the zipper. The fact that there was no direct paper trail in her personnel record about what had happened out in St. Louis was significant. Given all the stories, this meant that someone had extended himself, a pretty powerful someone at that. Powerful enough that Heinrich and the director were resorting to palace games to wedge her out. So who the hell might that be? he wondered. One of the dragons over at Main Justice?

He turned the chair slightly to see if she was awake, but she appeared to be dozing. Looking at her face in repose, he tried to imagine her laughing, having a good time, maybe splashing along a beach in sunny Southern California, Colley Lang, instead of Senior Special Agent Bitch Kitty Lang.

Hush Hanson was forty-six and had been with the Bureau for twenty-two years. He had never been married, and he lived a relatively quiet and introspective life in Washington. From Monday to Friday, he stayed in his condo in northern Virginia. On Friday evenings, he usually drove out to his small country place up in the Shenandoah Valley, where he enjoyed a weekend's worth of the physical labor required to keep a fifteen-acre homestead in good order.

He was at heart a solitary, shy man, whose height amplified a natural tendency to awkwardness, especially around women. He had known for years that he would always value his FBI career above the demands of marriage and a family, and he had also learned enough about women to know that they would expect just the opposite. It suited his nature to conclude that marriage was one of life's big decisions that had been made for him. He kept pretty much to himself on the weekends, steering clear of the county's frenetic social whirl and his neighbors' matchmaking wives. He knew some Bureau managers who had indulged in relationships with the growing population of attractive women in the Bureau, but with all the sexual harassment heat lightning going around, he wouldn't dream of starting something with another Bureau employee. As attractive as she was, Carolyn Lang would be no exception to what he considered a hard-and-fast rule of survival in today's Bureau.

He looked back over at Lang and felt his breath catch. She appeared to be sleeping soundly now. The magazine had slipped to the floor, and her skirt had ridden a long way up shimmering thighs. He stared at her exposed legs for several seconds like a teenaged boy, then, conscious of a warm flush rising in his neck, forced himself to turn his chair around again. He was both ashamed at his voyeurism and yet aroused at the sight of her body. Despite himself, he turned around again, slowly, but she had shifted in her chair and recovered her modesty, although she still appeared to be sleeping. In repose, her face was definitely softer.

He wondered again about what had been said in the director's office: This woman simply did not look the gunfighter or agent-provocateur type. Which proved once again how little he knew. He sighed, swiveled the chair back around, and tried to banish all thoughts of women from his head and to think about the case instead. At the moment, the most interesting aspect of it was that he, a senior headquarters official, had been assigned to run it. It was especially unusual for him, personally. After the incident in Baltimore, he had very carefully orchestrated his entire career to stay away from assignments that would ever put him back in a shooting situation. He had the impression that this career strategy had been tacitly supported by his Bureau supervisors over the years, almost as if they, too, had lingering doubts about fielding an agent who could do what he had done that afternoon.

The downside was that he had never been in charge of a field office. His expertise was in major conspiracies, special-counsel investigations, and complex cases that required close interagency cooperation within the federal government. It was an increasingly productive field for the Bureau, and he was a recognized as heavy hitter in that arena.

But this might be different. Someone had torn the heart out of a major railroad bridge and dumped an entire train into America's most important river. J. Kenneth Carswell was right, in a way: This should be National Security's operation. Except: Solving it would take the cooperation of so many government agencies that IITF's networks within the government were much better suited to handle it than NS. He sighed, wondering how he personally would perform if this thing ever got to the stage where they cornered some perpetrators. That will be a good time for me not to be there, he thought.

They arrived at the Cape Girardeau Regional Airport in eastern Missouri just before sunset, where they were met by special agents from the St. Louis Field Division Office. The Missouri Highway Patrol provided a cruiser to take Hush and Carolyn to the scene, where Capt. Mike Powers, head of the state police's Criminal Investigation Bureau, had taken charge. By the time they landed, Carolyn had changed into khaki slacks, a Pendleton shirt, and an FBI windbreaker identical to Hanson's. Her weapon, a Sig Sauer P-228, was holstered high on her right hip. She wore high-topped boots and carried a small leather purse that had a leather strap long enough to be worn diagonally across her chest.

Hush sat up front with the trooper to accommodate his long frame. After a twenty-minute drive through the deepening darkness of the Missouri countryside, they encountered the first police units at an at-grade crossing on a state road. Their driver made a left turn onto a right-of-way service road. About a mile down the dirt road, they encountered another cluster of emergency vehicles, and the trooper stopped the cruiser. Behind them, the three FBI cars pulled over and stopped. There were police, railroad people, some media troops humping television cameras, and what looked like Army soldiers milling around. Hush thanked the trooper and motioned for Lang to exit the cruiser. "The state police are being awfully nice," she ventured as they stood there for a moment among the throng of people headed down toward the bridge. The agents behind them began getting out of their cars.

"They'll want to keep tabs on us," Hush replied. "We talk in the car and the locals know what we're thinking."

He instructed the St. Louis agents to begin gathering facts from the cast of thousands that had gathered along the approach to the bridge. He noticed that a couple of them appeared to be giving Carolyn Lang a fish-eye look. He asked if Mr. Herlihy was coming out. One of the agents, who introduced himself as the supervisor of the Violent Crimes Squad, told him that Herlihy was on his way.

Hanson nodded. The presence of an assistant director in the field was unusual enough to warrant the special agent in charge to be present, even if Herlihy was a grade senior to him. The imposition of a headquarters official into what ordinarily would have been Herlihy's business would take some diplomacy. Hush confirmed his impression that the St. Louis agents were all studiously avoiding Lang. They would naturally be deferential to an assistant director, but they were clearly giving her the cold shoulder. He motioned for her to accompany him, and they began to walk down toward the river. The state police officers stood aside as they passed, their faces wooden and impassive. Suspicions confirmed, Hush thought, although the Bureau had been working hard these past years to improve relations with local law.

Ahead, the darkening sky was awash with flashing blue strobe lights and what looked like some big stationary searchlights illuminating the trees down by the river. There were several more military trucks, as well as state and county police cars all along the track bed. A cacophony of police and emergency services radios assaulted the tranquillity of the empty cotton fields on either side of the rail line. A National Guard Huey helicopter sat fifty feet away from the road, with three bored-looking crewmen perched on the skids, smoking surreptitiously. Hush walked purposefully through the swarm of vehicles, with Lang picking her way over the uneven ground close behind. As they approached the bridge itself, a county deputy waved them over. He was a big man with a beer belly and a beefy, sunburned face that remained red even in the growing darkness. A pair of highly polished sunglasses hung down from the button on his shirt pocket. Hush pulled out his credentials, as did Lang. The deputy turned a flashlight on the two sets of ID, then nodded and cleared them forward. Hush asked him who was in charge at the scene.

The deputy grinned. "Take your choice. We got your state cops, your sheriff's office—that's us—your Army Corps of Engineers, some guys from some national whatever safety office in Washington, a coupla dozen railroad dicks, and now you guys." He glanced over at Lang for a moment, wondering if he should amend the word *guys*. He apparently decided not to bother. "I saw Cap'n Powers up at the bridge a little while ago. I guess he's the senior guy from the state cops."

"Thanks, Deputy. Any coffee around?"

"You passed the state CP, but the Army guys'll have some. Over there."

They walked over to one of the two-and-half-ton Army Corps of Engineers trucks and cadged some coffee. There were several Army enlisted people standing around, apparently waiting for orders. Hush's understanding from the operations briefing book was that the Army Corps of Engineers and the Coast Guard shared responsibility for river bridges and barge operations on the Mississippi River system itself. The Union Pacific Railroad owned this particular bridge and the rights-of-way leading to it. The railroads were responsible for maintaining their bridges under the supervision of the Corps of Engineers. The Coast Guard treated a railroad bridge as both an aid to navigation, since lights could be mounted on a bridge, and as a menace to navigation, since tugs and barges could ram them if things went wrong out on the river.

By the time they reached the abutment on the west bank, there were dozens of police, Army, and railroad people milling around. A massive

Union Pacific flatcar wrecking crane was being backed down the east-bound tracks toward the bridge by a stubby switching locomotive, accompanied by lots of shouting as the road crew tried to get all the cops off the tracks. With the noise from the big diesel engine drowning out any possibility of conversation, Hush motioned for Carolyn Lang to follow him down to the riverbank below the bridge abutment. They threaded their way through a tangle of trees to the river. The ground was sloppy from the spring melt, and much of it had been ground into mud by all the people gathered on the bank.

The bridge structure towered over them. There were a dozen search-lights along the bank, driven by portable Army generators, illuminating the massive pile of wreckage out in the main channel. There appeared to be many people up on the bridge itself, which had four pier towers standing on this side. They could clearly see the twisted center span, still half-attached on the far side, sloping down into the current. There appeared to be a similar gaggle of emergency equipment and people on the far shore, although it was hard to tell because of the spotlights pointing in their direction from the east bank.

The Mississippi River was nearly two thousand feet wide at the bridge site. Hush marveled at its size; the maps gave no indication of its scale. Two Army Corps tugboats were standing off the pile of wreckage on the downstream side of the bridge, playing searchlights around the partially submerged pile of railcars. Some of the cars had already been swept downstream, coming to rest in the shoals along the west bank, with only their tops showing above the current. Hush found himself standing next to a burly railroad man, distinguished by a ball cap with the letters UP on the front.

"How in the hell are they going to clean this mess up?" he shouted above the din of engines.

The railroad man peered up at him and then shook his head, pointing to his ears. They won't be able to do it from the bridge, Hush thought. It looked to be almost a hundred feet high above the river. They would probably have to use a floating crane and recovery barges. Eventually, that would require divers. That would be a tough operation when the river was up and running. He looked along the bank and could see that the water was right at the edge of the undercut banks, lapping away at tree roots. He turned to Carolyn and signaled that they needed to go up on the bridge.

They clambered back up the riverbank and walked back inland until the angle of the track embankment changed from almost vertical to a slope they could negotiate. He dug his boots in and climbed up toward the graveled roadbed, using tufts of wet grass as handholds. When they reached the main-line grade, they stepped carefully through heavy gravel and then walked back down the tracks, stepping along the ties toward the bridge. The wrecking crane and its engine had stopped just in front of the second pier tower.

There were many more people up on the main-line grade, most of whom appeared to be railroad people. The wrecking crane was massive, and the air was filled with diesel engine exhaust that drifted across the blazing white lights in pungent blue clouds. Even at idle, the switching engine pummeled the night air. They were stopped at the west end of the bridge by three sheriff's deputies. The shortest of the three was hatless and held a Motorola radio in his hand. He had to bend his neck dramatically to see Hush's face.

"Hold up a second, bud," he shouted over the engine noise. "We gotta clear anybody going out to the middle."

Hush pointed to the FBI letters on his jacket, then dug for his credentials. The deputy glanced at Hush's ID perfunctorily, gave Lang's a longer inspection, and then spoke into the radio, clamped it to his ear, nodded, and motioned them through. Hush nodded and they walked out on the actual bridge structure along the center catwalk between the eastbound and westbound tracks. The catwalk was narrow and lined with uneven creosote boards that were not uniformly nailed down. They had to stop and turn sideways whenever anyone came by going the other way. There were some railway maintenance people walking disdainfully on the open-air ties above the catwalk, but Hush, who did not care for heights, felt more comfortable on the catwalk with its railing. They both held their ears as they brushed past the service engine and its crane. When they reached the last segment of the bridge before the downed center span, they encountered a barrier of yellow police tape that shunted all the pedestrian traffic to the downstream side of the bridge. They had to climb up to the eastbound track bed, cross it, and then drop down to the outboard catwalk. Hush could not figure out why a hundred feet of the upstream side had been taped off.

He saw a big man wearing the flat hat of the state police, whom he suspected was Captain Powers. When they finally pushed their way through the crowd and reached the western center span pier tower, Powers was discussing something with a harried-looking Army officer dressed in green fatigues and two coatless railroad men in shirts and ties and white hard hats. A fourth civilian was trying to talk on a portable radio. All four were standing just within the cordon of draped yellow crime-scene ribbon. With the top of the concrete pier tower between them and the switch engine, the engine noise was somewhat diminished. The big man broke off his discussion when he saw the FBI jackets, and he waved them over. Hush thought he heard the police captain say something about FBI as they stepped over the yellow crime-scene tape. Hush introduced himself, omitting his rank.

"Powers," the big man said, not offering to shake hands. "I assume you all are ready to take charge and tell your country cousins what to do?"

Hush was taken aback by Powers's overt hostility, but he tried to keep his expression neutral.

"Not exactly, Captain," he said. "The Bureau will be forming an inter-agency task force to find out who did this, but it's early days yet for us to be telling anybody anything."

Powers frowned at him. "Early days, huh? Inter-whatever the hell task force. You Washington types slay me, you really do. And who's this? Your private secretary?"

The other men on the bridge began to study their boots. Hush turned slightly to include Lang in the conversation, or confrontation—he wasn't sure which.

"This is Senior Special Agent Lang; she will be the deputy director of the task force. Which will include people from all the law-enforcement agencies involved, and from the marine safety authorities, railroad security, the relevant Washington agencies, whatever and whoever we need, Captain. Including the Missouri State Highway Patrol, assuming you're interested."

"Interested?" exclaimed Powers. He took off his hat and wiped his flushed face with a damp handkerchief. Then he shook his head, as if trying to control his temper.

"You just look around here; you tell me if we should be *interested* or not. Jesus H. Christ, Hanson, just look at this mess!"

They looked. The island of wrecked boxcars and tank cars was large enough to cause the river to divide on either side, sending up a wake of white foam tinged with leaking oil and chemicals from the pile. One of the Army tugboats was holding its bluff nose against the downstream edge of the wreckage. The engines of two boom boats bellowed across the surface of the river as the oil-spill team continued its efforts to lay out a floating spill-containment boom, although it was obvious to everyone watching in the glare of the searchlights that they were wasting their time. The current was simply too strong, especially as it divided around the mountain of drowned wreckage and created whirling eddies that buffeted the floating barrier. As they stared down, one of the boxcars was stripped off the pile by the current, rending the night with sounds of tearing metal and snapping beams as it slid down and was swallowed by the black waters. A minute later, cardboard boxes began to pop to the surface like confetti, only to be swept away downriver into the darkness beyond the searchlights. Everyone on the bridge stopped talking to watch. Hush turned back to face Powers.

"The initial reports say this was done by a bomb. May I see the evidence of that?"

"Don't believe us, huh?"

Hush just looked at him. "I didn't say that. I asked to see the evidence."

Powers stared back at him again for a moment, as if searching for some hint of a taunt, then relaxed slightly.

"Yeah, sure. All right. It's been a long night and it isn't even night yet. By the way, this here is Mr. Campbell. He's a bridge inspector for the Corps of Engineers, St. Louis District. This is Mr. Jameson, chief of security for the Union Pacific, and this is Mr. Canning—he's the chief engineer for roadways and structures for the UP. And over there is Major Williams, St. Louis District, Army Corps of Engineers."

Hush shook hands with all four of them, who made polite noises back at him. Powers's visible antagonism was out on the table for all to see, and Hush sensed that these men were waiting to see how the feds would act before showing their hands. Lang nodded politely at each of them as Hush introduced her, then smiled some sweet daggers at Powers.

The captain led Hush out to the edge of what had been the center span. The catwalk railings were bent over like limp spaghetti, and some of the huge rivet holes along the main beams had been deformed into large jagged tears in the metal. The concrete ledge that had supported the center span jutted out into black space. Hush had trouble looking past it.

"Smell anything?" Powers asked.

Hush *had* smelled something odd, but he had attributed it to the bleed-ing island of wrecked train below. Then it hit him.

"Sulfur."

"Yeah, sulfur. Now look here."

Powers crouched down against the outside beams of the pier tower and pointed a flashlight into a boxlike cavity. Hush pulled his own light and pointed it down into the hole. The interior of the cavity was white with residue. An even stronger stink of sulfur burned his nostrils: the smell of black powder. The sides of the steel box were concave instead of rigid right angles.

Hush stood back away from the blasted pin cavity. He looked up at the adjacent truss structure, indistinct in the shadowy darkness. Powers followed his look.

"Yeah," he said. "That's why all the tape. Let me show you."

They climbed back up to the track-bed level and then went through the pier tower aperture to the next span back from the center span. Pow-ers went down on his knees and pointed his flashlight into the space beneath the tracks, illuminating the main side girder on the upstream side of the span. Hush again put his own light where Powers was pointing. Even from there they could see that the top flange of the I beam had been cracked along its full length, going almost fifty feet back toward the west bank. The steel frame supporting the track bed was rippled and deformed along the same distance.

"Detcord?" said Hush.

"Detcord, Primacord, something like that. If they'd done this right, this span would have gone down, too, but most of the blast went into space. But as it is, they can't bring that crane out here. The UP guy says they'll probably have to replace this section of the bridge before they can begin to fix the center span."

Hush, down on one knee beside the captain, nodded slowly. The smell of chemicals wafting up off the river below was much stronger. "Damaged it enough to hold up repairs. Somebody knew what they were doing here."

"You got that right," Powers said, getting back up and dusting off his trousers. They climbed back to where the civilians were standing. Lang had her notebook out and was talking to the UP chief engineer. He con-firmed what Powers had said.

"That cracked girder means this next span is closed. The collapse of the center span probably also overstressed every truss pin all the way back to the west bank. We're waiting for my head structural guy to come, probably in the morning. They'll have to do deforms and alignment on the entire remaining structure, both sides."

The civilian introduced as Campbell snorted. "Don't need any structural guys to confirm that, Belon. This whole bridge is screwed. You'll salvage the pier towers, and that's about it."

The big switch engine shut down at that moment, as if it had been listening to them. There was a sudden relative silence, quickly filled up with the rattle of the emergency lighting generators and police radios.

"Was it timed or radio-controlled—what's the consensus?" asked Hush.

Powers rolled his eyes. "Consensus? Shit. We got a million opinions, but with all the federal shovels that're getting into this pile, a consensus is going to be out of the question."

Hush looked at him for a long moment, trying to stay calm. Lang stopped writing in her notebook.

"Captain Powers," he said, finally. "I think you're more tired than you realize."

Powers eyes widened and his neck began to swell. "Now you look here, mister—"

"No, Captain," Hush interrupted. "Agent Lang and I are *federal* officers. We're going to conduct a *federal* investigation of what happened here. I don't know what your problem is, but it's not going to interfere with our *federal* work for another minute. The Bureau would appreciate your cooperation and would prefer to work *with* you and any other local jurisdiction involved. But if you can't get around your hard-on against federal authorities and return this meeting to a professional level right now, I'll have the *federal* Army clear everybody off this bridge, and cordon off the bridge and as much of the county around it as I deem necessary. I can do that with one phone call from my flip phone. And I will do it, and when and if I do, your name will be featured prominently in the reasons why. Is all that clear, Captain Powers? You want me to explain it some more? Or are you ready to do police business?"

The other men tried to make themselves small within the taped enclosure. Lang was watching the red-faced state police captain carefully. Powers glared around at everybody, and Hush thought for a moment that the big cop was going to swing on him. Hush was considerably taller than Powers, but not quite as broad. Out of the corner of his eye, he thought he saw Lang's right hand begin to creep toward her hip. Powers must have seen the movement, too, because he did a double take, looked back at Hush, and deflated.

"Okay, screw it," he said. "You wanna be in charge, you be in charge. The Missouri State Highway Patrol anxiously await your orders, Mr. Washington Big Shot."

"All right, Captain. Senior Special Agent Lang will tell you what needs to be done. First we need to recover this crime scene."

Carolyn never missed a beat. "Captain Powers, I want the state police to get everyone off this bridge, both ends, except for your forensic teams and their federal counterparts. I want one command post to be running the recovery effort out on the river, preferably from this side. Our Laboratory people will be here at first light, at which time they will get a briefing from your people and the Railroad Safety Office people, after which they will work *together* until a preliminary report has been developed."

Powers just stared at her. Hush decided to pile on a little.

"And *I* want all those people standing around on the banks—Army, police, whoever they are—to be issued plastic trash bags and I want them to pick up any and every man-made object along the banks for five hundred yards downstream, both sides. Then I want those trash bags taken to a hangar at the local airport and logged as evidence. And after all of that is in motion, I want a meeting with you, the head of your forensics team, the senior Army Corps of Engineers officer here, and the senior railroad official. Let's say in one hour at the Army CP back there." Hush turned away to speak to the UP official. "Mr. Jameson, can your people help with setting up a proper security perimeter here?"

"Uh, yes, sir, we can," answered Jameson, looking sideways at Powers. "But we also need to continue with our recovery efforts down there, if that's okay."

"Yes, fine. But I want those tugboats to stay away from the bridge structure itself if they can—don't tie up any boats to the piers—that kind of thing. Maybe use one of those tugs down there as a floating command post for your cleanup, but leave the physical area around the bridge alone for now."

"Yes, sir, can do. We'll see you at the CP in an hour." He nudged Canning, and the two of them walked quickly back toward the west bank. Campbell stepped over to one side of the platform and began talking on a portable radio.

Hush looked back at Powers, who was still standing there, his jaw muscles working and his face set in an ugly expression.

"Well?" asked Hush.

Powers said nothing for what seemed like a very long time, and then he slipped out under the tape and shouted for one of his troopers to bring him his "goddamned radio right goddamned now." Major Williams took off his hard hat, wiped his forehead, and grinned at Hush. "I wouldn't do any speeding while you're out here in Missouri, if I was you, folks."

"That's not the way I wanted to start this thing out," Hush said to Carolyn. "But we don't have time for theatrics. This scene is pretty well clobbered as it is."

"Why you bagging up all that trash and stuff down there?" the major asked.

"There's always the chance, however slight, that we might recover some useful evidence. Not likely, I'll admit, but we've got to try. Carolyn, go find some of our St. Louis people, please. Take a look at their case book, and then go to the Army CP and tell whoever's in charge there what we're doing, and wait for me there."

She nodded and headed back along the catwalk toward the west bank. The three deputies gawked at her as she went by. Hush asked the Army officer to describe briefly how the bridge was constructed. The major took him over to the pier tower and pointed out the significant features of the truss design. He also explained how the pins had been mounted. They walked back to the next span so the major could show him an intact set of pins. Then they went back out to the edge of the center span to compare the damaged structure with the intact structure. When he was finished, Hush had a question.

"Tell me: How big a deal is this? What's the impact going to be on the railroad?"

Williams put his hard hat back on and looked back out over the river. "The UP operations guys can give you the answer to that; the Army Corps doesn't get involved in railroad operations per se. But I'd say it's going to be a serious disruption. All the big rail operators are running at near capacity these days."

"But they can always reroute across another bridge, right?"

"Well, yes, and no. There's something you probably don't realize: In the seven hundred miles between St. Louis and the Gulf, there are only six operation rail bridges across this river. Five, now, after this thing. In my opinion, this isn't going to get fixed anytime soon, although we've called in Morgan Keeler—he's the Corps' big kahuna expert on these Mississippi River bridges."

One of the deputies was walking up to the taped area. He held a portable radio in his right hand.

"Director Hanson?" he asked.

"Yes?"

"Lady wants to talk to you." He made a somewhat elaborate show of handing Hush the radio across the tape.

"Hanson."

"Sir, this is Carolyn Lang. I'm at the Corps of Engineers command post. The Army is organizing the bank search now. The state police will *not*—I repeat, *not*—be participating, apparently per Captain Powers's orders. The state police have agreed to establish a secure perimeter around the approaches to the bridge, and to keep everyone off the bridge except for the forensic teams. I've been informed that the senior bridge engineer for the Army Corps, one Morgan Keeler, is coming in by helo in about thirty minutes; he's been advised of the meeting. Special Agents Russo and Markham are on their way to your location now. Over?"

"This is Hanson; copy all. Request verify that the state police forensics team leader will attend the meeting."

"This is Lang; will do."

He handed the radio back to the deputy. "There will be two FBI agents coming out onto the bridge; please let them through," he said.

The deputy nodded curtly, spat a glop of chaw through the ties into the river, and walked back down the catwalk to his post at the end of the next span. The spat between the FBI and the state cops must be out on the local law grapevine, thought Hush. Oh, well.

He pulled out his flashlight and walked back to the concrete ledge, taking in the scene. He was careful not to step on the sooty concrete surface directly in front of the pin cavity. The saddle mounting in the cavity was completely deformed, but its base was still attached. There were deep gouge marks on the outboard side of the mounting where the end of the truss arch's girder had dragged over the side before collapsing into the river. He bent out over the side, shining his light down toward the water, and saw the remains of a ladder curled back over itself and hanging out over the water some twenty feet below. The ladder swayed back and forth in response to the eddies of the current tugging at its base.

Something fluttered in the updrafts around the concrete pier tower. A strip of cloth appeared to be caught between the ladder side and the concrete face of the pier about halfway up. He experienced a sudden wave of vertigo looking down the sheer sides of the pier tower with nothing between him and the river except the night air. He jerked his head back.

"Mr. Hanson?" said a voice behind him. Hush straightened and turned, to find the two agents from the St. Louis office standing outside the taped area.

"Gentlemen. Did Agent Lang fill you in on the bank search I've got going?"

"Yes, sir," said Russo. "Sir? We got some kind of problem with the state cops? All of a sudden, it's gotten kinda cold out there, and I'm hearing 'Fart, Barf, and Itch' talk."

Hush gave a thin smile. "The senior state guy resents feds," he replied. "I felt obliged to recalibrate him. I want you two to give some direction to the bank search: I want the bags marked with the general location of where the bulk of the material was picked up, referenced to the bridge—Such as 'west bank, one hundred yards downstream.' Like that. I want some coordination with the layout of the bags at the inspection site—we don't need a trash mountain. If there's enough room, lay them out in the same relative position as they were collected. And I want each bag positioned so that it can be dumped and the contents examined by our lab people."

"Yes, sir," said Markham. "Agent Lang said something about a hangar out at the airport?"

"That's the only place that came to mind," replied Hush. "I think I saw a couple of hangars out there when we came in. Like after an airplane crash—it's a big area, but still under cover."

"Yes, sir. We'll coordinate that. The Army's going to provide trucks, and the state cops have agreed to secure the building once the stuff comes in."

"Okay. Are those people giving Agent Lang any trouble back there?"

Russo looked over at Markham and smiled. "One of the local fuzz made a smart-ass remark," he said. "Lang walked up to him, wrote his name and badge number down in her notebook, asked him if he had a good lawyer, and then walked away. Guy looked like he was experiencing serious gas pains. Razor Pants hasn't changed much."

Razor Pants? They indeed remembered her. "Is Himself here yet?"

"I believe so, sir."

"All right. That's all."

The agents nodded and left. With an assistant director on their patch, some SACs would come out of a sense of protocol. Others, like Himself Herlihy, might come out like a territorial male dog. He was pretty sure Lang would be in for some discomfiture once Herlihy showed up. He went to find the Army command post.

Colonel Anderson massaged his temples. It was nearly 9:00 P.M., and the staff department heads sitting on either side of the conference table waited patiently. The operations department briefer, a young captain, stood at parade rest by the podium, his last slide barely visible now that the lights were back up. Anderson looked around the table.

"So," he said, "After what, three years of slogging through the EPA bureaucracy, fighting off all those protestors and hostile media, not to mention the Army's own paperwork, after all that, you're telling me we have to redo the route?"

The staff officers remained silent. Some of them were new, but a few, like Matthews, had been at Anniston long enough to appreciate the enormity of what the colonel was talking about. He looked over at Carl Hill, who sat, grim-faced, at the end of the table.

"Maybe they can get it fixed, Colonel," Matthews said. "Those railroad people seem to put a derailment back together almost overnight."

Hill was shaking his head. "You ever seen a Mississippi River railroad bridge, Tom?"

"I guess not."

Hill nodded. "They're huge. Not quite as big as the Rhine River bridges, but almost. And they're old. Big-assed truss bridges, lots of heavy steel and rivets and massive girders. Some of them clear a hundred and forty feet above the river for ship traffic."

"But they will have to repair or replace it, right?" Anderson asked.

"I don't know, sir. That's probably going to be more of a financial issue with the Union Pacific than an engineering question. The problem is that our route plan for twenty-seven thirteen is in the dumper. From a timing perspective, that's a disaster. The EPA's route approval was for a specific period of time. Ten more days, twenty-seven thirteen *has* to roll. We miss our launch window, those EPA tickets turn into pumpkins, and we start over."

There was an uncomfortable silence in the conference room. Matthews knew that neither Anderson nor Hill could talk about the other, and certainly more urgent reason for urgency. All of the other department heads knew about the plane crash, but none of them knew about the hot nukes.

"The transport containments are approved for fourteen days once the casings are out of their tombs and on board," Hill said, trying to cover the growing silence. "We can't keep the train elements in the assembly buildings next Thursday."

Anderson was tapping a pencil on the table. "And how long is the trip to Utah?"

"Sixteen hundred miles, sir. At an average speed of thirty-five miles per hour, the trip should take forty-five hours, or it would have, using the Cape Girardeau bridge route."

"And now?"

"With that bridge down, we'll have to recompute. And get a route modification approved. But either way, this train *must* go by next Thursday."

"Maybe we can keep this problem in-house," Matthews suggested. "Change the route once the train is out on the road. If somebody squawks, we could claim we did it for, I don't know, security purposes."

"My thought exactly, Tom," Colonel Anderson said. "But I'll need to clear that with Washington. There's no way to get a new route approved in nine days, so we're gonna need lots of top cover for this. Okay, that's it, gents. Tom, Carl, stay behind, please."

The conference room cleared quickly. Anderson asked Matthews to close the door.

"Tom, what's the status on the C-one thirty problem? Does that Colonel Mehle know about the bridge?"

Matthews sat down, running his fingers through his thinning hair. He'd been assigned as the base operations officer here at Anniston for almost three years. This would be his last career posting in the Army.

"Sir, Colonel Mehle's been out at the crash site all day. He may have heard about the bridge, but he probably wouldn't appreciate the significance."

"Reassure me," Anderson said, looking at both of them. "The fact that we have some hot nukes out at the strip remains close-hold?"

They both nodded. "Yes, sir. The CERT guys and the MPs know something's up, but they've been held at the scene, as per your orders."

"Carl, have you found the cars Mehle needs?"

"I can give him two, not four, Colonel. We can use those two vacuum-enhanced armored tank cars. We can classify them on the public manifest as mustard gas-contaminated rocket casings. We'll have to figure out what to do with the actual casings."

"Mehle said he wanted four cars. I wonder if there's some problem with putting two in a single car. Like too much plutonium close to more plutonium."

"I shouldn't think so, Colonel," Matthews said. "They were closer than that in the C-one thirty."

"That was before the crash," Anderson pointed out. "Okay, I'll have to run this by Mehle. I'll tell him that we have only the two big vacuum tankers; they'll have to do. He told me he wants to move the weapons to Building Nine soon."

"As soon as he does, they'll be more people in the loop, Colonel," Matthews said. "The Building Nine handling crews, and the ammo-car drivers. Once they see Geiger counters and dosimeters, they'll know it's not chemical."

Anderson frowned. "Maybe we can use Mehle's own team to handle the weapons within Building Nine. Maybe keep one senior civilian handling supervisor in the loop."

"And then quarantine the hell out of everybody," Matthews said. "Because if this word gets out, it goes without saying—"

"Indeed it does," Anderson interjected. "Okay, I'll call Washington, then talk to Mehle. Carl, for the moment, we'll say nothing about any changes."

"Yes, sir," Hill said. He got up and went over to the wall, where he pulled down an oversized map of the United States on which all the major rail routes were drawn. "Getting across the Mississippi is our problem. For what it's worth, there are five other bridges that can meet the time-distance route criteria. Cape Girardeau was our first choice because it didn't take twenty-seven thirteen through a metropolitan area."

Anderson nodded, staring at the map. "I can't see rolling twenty-seven thirteen through St. Louis or New Orleans," he said.

"So we're really talking three remaining candidates," Hill said, pointing at the map. "Memphis, Baton Rouge, and Vicksburg. Tom, do the Corps of Engineers people have any ideas of what happened to that bridge?"

"No, only that it collapsed with a train on it. The initial reports came to us from our route contact at the Corps of Engineers office in St. Louis. Big fornicating mess in the river right now, though."

"Which will reinspire every tree-hugger between here and Tooele to lay himself down in front of twenty-seven thirteen," Anderson said, shaking his head. "*Especially* if we have to go in for a route-mod approval."

"Well, now, Colonel, you have to admit—"

"I don't have to admit any damn thing at all, Tom," Anderson said in a hard-edged voice Matthews had not heard before. "A four-star general shared his thinking with me at zero dark-thirty this morning. That train's primary mission right now is to get Colonel Mehle's glow-in-the-dark Beanie Babies out to that Idaho National Engineering Laboratory. The CW train is officially second in the pecking order. In fact, Carl, your train's main mission now is to provide cover for those things."

Matthews saw that Carl Hill was about to pop his question about getting this all in writing. He caught Carl's eye and shook his head slightly, trying to communicate that this was not the time to raise that issue. He stood up before Hill could speak. "Yes, sir," he said quickly. "Understood, sir."

"Good," Anderson said. "We'll get guidance from Washington as to where to cross the river. Tom, you and Carl work up a new route. For now, we'll punt on the route-modification issue."

Anderson dismissed them and went into his office, closing the door behind him. Hill gave Matthews a "What the hell?" look, but Matthews gestured him out of the conference room. He waited until they were out of earshot of Anderson's office to speak.

"He's under enough pressure right now without our putting him a corner," he said. "Let's wait and see what happens; I'm personally not convinced that this is going to go the way Mehle wants it to."

"According to the four-star general, whoever the hell *that* is, it's going exactly the way Mehle wants."

"Yeah, for the moment. But the more people who get involved in this goat-grab, the less likely this secret is going to stay in its box."

• • •

The Army Corps of Engineers command post deuce-and-a-half truck had been replaced by a large semitrailer filled with communications equipment. Along one side of the trailer an olive-drab awning had been deployed, under which the meeting took place. There were no chairs or tables. The only light was that which spilled out from the open door to the CP itself. The attendees included Captain Powers, Hush, Carolyn Lang, the chief of the state police forensics team, the chief engineer of the Union Pacific Railroad, a lieutenant commander from the Coast Guard, and Major Williams. As the group coalesced around a temporary coffee mess, an Army helicopter landed a few hundred feet away in a flare of dust and landing lights. A single passenger, who appeared to be a civilian, debarked carefully under the whirling rotor disk and walked over to the CP. He was a tall, spare man with short gray hair, and he carried a leather portfolio under his arm. Hush had difficulty seeing the man's face as he stooped to get under the awning, but he got a quick impression of gray-faced austerity, perhaps even chronic pain. The man straightened up under the awning and took charge of the meeting. He nodded at the railroad people and at Major Williams as if he knew them all. He ignored Powers.

"Which of you is Assistant Director Hanson?" he asked.

Hush stepped forward. "I am."

The man turned and extended his hand. "Mr. Hanson, I am Morgan Keeler, senior bridge inspector for the Mississippi Valley Division, Army Corps of Engineers. I understand you'll be heading the federal task force to work this incident."

"That's correct. I've set some things in motion."

"So I understand."

As his eyes adjusted to the mixture of light and shadows under the canvas awning, Hush could see Keeler's face better. He confirmed his initial impression of an ascetic, hard-lined, almost gaunt face, with intelligent deep-set eyes under fine gray brows. Keeler had pronounced crow's-feet radiating from the corners of his eyes, a high forehead, and a long, prominent nose. When Keeler didn't say anything, Hush felt compelled to keep talking, which was not his usual style at all.

"The physical evidence up on the bridge has been only partially preserved," he said, not looking at Powers. "The collection effort along the banks is a very long shot, but maybe we can pick up something. What they used is pretty apparent."

"I've been told it was a black-powder device," said Keeler. He fished a pack of cigarettes from inside his jacket, shook one out, and lit up. Hush was struck by the man's intense eyes, glittering in the flare of a butane lighter. His age was indeterminate, fifties, maybe late fifties. Definite type A, Hush thought.

"That's correct, or at least that's what it smells like."

"Oh, it's black powder all right," interjected Powers. He stepped forward. "I'm Capt. Mike Powers, chief of the CIB, Missouri State Highway Patrol," he said. He shook hands with Keeler before continuing. "My forensics people have been out there for a few hours; they're reporting a form of black powder, probably Pyrodex, with some kind of high-order initiator. Of course, the FBI here will be putting their lab people on it, so this may all change. They've got the best lab in the whole wide world, you know."

Hush ignored the gibe. "Our lab people are due into the area shortly," he said. "I'm sure they'll confirm what the state police forensics people have found."

If Keeler had picked up on the tension between the state police and the FBI, he gave no sign of it. "All right," he said. "The forensics are your bailiwick. The structural analysis of what's left is mine. Major Williams, what's your status?"

"We're trying to get that mess in the river stabilized, Colonel. We're attempting to get any large-scale contamination contained, and then we'll begin to get the channel cleared out. The Coast Guard's marine safety office up in St. Louis is already reporting barge traffic backlog building up on both sides"

Hush noted the major's use of the title Colonel when he spoke to Keeler.

"Can barge traffic get by in the side channels?" Keeler asked.

"No, sir," offered the lieutenant commander. "The channel out there is smack-dab in the middle; water on either side looks plenty wide, but it's only about eight to ten feet deep, and that's at high water. We have to get all that wreckage out of there, and especially that downed span."

"Well, that's Corps business," said Hush. "Once I have the sweep made of the banks, which the Army is kindly going to help us with, since the state police are apparently otherwise engaged, our efforts will focus on the bridge itself."

Powers jumped in to defend himself. "The state police are just operating within their charter, especially since you people have taken over, Mr. Hanson," he said.

"Whatever." Hush sighed. "Mr. Keeler, anything else we need to co-ordinate?"

Keeler was looking at both Hush and Powers with impatience. "Not tonight. Just give me and the railroad engineers access to that bridge as soon as possible, before the current spreads the wreckage any farther downstream. The closer it is to the bridge, the easier it will be for us to pick it up, okay?"

"You're going to want to see the inboard span first, Morgan," said the railroad engineer. "We think they hit the main beam with Detcord. We're talking a river recovery."

"Detacord?" Keeler said. Then he sighed. "All right. You've got a team coming out?"

"At first light. They'll need to do some transit work on the truss structure from a land datum, and inspect pins and rivets, of course. But I predict we're not going to be able to use a crane set."

"Damn. All right, I need to go up and take a look," Keeler said. "I guess we've settled who's doing what to whom. Belon, let's you, me, and the Coast Guard here hunker down and get a channel-clearance plan of action going. Sounds like the cops have their hands full."

"I'll have my forensics team start wide and then shrink their examination to the explosion focus," Hush said. "That way, you can get going on cleanup ASAP."

"Appreciate that, Mr. Hanson. Have your team leader let the major here know when they can come on out to the end of the bridge."

Hush agreed and the meeting broke up. He turned to confer with Lang and the two agents. "Agent Russo, you take charge of the bank sweep. Get it under way tonight, while we still have all these people here. Agent Markham, I want you to work with the head of the state forensics team—I believe that's the short guy standing next to Captain Powers over there. Keep everything on a team-effort basis as much as possible. No reason to let Powers's attitude poison all the wells here. Have a car pick me up in the morning, say eight-thirty, at the motel. Questions?"

The two agents had none and left. Hush turned to Carolyn Lang.

"Let's call it a night. I'm going to send you back to Washington to-morrow morning to get the interagency group in motion. I'll be staying out here for another day or so, but there's nothing more for us to do here."

"I just hope that trooper and the car are still waiting back there."

"You think Powers might have pulled him off?"

"He's not exactly a happy camper right now."

Hush looked across the grassy area in front of the CP. In the harsh illumination from the light stands, Powers was talking to several of his state police people. His animated gestures and scowling expression said it all.

"Well, that's my problem, I suppose," Hush said. "Good moves out on the bridge, by the way."

She smiled at him. "Actually," she said, "I think he's harmless. Just a little testicular about the Bureau being here."

Hanson laughed. "I just hope the car is still there," he said.

As they were walking back up the track bed toward the county road, a large figure materialized out of the darkness, approaching them. Hush recognized Joseph Michael Edward Herlihy, special agent in charge of the St. Louis office. Herlihy gave Hush a warm greeting. When he saw Lang, however, his expression changed.

"Oh, for God's sake!" he said. "What in hell is *she* doing here?" He was speaking as if Lang weren't even there.

Hush felt Lang stiffen by his side. "Senior Agent Lang has been appointed deputy of the interagency task force," Hush replied.

Herlihy glared at Lang. "Really. Well, that's a big damn mistake. Lang on a task force? Of all the—"

"By the director," Hush interjected quietly.

Herlihy stopped in midsentence and then struggled visibly to contain himself. Finally, he took Hush by the arm and stepped a few paces away, turning his back on Lang. "I can understand their bringing in an AD to run this one," he said. "I've got no problems with that. My people tell me it's a big goddamned mess out there on the river. But you need to watch your back with that woman, Hush. She may be a Breast Fed, but she's poison."

"Well, I know there were some problems out here last—" Hush started to say, but Herlihy cut him off.

"Problems? That doesn't describe it," he said, making little effort to keep his voice down. "Goddamned woman came in with a big chip on each shoulder and a corncob stuck up her ass. She wasn't on board one week before we had an EEO complaint going. The guys absolutely hated her. I lost Hank McDougal, the best senior agent I had, to early retirement because of her."

"Water under the bridge, Joe," Hush said, trying to keep his own voice down. "Look: She's mostly going to work the Washington interagency venue. I'm sending her back tomorrow."

"Well, good," Herlihy said, making sure Lang could hear. "This state isn't big enough for the two of us, director or no director. Now, you got everything you need here? My guys said they got you rooms at the Best Western over in Cape Girardeau."

Hush nodded. "For the moment. The Army's helping us do a bank search—probably a waste of time, but who knows. Oh, I had a run-in with a state guy named Powers. Seems to have a hard-on for things federal."

Herlihy laughed. "Yeah, well, he's in contention for top cop in the state police. Probably had high hopes of having a starring role in this caper. Actually, he's not a bad guy. Just has a temper. You want me to talk to him?"

"No, it's my problem. I wouldn't mind having my own command center, though. You got a mobile out here?"

"Not really. I've got some Suburbans kluged up for comms, but that's about it."

"Okay, I'll use the Army CP for now," Hush said, looking around at the darkness. "You drive yourself out here? Powers gave us a state car, but he may have pulled the guy off."

"My guys can take you to the motel if you need," Herlihy said. He seemed to have calmed down; he was now speaking in a normal tone of voice. "I'm gonna go on up ahead here and see what my people are doing. What are your plans?"

"I'm bushed. I'm going to get some sleep." He described the arrangements with the Army, and Herlihy said he would try to meet them at the hangar in the morning. With one last glare at Lang, he stomped on down the track bed toward the lights.

THE HANGAR was already beginning to stink by the time Hush arrived Wednesday morning. One hundred and sixty-two bags' worth of riverbank treasure were lined up in orderly rows across the wide expanse of the main hangar when he stepped in out of the sunlight. Each bag sat on the concrete floor like the dropping of some obnoxious animal, sodden and stinking in individual pools of toxic-looking fluids. The smell made him reach involuntarily for his nose. Some hangar maintenance people were standing around in obvious dismay. A large trash-hauling truck was parked at the entrance to the hangar. Its two attendants watched impassively as they sat on the front bumper smoking their cigarettes. Herlihy's ASAC from the St. Louis office met him at the entrance, accompanied by three other agents. They were all dressed out in paper overalls, gauze face masks, and rubber gloves and were holding steel rakes.

Hush greeted them. "I suppose this noisome collection is being credited exclusively to me."

"Yes, sir," the ASAC replied. "Exclusively. The airport manager has asked that we do whatever we're going to do with all this . . . stuff—today if we can. He's had to move three aircraft under maintenance out of the hangar, and he'd like to get them back under cover ASAP. And it's going to get warm today, sir. Really warm."

"Got it. Are these the forensics people?"

"Yes, sir," replied the ASAC. He introduced two people from the Washington lab, and a third man from the state police forensics division.

Hush shook hands all around. The senior lab man pulled out a small bottle of Vicks, dabbed a bit in each of his nostrils, and then passed the bottle around. It was gratefully accepted. Hush donned a set of coveralls that reached to his knees. He led the group toward the first row of trash piles. The ASAC continued to brief him.

"Our explosives forensics unit got out to the bridge at two-thirty A.M. They pretty much confirmed what the state people found. Two specialists from our team are there now; the senior guy is Dr. Franklin. The other techs are getting some sleep. There're a couple of state cops up in the maintenance office. They said they'd deal with any intruders or press while we work this sweep. Uh, do we have some idea of what we're looking for, sir?"

"Nope," said Hush cheerfully. "I would really appreciate finding some bomb-making materials—wire, clocks, batteries, empty dynamite boxes, black-powder cans, signed credit-card receipts for gunpowder, a group photo of the bad guys, you know."

The others were grinning behind their masks.

"But what I really want done here is to go through each pile of trash and look for something that we would not expect to find along the riverbanks, or that might by some stretch of the imagination be related to a bomb on the bridge. I can't define what that would be—we'll all just make one pass through this, er, collection, and then we'll move on. I want to do this as a group."

They worked through the first row of piles, front to back, looking for anything that looked out of place. The riverbank had yielded up an eclectic collection of rubbish, which the forensics people pulled apart with the steel rakes. Bottles, plastic bags, wood debris, clothes, an occasional shoe, paper boxes, aluminum cans, a dead cat, tires—the standard decor of too many American rivers. At the end of the first row, they set aside two pieces of creosoted planking that had fresh splintered edges, indicating they came from the bridge deck. The second row produced nothing of interest, nor did the third.

The county trash people drove their noisy truck out to the middle of the hangar and then followed along behind the agents with their shovels and brooms. Halfway down the fourth row, Hush spotted something—a rag, a foot-long strip of cloth. It looked like it had been torn from a T-shirt. He reached into the pile and picked it up. Something about it keyed his memory, but he could not remember what.

"Sir?"

"Bag it, please."

They continued through the fourth row, then began on the fifth. They found several more pieces of wood from the bridge, much of it heavily soaked in what smelled like dry-cleaning fluid. At the end of the fifth row, one of the agents leaned into the pile and extracted another rag, nearly identical to the first.

"Good eye," said Hush. "See how it's been torn into a strip? It's like a makeshift bandage. And it's pretty clean, considering. It's keying something in my memory from last night, but I've lost it. Bag it up. Let's go on."

They spent an hour and half going through the rest of the detritus from the riverbanks, but nothing else of interest surfaced except for more pieces of the bridge catwalks. The hangar mechanics had a fire hose out and had begun to hose down the concrete floor by the time the agents had completed their search. They walked out into the sunshine for a quick conference.

"I don't know if that was productive or not," said Hush. "I just felt we had to make a sweep—you never know where physical evidence will turn up. I want those two rags analyzed for chemical residues: what's in them, and if the same thing is in both of them. The pieces of catwalk will probably confirm that they were exposed to flame and black-powder burning. You guys concur with the state that it was a black-powder device?"

"Yes, sir," said the older of the two FBI lab men. "Your nose could tell you that, but the residues confirm it. We'll be able to tell you what kind of powder, maybe who made it, and probably what was used for an initiator. I suspect either a blasting cap or a cap and dynamite combination."

"Big bomb? Something it would take a crew to carry out there?"

"Not necessarily," said the state forensics man. "That concrete cavity would contain a black-powder blast pretty well, and focus it on the movable part of the structure, which was the truss pin. That Keeler fella said that all they really had to do was blow off that pin, not blow the whole bridge down. That bridge collapsed because the main pin holding the entire structure was dislodged with two thousands tons of train on it. That wouldn't take a five-hundred-pounder."

"So the bombers knew precisely where to put an explosive device to do the max damage with a minimum amount of stuff."

"Yes, sir. These guys knew their bridges, too, I'd say. Without the train, it might not have gone down right away."

"OK, gents, thanks for the effort here. I'd like a ride back out to the bridge, and I'd like to have the forensics people go with me."

Hush spent the remainder of the day at the bridge, reexamining the scene and what remained of the physical evidence. The recovery crane engine set had been pulled back to the bank; apparently, Morgan Keeler had pronounced the inboard western span unsafe. The Corps of Engineers and the Coast Guard had a full-scale recovery effort under way down on the river, with a very large contract floating crane operating below. Three drowned boxcars had been lifted from the river and placed on a barge anchored just downstream of the bridge. Two other empty barges were anchored to the riverbank upstream, waiting to be moved into position. Three large and two small tugboats huffed and chuffed around the bridge piers, trying to stay clear of the heavy cables holding the crane barge in position in the current.. The engine noise was nearly deafening, even up on the pier tower. Everyone communicated with one another using pads and pens, since normal speech was nearly impossible.

Hanson spotted a third strip of cloth snagged on a pier tower's ladder; it looked similar to the ones found in the hangar search. He realized that this was what had triggered his memory that morning and had it retrieved as possible evidence. Toward two o'clock, they retreated to the base of the bridge for their first conference. They grabbed some sandwiches and coffee from the Army CP and were kicking around their findings when a state police cruiser bumped its way along the service road all the way to the base of the bridge. It stopped and Captain Powers got out of the right-front seat. He walked over to where the group was standing. Hush proffered a Styrofoam cup of coffee.

"Join us?" he asked.

Powers frowned but accepted.

"We were just wrapping up out here," said Hush, nodding up toward the bridge. "I think we've squeezed most of the evidence out of the scene, such as it is."

Powers nodded. "Yep. Looks to me like a bridge got blown up." Hush peered down at him, but Powers was keeping a straight face. The state forensics man was grinning into his coffee cup.

"I heard that all you found at the airport were two strips of cloth," Powers said.

"Yeah, and we got another one off the bridge."

"So?"

"We can't know that now, Captain," one of the Bureau lab men said. "We have to do some more work. You know, investigate. That's we do, remember? FB of *I*?" It was Hush's turn to suppress a smile. The lab guy was pretty quick. To his surprise, he saw Powers begin to grin. Then they were all laughing. Powers took off his state police hat, stomped some mud off his shoes, and then tipped his head sideways. Hush joined him at the base of abutment.

"Why I came out here was to invite you to have dinner with me," Powers said. "There's a pretty good steak house out near the county line. I think you'n me need to start over."

Hush's face lit up. "Hell of an idea, Captain. I was trying to figure out how to say the same thing."

"Glad to hear it. Name's Mike, by the way. I'll have a cruiser come by your motel—say around seven, if that works?"

"Works fine. Call me Hush."

Powers put his hat back on and headed back to his waiting cruiser. Hush, feeling much relieved, returned to the forensics team and gave them wrap-up instructions. He asked the agents to take him back to the motel, where he took a quick shower, put in a wake-up call for 6:30. He dropped on the bed in the cool darkness of the motel room. There had been no messages from Lang, so she was either making progress or unwilling to call for help if she wasn't. He had left a message for Tyler Redfield to provide all possible assistance. Tyler would know what that meant.

At seven o'clock sharp, a highly polished state police cruiser bristling with antennas swung under the motel's registration portico. Hush climbed into the passenger seat. The driver was a very large Highway Patrolman who appeared to be of Native American heritage, which, thankfully for Hush, meant that the front seat was pushed all the way back. The trooper tipped two fingers to his hat and then nosed the powerful car out onto the state highway. Hush contented himself with examining all the gadgetry on the consoles in front of him while the impassive trooper pushed the cruiser down the darkening road at a smooth eighty miles an hour. Radios, radar, computer terminal, pads of forms, emergency medical gear, shotgun—all the tools of the police trade. And a video camera, he noticed. He wondered if that was to film the bad guys or to protect the cop from the bad guys' lawyers. He had been on the paper side of things for so long, he had almost forgotten what a real cop car looked like. The steel grill between the front and back seats was missing, and it looked like the backseat was configured as a mobile command center, with two phones and a second computer terminal visible. This must be Powers's personal cruiser, he thought.

They arrived at the restaurant, a roadside stone and brick affair whose filled parking lot showed promise. The trooper let him out at the front door. Hush was conscious of some stares from a casually dressed young foursome headed across the parking lot. He had dressed in a dark suit, white shirt, rep tie, and shiny black wing tips. His height alone would have provoked a second look; his emerging from the state police car definitely did.

Powers was already at the table. He was dressed in a sports coat and tie, tan cavalry twill pants, and loafers. Hush noted that the sports coat was roomy enough to conceal a shoulder weapon. He wondered briefly if he should have been carrying, now that he was out in the field. The restaurant staff obviously knew who Powers was and they had given him a secluded corner table in the back of the dining room, which was decorated in dark woods, with a low-beamed white ceiling and brick walls. There was a large fireplace at each end of the dining room. The clientele ranged from solid-looking rancher types to young people dressed out as urban cowboys. Hush, as always, felt conspicuous as he squeezed himself into an armchair. An attractive young waitress appeared at the table as soon as he sat down.

"Double scotch rocks, water back," rumbled Powers. He raised his eyebrows at Hush.

"Same," said Hush. He normally did not drink hard liquor when he was in the field, but he sensed that Powers might still be taking his measure.

"Thank you, sir, and here are your menus. The specials tonight—"

"That's okay, Cindy," said Powers. "We'll order in a little bit."

The girl hurried away, returning in two minutes with their drinks. Powers tipped his glass in Hush's direction, then took a substantial hit, followed by a satisfied sigh.

"Nothing like the first one after a bitch of day," he said. "Now, first off, I apologize for being a state dickhead out there last night. It was unprofessional. There was no excuse for it, and none being offered."

"Accepted. And I apologize for acting like a federal dickhead. This is your turf and I didn't invade it correctly."

"Yeah, well, good. Now, I—I mean *we*—want to help. Blowing up a railroad bridge is a big goddamn deal here in Missouri. Not to mention what it's going to do to the Union Pacific traffic."

"They're not saying very much about that, are they?"

"They will, but it's a highly competitive business. Railroad boys're used to playing their cards pretty close. Now, look here: I know you guys are gonna run this, but we'd really like to be in it, 'cause I think we can contribute."

Hush nodded, putting his drink on the table. "Count on it," he said. "No matter what you've heard, the Bureau knows that state law always has a much better local picture than we do, unless we've been running a trapline for some time. But tell me, how's the law organized in this state?"

"We're the Missouri Highway Patrol. We've also got county sheriffs, and some city and town cops for those burgs big enough to pay for 'em: St. Louis, Kansas City, Jefferson City—pretty standard setup. We don't have a separate state bureau of investigation, like in Georgia.—that's what my folks do."

"So you're CID?"

"CIB," Powers said. "Bureau. Missouri has five bureaus—field ops, criminal investigation, technical, admin, and support. I run the Criminal Investigation Bureau. We have statewide jurisdiction to investigate, execute warrants, and make arrests, even where there's county or city law involved."

"Right," Hush said. Then he remembered what Herlihy had said. "Let me ask you this: Is there a political angle here? I mean, would it make a difference if, for instance, we find these guys and you guys make the collars? What I'm saying is, I have the authority to make that happen."

Powers leaned back in his chair, an approving look on his face. "Goddamn, Hush Hanson," he said with a grin. "A politically astute Fee-bee. I believe you just might be dangerous, partner."

It was Hush's turn to grin. "We do indulge in office politics from time to time, I admit."

Powers laughed harder.

"The only thing the Bureau *must* do," Hush continued, "is to get the credits right in Washington. That's the only constituency that counts for us."

"Understood. And you're pretty senior, right? An assistant director?"

"Right. My division was created to coordinate federal task forces when

the cases become complex. If we catch the bad guys, I do our standard
'We always get our man' press release in D.C. But if it makes the sun
shine out here for you guys actually to make the bust—say, perhaps, with
the cameras rolling—I don't have a problem with that." He paused for a
moment to sip his drink. "But that's assuming this is a local thing. If this
is, say, an Iraqi conspiracy, then it's going to get very federal."

"Yeah, okay," Powers said. "That works. Now, you guys think there's
some kind of a group who did this, right?"

"We're just getting started. We always assume a terroristic act like a
bombing is a group effort, if only because the logistics of bombing can
get complicated. Truth is, right now we've got zip-point-shit, other than
a small handle on the explosives."

"What's that Lang woman's role in this task force?" Powers asked,
finishing off his scotch.

"Senior Agent Carolyn Lang. She's out of the Washington headquarters, and she's been appointed as the task force deputy. She'll primarily
act as the interagency coordinator in D.C."

"Quite a looker," Powers said. "But a couple of Herlihy's guys were
talking. Said she was a ball-breaker."

Hush sighed. "I haven't worked with her very much, yet," he said. "So
that's all hearsay. Himself Herlihy certainly doesn't like her."

Power rattled the ice in his glass and nodded to himself. "Yeah, so we
gathered. Tell you something, though. The other night, when you'n me
had our little dustup? I was pissed off enough to want to hit somebody.
I don't know if *she* was aware of it or not, but her gun hand was in motion
about the time I was ready to pop. She's at least got the right instinct
about trouble."

Hush remembered. "That's good to know."

Then Powers surprised him. "Your nickname," he said. " 'Hush.'
What's that all about?"

"I've always made it a point not to talk too much. Someone made a
play on words a long time ago. I guess. It just stuck."

"Nothing to do with a shooting deal in Baltimore?"

Hush tried to keep his expression neutral. He wondered who'd been
running his yap. The Baltimore thing was ancient history, which was exactly where he wanted it to stay. "Nope," he said. "Nothing like that. I've
mostly been a Washington bureaucrat."

Powers smiled and said nothing for a moment while he glanced at the menu. Hush realized that Powers had been making some calls. Well, he thought, that was only intelligent. Hush asked him about the trooper who had brought him to the restaurant.

"That's Little Hill," Powers said. "People out here think he's an Indian, but his parents are Samoan. I use him as my personal driver. He can keep his mouth shut, and he's pretty handy if things get hinky."

"*Little* Hill?"

Powers grinned. "You should have seen his old man, *Big* Hill. He was a trooper, too." Then he tapped his menu. "So, how do you like your steaks?"

"I prefer them rare, depending on what that means out here on the range."

"Out here, *rare* means they cut its horns off, wipe its ass, and bring it to the table."

"Oh. Well, hell, maybe medium rare, then."

They talked casually during dinner, rubbing down the hard edges of their normal bureaucratic reserve with another round of whiskey. Powers filled Hush in on his own background in the state police over coffee, then paused when the waitress came to clear away the table.

"You said you were primarily a headquarters guy," he said. "I thought you had to spend a lot of time in the field to get to your level."

"That used to be true, but our business is getting so complex and specialized that some of us bubble up from inside the headquarters building."

Powers nodded slowly as he stirred his coffee. He appeared to be thinking about something for a minute. Then he looked back over at Hush.

"So, Baltimore. I've heard the folklore. I'd be obliged if you'd tell me the real story."

Hush had to think about it. He almost never talked about Baltimore, but Powers seemed to be a senior cop with a visibly low bullshit threshold. And they were going to work together. He felt a sudden impulse to tell him. Maybe it was all the scotch.

"I was a nugget agent, the junior guy on a drug-money stakeout," he said. "My two partners went into the house. I was the outside backup. It seemed to be taking a long time. When they didn't come back out, I went in. Without calling for more backup, as I was supposed to do. There was some shooting. It came out all right. Lots of paperwork. Got my ass chewed for breaking procedure, and rightfully so."

Powers was watching him carefully. "Way I heard it," he said finally, "was that the bad guys had your partners on their knees in the kitchen in the execution position. You came through the back door and shot all four of them. In the head."

Hush stared across the dining room. In the eyes, actually, he thought to himself, then quickly smothered that detail. But he couldn't smother the memory: four shots in the space of maybe three seconds, the first one, Herrera, dropping like a one-eyed stone while Hush was blowing the brains out of the fourth one. The shots coming so fast, he'd wondered at the time if he'd missed one of them. But he had not. One of the kneeling agents had wet himself when the shooting started. The other had taken several seconds to raise his eyes, look around, and then look at Hush, and it was the expression on that man's face that Hush would never forget. The silence in that kitchen turned charnel house had been profound. His nickname had taken on a whole new meaning after the incident.

"Well, something like that," he said, attempting to fill the silence. He shrugged. "It was a long time ago. I was just new enough that they forgave me. After that, they changed the procedure: Now you leave an experienced man in the backup position. If you ever need him, that's not the time for amateur night."

"And after your first four years, you applied for career path," Powers said. "Got off the street."

"That's right," he said.

"Because of the shooting incident?" Powers was looking at him with an expression that said, We're both cops and it's important that I hear this.

Hush hesitated. What had happened in Baltimore had changed his life. He had always been something of an introvert, but after that bloodbath, he had walled himself in, determined to contain the other Hush Hanson, the one who could snuff out four lives in three seconds with such murderous efficiency. It had been a totally clean shoot, and yet . . .

"Yeah. When I killed those four mutts, I learned something about myself," he said. "Something profoundly disturbing."

Powers waited, and then he said, "You found out you liked it."

"Liked? No, that's the wrong word, absolutely."

Powers wasn't put off. "Okay, so maybe not *like*. But it was a rush. It was the most exciting thing you had ever done, even if you felt bad about it later."

Hush nodded slowly. "I felt bad about killing four . . . people, if I can use that word. Of course, I felt good about saving my fellow agents." He paused. "I guess I had trouble believing that I had done that. In the blink of an eye." He was talking too much. Damn the scotch.

Powers nodded thoughtfully. "So you decided to get your ass off the street and go be a headquarters bunny."

"Had some help with that, I think," Hush said. He signaled the passing waitress for some coffee. "I think my bosses were just a little bit shocked, too. I went career path early and nobody objected. Anyway, that's the essence of it."

Powers could see that Hush wasn't going to elaborate further. He rattled the ice in his glass and took a final hit. "Appreciate the insight," he said. "Now, what the hell are we going to do about this railroad bridge?"

On Wednesday evening, Major Matthews was observing the assembly of the 2713 weapons train. He was standing in the third-floor observation gallery, an enclosed room with a large glass window overlooking the open assembly bay. The men working below on the train were dressed out in full protective gear. They were using a gantry crane to lift the contaminated weapons casings from a line of ammunition carriers into one of the specially armored railroad cars. Because he was up in the sealed gallery, Matthews was not required to have a protective suit on.

The assembly building was a large windowless four-story concrete structure with train-size steel doors on each end. Inside, there were facilities for loading ten railcars at a time. Two parallel siding tracks were embedded in the concrete floor, alongside which ran two other tracks. Outside of those ran two additional, narrower-gauge tracks, which were used by the smaller ammunition carriers. A thirty-ton capacity overhead gantry crane ran across the ceiling on suspension tracks at right angles to the rail tracks. The special railcars were classified as eighty-ton covered gondola cars, built to Army chemical-ordnance specifications to carry five-hundred-pound bombs, eight-inch howitzer artillery shells, ballistic rockets, or aerosol dispensing tanks. While the cars were being loaded in the assembly building, their tops and sides were dismantled and removed until the load had been assembled on lockdown racks, at which point the sides and top were put back on and onboard pressurization systems activated. Each of the assembly buildings was maintained under negative air pressure, and the single security-controlled entrance for humans was airlocked. The actual work area was a secondary pressure zone, ensuring that if there was ever an accidental release, any toxic material stayed inside the assembly area, while the primary pressure area protected the other people in the building. Anyone working out in the assembly area was required to be in full chemical protective gear: rubber suit and gloves, hood, face respirators, and emergency air canisters. Matthews knew that the protective suits made the work awkward and slow, but that wasn't necessarily a bad thing from a safety point of view.

The building's control room called. The colonel wanted to see him in Assembly 9. He walked to the hallway outside of the gallery and took an elevator to the ground floor, which was outside of the pressurized operating assembly area containment zone. Assembly Building 9 was a triple containment building, all the way at the back of the two rows of concrete buildings. It had been built to deal with the problem of "leakers," or weapons stored in the Anniston Depot whose internal casing integrity was suspect due to age or visible deterioration. The weapons did not actually leak anything, but the casings, many of which were over fifty years old, were rusting out and no longer certifiable for safe operational use. Assembly 9 was where they would assemble the two specially modified tank cars that were to carry the damaged Russian torpedoes.

He signed out through the security desk, went through the building's air lock, and out into the night air. To his left was the blank concrete wall of Assembly 3, and beyond it, two more of the large buildings. To his right was the extension of the main railroad line. Assembly 9 was three buildings back. The main rail connector line ran between the rows of buildings. When all the cars had been assembled, a switch engine would be brought onto the base and the train set out onto the main-line spur. It would then be hooked up to specially configured Army diesel locomotives for the run to Utah.

He walked down the empty concrete apron area that ran between the depot's ten assembly buildings. The days were already starting to get hot; the first hint of Alabama's ferocious summer heat was emanating from the still-warm concrete slabs of the buildings. Beyond the high wire fence surrounding the line of assembly buildings were trees: an entire forest of pines extending for miles out into the nine-thousand-acre reservation. Back out there, beyond the close-in woods, were the tombs, row upon row of heavily guarded, partially submerged concrete bunkers containing the remnants of America's chemical weapon arsenal. The United States had committed to the destruction of its entire CW arsenal upon signature and ratification of the Chemical Weapons Convention. The actual destruction process would take a decade or more, with each CW depot operating its own destruction facility. Every single weapon in all the storage depots around the country had to be inspected, certified safe for handling, exhumed from its bunker, uploaded onto an ammunition transport car, and taken into the destruction facility, where its contents would be extracted and burned. The casings, purged of their deadly contents, would then be assembled for transport by special trains to the Army's large scale metal destruction facility out in the Utah desert.

Colonel Anderson must have received a decision from Washington as to what to do about a new route, Matthews thought. In the beginning, the Army had planned to move the actual weapons out to Utah, which had precipitated a huge bureaucratic fight to get route clearance. Every environmental group in the country fought the Army tooth and nail to stop the shipments, while at the same time protesting vociferously that the Army wasn't moving fast enough to destroy the CW arsenal. The Army fought a damned-if-you-do, damned-if-you-don't situation. The proposal to move 2713SP from Anniston to Tooele, even considering the fact that its cargo was empty casings, had been no exception.

The Army made three arguments: First, the United States had signed the treaty, and it was thereby obligated under international law, which superceded domestic law, to destroy the weapons. Second, the weapons were binary-safe. That meant that, by design, every American chemical warhead contained not an actual chemical agent but, rather, the two main constituents of the ultimate toxic substance. Until the weapon was fired or launched, and subjected to G-forces, the main constituents could not mix to create an actual chemical weapon. Therefore, even if a train wreck occurred, and the train was carrying actual weapons, the worst that would happen would be a toxic chemical spill, as opposed to a nerve-gas or blood-agent weapon release. Which made the third reason even more important, for 2713's cargo was not even actual weapons, but empty CW cases. The only reason for all the special precautions was the remote possibility that some of the casings' internals had deteriorated enough to have been contaminated. It was a pretty good argument, except, of course, as Matthews now knew, two of the cars would be carrying something infinitely more dangerous than chemical weapons: damaged Russian nuclear weapons. About which, Matthews realized, Colonel Anderson and everyone else on the Anniston Depot knew exactly nothing.

Tom Matthews had one year left to go before he could retire on twenty, and he was therefore being a very careful man at this late stage in his otherwise uneventful career as a Chemical Corps officer. He had recognized for a long time that he would never make lieutenant colonel; the Army's Chemical Corps was in the sunset of its existence. He had, however, served his country honorably for almost twenty years and was very much dependent financially on getting safely to twenty and retiring from active duty with his military pension intact. He definitely wanted no part of shipping hot nukes across the United States, especially under a false pretext.

He reached Assembly 9 and saw that Colonel Anderson's car and driver were waiting outside. There was a second official vehicle parked next to Anderson's. He checked in with the guards just inside the first air lock and picked up his escort. From the outside, Assembly 9 looked like the other assembly buildings, but just past the security area there was a second, cipher-locked airlock, through which his escort admitted him to the internal control area. From there, they took the elevator to the control room air lock on the second floor. The control room was positively pressurized, and it had a set of windows looking down into the assembly area, much like the observation gallery from which he had just come. There were consoles that operated the gantry cranes, the main and auxiliary doors, and all the safety and security systems in the building. Since there were no train units in the building, no shift personnel were present and the consoles were shut down. The escort remained outside the control room.

Colonel Anderson was standing in the center of the room with Colonel Mehle. There were two other Army officers, both lieutenant colonels, whom Matthews did not recognize. He assumed they were part of Mehle's team. Colonel Anderson was looking somewhat uncomfortable.

"You called, sir?" Matthews said, deliberately addressing his question to Colonel Anderson.

"Yes. We have developments. First, Washington military intelligence reports that that bridge at Thebes didn't just fall down. It was sabotaged."

"Damn! Somebody blew it up?"

"Indeed. Second, I've had two teleconferences with General Whitfield regarding the bridge incident and the requirement to change the route for twenty-seven thirteen. He understands the time constraints, that we have to launch next week."

Matthews glanced over at Mehle. "Does the CG know about the new problem, Colonel?"

Anderson looked to Mehle, who answered Matthews's question. "No. General Whitfield has *not* been brought into the loop," he said. "And he's not going to be. This problem is being handled above his level."

Matthews took a moment to absorb what Mehle was saying. Major General Whitfield was the commanding general of the entire Chemical Corps. If he was being cut out of the Russian nuke problem, Mehle must have some serious top cover in the Pentagon.

"So then who is giving us authorization to ship damaged nuclear weapons on this train, sir?" Matthews asked. Mehle just stared at him. Matthews knew his question was bordering on impertinence, but he was also mindful of what Carl Hill had said about getting this in writing.

"I have had verbal orders from the office of the Chief of Staff of the Army," Colonel Anderson said, staring down at the floor.

"*Verbal* orders, Colonel?" Matthews asked, trying not to sound too incredulous.

"Confirmed by the commander in chief of the Special Operations Command," Mehle said. "What's the matter, Major? The orders of two four-stars not good enough for you?" Mehle's officers were giving Matthews fish-eye looks.

Carl Hill was right, Matthews thought. "Sir, we're talking about making a clandestine shipment of damaged nuclear weapons on the national rail networks. I guess what I want are orders in writing from someone qualified to approve that shipment," Matthews said. "So far, and I'm not trying to be insubordinate here, all I have are reports of telephone conversations."

Mehle's face started to get red, but Colonel Anderson intervened. "I understand your problem, Tom. I'll personally issue the train dispatch order for twenty-seven thirteen—in writing. We'll wordsmith it somehow to cover the special cars. But we have specific orders not to put anything in writing about the nukes. From the top."

Anderson looked at Matthews as if to say, Trust me, and Matthews was inclined to do just that. He knew that Colonel Anderson wasn't the type to hang his subordinates out. Mehle, on the other hand, appeared to be a different proposition.

"Yes, sir," Matthews said, deciding to wait until he could talk to his boss alone, without the Special Ops people around.

Anderson breathed a small sigh of relief. "Right," he said. "Okay. The route problem, of course, is how to get the train across the Mississippi. The CG agrees we will roll twenty-seven thirteen on the original route up to the Birmingham junction, but then we're to cross the river at Memphis. By his people's computations, that allows the original transit window to remain almost intact. You and Major Hill will need to double-check that."

"Yes, sir," Matthews said, waiting for the other shoe to drop. Mehle was listening to all of this with visible impatience.

"And further, the CG has given orders that we will not—repeat, *not*— announce the route change prior to departure. He feels that in light of the Thebes bridge sabotage, the Army's agreements with the EPA and the state agencies are now subject to 'changed security circumstances.' If necessary, General Whitfield says he can get a national command authority warrant to move this train."

I'll just bet he can, Matthews thought, but the general won't know why it was so easy to get one.

"The presence of the Russian weapons is not to be disclosed to anyone, Major," Mehle announced. "All of the additional security arrangements are to be predicated on the inclusion of two special cars containing possibly contaminated chemical-ordnance casings. Is this clear?"

Matthews took a deep breath. "I can see how we can duck the federal EPA, Colonel," he said. "But you're talking about making a route change on the fly. If I understand the process, you'll have to notify at least the state authorities. Major Hill tells me that the railroad traffic-control people won't clear a toxic block down the line without those state agency tickets."

"Yes, I understand that. But not in advance. What Washington proposes to do is to launch the train on the original route and then do an emergency route modification and go via Memphis. With, of course, no notice to the public. That goes without saying."

"Yes, sir, absolutely," Matthews said as he mentally worked through the possibilities of the word getting out that they were changing the route.

There would be absolute hell to pay if it did, even without the new problem.

"My people have flown in new containments for the weapons," Mehle said. "Your safety people are now training our people on how to run one of those ammunition carriers, and we're bringing in other Special Operations Command people to do the uploads here in Assembly Nine when the time comes."

"I assume someone's come up with a cover story, Colonel?" Matthews asked. "You replace all of our people with your people, and the whole base is going to be talking about it."

"We've discussed that, Major. The cover story is that the C-one thirty was carrying some Iraqi materials recovered by the UN inspection teams. We're dropping some hints that it's chemical, but that we're treating it as biological just to be extremely safe."

"Your people were wearing dosimeters at the crash site, Colonel," Matthews said to Mehle.

"Not anymore," he replied. "At least not where anyone can see them. We're not actually saying what's in these new containments, but if there is speculation, we want it to be chemical."

Matthews nodded while he thought about Mehle was proposing to do. The original route had been from Anniston to the Birmingham, Alabama, junction, then northwest to the isolated bridge at Cape Girardeau, Missouri, and from there continuing northwest out toward Utah. Going through a city the size of Memphis raised the safety stakes considerably.

"Very well, sir," Matthews said to Anderson. "Carl and I will recompute the new route. We'll need to pick the best time to go through Memphis, as that will be the only metropolitan area we'll transit. I'll have the route parameters for the morning staff meeting."

"Good, that's settled, then," Anderson said, obviously relieved that Matthews had not balked.

Mehle gave Matthews another hard look and then took his assistants downstairs. Matthews started to leave, but Colonel Anderson appeared to have something to say. He moved to the windows overlooking the empty assembly bay below. In the subdued lighting of the control room, his face looked tired and drawn.

"This is a mess, Tom," he said. "There's a lot of back-channel stuff going on that you don't know about."

Matthews took some care with his answer. His boss was being squeezed pretty hard by the top brass and probably also by Mehle. He did, however, feel obligated to express his reservations. He explained the radiation dangers of a tritium-gas leak and told the colonel what he remembered about the nuclear weapons school descriptions of poorly assembled Russian weapons. Anderson shook his head slowly.

"I know. Actually, Mehle's been pretty up front with me about the hazards. But the Army's kind of stuck right now: Apparently, Washington's put another airlift out of bounds after this accident. These nukes, fortuitously, from Washington's point of view, landed right here on a special weapons depot—where there's a high-security train being assembled to go pretty damn close to where the weapons were bound in the first place."

"Yes, sir, but we've been totally above board about this train. What happens if we get caught moving these things undeclared on the public rail network?"

Anderson gave him a bleak look. "Well, we just better not get caught. That business about getting written orders—was that Carl Hill's idea?"

The colonel knows his people, Matthews thought. "Yes, sir. But I share his concerns. And, with respect, so should you."

Anderson gave him a cool smile. "I appreciate your concern, Tom. I'll make sure you're covered. I'm the one on the hook for this little caper. I just hope our bosses know what the hell *they're* doing."

Matthews looked down into the darkened assembly bay. That makes two of us, he thought.

5

A COLD, SODDEN RAIN was drizzling down in the Illinois Central Railroad switching yard, East St. Louis, Illinois, when he stepped out of the shadows of a round house, carrying an Army-surplus duffel bag. He was dressed out in regulation Illinois Central rain gear and hard hat, and he looked like any other graveyard-shift brakeman. Given the weather, he had a better than even chance of not encountering a single living soul out here in the yards, not at this hour, but he wanted to look the part just in case. He humped the heavy duffel bag across six sets of tracks, slipping between all the parked blocks of cars, trying to keep his feet dry. The first six tracks, known as the forwarding yard, were staging areas for blocks of cars that had been pushed over from the Missouri side. Seven through twelve were for trains going back the other way, with track seven being the next block to move. When he reached the seventh track, he took one final look around, then swung the duffel up onto the back platform of a Norfolk Southern tank car and climbed up after it. He shoved the bag into the shadows beneath the round-down of the tank but made no special effort to hide himself. Switch crews rode the blocks over the bridge all the time. He could see only the top of the MacArthur Bridge in the gloom and rain; the rest of it was obscured by hundreds of boxcars, coal hoppers, single and double-stack flatcars, tank cars, gondolas, and the occasional switching engine rumbling through the darkness.

The East St. Louis yard was huge, nearly four hundred acres of switching leads, parallel sidings, a hump yard, and the roundhouse, all marking the confluence of eight national and regional railroads. Its main function was the assembly and dispatch of trains that would be crossing the Mac-

Arthur railroad bridge at St. Louis, bound for the western United States rail network. The Terminal Railroad operated a smaller version of the Illinois yards over on the Missouri side. Its switch leads were nested underneath the elevated I-55 expressway. The MacArthur, which soared over one hundred feet above the Mississippi, was almost continuously busy as trains from the east were disassembled on the Illinois side, reassembled into blocks with cars from other railroads, and then hooked to the switch engines to be pulled across the high, arching bridge into the Missouri yards. There, they would be linked up with the main-line engines of the Union Pacific and the Burlington Northern Santa Fe railroads. Eastbound trains were unhooked, assembled into blocks, pushed across the bridge, and reassembled on the Illinois side. The bridge also carried road traffic, although the lanes were so old and narrow that there was very little vehicular traffic except during the busiest times of the day, when the shifts changed.

A succession of rumbling clunks cascading through the line from ahead signaled that this block was moving out. He grabbed a handrail, and a moment later his tank car jolted into forward motion, the solid steel wheels hissing and screeching on the wet rails. He looked at his watch. The wonders of centralized rail traffic control, he thought, and then he relaxed. Train speed across the bridge was never more than about three to five miles an hour; like most of the river bridges, the MacArthur was an old bridge, and the blocks often reached past both ends of its mile-long span during these transfers. He sat down on the top step, making sure to keep his feet in as the string banged its way through several switch points. The heavily loaded cars swayed uncomfortably, looking like a conga line of drunks, before merging finally with the bridge approach line. As soon as they were on the approach line, another block coming down from the Missouri side blotted out the night sky in front of him. The wet metallic sides of the cars on the eastbound line clacked by right in his face.

He waited until he felt the angle change as his tank car started up the approach incline; then he shoved the bag over to the far right-hand side of the tiny platform. He followed it over. Dressed as he was and with the bad weather, he wasn't really worried about anyone seeing him, but he had been a little surprised to find no extra security in the yards after what had happened a hundred miles downstream. That will change after tonight, he thought. But that was all right: He'd figured all along that he could get two before security really tightened up. The railroads were consistent in their arrogance. They'd still be staring at the mess at Thebes like some large, slow animal who's been shot from a distance and is still wondering why it's sitting down. Besides, this was the last bridge on which he would need direct, physical access.

He settled in under the round-down of the tank and looked out over the river. He could see the lights of St. Louis on the other side, its gleaming arch only partially visible as it soared into the low-lying night mist. The garish lights of the casino boats up beyond the interstate bridge threw a blaze of reds and whites across the black surface of the river. The approach bridge was a mile long, curving around from a north to a west heading as it made the approach to the high bridge, rising slowly to meet the first arched truss. He could see the glow of some aircraft warning lights pulsing silently above him in the mist, indicating the very tops of the main bridge.

Twelve years ago to the month almost, he thought, closing his eyes to the vista below. He could still vividly remember the Highway Patrol car pulling into his driveway, a trooper and a sergeant getting out, their faces like thunderclouds. He, standing in the doorway, suit coat, car keys, and briefcase in hand, on his way to the office, dropping the briefcase when he saw their faces, knowing even before the older man spoke that his world was about to end. "All of them," the sergeant said. He had kept asking, "All of them?" And the sergeant replied, "Yes, sir, we're terribly sorry. Is there someone we can call, sir? Don't you think you better sit down, sir?"

He opened his eyes. The visibility conditions were just about perfect. He slipped out of his bright yellow rain gear, rolled it into a tight cylinder, and stuffed it into his waist pack. He kept the hard hat on. He was wearing a set of dark green workman's overalls, the waist pack, black leather gloves, and Army surplus–style laced boots. He had a large hunting knife strapped in a sheath on the outside of his right leg and he wore a black knit watch cap under the hard hat. Fifteen minutes after beginning the ascent of the approach bridge, his tank car was approaching the center span. On this bridge, unlike the one at Thebes, the center span was an arch suspension segment. The flat track bed was supported by a two-hundred-foot-long platform, which in turn was suspended beneath the lofty center arch by four-inch-thick steel cables hanging down from the arch to the track-bed support platform. The cables were spaced every three feet, which meant there were more than sixty-five cables on each side. There was a solid-walled catwalk running both inside and outside of the cable-connection fixtures.

He gathered himself and the bag over to the edge of the tank car's platform. When the car reached the approximate center of the span, he let the bag drop as gently as he could onto the catwalk. Then he jumped down after it, grabbing the top edge of the wall with his gloved hands and quickly flattening himself against the solid wall. The passing cars were only three feet away from his back, and he had to be careful that some oddly shaped car didn't come along and take his head off in the darkness. Using his feet, he pushed the bag closer up against the wall, and then, when the space between the next two cars allowed, he climbed over the three-foot-high solid wall between the inner and outer catwalks, pushing himself between two adjoining suspension cables. The catwalks were made of steel grate on this bridge. They were very slippery. Gauging the next car's width, he hauled the bag up over the wall and laid it down on the outer catwalk.

Once there, he looked both ways, just to make sure yard security wasn't out for a midnight stroll across the bridge, and then opened the bag. He began to extract the Detacord, some three hundred feet of it this time, from the bag. It had been coiled into the duffel like a Slinky toy, and when he had half of it out, he took out his knife and sliced through the bag to expose the back half. He set aside a cigar box–size package and a long black Maglite flashlight, then pitched the empty bag over the side into the darkness. Then he uncoiled the Detacord. Each of the suspension cables ended in what looked like a massive upside-down tuning fork. At the bottom of the fork was a three-inch-diameter lateral pin. Suspended from the pin was a vertical steel bar, which in turn held up its section of the track-bed deck. He wove the Detacord through the small aperture that was just above each pin, threading it through a succession of holes for the entire length of the deck. He worked silently, perspiring a little with the effort of pulling the long, oily cord through all those cables. In theory, the Detacord explosion would spread the two arms of the tuning fork–shaped suspension fixtures, releasing all the pins.

The westbound train kept on coming, clacking, squealing, and thumping its way past him in the darkness. He kept watch as he laid out the explosive, checking to make sure that when the end of this string came up, there weren't a couple of brakemen hanging on to the last car. The eastbound train was still making its way down toward the Illinois side, its cars audible but not really visible behind the seemingly endless block chunking west in front of him.

It took him ten more minutes to lay out the entire length of the Detacord, which now extended in both directions from the center of the span to each end. The eastbound string had passed on by; now he had to wait for the westbound string to finish going through, because there was no way to get to the other side of the span without crossing both sets of tracks.

He had one other thing to do. He walked back to the Missouri side of the center span and stepped through the aperture of the pier tower, the towering boxcars rocking by inches from his head. He went another ten feet, then knelt down to tape the small box under the westbound track-bed support girder. From another pocket in his waist pack, he pulled out a coil of black bell wire and strung it underneath the catwalk. He pulled it back to the pier tower, where he tied off the end to a cross-tie, trying hard to ignore the sixty-ton cars rolling by three feet over his head. He went back to the bundle, carefully pulled out a foot-long hank of wire with a ring on the end, and connected it to the long wire. He let go of the short wire and it tensioned back up into the bundle. Being very careful of where he put his feet, he went back to the center span. He crouched at the Missouri end, squatting up against the base of the steel tower supporting the truss arch overhead, where he had tied off the Detacord. He had left just enough cord to be pulled under the two sets of tracks to the other side of the span.

The rain was heavier now, and he was a little worried about making the electrical connections in all this dampness. He leaned back against the cold, wet concrete and took a deep breath. His heart was racing a little from the exertion of pulling the Detacord. The air up on the bridge smelled faintly of ozone from the diesel-electric engines, overlaid with the sour stink of heavy grease and old iron. The lights of the city upriver brightened as the clouds lifted momentarily, reflecting a bronze glow off the great arch. For an instant, he felt totally exposed, until he remembered how small he was in comparison to the massive steel structure looming all around him. But nor for long, he thought. The sides of the heavy boxcars rumbling past toward Missouri looked like frames of a silent film running sideways in the reflected light. He tried to generate some sense of excitement at what he was about to do. The Thebes bridge had been a piece of cake, and this one was shaping up the same way. Get on the bridge, lay down the explosives, and then just leave. Just like he'd planned it. But he felt neither pride nor any sense of accomplishment at how easy it had been. So far, anyway. He waited alongside the tracks for the last car to go by, mentally counting down the remaining boxcars—three, two, one, zero—and began to stand up. That's when he saw the security guard.

The man was walking down the center catwalk, his hands in his pockets, his face an indistinct white blur under his hard hat. In the second before the guard saw him, he dropped the hank of Detacord, picked up the big flashlight and snapped it on, pointing the bright white beam into the other man's face. The guard stopped and threw up an arm against the sudden glare.

"All right, what the hell are you doing up here?" he yelled at the guard as he stepped closer across the tracks. "Keep your hands in sight! Both hands!"

He got within three feet of the guard before the other man recovered from his surprise and started to say something, at which point he hit the guard in the temple with the barrel of the heavy Maglite. The man dropped like a sack of potatoes onto the catwalk, his hard hat rolling out onto the track bed.

He discovered that his hands were shaking and his heart tumbling with adrenaline. He had attacked reflexively, without the first thought. The guard lay terribly still on the catwalk, the bruise on his temple visible even in the darkness. He wondered if he had killed the man. So what if you have? a voice asked inside his head. Get on with it. A long train whistle blast down below got his attention. The headlight of the next eastbound string was already illuminating the lower approaches.

He moved quickly. He rolled the man over onto his side and saw that he was wearing a radio. He ripped off the shoulder microphone and threw it into space. He checked quickly to see if the man was still breathing, and whether or not he had a gun. No weapon; short, shallow breaths. He let the man's head drop back down onto the deck of the catwalk, then retrieved the segment of Detacord. He pulled it under the first set of tracks, across the intervening platform, and then under the eastbound tracks. The only portion of the cord visible was the segment that went over the solid walls along the catwalks, but it was black and they were covered in soot. Once over on the downstream side, he tied off the cord to the first suspension cable and then hurried up the catwalk to find the other bag, which he had dropped off an hour earlier while riding an eastbound string. Keeping an eye on the train that was inching its way up onto the approach bridge, he repeated the entire layout, threading the cord snakelike in and out of the suspension cable attachment points, pressing its oily surface tightly against each connecting rod, until he had the entire length of it stretched out. His mouth was very dry and his heart was still racing. But he was not afraid, only anxious to be done before he had to do something about the guard. A part of his mind had been considering that problem. Should he just throw the man off the bridge?

He looked over into Illinois and saw the next westbound block starting up the mile-long approach bridge, the switch engine's yellowish headlight probing the wet tracks ahead. He took the detonator assembly out of the duffel bag, kicked the second bag over the side into the river below, and made the connections. Nothing complicated here: detonator-receiver box, blasting cap, and a lot of duct tape. He kept an anxious eye on both trains now, gauging how much time he had before he absolutely had to move the security guard's inert form.

He clamped the final wire, rechecked the connections, and then scrambled back over to where the guard lay on the westbound track. Flashlight held in his armpit, he tapped the man's testicles with his boot to make sure he was still fully out; then he dragged the guard onto the catwalk and pulled him over to the concrete edge of the pier tower. By the time the first straining engines came abreast of him on the westbound track, he had the man curled into a dark ball, his face turned away from the headlight. From this position, the unconscious guard ought to survive what was going to happen to the center span. He had decided not to kill the man: His target was the railroad, not their people. Unless they got in his way.

He hid himself down at the track-bed base of the pier tower, holding his ears until the engine set was well past the center span, and then swung over the wall and hopped the first tank car that came abreast of him. As soon as he did, however, the train slowed and then ground to a stop. Now what? he wondered, although he knew the trains often stopped up here, awaiting switch windows in the receiving yard. Then he had an idea. He jumped down off the platform of the tank car and scuttled back to where the security guard lay in a dark heap. He grabbed the man under the arms and pulled him across the tracks and up onto the tank car's platform.

He scampered back onto the next tank car in line, just in time, too, because here came the next eastbound train, its engine throwing a blaze of yellow light all over the center span catwalks about thirty seconds after he had swung aboard. Next to the massive steel connections and cables, the spidery trace of the Detacord would have been invisible to even an interested observer. Then he remembered he'd left the guard's hard hat. Damn it! He had left it on the tracks. Would they see it? Worse, would they stop?

He heard a cascade of thumps and bangs climbing the bridge below him as the slack came out, and then his tank car lurched into motion again as the train started down the Missouri side of the bridge. He was anxious now to get off the bridge and into firing position. He shrugged back into his rain gear, which he pulled on over the now-empty waist pack. To his great relief, it looked like the eastbound train had kept moving. Maybe they had seen it, maybe not. It was just a hard hat. Hopefully they had not reported it.

Relax, he told himself. Breathe. Focus. You're not done yet. He looked across the coupling to where the security guard's inert form lay on the next car. Still out cold. Good. Either they'd find him down in the switch yard or he was going to make a long train trip. But at least he would not be on the bridge.

Once the block of cars banged to a stop and the engines had been disconnected, he hopped off the tank car and crept carefully through the maze of parked railcars. Big trucks banged noisily over the expansion joints in the elevated expressway running over the top of the Terminal switching yards. He slipped between the blocks of cars carefully, checking constantly to make sure a string wasn't about to jolt into motion. He also could not afford to collide with another yard bull. A distant switch-tending crew appeared as yellow blurs in the rain, their flashlights darting here and there as they confirmed couplings in the hump yard. He put his head down and kept moving, just another yellow-slickered figure going about his business in the switching yard. He tried not to think about his close call up on the bridge. If he hadn't seen the guard first . . .

It took him twenty minutes to get to his truck, where he took off the waist pack before climbing in. After watching through the rain-streaked windows for another ten minutes and seeing no one else in the employees' parking lot, he started the truck. The rain had become steadier, so he felt reasonably safe in backing out of the row of parked pickup trucks and driving slowly down toward the main access road, even though it wasn't time for shift change. He would be most vulnerable to a challenge when he passed the main control building, but all the windows faced out on the switching yard like an airport control tower. He also knew that, given the scale of the operation that was going on, there were very few people involved. Four in the main control room, maybe six two-man engine crews, about a dozen brakemen out on the tracks, and probably two yard bulls, who, on a night like this, would be cooping up in the security shack, more than likely. Perhaps most amazing, there was no gate or security checkpoint at the main entrance to the switching yard. There were probably too many big rigs coming in and out of the yard to allow for any practical check of each vehicle. But that is all about to change, he thought. Smug bastards are in for a real wake-up call.

He nosed his truck slowly past the control building, waited for a block of cars to creep by on a side line that crossed directly in front of the main entrance, and then drove out of the yard into the south side of St. Louis. He drove directly down South Twelfth Street, through the industrial area and toward the elevated spaghetti junction where I-44 and I-55 merged. When he reached the Chouteau Avenue intersection, he pulled in behind a parked semi rig. He ran through the wiring lash-up in his mind's eye, and nodded in the darkness. The Detacord would sever all but a very few of the suspension cables, which should mean that the weight of the center span would be enough to drop it into the river. With a train on it, there was zero chance that the span would survive the blast. Two trains, even better. But first he had to set up his transmitter, then take care of the vehicular side roads on the MacArthur Bridge. He didn't want some civilian to be taking a midnight spin across the deserted bridge road when the center span came down.

He pulled the transmitter box out and entered the settings. Leaving it on the seat next to him, he pulled back out and made a right on Chouteau, went down one block, and then made another right to swing onto the approach ramp for the MacArthur Bridge side roads. Seeing no other traffic coming or going, he stopped at the bottom of the ramp, piled out of the truck, and grabbed four red traffic cones out of the bed. He set these up to block eastbound traffic on the ramp, then got back into the truck. He hurried now, going faster than he normally would on the narrow lane. The side roads climbed alongside the track bed until about one-third of the way up the arch, and then the track bed rose higher, ending up running thirty feet higher than the parallel roadbeds at the midpoint of the bridge. All he could see of the center span was its bottom. As he drove down the Illinois side, the two spans merged again and he saw that a westbound coal train was bumping slowly up the long incline. Good, he thought. A nice heavy string.

When he reached the bottom of the Illinois side ramp, he stopped again, this time in the middle of the road. He looked for approaching traffic, and seeing none, he got out. He grabbed four more orange cones, hopped over the cement divider, and blocked off the westbound approach ramp. He was perspiring now despite the cool air: Time was becoming critical. The cones should stop traffic just long enough, until some trucker got on his cellular and a cop came to see what the problem was. There shouldn't be any patrol cops out here at this hour, unless the railroad police had discovered that their man on the bridge was off the air. And even then, the railroad cops should be searching the rail bridge, not the roads.

He jumped back in his truck and drove on down the remainder of the ramp to South Tenth Street in East St. Louis. From there, he could access the connecting ramps to the Interstate 55 bridge, which was a third of a mile upstream of the MacArthur. There was almost continuous heavy truck traffic on the interstate bridge, both ways, but that did not matter now. He drove under the interstate and then up onto the westbound approach lanes of the I-55 bridge to head back into the city. The arch of St. Louis was directly in view now, sparkling in the reflected lights of the casino boats down on the riverbanks below. The rain had petered out for the moment. Low clouds scudding along the river appeared to be polishing the top of the arch.

He looked over at the MacArthur as he merged onto the interstate bridge, surrounded now by squadrons of semis headed west. He changed lanes over into the far left one so he could have a clearer view of the MacArthur. He frowned when he saw flashing blue police lights down on the MacArthur's East St. Louis side; someone must have reported the cones. Then he concentrated on the bridge. He was in luck. It looked like there were *two* trains crossing the hump. He kept one eye on the road while he looked hard for engines, but he saw no headlights up there. Just cars. Perfect. Just a few more seconds now.

He looked right to make sure there wasn't a curious truck driver staring down into the pickup truck. When he reached the midpoint of the expressway bridge, he picked up the transmitter, lowered his driver's side window, pointed the transmitter like a television remote, and shoved the detent switch to the top of the box. Two flashes of red-yellow lightning erupted all along the bottom of the center span before disappearing into a fuming cloud of smoke and dust. He swerved out to the right when he felt his left-front wheel rubbing along the curb, provoking a howl of protest from a semi coming up in the next lane. By the time he was able to look back at the bridge, the center span was smacking the river below in a gigantic belly flop, smashing a sheet of white water two hundred yards out to either side. The span was followed down by a cascade of coal cars tumbling into the maelstrom. From this distance, they looked like toys, falling one after another in a silent chain of annihilation.

Brake lights were flaring ahead, and he had to stomp down hard on his own. There was a blaze of lights in his mirror and another protest of air horns and brakes behind him, but everyone on the interstate bridge was slowing to gape at what was unfolding downriver. He wanted to change lanes and get the hell out of there, but he knew that would call attention to his truck when the rest of the world was rubbernecking in stunned amazement. He slowed down to a crawl and watched the trains pull themselves to destruction in the river.

"That's two," he said aloud.

Hush got back to his condo at the Belle Haven Apartments in Alexandria, Virginia, just after 4:30 A.M. eastern time, bone-tired after a rough jet flight back from Missouri through a nasty low-pressure system. He took a long, hot shower and made some coffee. He thought about calling Carolyn Lang, but it was far too late. He had had a long, teleconference with her about the progress of establishing the interagency task force. The case, which did not yet have a name, had been designated a special, so the first meeting was scheduled for four o'clock Thursday afternoon. That's today, he reminded himself. As he was stirring his coffee and thinking about the mess out in Missouri, the phone rang. He looked at his watch: 5:15. Bureau operations already knew he was back, so who was this?

"Mr. Hanson, this is Carolyn Lang."

Surprise, surprise, he thought. "Yes?" What is she doing up at this hour? he wondered.

"I checked with operations. They told me you just got in, and I'm sorry to—"

"I'm still up. In fact, I just suppressed the impulse to call you. What's happened?"

"There's been another one. Another bridge. This one's in St. Louis. It's a railroad bridge, the MacArthur."

"Son of a bitch!"

"Yes. The first reports say the center span was blown up, or down, I suppose. Dropped two coal trains into the river."

"*Two?* Damn! Which railroad?"

"Rail*roads.* St. Louis is a major rail gateway. There are apparently eight lines that use the big switching yards on the Illinois side, and three more on the Missouri side. I called that Canning guy from the Union Pacific as soon as operations called me—he's the chief engineer, remember? He said this was beyond serious: This will cause major national rail-traffic disruption."

Hush remembered his trips to St. Louis. He had seen what looked like hundreds of acres of rail yards down by the river. "Is that the only railroad bridge in St. Louis?"

"*In* St. Louis, there are two: the MacArthur and the Merchants, but the Merchants is under renovation, so effectively there is—was—just the one. Canning said there are three other bridges within two hundred miles north of the city: at Quincy, Louisiana, and Hannibal, Missouri. Quincy is a tonnage group seven like the MacArthur, but the switchyards at Quincy are much smaller than at St. Louis."

"Refresh me: What's a group seven?"

"Canning explained that. Rail lines are grouped into categories, one through seven, as a function of how many millions of gross ton miles per mile they carry. Group seven means more than forty million gross ton miles per mile of track annually."

Hush was having trouble assimilating gross ton miles per mile, but he got the picture. He remembered that the Cape Girardeau bridge had also been a group seven line.

"These guys know what they're after, it seems."

"Yes, they do. Canning said there are seven yards on the Illinois side, and four more on the Missouri side. Basically, he said Chicago traffic north of St. Louis was still in business, railwise, but that the southern tier of the country would be hurting, and hurting bad. And soon."

They should have put out a security alert on every damned bridge on the river, Hush thought. He had just assumed the railroads would have done that.

"Mr. Hanson?"

"Yes, I'm here. Just trying to think. Okay, we'd better move up the interagency meeting to this morning. But we're going to have to get on it early. You'll have to call around and see who can make it and who can't. Where are you?"

"I'm at home. In Old Town."

He hadn't known where she lived. "Well," he said. "We're neighbors. I'm at the Belle Haven."

"Yes, I know," she said patiently. He was surprised that she knew, and then he realized he shouldn't have been.

"Okay," he said. "I'll send for a car. Give me your address and I'll have someone pick you up. Forty-five minutes enough time?"

After the interagency task force meeting Thursday morning, Hush called a postmortem debrief session in his office with Carolyn Lang; Ben Fenton, the senior rep from the Bureau operations center; Carter VanKampf from the intelligence section; and his own admin deputy, Tyler Redford. The first formal meeting of the interagency group had been necessarily a hurry-up affair, with very little hard information to put out and lots of high-level hand-wringing. There had been no lack of interested parties: From the Department of Transportation, there had been representatives from the Railroad Administration, the Surface Transportation Board, the Coast Guard, and the National Transportation Safety Board's Railway Safety Office. From the Defense Department, there had been reps from the Corps of Engineers, the Defense Intelligence Agency, and the Army National Guard. The Secret Service had sent intelligence and explosives specialists. From within the Bureau itself, there were reps from Info Resources, the Laboratory, CID, Public and Congressional Affairs, National Security, and a bright young executive from the director's office. Senior Agent Lang had served as chief scribe, and Hush had given the briefing, short as it was. Operations handed out the pertinent communications numbers for the command center, and the next meeting had been set up for Friday at three o'clock.

Hush had deliberately kept it as short as possible, mostly because they had very little hard information. It was agreed that the Bureau would handle media on the progress of the case, while Transportation would deal with media on the effects of the bombings. It was also agreed that reps from the major transcontinental railroads needed to be folded into the task force as soon as possible. The Transportation rep had taken that one for action.

Hush's own office was on the tenth floor of the high-rise section of headquarters, with an oblique view of the building's central courtyard. The more senior assistant directors were all on the seventh floor, but as acting assistant director, Hush did not yet rate a presence on the executive level. His desk was at one end, and there was a small conference table with six chairs at the other. On one end wall was a bookcase; on the other was a wall-size map of the United States. Hush sat at his desk, reviewing Lang's notes.

"Ben, we have anything new on the St. Louis incident?"

Ben Fenton, who was a supervisory special agent in the operations division, consulted a Teletype that had been delivered as the task force meeting ended. "Missouri police think it was Detcord this time. The blast severed all the suspension cables holding up the center span simultaneously, dropping it straight down. Lots of witnesses to that from the interstate highway bridge upstream. They all said the same thing: horizontal flash, like red lightning, and then the bridge dropped straight down and hit flat."

"Anyone injured?"

"There is a railroad policeman missing. The UP had apparently put a guy on random walking patrol up on the bridge after the Thebes bombing. He checked in with his control forty minutes before the blast, with nothing to report. A switchyard engineer crossing the bridge reported seeing a hard hat on the track bed, but no one can say whose it was, and it went down with the bridge."

"Well, I guess we should assume he was on the bridge when it let go," Hush said. "Or maybe he surprised the bad guys. That ups the ante somewhat. How many cars went into the river?"

"Railroad people estimate one hundred and five; sixty-seven fully loaded coal cars, and the rest a hodgepodge of mixed freight, empties, and what they call flat stack cars. Same deal as last time: They apparently waited for the engines to clear the bridge. Local EPA unit is already in it for a spill-damage assessment, although this doesn't look as bad as

Thebes from their perspective. Mostly coal. The barge channel is clobbered, though, which doubles the impact."

The room was silent as they digested this news. Hush doodled on his desk pad and then asked the central question. "Okay, so who the hell is doing this?"

VanKampf shook his head. "We've pulsed the national databases for I & W and come up with zip. Carswell's people are drawing a blank. Ditto for known foreign terrorist groups' MO's. A couple of remote possibles for domestic militia groups, although only on the 'attack the government infrastructure' theme, and they're both better known for talking about targeting buildings."

"Maybe this is just a 'matter of time' deal," Fenton offered. "You know, only a matter of time before the nutcases start hitting the national power grid, the telephone system, or, now, bridges."

Hush looked over at his task force deputy, who appeared ready to say something. "Senior Agent Lang?"

"Cui bono," she said. "Who gains? Or perhaps the converse. Who gets hurt?"

That prompted a moment of silence.

"Yeah," VanKampf said "You're saying maybe we should expect a ransom or extortion note of some kind: Pay us X millions and we'll stop blowing up the bridges." But Hush was focusing on the second of Lang's questions: "Who gets hurt?"

"Two group seven bridges, no notes, no claims," he said. "Seems to me that, so far anyway, no one is trying to *gain*. Who gets hurt, on the other hand, is something we *can* identify. We have two rail bridges down, two big, important bridges. Important because there are so few."

Hush got up and went to the map. "There are—were—only six operational main-line railroad bridges across the Mississippi River in the seven hundred miles from St. Louis on down to New Orleans—here at St. Louis, Thebes, Memphis, Vicksburg, Baton Rouge, and New Orleans. There are two more, one at St. Louis, and one at Memphis, which were out for repairs for at least a year."

He went back to his desk to retrieve a book. "This is the *U.S. Railroad Traffic Atlas*, which I'm told is the definitive public reference. From St. Louis on down is the band of geography where about forty percent of America's east-west freight rolls. Over six bridges. Now there are four. That's a thirty-three percent reduction in southern-tier capacity."

"It might be more significant than that, sir," Lang said. "I talked to the chief engineer of the UP again. Every bridge would be a bottleneck without the switchyards. The yards allow them to do centralized traffic control without clogging up the east-west lines that lead to the bridges. The Thebes bridge had two siding tracks where trains could wait on each side, but this St. Louis complex is a major switching hub, with over three hundred sidings."

"Then this is real trouble," Tyler Redford said. "That Surface Transportation Board guy said the railroads are operating at or near full capacity already, remember?"

"Okay," Hush said. "That answers the question 'Who gets hurt?' So, maybe the bridges aren't the targets—maybe the railroads are the targets."

"It could still be an attack on the whole country," VanKampf said. "Yeah, the railroads get hurt, but as a consequence, the whole economy stalls out because goods can't move. Think about it."

Hush sat down at his desk. "We're going in circles here, troops. Look, we're setting up in Situation Room Four. Carter, how about contacting your security counterparts at the major railroads. See if we can get them in here for an exchange of information. Off the record if their lawyers are goosey. Ops, we'll need some good railroad-route maps in Sit-Four. Tyler, verify that the appropriate comms are terminating in Sit-Four and that we have twenty-four-hour manning there. Once they're in place, have them begin to work up the basis for a string of press releases. We need to keep feeding the media beast or it will start speculating in Technicolor."

He paused. "Anybody think of anything else?"

There were shaking heads all around. "Okay. Senior Agent Lang and I are going back out to Missouri."

Carolyn Lang said she had to talk to VanKampf for a minute. Tyler Redford stayed behind. Hush gathered some of the reports into his briefcase, and then asked Redford how Lang had done setting up the interagency group.

"Fine," said Redford. "I gave her a few pointers, but mostly, she just ran with it."

"Anybody in particular give her any trouble?"

"Carswell's National Security division is all bent out of shape," Redford replied. "But he's pissed at us here in IITF, not her. No, with her looks, who would give her trouble? The guys I saw her talking to were falling all over themselves. She did fine."

Hush leaned back in his specially constructed office chair and closed his eyes for a minute. So Carolyn Lang, whose networks were not so good here in the building—according to her, anyway—had done just fine? How very interesting, he thought. He wondered briefly if there was another game being played by the deputy director, a game within a game. The phone rang, interrupting his thoughts.

At noon on Thursday, Matthews was having a quick lunch at the Officers Club when he was alerted by his beeper to call into the Anniston ops center. He reached the duty officer on his cell phone.

"Major Matthews, we've just received word from the Army Ops Center in Washington: A big railroad bridge in Saint Louis has been sabotaged."

"Good grief! Another one?"

"Yes, sir. No details as yet. I've notified Colonel Anderson. He said he wanted to talk to you, sir."

His heart sank a little. "Naturally. Okay, I'm on it."

He had left Colonel Anderson's office an hour ago, when he and Carl Hill had presented the recomputed route for 2713, using the Frisco Bridge at Memphis. The new route was actually two hours shorter than the original Cape Girardeau Thebes crossing route, which gave them some more flexibility for the divert to Idaho. That was the good news. The bad news was that they were still taking extremely dangerous cargo through a metropolitan area. Anderson had listened gravely to his objections and had then directed them to time the launch of the train to run through Memphis at around 0300 in the morning, minimizing vehicle cross traffic and the number of people who would be out and about along the route. Matthews had gone away unsatisfied. As he headed back to Anderson's office again, he decided he would try one more time.

When he got there, however, he found Colonel Mehle instead of Anderson. "Close the door," Mehle ordered when Matthews knocked and announced himself. "I take it you've heard about the MacArthur Bridge in St. Louis?"

"Yes, sir. Sir, where is Colonel Anderson?"

"Colonel Anderson did not send for you. I did. Colonel Anderson tells me that you and Major Hill have some problems with what's going on with twenty-seven thirteen."

Matthews knew he had to be careful here. He did not like the fact that Anderson wasn't here. If Mehle felt empowered to use Anderson's office this way, something important had changed. "Yes, sir, I guess that's true," he said.

Mehle's expression darkened. Matthews decided to plunge ahead anyway. "I think we're taking some real chances by amending the route in the first place, Colonel. Taking hot nukes through a city is way out there."

"In your opinion."

Matthews hesitated. "Yes, sir, in my opinion. I have been working this route-clearance problem for three years, Colonel."

"So I've been told, *Major*," Mehle said, emphasizing the title Major to make sure Matthews understood who was the major in the room and who was the full colonel. "Do you not think our superiors in Washington have taken these concerns into consideration?"

"Well, yes, sir, I suppose they have."

"You *suppose?* Well, let me confirm your supposition. I'm only temporarily attached to the Special Operations Command. My permanent billet is on the National Security Council staff. Does that tell you anything, Major?"

"No, sir."

"*What?*" Mehle shouted. "Are you really that stupid? Do you know what the NSC is? Do you know what kind of access I have?"

"The same kind of access that Ollie North had," Matthews replied evenly. "And look where that got us."

For a moment, Mehle looked angry enough to get physical. He started to say something but then closed his mouth. He took a deep breath and sat back down.

"What I must know, Major Matthews," he said, "is whether or not you are on board. You have—what, not quite a year to go to your twenty?"

Ah, Matthews thought with a tingle of apprehension. "Yes, sir," he replied, his voice catching.

"Then let me suggest that the best way for you to get from here to there with your pension intact is to put your head down and carry out the mission at hand. Your reservations about this project are duly noted, but the time for such input is past. The decision has been made by the competent higher headquarters. We're going to run this train and solve the Army's problem. Is that clear?"

"Yes, sir. Very clear."

Mehle looked at him for a moment. "I acknowledge this business is not without risk. The presence of the special weapons in this train is, however, a military secret, and I expect that secret to hold until the train reaches its new destination. If you have a problem with keeping that secret, now's the time to say so."

"No, sir," Matthews said. "I've never broken security in nineteen years of service and I'm not going to start now."

Mehle stared at him for a moment. "All right, Major. As Colonel Anderson said, the train dispatch order will be in writing and will cover your ass as well as Hill's. Do I need to calibrate Major Hill, or can you take care of that?"

"I'll talk to Major Hill, sir."

"All right. Anything else bothering you?"

Matthews hesitated. "Sir, what about these bridge bombings?" he asked. "Doesn't the fact that someone's attacking railroad bridges on the Mississippi bear on the risk?"

"That's Washington's call to make. The FBI is on the case, and they'll get these bastards, whoever they are. It's our job to execute policy, not to question it. Get me a status report on the twenty-seven thirteen build by seventeen hundred today."

Matthews blinked. He did not work for Colonel Mehle. "Sir, you mean Colonel Anderson?"

"Colonel Anderson is away on temporary assignment. I'm in command of this mission. You will make all reports on twenty-seven thirteen to me until further notice, Major. Dismissed."

On Thursday afternoon, he drove his pickup truck slowly down a bumpy two-mile-long dirt lane that ran between two six-hundred-acre cotton fields. The vast flat expanses of black dirt, dotted here and there with small stands of bare-limbed trees, should have been depressing, but to him the isolation they represented was almost comforting. He had lived in the small riverside cabin ever since the accident. A reclusive artist had lived there before and then committed suicide out in the yard. Because of that history, and the fact that he offered to pay in cash each month, he had been given a very good deal on the place.

The lane led down from the county road to a small hummock of land fringed by a stand of trees right along the Mississippi, high enough above the river to escape the annual floods. There were no levees on this side of the river, so the wooden cabin had a view of the entire river through the trees. The cabin was small: a single combined living room, dining room, and kitchen area, two bedrooms, one bath. There were covered porches on three sides. The cabin was built up on concrete block piers, which provided three extra feet of insurance against a flood. Out back was an old shed-barn he used as a tool shop and a place to park the pickup truck. Next to the barn were a few ramshackle outhouse-size sheds filled with moldering garden tools. The cabin had well water, septic, phone, and electricity. The nearest people were up at the main farm complex some three miles away.

To one side of the cabin, there was a small fenced-in vegetable garden, which produced indifferently because of all the large trees surrounding the house. There was a slant-door tornado shelter right behind the back steps, which led down into a cool dirt hole that had doubled at one time as a root cellar. Like everyone else in the county, he had spent some time down there during those deep summer nights when end-of-the-world thunderstorms swept in off the Great Plains and the kitchen radio began squealing tornado warnings.

The river had cut steep fifteen-foot-high banks down beyond the trees, some three hundred feet from his back porch. The boat was chained up in a small ravine cut by the runoff ditches coming out of the table-flat cotton fields. The Mississippi was three-quarters of a mile wide behind the cabin, with the main shipping channel over nearer the Illinois side. There was an almost constant hum of marine diesel engines from the big pusher tugs as they drove thousand-foot-long barge strings up and down the river, twenty-four hours a day. The barge strings carried nearly thirty thousand tons in their deep bellies: cargoes of shell corn, wheat, soybeans, coal, cotton, fuel oil, raw lumber, and sheet metal: lifeblood commodities that flowed out of the midwestern United States to feed, house, and clothe half the world. At night, the engine sounds were louder; the barges and their mighty tugs seemed to crawl upriver, their multicolored lights blacked out by downsteram traffic, which slid unnaturally fast over the shimmering black waters. He often spent hours on the bluff, just watching, listening. And remembering.

He was returning from a shopping run up in Festus, some twenty miles away. He loved the exotic names of the towns along or near the great river: Cairo, Herculaneum, Memphis, Karnak, New Athens, Thebes.

Thebes.

A cold wave of satisfaction washed over him as he parked at the cabin. He sat in the truck for a moment. Thebes had been perfect. St. Louis almost perfect. The security guard had been reported only as missing. He was sorry for that, but it was unavoidable—perhaps inevitable given the scope of what he was going to do. And he *was* going to do it. Finish it. And if he died doing it, well, it wasn't as if he had a lot to live for. He closed his eyes and let the scene form in his mind for the ten thousandth time: Kay's station wagon, blackened, shattered almost beyond recognition, crushed, shredded—the words came at him like flaming arrows. Random yellow plastic body sheets stuck here and there to cover the gory pieces of what was left of his family, plastic so there would be no stains, you see. Like so much meat through a grinder.

And those huge diesel locomotives just sitting there five hundred yards down the track, totally indifferent, uncaring, the front engine unmarked, actually, the ram steel cowcatcher assembly on its nose showing little more than paint scratches. Still running, as if anxious to get on with business, impatient at being delayed by this crushed and crumpled *annoyance* that was smoking and leaking alongside the tracks a hundred feet down from the crossing. The police and the railroad officials comforting the *engineer*, for Chrissakes, while what was left of his wife and two kids dripped into the rain ditch.

He again saw the crossing, blocked by the mile-long string of boxcars. The at-grade crossing, where the lights did not work—or worked only some of the time. They had been flashing by the time he got there, but later, much later, his lawyer had found one witness who claimed they were not working until the train had finally been stopped. But that person had not seen Kay start across.

And the railroad people: stone-faced suits. Million-dollar lawyers, whole platoons of them. "We deeply regret this family's loss, Your Honor, but people do this all the time, try to beat the train. It's going twice as fast as it looks and it's half again closer than it looks. Something about the optical illusion created by the parallel tracks. No, there were no gates, but there were lights. Other cars stopped. She did not, Your Honor. That's the sum total of it. She tried to beat the train. And she lost."

And he lost. Not one lawsuit, but two. Four years of litigation. Every cent he had. Their house, his savings, everything. And then they sued *him*. Damages to the engine. Lost revenue. Recovery of legal fees, for on-staff attorneys. They garnished his pay and the banks took everything else. And he was still paying them. Would be paying them for life and probably after he was dead, from the proceeds of his life insurance.

His one witness had testified the lights were not working on the state highway side. "Then why did you stop, sir?"

"Saw the cars on the other side stopped. Looked for a train, and there it was."

"Did the lady stop?"

"Not sure. She might have. But then the train was there and she was there and her car was rolling around in front of that engine like a dog under a truck—and I don't want to talk about this anymore, Your Honor, got bad dreams enough."

And so he lost.

He opened his eyes.

And now, by God, if there was a God, *they* were going to lose. He was going to take a chain saw to their corporate throats. He was going to stop the trains, stop up the entire national railway system. Bring the country to a standstill if he had to. Didn't matter to him. Nothing mattered to him now.

He felt his fingers burning from his grip on the steering wheel, his jaw hurting as he ground his teeth. I am going to destroy them all. I know exactly how to do it, and I am going to do it. All by myself. Each one has been planned out in infinite detail. The bridges climbed. The ground reconnoitered. The line operations memorized. The explosives stolen. The electronics built from scratch. The hate, the cold, lethal, poisonous hate, nurtured like some deadly night virus deep in his brain.

He took a deep breath, then another. He forced his body to relax, one finger, one hand, one arm at a time, as he released the steering wheel. One at a time. Just like the bridges.

The next one will be tougher, he thought. They were fully alerted, and now, of course, the FBI was in the game. In his experience, the FBI was equal parts bureaucracy and investigations these days, but its sheer size and resources made it reasonably effective. Eventually, they'd figure it out, and then there'd be some government cars rolling down his dirt road one early morning. He had made some interesting provisions for that eventuality, but right now, he figured they'd be flailing: The television news spoke of a big government task force, high-level meetings in Washington, the media going crazy with terrorist bullshit, sincere-looking government spokesmen bobbing and weaving while their principals tried to figure out the who, why, and what of it. And what the hell to do next. But he had one huge advantage: He had had twelve years to plan his revenge. The arrogant bastards had never so much as put up a fence around the bridges; it was almost as if they were daring someone to try them on. Well, here I am, he thought.

The sunset flared briefly along the bottomland, a sudden final blaze of orange light, fading to red even as he watched, turning the trees black and the river into a fiery sheet of flickering hues. It reminded him of the red-hued lightning flashing along the base of the MacArthur span, and the way it had lit the river like an enormous flat board.

Two down, four to go. A vision of Kay and the kids, laughing, happy, alive, floated across the windshield in the afterglow of sunset. As alive then as he was now dead inside.

All he had to do was do it.

"No problem," he said out loud.

6

ON FRIDAY MORNING, Hush and Carolyn Lang stood on the Missouri side of the broken span, staring down at the now-familiar pile of wreckage in the river below. A cold front had moved in behind the rain, and it was a blustery, raw day up on the bridge. The MacArthur was higher over the water than the bridge at Thebes, but the sodden mound of smashed railcars looked about the same. The police had strung safety ropes across the gaping center span area. Two rows of black steel cables dangled uselessly down from the undamaged overhead arch, looking like hangman's nooses as the wind moved them fitfully back and forth. Two agents from the St. Louis office were talking to some hard-hatted railroad structural engineers. There was a collection of emergency vehicles down at the base of the bridge, and a similar collection of flashing blue lights visible over on the Illinois side. Captain Powers stood with one hand on the safety rope, the other pointing out at the cables.

"Detcord again," Powers said, almost shouting over the wind. "Sliced all the cable connections right through, and the span went down like a stone. We've got a shitload of witness statements this time."

"Any more word on the missing security guy?" Hush asked.

"Nope. The UP had him up on the bridge as a rover. Each of the companies who terminate in East St. Louis was going to take turns assigning somebody to the bridge. I suspect they're gonna tighten it up a lot after this."

Hush surveyed the wreckage below and shook his head. He stuffed his hands into his windbreaker. Carolyn Lang was huddled against the steel wall of the pier tower, talking on a cell phone to Washington. They had flown out late Thursday afternoon and checked into a hotel in downtown. St. Louis. SAC Herlihy had come to their hotel to pick them up this morning. Herlihy had wanted Lang to ride in one of the other cars, but Hush had pointedly insisted she ride with him. Herlihy had not been pleased. Well, he is just going to have to get over it, Hush thought. He wasn't going to have Lang subjected to any more bullshit, not when this case was growing, instead of getting smaller. There was already some heat beginning to come down from the director's office. Herlihy and a couple dozen of the St. Louis violent crime squad were over on the Illinois side, interviewing everyone who had been on duty in the big gateway switch-yards the night before.

Keeler, the Corps of Engineers' senior bridge inspector, arrived at the western end of the center span, having ridden what looked like a pickup truck mounted on hydraulic rail wheels up the three-quarter-mile approach track. He was accompanied by the Union Pacific Railroad's maintenance-of-way engineer, his district superintendent, and a youngish-looking Army officer wearing starched fatigues. Hush and Powers walked across the remains of the track bed to greet Keeler. Lang stayed on the phone.

"We meet again, Mr. Hanson," Keeler said. "And so soon."

"That does have me worried, Mr. Keeler," Hush replied. Keeler introduced the UP engineers and the officer, who was an Army Corps of Engineers structural specialist. They went over to the nearest of the severed cables. Keeler put on heavy gloves and pulled on the dangling cable, without much effect. It was four inches in diameter and nearly forty feet long. It must have weighed several thousand pounds. Keeler waited for the wind to blow it back in his direction and then quickly examined the burned, melted ends of the attachment shackle.

"Detcord," he pronounced.

"Eureka," Powers muttered sotto voce.

If Keeler heard him, he gave no indication. He straightened up. "Did they tag the adjacent inboard span, like at Thebes?" he asked.

Hush and Powers looked at each other, and then at the two structural engineers. Obviously, no one had thought to check. Keeler and the engineers moved over to the other side of the pier tower and began to poke around the base of the track bed, working their way back toward the Missouri end of the next span. Carolyn Lang came over, clutching the casebook to her chest, and asked Hush what they were doing. As he was starting to explain, they heard someone yell, "No-o-o!" followed instantly by a flash of heat and a very loud blast that shook the track bed and knocked them backward.

Hush thought he heard Lang yelp as a nasty-looking cloud of gray-black smoke enveloped them before blowing downstream off the bridge from behind the pier tower. When the smoke cleared, she was staring down at the middle of her blouse, where a red stain was beginning to blossom between the zippers of her windbreaker. Then she dropped her phone and the notebook and began frantically grabbing at the buttons of her blouse. Before Hush could do anything, she was ripping the buttons open and fumbling inside her blouse. She extracted a bloody bit of metal and quickly dropped it, swearing as she did so, as if it was hot. Hush saw a small bleeding welt between her breasts before she got herself covered back up.

"Damn! That burned!" she said to the astonished Hush. He reached down between her feet and recovered the bit of metal, and then her notebook. He couldn't see the phone. When he straightened up, they both saw that the thick notebook had a jagged hole torn right through it. When Lang saw the hole, she turned pale. He took her arm and pushed her gently back toward the face of the pier tower.

"Sit down," he ordered. He pulled out his handkerchief and pressed it over the welt between her breasts, then put her right hand in place to hold it there. "Put your head down," he said. "All the way down. There. Between your knees. You're okay. And very damned lucky! Now, deep breathing. Slowly."

Leaving her sitting against the concrete wall of the pier tower, Hush ran through the track-bed aperture and stopped abruptly. Keeler was standing twenty feet back down the track bed, whose upstream side was now sagging visibly at the point where it connected to support ledge of the pier tower. There was a large hole in the track-bed platform at that point, alongside which lay the gory remains of the young Army officer. The upper part of his body was literally gone. The district engineer, who had been on the other track and partially shielded by the catwalk barrier, was sprawled backward across the rails, trying not to fall through the ties to the river below. When he pulled himself back onto the bridge deck, he held his head in both hands. There was blood streaming down his forehead from multiple scalp cuts.

Powers, who had been shielded from the blast by the concrete of the pier tower, was already on his radio as Keeler shifted carefully over to the eastbound track and began climbing back toward the pier tower, his face ashen. Hush, realizing that the Army officer was beyond help, went back to see about Lang. She was still sitting on the track bed, holding his handkerchief to her chest. He decided to stay with her, as this was not the moment for her to see the remains of the Army engineer. Even with the wind, there was a strong smell of explosive, interlaced with the nauseating odor of burned flesh. He knelt down beside her and held her other hand. Her face was still white, but her expression was clearing.

"Kee-rist, what a breeze, as the parrot said," she declared, looking down at the red-stained handkerchief against her chest. "What the hell happened?"

"Looks like our bad guys left a booby trap behind," Hush said. "Powers has called for some medical assist. Thank God for the casebook."

"Amen," she said, looking down at the handkerchief again. "Gives new meaning to the words *booby trap*, doesn't it?"

She was trying to keep it light, but it wasn't quite working. Her expression was definitely wobbly. He decided not to say anything about the Army officer just yet. A moment later, Powers came around the pier tower, saw Lang, and hurried over. The uninjured railroad superintendent had taken one look at the Army officer's remains and vomited. Then he pulled himself together and went to help Keeler, taking off his jacket and then using his own shirt to help bandage the injured man's head. Powers, the only one of them on the bridge with a radio, had called in Lang's injury when he saw her holding the bloody handkerchief pressed against her front.

"Is that serious?" Powers asked, looking down at Lang's red-stained blouse.

"I don't think so," Hush said. "This is what hit her, and it went through the notebook first." He handed over the bloody bit of metal to Powers, who looked at it and then wrapped it up in a rubber glove he pulled from his pocket.

"What happened?" Hush asked.

Powers shook his head. "We were looking for anything out of order. Any signs of blast damage on the other side. I heard Keeler yell something and then—whammo. You saw the Army kid?"

"Yes, goddamn it." They could see another maintenance truck starting up the approach track from the Venice switchyards down below, its yellow strobe light flashing urgently. Morgan Keeler came through the track-bed aperture. His face was still pale, and he was rubbing his lower jaw with his left hand. He stopped short when he saw Lang, but then he spoke to Powers.

"Captain Powers, if you can talk to that truck, get them stopped before they hit that span. That whole segment may very well collapse."

Powers got back on his radio while Hush knelt back down by Lang.

"You okay?" he asked. She nodded her head. She pulled away the red-stained handkerchief, and they both studied the welt. Hush tried not to notice the swell of her breasts on either side.

"It broke the skin, that's all. Stings more than hurts," she said, closing her blouse and jacket again. "Is anyone else hurt?" she asked.

This time, Hush told her that the Army officer had been killed. She swallowed hard at that news as she pulled the edges of her jacket tighter across her chest. Her hands were shaking. She'd had a very close call, and she knew it. Keeler stared back through the aperture, a bleak expression on his face. Hush tried to erase the horrific image of the young Army officer's body. They could see the truck stopping at the beginning of the next span. Two state troopers carrying medical first-aid bags got out and hurried up catwalk on the eastbound side. Powers went to meet them.

Hush felt a wave of nausea. Been desk-bound too long, he thought. "What's this do to the bridge?"

"I'm afraid it's basically the same thing as Thebes," Keeler said. "It means the railroad can't put big repair equipment up next to this center span, on this side, anyway. They'll have to fix the inboard span first, then this one. Shaped charge, I think. This bridge is going to be down for a long time."

"I understand the Merchants Bridge is also out of service," Hush said after a few seconds. "These guys aren't amateurs, are they?"

Keeler shook his head but did not answer. Carolyn Lang got up, still holding the handkerchief inside her jacket. One of the state troopers appeared. He was wearing white rubber gloves and bringing Lang a large gauze bandage. Powers was right behind him.

"The other guy's cut up, but we don't think it's life-threatening," Powers said. "I've called down to the yard on the Illinois side and informed the control center. My people have sent for our bomb squad to come up and examine the entire bridge. Oh, and Mr. Herlihy has been informed."

"Thank you," Hush said. "Mr. Keeler here thinks it was a shaped charge."

"I initially thought concussion grenade," Keeler said. "But that's heavy steel framing. And the damage to that man's body . . . too big for a grenade."

Lang zippered up her FBI windbreaker over the gauze bandage, and the troopers went back to lay out a body sheet over the remains of the Army officer. "Okay," Hush said. "We're going back down now. The media are going to go high-order with this. I need to get Agent Lang to a hospital, and then we probably need to talk to Washington."

"What you need to do is find these sons a bitches," Keeler said forcefully. "These bridges are irreplaceable."

Keeler was taking the attacks on the bridges personally, Hush noted. He recovered Lang's phone and then took her by the arm. "We know, Mr. Keeler. Believe me, we're working on it."

Hush was grateful for the body sheet as he escorted Lang past the gaping hole in the track bed and walked her carefully over to the east-bound track of the next span. The troopers were still gathered around the injured engineer. Another truck was coming up the tracks with yet more people. Hush waited for them to unload and commandeered it for a ride back down to the switchyards, where Herlihy was waiting for them with a couple of Bureau cars. There was a small crowd of railroad people standing around at the base of the bridge, as well as several more state troopers. The media won't be far behind, Hush thought.

"What happened up there?" Herlihy asked, looking askance at Lang's white face and bloody fingers.

"A leave-behind bomb. That bridge inspector, Keeler, and an Army guy were examining the next span to see if they'd damaged it, too, when the Army guy apparently pulled a trip wire. It took him apart and blew out the next span's supports. Keeler says the bridge is down for a long time. Agent Lang here got hit by a piece of shrapnel, but it appears to be superficial. Can one of your people take her to an ER?"

"Absolutely," Herlihy said, an uncomfortable expression on his face as he looked at Carolyn. He called an agent over and Carolyn left with him. Hush called after her that he would meet her at the hospital.

"She okay?" Herlihy asked.

"Do you really care?" Hush retorted.

Herlihy's face reddened. "Look, goddamn it, she was a major thorn in my side out here, but she's still an agent. Yes, I care."

"Sorry," Hush said. "But you've been in her face since the Thebes thing. She's not a threat to you, you know."

Herlihy gave him a sardonic look. "You think that's what it was? That I felt *threatened* by Carolyn Lang?"

"Don't know what you *felt*," Hush replied evenly. "Only how you've been acting."

Herlihy shook his head. "Hush," he said, "for an assistant director, you are some kind of naïve. I'm not the one threatened by Carolyn Lang. You just wait. She's just biding her time, and then—wham. Pearl Harbor. You'll see."

"I don't have time for that shit, Joe. *We* don't have time for it."

Herlihy exhaled forcefully. "Okay," he said. "But don't say I never warned you. Anybody called Washington yet?"

"I'm about to," Hush replied. He steered Herlihy away from the crowd. "This thing is getting out of hand, and we're nowhere with it."

"Got that right. The state guys are ripshit. And guess what's next." Herlihy pointed upriver to the I-55 bridge. A television news van was already parked at one end of the bridge; another one was pulling out and headed their way. Herlihy ordered his people to keep the media types out of the switchyards, both sides. Then he extracted a big cigar and lit it up in a cloud of blue smoke. Hush, not a smoker, inhaled some of it to clear his nostrils of the smell of death on the bridge. They began walking to Herlihy's car.

"The railroad people have anything to offer?" Hush asked.

"Shit no. They're all so worried about how the bridge being out of service is going to affect their 'competitive position.' That seems to be the phrase of the day. Mostly, they're all going in tight-assed little circles. My ASAC says when they heard about the Army guy getting blown up, the first thing they did was send for their lawyers."

"They weren't too forthcoming at the first interagency meeting, either," Hush said. "Didn't want to send a rep because it might compromise their liability position. That kind of stuff."

"Let's go back to my office," Herlihy said. "You can make your calls. Then go check on Razo—Senior Agent Lang." He stopped. "A booby trap," he said. His mouth twitched.

Hush just stared at him.

"Okay, okay," Herlihy said. "I'll be good. Promise. I'll even drive."

Major Matthews was at home having lunch when Carl Hill called.

"We've received the execute order from Washington," Hill said. "Begin route assembly this afternoon. Do a load audit on Monday. Launch is set tentatively for next Tuesday."

"Got it," Matthews said. There was a pause on the line.

"Tom, I need to ask you something."

Matthews felt a tingle of apprehension. Hill had been extremely busy redoing the route orders and supervising the assembly of the train. Matthews had not yet had a chance to 'calibrate' him, as he had promised Mehle, mostly because *he* was the one Mehle had threatened, not Hill.

"Yeah, Carl?"

"What's going on with this Mehle guy? Suddenly, I'm making reports to him instead of to Colonel Anderson. Then I went down to Assembly Nine? Tried to get in there a little while ago? The security gomers tell me I'm not on the current access list. They said you were. I'm the goddamned train master, for Chrissakes—what's going down?"

"Assembly Nine?" Matthews said, stalling for time. That idiot Mehle, he thought. His wife, who was across the room, was pretending not to listen. "Carl, I guess we need to talk."

"Well, what's going on in Assembly Nine is no damn mystery to me. That's where they're taking their problem children to do the upload. But they can't keep me out of there."

"Where are you now?"

"I'm back in operations."

"I'll be right over. Meet me out front. And don't talk to anyone else."

Twenty minutes later, they were standing side by side against Matthews's car. Hill was kicking a piece of gravel around with the toe of his boot while Matthews explained what had happened in Anderson's office.

"So he's really an NSC staffer," Matthews concluded.

"Big deal," Hill said. "That doesn't mean he isn't a nutcase. Especially in this administration. And where is Colonel Anderson? Nobody's seen him for the past day."

"Mehle said he went TDY back to Washington. Look, this guy Mehle has some serious pull. He's still got the CERT and all those MPs deployed out at the airfield, and I haven't heard bitch one from Fort McClellan. We need to be really careful around this guy."

"Well, I'll tell you what," Hill said. "I don't like it. I don't like changing the route in secret, and I don't like taking damaged nukes through Memphis, and I don't like some Washington weenie coming down here and throwing his weight around."

Matthews had been afraid of this. "Just hang in there, Carl," he said. "They're bringing special containments in for those weapons, and your two armored tank cars will make it an even safer proposition. Washington is probably more afraid of an incident than you are."

"That depends," Hill said, kicking at the curb, "on just exactly who in Washington is authorizing this shit."

.

Using Herlihy's office in the Abrams Federal Office Building, Hush and the SAC spent forty-five minutes on the speakerphone with Tyler Redford back in Washington, detailing the preliminary findings on the MacArthur Bridge bombing and informing him of the second bomb incident. He instructed Redford to contact the appropriate people in the Transportation Department and request authority to put out a general security alert for the reminder of the Mississippi River railroad bridges, north and south of St. Louis, to include the possibility of putting National Guard troops into the equation. Redford confirmed that the railroads, purportedly because of proprietary business concerns, were doing the armadillo on any assessment of the impact of losing two bridges. Further, they would probably *not* be receptive to the idea of federal troops, in that their railroad police had exclusive jurisdiction on the rail system and they did not want to set any precedents. Hush groaned aloud; a crew of mad bombers was taking down their lifelines, and they were throwing lawyers at the problem.

Redford told them that the burning question around Washington was, of course, what the FBI was doing about it beyond holding interagency meetings. Herlihy piped up that the state police were combing their own databases for any persons or person who might fit a bomber profile, but so far, they had come up empty. The serious irregular militia gangs were all pretty much farther west of Missouri. Redford reminded both of them that national press interest was building fast and that the director was getting some pointed questions from his congressional oversight committees. Some of the television talking heads were beginning to predict economic disaster if the rail system sustained any more hammer blows like these two, and so on.

Redford also had some statistics from the Transportation Department. The MacArthur Bridge reportedly handled an average of twelve heavy trains an hour, going both ways, twenty-four hours a day. A hundred-car train moved close to eight thousand tons of cargo. Factoring in a 50 percent empty car rate on the bridges, that meant nearly one million *tons* per day of transcontinental freight was going to have to be rerouted onto other bridges that were already at capacity, and, in some cases, using less capable regional track systems.

Hush acknowledged all that and closed with a strong recommendation that the first thing to do was to secure the remaining bridges. Railroad police, state police, feds—the interagency group could take their choice but there couldn't be any more of this totally unrestricted access to the bridges.

"You're saying they had *no* security?" Redford asked.

"They had one guy patrolling over a mile of bridge in the dark and the rain, and he's missing right now. There are no real physical barriers to access, to either the switchyards or the bridges, other than an unsupervised chain-link fence. That Thebes bridge was out in the middle of nowhere: They could have driven a van right out onto the damn thing and no one would have seen them. So we desperately need to get them secure."

"Got it, boss," Redford said. "I'll teleconference with the IG principals right away."

"Right, and if the major railroad companies don't want to cooperate, let's get Transportation to stop asking them and start *telling* them instead. Hell, I guess the government could always nationalize them, or at least the bridges."

Redford took a moment to digest that comment, and Hush realized that his suggestion might have been just a bit extreme. They concluded the conversation, and Herlihy sent out for some coffee. One of the office secretaries stuck her head in and reported that the local television was running tape about the bridge explosions on the midday news. Herlihy groaned and switched on his office television.

Captain Powers was being interviewed by a breathlessly beautiful blonde, who was having a tough time keeping her hairdo in place in the wind that was blowing through the switchyards. Powers was doing a professional bob-and-weave act. Yes, this was the second railroad bridge to be attacked in a week. Yes, there had been another bomb explosion on the bridge this morning; one person had been killed, name awaiting notification of next of kin, two injured, no further details. The impact on the national rail system? That would have to be determined by an interagency group in Washington. Was it true that freight shipments were already being delayed? The railroads would have to answer that. Was the FBI involved? Yes, and they were all working very closely together. Did the FBI have any idea of who might be responsible for these attacks? All law-enforcement agencies involved were actively developing several leads. Was there full cooperation between the Missouri Highway Patrol and the federal agencies? Absolutely. Did FBI believe this was the work of terrorists? The FBI would have to respond to that. We are keeping all our options open right now. Powers then said he had to go.

As Hush watched, he found himself thinking about Carolyn Lang. She had received a pretty nasty shock up there on the bridge this morning. Absent the notebook, that fragment would have blown a hole the size of a quarter right through her heart. The other thing that bothered him was what Herlihy had implied: that Lang posed some kind of threat to *him.* Did Himself know about the director's palace games? For all the noise about Carolyn Lang, Hush had seen nothing but entirely professional behavior. He realized he wanted to get out of the office and go see how she was doing.

"Not bad," Herlihy was saying, switching off the set. "He gave away nothing that hadn't been available to someone watching from that other bridge."

"Powers is okay, I think. We regrouped after our initial hydrant-watering episode on the bridge. Went to dinner, had a drink. I told him we'd cut the state guys in on as much glory as he needed for political purposes, and that seemed to calm him down."

"Know how that is," Herlihy said. "Although there ain't much glory in sight right now. Who the *hell* is doing this?"

Hush could only shake his head. "I'm going to go check on Lang," he said, getting up.

Herlihy started to say something but then put an elaborately innocent expression on his face.

"What?" Hush asked.

Herlihy told Hush to close the office door. "Would you be doing that if she were a he?" he asked.

"Yes, actually, I would. For Chrissakes, Joe. She works for me. She was injured in the line of duty. Just because you hate the idea of female agents doesn't mean I have to be professionally indifferent."

Herlihy gave him an amused look. "Is that an AD speaking, or is this between us ordinary assholes here, Hush?"

Hush waved his hand. "All I'm saying is that if the boss has a hard time with the concept that women make just as good agents as men do, then his subordinates are going to take their cues from him. I think that's probably what happened out here."

"Bullshit," Herlihy said immediately. "I've had women in this office since I've been SAC, and none of them have felt inclined to go to the barricades. Not until *she* showed up, anyway. You've been away from the trenches too long, Hush. You were never a SAC. You don't know what it's like to have a fuse-lighter like Lang come in and start some shit. She was like a virus, infecting the whole goddamned organization."

Hush mentally acknowledged Herlihy's point about his never having had field command. Besides, he needed to be more careful: Herlihy and the current director went way back, as was the case with many SACs, which is probably why Lang had been transferred and Herlihy left untarnished by the problem.

"Plus," Herlihy continued, "the guy who should have been moved up to ASAC here, Hank McDougal, the guy I was grooming to replace me one day, took an early out. Because of her. You think about that."

"Meaning what, exactly?" Hush asked.

"Meaning she leaves bodies in her wake, that's what."

"I hardly think she and I are in some kind of competition, Joe," Hush said, and then immediately he remembered that in a sense, they were.

"Yeah, but you're single, aren't you?" Herlihy replied, wagging a finger at Hush. "And she's for damn sure single. And while I personally can't see any man ever warming up to the likes of Carolyn Lang, you better watch your ass. People will take one look at her, and then they'll talk. That's how shit starts, Hush."

Hush threw up his hands in a gesture of surrender. "Point taken. But I'm still going to go see her. In the meantime, where the hell do we go from here, Joe? Our intel guys have nothing. Not even the usual loonies are claiming, and now the railroads are going to lawyer up."

Herlihy sat down heavily in his oversized chair. His office was large, and the direct access to the conference room made it look even larger. Beyond the closed office door was one floor of the main office area, where the St. Louis agents were working at desks and answering telephones. The FBI offices occupied two more floors. Before Herlihy could answer, his phone rang. He listened for a moment, then hung up.

"Problem's solved. Lang's back in the building. You need an office? I can evict somebody."

Hush realized that Lang's return was going to be awkward, both for Herlihy and his people and for her. The fact that they had an assistant director in the office wasn't helping.

"That's okay," Hush said. "They're going to want me back in Washington pretty quick. I want to go back out to the rail yards and talk to some people, see the ground again. We'll get out of your hair. If you can detail me a car—"

Herlihy offered to provide both a car and driver, but Hush wanted to operate independently for a while. He went out to meet Lang in the reception office while Herlihy got on the intercom. She had changed clothes, but otherwise she seemed none the worse for wear. The top of a bandage, framed by a brown stain of Betadine, was visible in the V of her blouse. When they went downstairs, an agent was waiting curbside to turn over the keys to a late-model Ford Crown Vic. He gave the keys to Lang, nodded at Hush, and went back inside the building.

Lang walked over to the car and opened the right-rear door. Hush smiled at her and got in the right front seat instead. "I'm too tall to fit in the backseat of anything," he said.

Lang said nothing, closed the rear door, and walked around to get in.

"Are you okay to drive?" he asked her as they joined traffic.

"It was superficial. I think I was mostly frightened. Especially when I realized . . ."

"Yeah, I think that's precisely right. You up for lunch?"

"I don't often eat lunch. But if you—"

"Well, I was thinking you might need a good scotch. And then lunch, if only to keep up appearances—it being the middle of the day."

She looked back at him, and for the second time he thought he saw a flash of warmth.

"A scotch. In the middle of the day."

"Yep. Maybe even a double."

"Sounds wonderful. But then you'll have to drive, Mr. Hanson."

"I can probably handle that," he said.

They found a restaurant on the bluffs just north of the riverboat casino row, shucked their FBI windbreakers, and went in for lunch and Lang's badly needed scotch. Over coffee, she brought him up to speed on what she had learned from the agent who took her to the ER. Herlihy's team canvass in the switchyards had confirmed the total lack of security for the bridge.

"So in terms of real security to prevent or monitor physical access, say in the face of a determined terrorist group?"

"They have nothing. They do have video-surveillance systems in the yards, but they're focused on trains, not intruders. They're monitored at the district control building. Those yards, the bridges, and probably even some of the rolling stock are wide open to someone who knows what he's doing."

Hush stopped eating. *"Someone?"*

She stared back at him and nodded slowly. "That's what I've been thinking. What if this isn't a group? What if it's one guy?"

He thought about that. "Go on. Based on what?"

She frowned. "You mean evidence? Facts? I don't have any. No, I was just thinking as I stood up on that bridge, before that poor man was . . . was . . . well, blown to pieces, that *I* could have planted Detcord on those cables. *I* could have set up a booby trap like that. I mean, I wouldn't really know how to do that, but one knowledgeable person could do it. All of it. And one person would be able to move easily through those switchyards and up onto that bridge, especially at night."

"Where as a whole herd of people, or their vehicles, might be seen."

"Exactly. Especially if he was dressed like the people who work there."

"Or was one of them," he said. "Maybe a trainman? Some employee with a grudge?"

"That's right. Neither our intel people nor the local cops have surfaced anything on any known group. I think we should pull the lone perpetrator string."

Hush thought some more. They had all just naturally assumed it was a group. A terrorist cell. The antigovernment militia fringe, maybe. Except it was the railroads that were being hammered, not the government.

"I think we need to get back to Washington," he said. "Tonight. But first, let's go find that bridge inspector, Keeler. See what he thinks of the feasibility of your theory."

She glanced at her empty glass and handed the car keys across the table. Their eyes met and held for about one microsecond longer than necessary.

"Better?" he asked.

"Much." She paused. "I was scared up there. Not during, but after. If it hadn't been for the notebook . . ."

"Been there. Makes you think about what's important, doesn't it?" he said. "Let's go find Keeler."

They checked back by car phone with the field office, who tracked Morgan Keeler down to the Union Pacific operations center in the gateway yards on the East St. Louis side. He was attending a meeting of the railroad operations people, who were assessing the impact of losing both the Thebes and the MacArthur bridges. As they drove into the switchyard complex at just after 3:00 P.M., they couldn't help but notice that virtually every siding was full—and that no one challenged their entry into the yard.

"Looks like the start of gridlock to me," Hush observed as their car bumped over the potholed parking lot out in front of the windowless operations center. The center looked like a blockhouse, but there was no security station inside the building. There wasn't even a receptionist. A brakeman standing inside the door asked them to wait while he found out who would be available to speak to them. He came back and asked them to follow him upstairs to the main operations control room. They were met by the superintendent for the East St. Louis operation, who introduced them to the other people in the room.

There were about twenty men standing around a row of consoles occupying the center of the large windowless room. The walls were fifteen feet high and covered with multicolored track diagrams, across some of which white and yellow lights were moving slowly. A track radio circuit was chattering away somewhere on a speaker, and eight console operators continued to work, muttering urgently into lip mikes, while ignoring the crowd standing behind them. Two bright red lines up on the boards represented the MacArthur and the Merchants bridges. Two other men over in one corner were arguing forcefully with a third man, who was holding a telephone handset in each hand.

The superintendent introduced the railroad men present, which included reps from the Union Pacific, Illinois Central, Norfolk Southern, Burlington Northern Santa Fe, CSXT, Gateway Western, and Conrail. Morgan Keeler and an Army colonel in uniform were there for the Army Corps of Engineers, along with a grim-faced civilian from the Surface Transportation Board in Washington.

"Excuse the interruption, gents," Hush said, introducing himself and Carolyn. "We're here to talk to Mr. Keeler, but it can certainly wait until you're done."

A large red-faced man with a Union Pacific badge acknowledged Hush. "We're just about done here, Mr. Hanson," he said. "We're in the blivet management stage right now, if you know what I mean. Trying to put a hundred pounds of train into a one-pound sack."

Hush nodded. "I saw an awful lot of trains stacked up in the yards," he said. "What's the immediate fix?"

"The immediate fix would be to run some of it down to Thebes," the UP man said pointedly. "Failing that, we're gonna have to start prioritizing so we can decide what's going to go across the bridges up north of St. Louis."

"In other words, it's a mess."

The red-faced man snorted. "Right now, we have about six hundred and fifty cars arriving here. Every hour. Until we get a reroute plan up and running, the UP's priorities are not exactly everyone else's priorities. It's going to be a full-scale cluster fuck. Excuse me, ma'am."

Hush was quick to fill the small embarrassed silence that followed. "The Bureau's working it as hard as we can," he said. "Here at Thebes, and in Washington. And we're getting excellent cooperation from the state and local police."

"What's this I heard about a second bomb up there this morning?" another man standing next to Keeler asked. Hush noticed that Keeler seemed impatient with their interruption. He explained to the group what had happened, and that Agent Lang had been hit by a piece of shrapnel. There were expressions of sympathy around the room.

"Do you have any suspects yet?" another man asked.

Hush hesitated. The correct Bureau answer would have been that they were developing several substantive leads, but he decided not to bullshit these people.

"No. I'd appreciate that staying in this room, but the real answer is no. We have a few fragments of physical evidence from the Thebes bridge, and I suppose we might get some more out of this one. But right at the moment, there are no groups claiming responsibility, and our intelligence people have come up empty, at least on the first go-round. Like I said, we're working it hard. That's usually the only thing that produces results in police work."

"Gentlemen, the Corps of Engineers needs an answer," Keeler said from the side of the group. "Do you want us to lay down a temporary floating bridge?"

The CSXT man intervened immediately. "Not unless you're prepared to open it fifty percent of the time. We have a barge jam building already, and that's going to get a whole lot worse once the channel at Thebes is reopened."

His reply sparked an immediate argument. Hush was able to deduce from the ensuing conversation that the CSXI operation also ran a huge barge fleet on the Mississippi, while the other railroads did not. Keeler threw up his hands. Hush gave him the high sign to join him and Carolyn back out in the hallway, where he explained Lang's theory of the single perpetrator. He asked Keeler if he thought it physically feasible for one man to do what had been done to the bridges. Keeler had to think about it for a moment.

"Yes," he said finally. "He would have had to do a hell of a lot of recon on these particular bridges, things like traffic density, the bridge design, and the security systems."

"What security systems?" Lang asked.

Keeler looked down his nose at her. "Well, I guess you're right there. The yards and lines are patrolled, but the bridges . . ."

"The bridges are wide open," Hush said. "I hope all those guys in there have been adressing that problem."

"If they have, I didn't hear it," Keeler said. "They're all trying to figure out how to move *their* trains and to hell with the competition. The UP guy had it right: Railroads simply are not used to cooperating with one another this way. Technically, at the track and yard level, they do it all the time, but always within the context of a rate and tariff structure. The rest of the time, they enjoy cutting one another's throats."

"You're the government's senior bridge engineer out here on the southern half of the Mississippi," Hush said. "If we lean on the railroads to implement tighter security, or maybe threaten National Guard intervention, would you be willing to conduct an urgent security inspection of the remaining bridges? See if there are any more bombs planted, or evidence of tampering?"

"Certainly," Keeler said. "I'd planned to do that anyway, once I got someone's attention. But don't confuse *urgent* with *quick*."

"What do you mean?"

"There are four operational bridges left south of here. Memphis, Vicksburg, Baton Rouge, and New Orleans. With the exception of Vicksburg, they are monsters. As large as or bigger than the MacArthur here. I'd suggest you *direct* the owning railroads do a security sweep on each one, and then I'll follow up with a detailed inspection."

"I agree. I'll surface that in the interagency group in Washington tomorrow."

"Tomorrow's Saturday," Keeler said.

"So?" Hush replied. "If what I saw in there is any indication, we'll probably be meeting Sunday, too. I have the sense that the national rail network is going to be in trouble."

Keeler nodded. "Not going to be—it already is. And it's complicated by the fact that the railroads are going to make cooperation very hard. Nature of the beasts."

"Can the Army really put a floating bridge across the Mississippi?" Carolyn asked.

"If they can pontoon-bridge the Rhine and run tank columns across it, they can bridge the Mississippi," Keeler said. "It would not be a trivial undertaking, though. And the barge problem complicates things." He turned to Hush. "So you think a lone ranger is doing this?"

"We can't rule that out," Hush said. "In a way, I wish we could, though."

"Why?"

"Find one guy, operating along nearly a thousand miles of river? We like to think we're good, Mr. Keeler, but I'm not sure we're that good."

• • •

Major Matthews stood in the control room of the Anniston Depot's rail operations tower, watching the yardmaster and his team of three dispatchers move the seventy-eight specially modified railcars into position on the main siding. From the outside, the tower looked much like an airport's control tower. There were deeply tinted windows on four sides, a small forest of aerials on the roof, and an unobstructed view of the entire switchyard. The ten assembly buildings stood like faceless sentinels just beyond the track complex. Dispatchers were in radio contact with the control rooms in each of the assembly buildings and with the brakemen and switch switch-tenders out in the yard. A single yard diesel was being used to pull each string out of the assembly buildings and then to "kick" them into the train, where individual brakemen confirmed the couplings. A dozen MPs from nearby Fort McClellan watched over all the movements as they patrolled the switchyard. From all the activity, no one could have guessed it was a Saturday.

Carl Hill entered the control room from the outside stairway. He spoke briefly to the yardmaster and then went over to where Matthews was standing by the windows.

"Engines are coming in," he said, pointing to the windows behind them. Matthews turned to watch. The main rail line running past the Anniston Depot was a tonnage group seven Norfolk Southern line connecting Atlanta to Birmingham. The main line ran close to the main entrance of the depot, but outside the security perimeter. The depot's switchyard terminated in a single spur next to the assembly buildings. Matthews could see three large diesel engines, coupled together, backing ponderously down the spur toward the first rail security control checkpoint.

Hill said that the engines were four thousand horsepower, six-axle road switchers. They were painted out in flat black, with U.S. Army serial numbers in place of company logos. The locomotives were also armored, with sloping, instead of vertical, steel skirts, slitted plate steel over the side windows, and specially articulated steel plates hanging down to cover the wheel trucks and sanders. Where there ordinarily would have been a small platform at the back of the engine, another armored cab had been installed to accommodate a two-man security detail, hard points for automatic weapons, and a military communications pod.

"Why three engines?" Matthews asked.

"This train is officially classified as 'heavy.' We'll have car weights ranging from ninety to one hundred and twenty tons, depending on the casings being carried."

"How fast can it go, then?" Matthews asked. His knowledge of trains was restricted to what went on inside the the depot. Commercial railroad operations were Hill's specialty, and, as train master, Hill was going to ride the train west.

"No way of telling that," Hill said. The engines were through the first checkpoint and now approaching the internal checkpoint. Massive steel gates were sliding closed at the outside perimeter. "We have to calculate the route using average speeds," he continued. "Taking into account delays, traffic stops, siding time—the list is potentially endless. The average freight train in this country is sixty-nine cars, weighs out at twenty-six hundred tons minus the engines, and averages speeds of only twenty-one point five miles per hour."

"That's all?"

"The key word here is *average*. Out on the flat, those three engines could pull this train at seventy, eighty miles per hour. The real reason for three engines is that out west, thar be big hills."

The engines were now backing through the internal gates. Matthews realized that only one of them was actually running.

"Why is the assembly taking so long?" he asked.

"Because we're in the process of doing a baseline thousand-mile inspection on every wheel of every car out there. Plus all the air brakes and general mechanical gear. Also, in the case of twenty-seven thirteen, sealant systems and security tags. Actually, we're almost done with all that. But we'll have to stop and do the wheels again during the run to Utah. Every thousand miles. Federal Railroad Administration rules. You hope and pray for no bearing or wheel failures."

"And if you get one?"

"We obviously can't unload a car outside the depot. If we get a hot box, we'll side it out, post a lot of guards, and then wait for the nearest rail-capable military installation to send an engine with a maintenance crew. Those wheels weigh eight hundred pounds—*each.* It's not like changing a flat."

The engines were all the way inside the depot perimeter now and were approaching the tower, whose windows began to rattle as the lead engine drew near.

"So what's the scoop on these bridge bombings?" Hill asked. "Washington still insisting on going ahead with this thing?"

Matthews nodded. He looked around to see who might be listening; there were four other people in the control room.

"And they're definitely not going to announce the route change until the train's on the road?"

Matthews nodded again

Hill shook his head. "Right through beautiful downtown Memphis."

Don't say it, Carl, Matthews thought. Just a couple more days and we can get this monkey off our collective backs.

7

ON SUNDAY MORNING, Hush was pacing the floor in the main outpatient waiting room at George Washington University Hospital while he waited for Carolyn Lang to get back from the pharmacy. He was surprised to see how many people were in the hospital, but then he remembered that it was Sunday morning after a Washington, D.C., Saturday night.

Their flight back to Washington Friday evening had been uneventful, and he had had his official sedan drop her off at her town house in Alexandria before letting him out at the Belle Haven. She had seemed all right after the incident on the bridge, but he did remember that she had been fingering the bandage on her chest in the car. He was willing to bet that it hurt more than she let on.

Saturday morning, they had convened the interagency group for an urgent session in the wake of the MacArthur Bridge bombing. The meeting had been frustrating, with a lot more questions being asked than there were answers available. Redford succeeded in coaxing the railroads to send reps, but the major companies, CSXI, Norfolk Southern, Union Pacific, and the Burlington Northern Santa Fe, had been represented by lawyers, most of whom had been operating in a shrill transmit mode. The Bureau had been able to announce just about nothing in the way of progress, and there had been a lot of dark talk from the Department of Transportation people about the need for stepping up the size and scope of the investigation. A twenty-something gunfighter from the White House staff had wondered aloud if perhaps the Department of Defense might not be better suited to handle this case, a suggestion the DOD rep, smelling a no-win situation in the wind, quickly quashed.

The long and the short of it was that they had nothing to go on other than explosives forensics, which unfortunately had translated into no leads. The Pyrodex used on the Thebes bridge was as common as dirt, and Detacord, by its very nature, left nothing but a black smear behind. The three rags, showing traces of blasting cap explosive residue, were still under origin search analysis. The bomb that had dismembered the Army officer had been a combination blast and shaped-charge device, which probably was military in origin. It revealed that the perpetrators knew how to set up a shaped charge, but that was about it.

Hush had elected to keep the one-man theory secreted in the casebook for the time being. If they did decide to go that route, they would stay publicly with the group conspiracy theory, thereby lulling their lone ranger into a false sense of security. Within the FBI, Carolyn's theory had been met with barely polite skepticism, especially from Carswell's National Security rep, who stoutly supported the terrorist group theory. Hush sensed that individual divisions within the Bureau were beginning to circle the wagons as the railroad bridge case evolved into one of those memorable shit storms from which no one profited.

He stopped pacing and sat down in one of the few empty chairs to try to think. The hospital paging system went on nonstop, making thought difficult. At midafternoon Saturday, he had gone from the director's office back to the IITF conference room, where he discovered Lang looking a little ragged around the edges. She thought she might be in the initial stages of an infection from the shrapnel wound. Her face was flushed and she could not keep her hands off the bandage. Hush had ordered her taken over to GWU Hospital, where they admitted her overnight to get a jump on any infection. He had called to check on her this morning and found out she was being released, whereupon he left a message for her that he would pick her up.

He looked at his watch. She'd been gone almost an hour on what should have been a simple pharmacy pickup. As he waited, he tried to analyze his own motives for being at the hospital. He kept thinking about Herlihy's comment about whether he would be doing this if the agent involved were a he and not an attractive she.

Well, that certainly was a question. Actually, two questions. First, there was the matter of the director's unspoken orders to discredit Lang if he could. He knew that he could; all he would have to do would be to let the current antagonism toward her work its poisonous magic and withhold his support when people gave her trouble. Especially now that she had put forth her own theory about the bombings. Carswell and company would be only too happy to squash her theory and her along with it. The bothersome question was, Did he want to do that? So far, she had not put a foot wrong, professionally, and had come up with the one idea that might end up defining their search.

The second question was personal and more perplexing. Hush found himself torn between his normal reticence around attractive women and his growing interest in Carolyn Lang. He had only to look in any mirror that didn't cut off at the level of his tie to know that he looked a lot like most people's vision of Ichabod Crane. Carolyn Lang, on the other hand, was a pretty slick package. And yet here he was, an assistant director, waiting to give a female agent who was junior to him a ride home because—why? It wasn't as if she'd been encouraging his personal attention. He wondered if he wasn't indulging some latent desire to play with fire.

"Ready to go if you are," a voice said from above him. He looked up, to find Carolyn standing right in front of him. She was carrying a white pharmacy bag in one hand and her purse in the other. She had fixed her face somewhat and looked a lot more alive than when he had seen her earlier in the morning. She was wearing the same business suit she had been wearing Saturday at the meeting, which had a fairly tight skirt. Hush, face-to-face with that lovely figure, found himself looking for a fraction of a second longer than he should have.

"Right," he said quickly, getting up. He immediately towered over her, but she did not move back, and for an instant they were standing very close.

"Great," he said, clearing his throat. She turned sideways, a faintly crooked smile on her face, and moved toward the entrance, her thick blond hair swaying slightly and leaving a subtle trace of perfume in her wake. He tried not to look like an oversized puppy dog as they left the waiting room, pursued by several frankly admiring looks from the other men in the waiting room.

Her house in Alexandria was on Union Street in Old Town, about two miles upriver from his apartment building. It was a large three-story brick town house, situated in a row overlooking the last block of shops fronting the Potomac. She invited him to come in for a cup of coffee. He thought about demurring even as he heard himself accepting.

"Wow," he said when they were inside. The interior decor was sumptuous.

"I'm single and I was a finance major in college and graduate school," she said over her shoulder, answering his implied question. "This long bull market has been very profitable for me."

He followed her back to the kitchen area, where she set coffee makings in motion. He could see a spacious brick-walled garden behind the house, framed by large trees that towered over the back wall. There was an ornate brick patio and some expensive-looking patio furniture surrounding a covered hot tub.

"These clothes and I smell of hospital," she said. "I'm going to change. The coffee will be done in a few minutes. Help yourself."

As someone who liked to cook, he examined the kitchen in detail, taking care not to collide with a rack of cookware that hung dangerously low from the ceiling. She was back in fifteen minutes, as he was finishing his coffee. She had appeared to have showered, and she had indeed changed clothes: She was now wearing a white one-piece bathing suit, sandals, and a long-tailed white gauze shirt buttoned casually over the bathing suit. He tried not to stare at her lush figure, looking at the large white bandage instead.

"They put some stitches in?" he asked.

"Nope," she said, bending over as she searched the refrigerator for some cream. "Just an IV drip and a few liters of antibiotics. The docs said we caught the bugs in time."

She turned back around, got some coffee, and added a large dollop of cream. "Let's go outside. I'm desperate for some sun."

He followed her out the back door, resisting his automatic urge to duck: The doors in this house were at least seven feet high. She dusted some pollen off the chaise, then flopped down. He chose one of the chairs and tried not to spill his coffee. A blue jay swore raucously at them from the high brick wall.

"So," she said, unbuttoning the white blouse and kicking off the sandals. "Welcome to my garden."

He nodded and mumbled something while he stirred his already thoroughly mixed coffee. He was feeling a bit on edge, and he wondered if it was the caffeine or being alone with Carolyn Lang. She was holding her coffee mug up under her chin with both hands and looking at him with cool, speculative eyes over the rim. They appeared to be deep green in the bright sunlight. He found himself at a complete loss for words: Hush to the max.

"I sense you're uncomfortable being alone with me," she said. "Are you married?"

He gave a quick laugh. "Not hardly," he said, his throat a little dry. She was arranging her body on the chaise in small liquid movements, and he was trying his damnedest not to watch.

"Why do you say 'Not hardly'?"

"I'm not exactly your classic ladies' man."

She shrugged and smiled. "So you're very tall," she said. "And I suppose that makes you feel awkward and therefore unattractive. It's funny how you men do that."

"Do what?"

"Men appreciate women mostly for how they look, initially anyway, and then assume we do the same thing. You are not an unattractive man, Hush Hanson."

He smiled at her, not knowing how to respond.

"You're known for being a consummate Washington operator, and you've managed to work your way up to assistant director in less than a hundred years. Relax. As they say in the Army, take your pack off. Or at least your tie. I won't bite."

He put down his mug. "Yes, well. Thank you for all the compliments. I'm constantly perplexed by all this gender tension in the government these days. If Heinrich were sitting up there on that wall, he'd be asking if I was out of my mind."

She laughed. "If Heinrich were sitting up there on that wall, he'd be trying to look down my bathing suit," she said. "Not that that would be such a pleasant sight just now." She cocked her head to one side. "Look, I fully realize that I'm on probation with this assignment, so I'm not proposing that you and I get together. I just wanted to say thanks for being . . . you. For being Hush Hanson, Mr. Straight Arrow."

He started to say something, then hesitated. She just waited. He decided just to come out with it.

"I guess what I'm trying to say is that it's been a little bit distracting to have you involved in this case. I understand that's my problem and not yours."

"And I suppose my reputation at headquarters isn't helping matters."

"No. Yes. I mean, well, take the way Herlihy acted out there in St. Louis. I was really surprised at that."

"That's Herlihy's style. But now I'm curious: Did I hear him warning you to watch your back around me?"

He quickly tried to recall how near she had been when Herlihy had indeed warned him about her. Near enough, he thought. "Yes, he did."

"Thought so. Let me ask you something else: Is there any reason *I* should be worried? As in, has someone senior assigned me to this cat roundup in the hopes that I'll fall flat on my face?"

Damn, he thought. She knows. But how could she? He wanted to tell her the truth, but his Washington instincts were screaming at him to duck the question.

"The deputy usually doesn't feel obligated to explain his assignments," he said carefully. "As you may or may not know, I'm kind of on probation, too."

"How so?"

He explained his "acting" status. "But if we do manage to pull off a success with this case, it will have a direct bearing on both our futures."

"Nicely done, Mr. Hush Hanson," she said with a grin. "I can see why you've survived so well for so long." For a moment, he caught a glance of the Colley Lang he'd not been able to picture before. He tried to grin back, although he wasn't entirely sure what she had meant by her comment. She leaned forward to put her mug on the ground and winced.

"Still hurts?"

"A tiny bit."

He started to get up. "I should probably go, then," he said.

She reclined on the chaise again and rubbed her eyes for a moment. "What happened up on that bridge," she said, as if he hadn't spoken, "Thing like that, what happened to that poor Army guy, it all makes one think about things."

"You were lucky. With that notebook."

"Do you know they framed it down at the Academy at Quantico? I can just see the sign: ALWAYS CARRY YOUR NOTEBOOK." She laughed. "But yes, it scared me."

"It always does, when you get shot at. Basically, you got shot at."

She opened her eyes. "I've heard some stories about you. Something in Baltimore."

"That was a long time ago, Carolyn. When I was very new to this business."

"Would you tell me about it?"

He took a deep breath and let it out. Domingo, Herrera, Santos, and Belim. The names surfaced unbidden, hovering like ghastly trophies at the back of his mind. One-eyed heads on a wall. The sun was getting hot in the confined space of the walled patio.

She pointed at the bandage between her breasts. "This qualifies as a near-death experience, I think. You were a very steadying influence up there on that bridge. I'd like to know where all that nerve comes from."

He hadn't talked about Baltimore to anyone for many, many years. Wait—yes, he had. He'd told Powers. "Steadiness under fire is a matter of self-control more than nerve, I think," he said quickly, trying to make it clear that he didn't want to go into detail.

She waited. She seemed to have the ability to make him want to fill up such silences. You don't know her, a voice in his head warned. But I want to, he thought. So he told her what he had told Powers.

She nodded thoughtfully. Her eyes were bright with interest, and possibly something more, almost as if his story had excited her. "What did you feel, doing that?" she asked.

"Numbness, mostly. It was all adrenaline, perceived time bogging down, a sequence of gun-sight pictures framed in very loud noises. Afterward . . ."

"Yes," she said, nodding slowly. "I can just imagine."

"No, you can't."

She nodded again, agreeing with him. Her face was slightly flushed, and he became conscious of a physical tension rising between them. Then she sat up, slipped off the shirt, and produced a tube of lotion.

"So, what happens next?" she asked as she began to put the lotion on her arms and the front of her legs. She was doing it slowly and with lavish attention, stroking her long legs and rubbing the lotion in large circles along the smooth muscles. Hush was mesmerized; he was also confused by her question.

"Next?" Did she mean with the case? "Well, next, I'm going back into the office. I'm going to try to figure out what we can produce besides hand wringing meetings with other government agencies. I want to think through your idea of it being one guy doing this."

She nodded and then rolled over on the chaise. She extended the tube out behind her. "Would you mind? Then I think I'm going to crash for a while. Take a day to recuperate, and I can go back in tomorrow."

Hush hesitated, then got up and pulled his chair over right next to the chaise. She lowered the headrest portion to the horizontal position and stretched out full length, cradling her head in her folded arms, her face turned partially away from him. Hush started up around her neck, holding her luxuriant hair to one side while he worked lotion into her skin. Even in the bright sunlight, the flesh on her back and shoulders appeared unusually white. She was finely muscled, though, showing evidence of frequent workouts.

"I hope this is sunblock," he said, suddenly anxious to break the silence as he stroked her body. She made a small noise of agreement.

He spread the lotion on her upper back and shoulders for as long as he could, working his fingers under the straps of her bathing suit, before moving to her legs. He started down at her feet, then began to work upward. He tried to remember the last time he had laid hands on a woman's body, and he realized it had been a long, long time. Don't be an idiot, he told himself. She just wants to avoid a sunburn. He began to feel a little bit ridiculous, perched at the edge of the chaise in his suit like some kind of folded-up grasshopper. And yet . . . Her eyes were closed and there was just the hint of a smile on her lips. He reached the back of her knees, paused, and then kept going. Her breathing changed, and he could see that her fingers were holding on to the fabric of the chaise.

He caught a change in the expression on her face. She was definitely getting turned on. He shifted again in his chair and changed the movement of his hands to a more rhythmic motion, stroking her thighs lengthwise instead of in circles, doing this for several minutes, until he reached the edges of her bathing suit. She was gripping the metal tubing of the chaise now, and there was a tension in her muscles that hadn't been there before. He checked her flushed face again, just to make very, very sure, and then he put his entire hand, balled into a gentle fist, down between her thighs, letting the hard edge of his wrist slide slowly against her. She moaned deep in her throat and then locked his wrist between her legs, and then she was the one doing the moving, her hips undulating slowly and then in increasing urgency as he splayed the fingers of his hand against her groin and then just held her while she took herself up, riding the hard sinews of his right forearm until her whole body went rigid and the side of her face turned crimson with the exertion of an orgasm that shook her from head to toe. She gave a great grunt of pleasure and then began to relax along her full length, her breath catching on each exhalation until she finally swallowed a couple of times and then went limp. He withdrew his hand and went back to stroking her, this time massaging her neck and shoulders, making his touch lighter and lighter as she drifted down into a deep sleep.

He got up, being careful not to disturb her, and rearranged his own tumescence. He scanned the visible windows on the adjoining town houses to see if anyone had been watching, but the patio walls afforded a great deal of privacy. She was asleep, her breathing deep and regular, with the only signs of her previous exertion being a fine sheen of perspiration at the base of her neck. Taking great care to make no noise, he picked up his coffee mug and went back into the house. He put the mug in the sink and went through to the front door. He made sure it would lock behind him, then closed it gently. He exhaled forcefully and walked to his car through bright sunlight, positively amazed at himself.

On Sunday night, Matthews and Hill joined Colonel Mehle and his people on the observation gallery of Assembly 9. Below them, the suited-up crews on the assembly floor prepared to mate the top half of the first special weapons car to the bottom half, which carried the Russian weapons. The car was a modified pressurized chemical tank car, sixty-five feet long and capable of carrying seventy tons. The tank had been cut in half longitudinally, allowing the top half to be lifted off for loading. The car had a double shell: an outside skin of highly polished aluminum and, inside, a steel pressure vessel. Nested in the lower half were two dark green containers, locked down on a framework of hydraulically suspended racks. The remainder of the car's interior was empty. The containers themselves were thirty feet long, four feet in diameter, and rocket-shaped, with umbilicals at each end and an instrument pack mounted on the top. Matthews could see black squares on the containers where the RADIATION HAZARD decals had been painted over. A makeshift array of lead plates had been erected between the weapons. The instrument panel on each of the containers had white, yellow, and red lights at the top. There were duplicate instrument panels mounted on one end of the car's upper half, one for each of the embedded containers. Only the white lights were illuminated, which Matthews assumed meant that conditions were normal within the containers. None of the assembly people in full protective suits below appeared to be paying any attention to those indicators. One worker stood at each corner of the tank car, guiding the fifteen-ton steel half cylinder with ropes as the overhead gantry inched it down over the mating pins. The entire evolution was being in done in exaggerated slow motion. Matthews glanced at his watch.

"Are those Anniston people down there?" Hill asked in a low voice. Mehle and his people were consulting a roll of plans over to one side of the room.

"Mehle's people. The supervisor at the far end is one of our people. The rest of the Assembly Nine crew was excused once the cars were set up."

"And no one's going to talk?"

"About what? Mehle's people dropped some hints that the C-one thirty was carrying some hot stuff; the current speculation is that it's biohazard from one of the government labs. Ebola virus. Anthrax. Rumors like that. Our crew was only too happy to turn it over to Mehle's people. How close are we on the rest of the train?"

"The dispatch audit's almost done on the main train," Hill said. "Tomorrow's the big day, I guess. The wheel inspection is completed."

"And security?" Matthews asked. "With respect to these two specials?"

Hill simply nodded. Matthews gave him a sideways look but didn't pursue it.

The upper half was coming down into position now, and some of the corner men were pulling hard to line up the holes and pins. "I'm still worried about these bridge bombings," Hill said. "From watching the network news, the FBI is clueless."

"I heard that the government has put extra security on all the Mississippi bridges. Hopefully, that will slow them down."

"First Thebes, now the MacArthur up in St. Louis. If they're working their way downriver, guess which one would be next?"

Matthews recalled the map in Anderson's conference room. The next one would be the Frisco Bridge at Memphis. "Then we'd better get a move on," he said.

"I don't think the railroads are going to buy the route mods," Hill said. "I think they'll sideline the whole train the first time we file for Memphis without EPA tickets. Plus, there's a ton of traffic congestion building out there."

"Maybe we need to tell Mehle that, then," Matthews said.

Hill grunted. "You tell him. One of his guys told me that if necessary, he'll extend that biohazard rumor to the traffic-control people once the train is rolling. Then no one will want it stopped, anywhere."

The upper car casing landed on its pins with a ponderous thump felt throughout the building. Matthews felt a sense of relief. One down, one to go.

"Well, hell, whatever works, I guess," he said. "But I'm glad I'm not going to ride it."

Hill gave him an unfathomable look.

8

MONDAY MORNING had gone by for Hush in a blur of meetings and general brainstorming around headquarters about the bridge bombings. He had returned to the office Sunday after leaving Carolyn's house, in order to have some time alone to prepare for the kind of Monday that a major case always generated. He had spent the rest of the day at his office and in Situation Room Four, poring over the reports from the two scenes, talking to the watch officers, technical people, and intelligence analysts. There had been a brief teleconference of the interagency group, primarily to listen to two other agencies describe the building chaos in the national railroad system.

Carolyn Lang had returned sometime Monday morning after first stopping by the headquarters medical office to have a nurse change her bandage. She had immediately been closeted with Tyler Redford as he prepared to get further involved in the public-relations program. Hush had not actually gotten to see her until mid afternoon, but it was in a meeting and she was all business, giving him no hint of what had happened out on her patio the day before. Hush had found himself at first disappointed, but then at a break, he had handed her a cup of coffee and she had said, "Thanks, I needed that," flashing an intimate smile at him. Then the director's office had called and he had been jerked back into the bureaucratic waterfall.

It became clear by the end of Monday that two competing theories were developing on the case: Within IITF, Hush and his team wanted to focus on the one-man theory. Carswell's National Security Division was touting the terrorist group theory to anyone who would listen. Hush tried to take the front office's pulse on the developing split, but Wellesley had been evasive. Hush had then gone to the fitness center to work out and de-stress. His main accomplishment of the day turned out to be getting Mike Powers designated as the central coordinator of the two state police forces assigned to the case. By 8:30 that evening, Hush had had enough. He was gathering some papers into his briefcase when Carolyn Lang appeared in his office doorway.

"Why don't you take the rest of the day off?" she asked.

He smiled. "I'm just declaring victory before someone else declares defeat," he said. Framed in the doorway, she looked delectable. "You're looking better."

It was her turn to smile. "I'm feeling better," she said. But then she turned serious. "This thing with Carswell—we're not going to be able to keep it from the interagency group much longer. The Public Affairs Office is asking the seventh floor how to play it, and the silence is getting loud."

"Do we have a name yet for this operation?" he asked.

"Not that I know of."

"Let's call it Trainman. I heard the director use that word a few days ago. Tell Wellesley. Call it Operation Trainman and let people know where the word came from."

"Train*man*, as in singular. And that way we emphasize our theory over theirs."

"Exactly. Hell, it's worth a try. Carswell swings some serious weight in this building, but maybe we can get the jump on him."

She nodded. "I'll take care of it. But you know we're all kind of spinning in place here."

"I know. If it is an individual, we need some way to reach into the weeds and find him. I'm going to go home, have a scotch, and try to think of one or two."

She looked at her watch. "I've still got to meet with the Public Affairs Office; they've been told to run a full-fledged press conference tomorrow, and they're flailing, not surprisingly."

"We're all flailing. I just hope this bastard's all done."

"I'll bet he isn't," she said.

He lay on the back side of a gravel pile in the darkness, examining the Memphis bridges through binoculars. It was Monday night. He had cut through a chain-link fence surrounding the gravel pits an hour ago, and had taken his time crawling across the mounds of gravel and rip-rap until he found a good vantage point. The Memphis railroad bridges were three quarters of a mile away downstream. There were two: the Harahan and the Frisco. The Harahan was the nearer bridge, but it was not his target. It was being redecked and would be out of service for another eighteen months. The Frisco, just downstream of the Harahan, was a trussed arch bridge with a single track in the middle. To his left across the river was the city of Memphis. The rose quartz lights of the newer interstate high-way bridge, just below the Frisco bridge, back-lit his target. The night was clear and calm, and the visibility was perfect.

Much too perfect, he thought, as he counted the security people loung-ing about their vehicles near the side-road approaches and under the bank abutment on the Arkansas side. They had rigged extra security lights all along the bottom of both bridges up to the first abutment, and he was pretty sure there were walking patrols on the bridge itself, probably up there along the catwalks, where they could stay out of sight. If they were smart, they would be using infrared to scan the river approaches and the surrounding fields. He kept himself low in the gravel, scrunched down on the reverse slope of the mound, his body enveloped by the smooth, warm stones so as not to offer night-vision devices a contrasting target. The FBI had undoubtedly issued a full security alert after the St. Louis bridge went down, as evidenced by all the Suburbans and top-lighted Broncos nosing here and there along the levees. The drivers kept stopping to talk with the cluster of men who were supposedly keeping watch under the bridge. He was pleased to see a small fire burning in a barrel up against the massive concrete abutment; that meant the men would gravitate there as the night wore on, which hopefully would keep the casualties down when he finally attacked.

The contrast between the Tennessee and the Arkansas sides was dra-matic. On the far bank were the bright lights of Memphis. On this side, there was mostly darkness. Farther to his right were the lights of West Memphis, but between the two was a wide expanse of river delta, low marshes, and levees. The tracks from the two bridges came together about a half-mile west of the main channel. Behind him, just north of the silent gravel mine, were the lights of a phosphate plant about four miles upriver. Out on the main channel there was the usual procession of big barges, behind which brightly lighted large tugs thrummed the night air as they worked the strings up the river current. The main difference between now and all the other times he had reconnoitered this bridge was the non-stop train traffic rumbling across the Frisco, courtesy of a 30 percent reduction in Mississippi River bridge capacity during the preceding week.

He put down his binoculars and scanned his watch. About time to begin, he thought. He had reviewed tonight's plan several times in his mind as he had driven his pickup into Arkansas. They had been slow to react when he dropped the Thebes bridge. That had made the MacArthur easier than it should have been, much easier. But for this, the third target, he had planned on there being full-scale security, which is why he was going to do this one from a distance.

He pressed the light on his watch again and then slid carefully back down the pile of gravel. He froze as he heard a security truck come bumping down the levee towards the gravel mine, its headlights sweeping the chain-link fences and the parked gravel trucks. It stopped long enough to illuminate the partially filled gravel barge that was canted against the riverbank, and then it ground its way in four-wheel drive down the levee approach ramp and headed back toward the bridge. He got up and concentrated on keeping mounds of gravel between him and the bridges as he withdrew.

Forty minutes later, he was back in his pickup truck, which had been hidden near the base of the levee in a dense grove of trees. He dusted himself off and climbed into the truck, whose cabin light had been disabled. Keeping the lights off, he drove slowly upriver, away from the bridges, toward the road at the county line, which was about halfway between the phosphate plant and the gravel mine. He turned left onto the dark two-lane road and headed west for about a mile, where he came to the entrance of the Memphis Water Authority's water-treatment plant. He was counting on there being no traffic on this road until shift change at the phosphate plant, which gave him two hours.

He turned onto the gravel road leading to the locked gates of the water plant, and then drove carefully around the perimeter fence until he reached the back of the plant. This was not a sewage-treatment plant, but, rather, the drinking water intake preprocessing plant for the city of Memphis. The installation took in river water just upstream of the huge phosphate plant, settled it out in large lagoons, and then centrifuged and prechlorinated the water before sending it out through a twenty-inch main to the final filtration and distribution plant in Memphis proper. The intake plant occupied some twenty acres, most of it in the settling basins. There was a windowless concrete building in the center of a cloverleaf of four ponds. Inside the building were the main intake pumps, a valve distribution network, the chlorine injection and heating bank, and transfer pumps to send the water out of the plant and across the river to Memphis. Outside was another valve bank and a five-thousand-gallon propane tank. He knew that the plant was unmanned and monitored remotely from the central municipal water plant over in Memphis. It was basically a continuous process that humans checked physically only once a day. If there were indications that something was going wrong after hours, the water company control center would shut the intake system down remotely and send someone out the next morning, The standpipes in Memphis contained easily enough water for two days' consumption. He was counting on that last fact.

He parked the truck at the back fence beyond the farthest pond, grabbed the big bolt cutters out of the bed, and then walked back around the fence. He had verified that there were no electronic security or intrusion systems at the facility. He came to the locked gates, which gave access to a causeway road running between the settling basins out to the control building. They were secured by a simple chain and padlock, which he cut with the bolt cutters.

His plan was simple. He was going to close the valves on top of all the chlorine bottles that were mounted in a line along an outside wall. The pressure drop would show up as a chlorine injection system fault over at the control center in Memphis. They should react by shutting down the main transfer and river intake pumps, idling the plant until the day shift could check it out the next morning. When he heard the machinery shut down, he was going to go to the other side of the building and close the discharge isolation valve on the twenty-inch transfer main that carried the clarified water over to Memphis. Once he had the system isolated, he would open the dump valve on the transfer main and let the entire transfer main drain down into the nearest settling basin. The transfer main did not go under the river, it went over the river, suspended directly beneath the Frisco Bridge.

After shutting off the chlorine, he went back to retrieve the truck and drove through the gates, which he then closed. He drove to the building and parked next to the propane tank. As he waited for the shutdown to occur, he made a quick surveillance check around the building's outside walls. There were white security lights on the four corners of the building, which had the perverse effect of putting the building itself and his truck in full shadow. There was still no traffic out on the county road. He could just see the aircraft warning lights on the tops of the bridges over the trees surrounding the water-treatment plant. Finally, he heard the big pumps inside the building start to wind down, and then the aeration fountains out in the basins began to subside.

He gave himself five minutes for the pressure to bleed off in the big lines. Then he walked over to the transfer main valve bank where it came through the walls of the building. He cracked a small drain valve at the base of the big twenty-inch gate valve. A jet of water blew out forcefully onto the concrete for about three minutes before it began to subside to more of flow than a jet. This meant that the pressure on the gate disk inside had been equalized. He used the bolt cutters again to cut the security chain on the big valve's handle. Then he wedged the arms of the bolt cutters into the valve wheel handle, and, with a great deal of effort, closed off the transfer main isolation valve. This ensured that if the system were started back up, what he planned to do with the pipe would not be interrupted.

He cut away the chain on the twelve-inch drain-down valve and forced it open, grunting again with the effort of turning the huge valve. A boil of water started up in the darkness about ten feet away as the twenty-inch-diameter transfer pipe began draining down. He sat back on his haunches to make sure he had a good flow going, because this was going to take some time. It was nearly two miles from here to the bridge, and almost another mile of piping from the end of the bridge approach ramps to the Memphis side. He wasn't sure if the Memphis side of the pipe would siphon over the hump and into the piping on the Arkansas side; that would depend on whether or not the discharge of the transfer main in Memphis was a vented piping system or not. But it didn't matter; all he really needed to do was to drain out one-half the pipe. Half a bridge was as good as no bridge at all.

He thought about the preparations for his campaign as he waited. Getting explosives had taken some time and care, but, given his business, he had known where and when various kinds of blasting supplies were stored. He had been always been very careful to lift only small amounts from any one site: a single stick of dynamite, two blasting caps, never more than a pound of anfo, the ammonium nitrate-diesel fuel paste, when he found some. The only large thefts had been when he had taken entire reels of Detacord, because it was tough to splice without the proper connectors.

His policy over the years of taking only enough to do the job ensured that there was never a hue and cry about large quantities of missing explosives. And then the hours and hours of reconnaissance, figuring out the rail-traffic patterns, physically exploring the bridges, creeping around in switchyards at night to see what, if any, security was really there and to rehearse his moves, figuring out where to stash the explosives and what were the best routes in and out of the target areas. Not all of it had been done at night; some of it he had done in broad daylight. The railroads might be hell on hoboes, but their infrastructure security was nonexistent.

He took some grim satisfaction in what he'd accomplished so far. He was smack on his time line. After this one, they'd assemble a real security perimeter at Vicksburg, but he'd break the sequence and go to Baton Rouge instead. Then maybe back to Vicksburg, or down to the Big Easy. The plan got looser the further it extended, because eventually they'd figure out who it was and be after him. A train whistle sounded in the distance from the south end of Memphis. It was a long, plaintive wailing sound, as if the train knew what was coming.

When he heard the rumble of air in the big transfer main, he closed the drain-down valve and went back out to the bed of the pickup truck. There he undid the straps on a tarp and pulled it off, revealing a triple-tank acetylene welding rig. He slid the tanks carefully down from the bed of the truck on a board ramp. Once he had all three tanks on the ground, he rolled them over next to the pump house. Instead of one green oxygen tank and two yellow acetylene, there were three oxygen tanks. He lifted the ends of the tanks to lean them against the propane tank, then returned to the truck to pick up the ignition and timing package. He felt somewhat exposed, walking around out there in the security lights, but he was pretty confident that no one would be watching or coming. The air beyond the ponds was still clear and the starlight plentiful. He stood still when he thought he heard a vehicle go by out on the county road, but then he decided it was sound carrying across the river from the Tennessee side. He permitted himself a small smile; this one was going to baffle the hell out of them. Then he set to work.

An hour later, after crossing the river on the Interstate 55 bridge into Memphis, he pointed the truck up onto a levee on the north end of the city, almost directly across from the gravel mine on the opposite shore.

He stopped at the top of the levee access ramp, shut off his lights, rolled down the window, and lit up a cigarette. The mounds of white gravel across the main channel were visible only as gray humps in the darkness. The bridges loomed to his left, not quite a mile downstream, where their eastern ends disappeared into the cluster of lights that marked the Memphis industrial area.

Using binoculars, he could still make out the lights of the security vehicles along the western base of the parallel bridges; that barrel fire under the western abutment was still going. He glanced at his watch. Anytime now, he thought. He didn't expect to bring the Frisco bridge down, but it should be seriously damaged. And he was going to get some help, he noted with satisfaction, as the headlight of a train made its way out onto the main span from the Arkansas side.

He checked his watch again. Come on. Had he set the timer correctly? Were the batteries fresh? He reviewed a dozen details but knew he had done it correctly. The air that was already in the pipe would form a perfectly sufficient explosive mixture with propane; boosting it with oxygen really ought to do the trick. Three fully pressurized tanks of welder's oxygen contained over seven hundred cubic feet of pressurized gas. He had connected the welding rig's triregulator valve to the bleed valve on the propane tank. Then, using a low-pressure, four-inch fueling hose, he had connected the propane tank's fill connection to the pressure-equalizing bypass valve on the water transfer main. As he drove his truck over the river, the two-thousand pound pressure in the oxygen tanks was driving five thousand gallons of vaporized propane into the transfer main. With that isolation valve closed, the gas mixture could only go in the direction of Memphis, flooding the pipe suspended beneath the Frisco Bridge with a violently explosive mixture. He had allowed an hour for the explosive vapors to migrate through the transfer main, at which point a tungsten filament, threaded into a gauge connection, would be ignited by the timer. Anytime now.

He scanned the bridge again, looking for signs of the cops he knew had to be up there. A tug and barge string swam into his vision, the tug's masthead towing lights bright white against the glimmering backdrop of the black river. When the explosion came, he almost missed it. An intense yellow-orange fireball erupted from the ground on the other side of the river, somewhere beyond the gravel pits. It flashed through the trees, bulleting like some enraged dragon directly to the base of the Frisco

Bridge, and then ripped across it, the glaring bolus of flame illuminating every element of the truss, throwing even the individual girders and each car of the train into dazzling relief, pursued by a continuous thunderclap of sound that reverberated across the entire Memphis waterfront. It happened so fast, his vision was left with nothing but a green aurora. The roar of the explosion echoed up and down the river for several seconds.

He closed his night-blind eyes for a moment, and then looked again. The bridge was enveloped in a cloud of dust and smoke, pierced by the sounds of deforming steel beams and railcar brakes. Flaming objects plummeted out of the cloud down into the river, raising hissing boils of steam over the water. He started up the truck and backed off the levee. As he drove away, he tried once more to feel some sense of victory, but there was only the familiar hollowness in his heart. Thebes. St. Louis. Now Memphis. Three down, three to go. They said revenge was a meal best enjoyed cold, and cold it certainly was. Behind him the first blue emergency lights were beginning to close in on the base of the bridges.

9

THE PHONE STARTED ringing just after 2:00 A.M. Tuesday morning. Hush had to fumble for a moment to find the beside light switch and pick up the phone.

"Hanson," he said. His voice was hoarse.

"Mr. Hanson, this is Agent Styles in Sit-Four. We've just had a report of another bridge getting blown up."

"Oh no!" Hush exclaimed, sitting up now and wide awake. "Where?"

"Memphis, Tennessee, sir. The Frisco Bridge. It's owned by the Burlington Northern Santa Fe, but there are five railroads that use it."

Hush rubbed his eyes. Everyone had been alerted, and the companies had all put on extra security. "Do we have any details?"

"No, sir, we don't. Just that the bridge has been attacked, and that there are probably personnel casualties."

"Send me a car, please," he said, swinging out of bed. He started to place a call to Carolyn Lang, then thought better of it. She had still been in the building when he'd left, and she was still on the antibiotics. He decided to let her sleep and come in at the normal hour, when he would be probably be starting to fade. Another bridge: This was terrible.

Situation Room Four was full of people when he got to FBI headquarters, with agents taking information over the phones and compiling reports. The senior agent on watch gave him a quick briefing. Most of the security forces had been either under the bridge or actually on it when the blast let go. This time, the bridge had not actually been dropped, but there had been a heavy grain train on the span at the time of the explosion. First reports described a simultaneous explosion along the full length of the bridge; another report said that there had been secondary explosions underground in the vicinity of the bridge approaches on *both* sides. The Sit-Four people were still trying to sort it all out.

"What's the status of the bridge, then?" Hush asked.

"The bridge is standing, but there's a train dropped halfway through the track bed along the full length of the bridge. They can see wheels hanging out over the river. No word on structural damage, but they've stopped barge and other shipping traffic until they know what the hell they have out there. There's a second, parallel bridge there, but it's out of service."

The director would be outraged, Hush thought. This was probably the time to escalate this case to the National Security Council, as his nemesis, Carswell, would no doubt be suggesting in a few hours. And they still had nothing. He suddenly did not want to attend any more interagency group meetings. He wanted to get out to the Mississippi and go after this guy until he caught him. He walked over to the big wall map that they had acquired from the Railway Mapping Service.

There were large red pins stuck in three places along the river. Three bridges in a row. Thebes, St. Louis, and now Memphis. As if their guy was working his way down the river. Their guy, he thought. Are we sure of that? He had not been very successful in the ideas department last night. His thoughts had kept turning to distracting images of Carolyn Lang on the chaise. He ran his finger down the map, along the thick blue line representing the river. The next target would logically be Vicksburg. What in the hell would provoke a lone individual to bomb railroad bridges? It was much more likely to be a group, and yet they had none of the indications they should be getting if it was a group.

"Mr. Hanson, sir?" an agent called. "I have a Morgan Keeler on the phone?"

Hush took the call at the central desk, holding one finger in his off ear to block out the noise around him.

"Hanson?" Keeler said. "I just got word from our operations center in Baton Rouge. I can't believe what I'm hearing."

"We're not too thrilled back here, either, Mr. Keeler. Where are you now?"

"I'm in St. Louis at the Coast Guard Marine Safety Office. I'm hoping to get a helo to take me down to Memphis, sometime around first light.

We've got to stop this. These people are wrecking the national rail system. You can't believe the congestion that's building up around the St. Louis yards, not to mention barge traffic. Everyone's going nuts."

"I know the feeling, Mr. Keeler. It's getting kind of crazy around here, too. It's going to get worse when official Washington wakes up. I'm thinking of leaving town."

"You might as well," Keeler said. "That task force of yours isn't exactly setting the world on fire, is it?"

Hush didn't reply to that, feeling it was almost self-evident.

"You remember that we had a theory?" he said finally. "That it's not some terrorist gang. That it's one guy doing this?"

"Yeah, I remember."

"Any more thoughts on that?"

It was Keeler's turn to be silent for a moment. "I still think it's feasible," he said finally. "Although I need to go see this thing at Memphis. What I'm hearing doesn't make sense right now. Tell me you have a suspect."

"Nope, but it makes a difference as to how we work it. You catch terrorist groups by their MOs and with an accretion of good intelligence over time. An individual is a tougher proposition unless he calls in for ransom money or political demands, something like that. What's bothering you about the Memphis attack?"

"The reports of underground explosions. That doesn't make sense, but of course I haven't seen it yet. What I can tell you is that he would have to have had explosives prepositioned long before the railroads put the extra security on. We've had bridge inspectors all over these structures looking for bombs ever since St. Louis."

" 'We' meaning—"

"The Corps of Engineers and the railroad engineering people."

"Right. We're trying to get word to Captain Powers right now."

"Wrong state," Keeler said. "The Frisco runs between Arkansas and Tennessee."

Hush told him about Powers's appointment as interstate police coordinator. "He'll bring the Arkansas and Tennessee state police up to speed. They'll listen to him quicker than they'll listen to us feds."

"All right. What's *your* plan?"

"I'm going out to Memphis. I guess I'll see you there?"

"Right," Keeler said. "And, look, somebody better beat the drum to protect the Vicksburg bridge. If he's running down some kind of a plan, that's the next one south of Memphis."

"We know," Hush replied. "I was just looking at that. We may put the damn National Guard on it by the end of the day."

"If that's what it takes, put the Guard on all of 'em," Keeler said. "Listen, Hanson, I take this shit personally. As far as I'm concerned, these are *my* bridges. I've been hounding the major railroads for going on twenty years now just to get them to do the *minimum* necessary to keep these beautiful old things from falling down. So hurry up and get this bastard."

Hush said he would and hung up. He thought about facing the director and the rest of the ADs sitting in judgment around that executive conference room table in a few hours. Having to explain that they had developed no suspects or even leads. It was not an appealing prospect.

"Agent Styles," he called across the room. "Get me air transportation to Memphis, and I want to be wheels-up at daybreak."

"Yes, sir," Styles said. "Will you be making the notification to the director and the deputy director, sir?"

"Yes, I will. But from the airplane, if you catch my drift."

Styles grinned and got on the phone. Hush went back to the main table and reread the reports coming through from Memphis. In the back of his mind, he concluded that he needed to get out not only of headquarters but of Washington, as well. From now on out, he had better remain in the field if he hoped to get this guy and also keep his job. The question was, What should he do about Carolyn Lang? Leave her here to coordinate the efforts of the interagency task force? That's what the deputy would normally do, he thought; it's why you have a deputy. On the other hand, it seemed unfair to her: She had come up with the idea that it was probably a single perpetrator, which was looking more and more like the right track to him. And it would be Lang who would have to deal with Carswell and go in and listen to the director raise hell about the lack of progress, while he, Hush, folded his tents and slipped away into the desert night.

He put the sheaf of Teletypes down and stared at the map. It had started at Thebes, then moved to St. Louis, and now to Memphis. If it was one guy, he both was mobile and probably had prepositioned everything he needed a long time ago, just as Keeler had said. He wondered if the guy was going to try to take out *all* the railroad bridges crossing the southern Mississippi. You mean the three bridges still standing, he chided himself. What in the *hell* was this guy after? The action so far covered a span of 250 miles. He called Styles back over.

"Get word to the Memphis office that I want a node of Sit-Four set up in Memphis. Second, tell them I'll want to convene a meeting at around five o'clock this afternoon with SAC Memphis, SAC St. Louis, Captain Powers and as many reps from all the state police as he wants to bring, and also that Corps of Engineers bridge expert, Morgan Keeler."

Styles was writing furiously in his notebook. Hush gave him a moment to catch up. He explained to Styles why he had not called in Lang yet.

"Tell operations that I'll make the incident notification call to the director from the plane. Once I've done that, I'll notify Senior Agent Lang, say around six-thirty A.M., and tell her to take charge here in Washington with regard to the interagency task force. We'll feed Sit-Four with as much information as we develop from Memphis, and she can work the Washington web. In the meantime, notify Tyler Redford of what's happened. I want him to help Lang as much as possible."

Hush put a secure call through to the director at his home once he was airborne and safely one hour out of Washington. He had thought about going through the deputy director but had decided to hell with it. He was an assistant director, not an assistant deputy director. He described what they knew about the destruction of the Frisco Bridge, listened to some outraged fulminations, and then outlined his own plans to take direct charge in the field while leaving Lang behind to run the Washington circus that was soon going to develop. To his surprise, the director agreed with that move. Hush took the opportunity to describe their theory that it was one man and not some terrorist cell, primarily because the intel people had come up with nothing. He described Carolyn Lang's analysis.

"She reversed the old 'Who gains?' question," Hush said. "He's figured out how to do the maximum damage to the rail network by concentrating on their Achilles' heel: the big bridges on the Mississippi."

"You figure he might be a trainman himself? Somebody inside one of the railroad companies? A disgruntled employee?"

Hush picked up on the word. It was the second time the director had used it. "We had the same thought, sir, and we're calling it Operation

Trainman. Whoever he is, he seems to know a hell of a lot about their operations around these bridges. And he's apparently had pretty good access, at least at Thebes and St. Louis."

There was a moment of silence. Then the director asked how Lang was doing.

"Very professional, actually. I think she's just about recovered from her injury in St. Louis. She's probably going to hate me for leaving her back there."

"That's her job as the task force deputy," the director replied, sounding entirely awake now. "Listen, we're starting to take some heavy flak over these incidents and the lack of progress in the case. So far, I've been able to say to people at my level that if anyone has any bright ideas, please step forward, but that's not going to cut it for much longer. We need results, and fast. We're also hearing from the White House. Railroads are not trivial political entities."

"Yes, sir," Hush said. "That's why I'm going to the river. I plan to stay out there until we break this thing."

"Sooner rather than later, Mr. Hanson. Keep us informed. I'll want an update on Operation Trainman from Lang as soon as I get in this morning."

Hush put down the phone and took a deep breath. He looked at his watch. Carolyn was going to hate him for this. In another hour, he would be in Memphis. He'd planned to call Carolyn just before landing, but after what the director had just said, he decided now was as good a time as any. The director was calling it Operation Trainman. He could at least start the call with something positive. Yeah, right.

Matthews was just finishing up his morning shave when a call came through from the operations center. Colonel Mehle had just called an early staff meeting on the 2713 train. Everybody was to be standing tall in the CO's conference room in thirty minutes.

"Now what?" Matthews asked the duty officer.

"That colonel got a high-precedence 'Personal for' message in from the Pentagon fifteen minutes ago; one of the comm center guys had to take it over to his BOQ room. That's all I know, Major."

Matthews thanked him and hurried to get his uniform. His wife was still in bed, but she woke up when he started fumbling around in the dark closet. She turned on the overhead light in the bedroom and automatically switched on the morning news. Matthews had his shirt on when he heard the announcer talking about the Memphis bridge. He stepped out of the closet and stared in growing horror at the early-dawn pictures of the Frisco Bridge.

"Son of a bitch," he muttered. One of the 2713 engines had come up with an electrical problem the day before, and they were still waiting for parts. Now this.

"What's the matter?" Ellie asked, still not quite awake.

"That bridge was our route for twenty-seven thirteen across the Mississippi. First the engine problem, now this. Mehle's gonna have his hair on fire."

"What will happen?" she asked.

"I'm guessing we'll have to hold twenty-seven thirteen. *And* figure out another route. This shit with the river bridges is getting serious. We're also running out of time." He grabbed the rest of his uniform and left the bedroom before she asked why.

Hush landed in Memphis at 8:30 A.M. An hour and a half later, Powers was taking him for a tour of the water plant.

"Here's where they set the damn thing off," he said, pointing to the burned back wall of the control building at the treatment plant. The remains of a ruptured propane tank opened ragged, blackened metal arms as if to embrace the equally blackened concrete. A three-foot-deep trench had been ripped through the earth in the direction of the bridges. The ruptured raw earth reeked of propane gas. Powers was accompanied by the heads of the Arkansas and Tennessee state police CID teams and a cluster of officials from the Memphis waterworks. Several FBI agents from the Memphis office were standing around observing the Arkansas state police crime-scene team do their thing.

"That open trench leads directly to the bridge," the waterworks man said. "It used to be a twenty-inch water main—the intake supply from the plant here to the Memphis water system."

"Water main?" Hush asked, looking around. What the hell does a water main have to do with a bridge bombing? he wondered.

Powers answered his unspoken question. "What the waterworks people *think* they did was to drain down the transfer main and then, somehow, backfill it with propane."

"But why?" Hush asked.

"Because that big pipe went over the river suspended under the track bed of the Frisco Bridge."

"Ah."

"Yeah."

"Probably propane and some kind of oxidizer," offered the Arkansas CID chief. "Propane alone wouldn't git it. We're gonna have to inspect that tank, soon's we find the rest of it. Might be out in those lagoons. Or up on Mars."

"But would that be big enough to blow up a big bridge like that?" Hush asked.

"*Hell yes,*" the waterworks engineer said. "You figure: a twenty-inch-diameter pipe, maybe four thousand feet long under that bridge, filled with propane and some kind of oxidizer? Or even air, for that matter. Only had to get eleven, twelve percent concentration. Think of it as an eight-, nine-thousand-cubic-foot pipe bomb. A real crowd pleaser."

"Damn," Hush said, trying to visualize it.

"Yeah. Only reason the bridge is still there is that most of the explosive force went out into thin air. But the bridge people say it was enough to unzip the track bed."

"The pipe was right under the tracks," Powers said. "The main bridge structure appears to be intact, but the track bed looks like blackened redfish. And there was a train on it. That Army Corps bridge guy, Keeler, is up there right now."

Hush stared down at the trench as a conclusion crystallized in his mind. "Railroads," he muttered. "He's not after the bridges. He's after the railroads."

Powers took Hush by the elbow and steered him away from the crowd. " 'He'?" Powers asked.

Hush quickly explained what at least his part of the FBI was thinking, then asked Powers if he could coordinate getting all the police reps to meet with him that afternoon in the Memphis FBI field office. He told Powers he was setting up a local command center in Memphis, and that the FBI thought the bridge at Vicksburg might be next.

Powers said he could set up the meeting, and then he suggested to

Hush that they go over to the bridge itself. Hush detailed the senior agent from the Memphis squad to find out how the state forensic teams were going to organize their efforts. While he waited for Powers to confer with the two state CID chiefs, he walked around the water-treatment plant. There were no other real signs of damage other than the propane tank and that ugly trench that ripped through the earth like some awful wound. Based on what was left, he estimated that the tank had held several thousand gallons of propane. As a gas, propane was heavier than air, so their bomber had had to pressurize that tank with something—compressed air, maybe—connect it to the big water main, and then wait. But it wouldn't take very elaborate piping or hoses to do it: None of this was high-pressure engineering. Hush knew the bridge had been heavily guarded, and, apparently, so had their bomber. And he knew something else, too, Hush thought: He knew that all bridges carried utilities, such as phone trunk lines, water pipes, and sometimes even petroleum-product pipelines. The bigger the bridge, the more pipes and cables running underneath. He looked over at the lab people poking around the tank.

Operation Trainman. Carswell would be pissed, but they had the director's blessing now. In fact, he thought the director's original instincts might have been right all along. Their perpetrator seemed to know everything he needed to know about his targets. In this case, he hadn't gone anywhere near the bridge; he had sent his explosive blast down a twenty-inch-diameter water main, from a safe distance, creating a total surprise for the people guarding the bridge.

A second thought occurred to him: The first two bridges had been done by carting explosives up onto the bridges. This one, however, would have required really extensive preplanning. The Trainman knew that by this point in his campaign, the security would be increasing. Which meant, in turn, that he would no longer be able just to waltz down to a bridge at night and wrap it in Detacord. This further confirmed Hush's suspicion that this was a campaign directed against the nation's railroads and their trains, not the bridges. The bridges were simply a way to wreck the railroads. There were only three left in the southern tier: Vicksburg, Baton Rouge, and New Orleans. The Transportation Department was estimating that the railroads had lost something approaching 40 percent of their transcontinental capacity. It must be getting really interesting in Washington about now, he thought.

He looked around to find Powers, but the captain was still talking to his counterparts, one of whom was on his cell phone. Hush got out his own cell phone and called Sit-Four back at FBI headquarters, where he asked for Lang. The watch officer told him Lang was in a meeting with the director and the executive board, but Tyler Redford was there.

"Tyler, you getting any interest in this morning's news?" Hush asked.

"Oh, dribs and drabs, here and there," Redford said, going with it. "Heinrich's been in here foaming at the mouth about once an hour, the White House staff is sending a permanent rep to 'enhance coordination' with us here in Sit-Four, the National Security Council is meeting this afternoon, the National Guard is probably going to be tasked to provide military-level security for all the remaining Mississippi River bridges, and we've taken over Sit-Five to accommodate all the extra high-priced help. Other than, not much going on, boss."

Hush had known Redford and his wife, who worked in the Bureau's Personnel division, for a long time. "Sorry I'm missing all that," Hush said. "How's Lang holding up?"

"Based on the amount of crap she's taking from the head shed, I would have to predict that she does not love you anymore," Redford replied. "She's getting to spend a lot of time with Heinrich. Interestingly, people who should know are beginning to talk that maybe she's actually angling to replace you."

"Keep in mind whom you're talking about, Ty. Besides, she wants to get closer to a lizard, she's welcome to it."

"That's thunder lizard to us peons, Hush. Look, this thing's getting squirreley, and the more agencies we get into the game, the more the director huffs and puffs about the lack of progress. Carswell sits there on the sidelines, agreeing with him at every opportunity. If you have anything at all, we need it here, and we need it bad."

Hush described the method of the latest attack. "Tell all concerned that we'll have some word late this afternoon," he concluded. "And make sure they guard the hell out of the bridge at Vicksburg. This guy is on a roll, and Vicksburg is the next one downriver. Get word to Lang I'll try to reach her in Sit-Four around noon."

Hush heard the sound of a door closing, and suddenly the background noise at Redford's end had disappeared. "I'll tell her, Hush," Redford said. "But you make sure you interface personally with the director or at least Heinrich. I don't like what I'm hearing about that woman."

"It doesn't compute, Ty. Would you want to take over this tar baby just now? I mean, look: when I called her this morning, she wasn't exactly jumping for joy at the news that I was coming out here and leaving her there."

"I know," Redford said. "All the same, watch your back and keep a line open to the seventh floor. I gotta run—the new White House bunny is here."

"Is she pretty?"

"It's a he, I think."

Powers's cruiser bumped its way over a temporary steel plate bridge covering the ragged gash in the earth where the water main had been buried, then drove through a cordon of emergency vehicles and more police at the base of the Interstate 55 highway bridge. The two-railway bridges, were just beyond. They checked in with a mobile CP borrowed from the Memphis city police SWAT division, which was parked across an at-grade spur crossing under the bridge. A Union Pacific three-engine set with what looked like an infinite line of boxcars behind it was stopped and shut down on the tracks fifty feet away from the CP. As they got out of the car, the smell of propane and blackened raw earth was strong in the air. The trench was already filling with river water.

The scene was becoming all too familiar to Hush. There was a crowd of emergency vehicles, police, railroad types, some spectators, the Corps of Engineers, the Coast Guard. All the usual suspects, he thought. He could see a similar congregation across the river on the Memphis side, where sparkling yellow and blue strobe lights were clustered around the foot of the bridge. The arrival of an FBI assistant director caused something of a buzz among all the cops as the word got out over the tactical radios. Powers and Hush, accompanied by the ASAC from the Memphis office and several Arkansas and Memphis police, walked up the track bed onto the bridge approach track itself.

At first glance, the bridge did not appear to be badly damaged, but then Hush saw where the water main pipe had joined the track bed, and from that point on up, it looked like a giant had taken a can opener to the track bed. Most of the ties were shattered or burned, and the rails drooped between segments of the bridge truss. There was a line of grain-hopper railroad cars up toward the hump, each of them sitting at a different angle, with some appearing to be half the height of the adjacent car.

A weary-looking Morgan Keeler came walking down the track bed to meet them, apparently oblivious to the condition of the ties. Hush knew he would not have been able to do that.

"Mr. Hanson," Keeler said, taking off his gloves and coming forward to shake hands. He was wearing an Army green jumpsuit and a white Union Pacific hard hat. He pushed the hard hat back on his head so he could look up at Hush.

"Mr. Keeler," Hush said. "We've got to stop meeting like this. What've we got this time?"

"One very clever devil, if your one-man theory is correct," Keeler said, looking back up the track bed to the end of the derailed train. "Wait till you see what it did."

"Is the bridge going to come down?"

"Don't know yet," Keeler said. "The track bed is ripped to pieces. They might be able to route a wrecking crane up there and retrieve the cars, but they'll probably have to rebuild the track first. Fact is, we really don't know yet what it did to the bridge structure."

"But you think it won't fall down."

"Well, maybe. That's a heavy grain train up there. Several thousand tons being supported directly by the truss elements, which were not designed for that. We find deformed pins, rivets blown out, stress fractures in the I beams? New bridge."

Hush swore softly. Powers tugged his sleeve. "We need to reconstruct how he did this thing, and that didn't happen here," he said.

Hush thought for a moment. Powers was right. The attack had taken place at the waterworks. The shattered track bed was simply the result.

The Memphis ASAC spoke up. He was a thin, pinch-faced man named L. Watkins Thomas, who appeared to be much older than Hush. He had already explained to Hush that the Memphis SAC was on medical leave. "We're working that scene with the Arkansas people, Mr. Hanson. Whoever did this cut their way into the treatment plant, operated some pretty big valves, and then somehow pressurized a big propane tank to deliver an explosive gas mixture into the water main. Lots of opportunities for physical evidence there, and traceable systemic knowledge."

"Traceable what?" Powers asked.

"It took some specialized knowledge to do this," Thomas said. "They had to know about the water main, they had to know no one would come out there until the next morning just because they shut off the chlorine, that a propane tank supplies gas by evaporative action and not tank pressure, and that propane by itself wouldn't do the job."

"And they'd have to know what would happen to the bridge when that pipe blew up," Powers said.

"Right," said Thomas. "So we're looking for a group—or an individual, I guess—who would know all those things *and* have the opportunity to act on that knowledge. And a reason for doing so. Traceable *systemic* knowledge."

Hush nodded. Thomas was focusing on the case in front of him. Which is what *you* should be doing, he told himself. "Mr. Keeler," he said. "If you had to put this bridge back in service, could you do it?"

"Depends on how safe you'd want to be," Keeler said. "If they can get at them, the railroad people could get these cars off pretty quick. But they'll have to rebuild the track and ties up to the end of that train up there first. Then the laborious part: send up a crane, pick up a car, back down, put it on a recovery frame, send up a rail train, repair one car length of track. Back the rail train off, send up the crane—like that. But the bridge—"

"Yes, I understand, the truss structure might have been damaged. But if you *had* to get this thing back in operation, how long would it take?"

Keeler looked at the senior maintenance-of-way engineer, who shrugged. "Wild-ass guess?" the engineer said. "Round the clock, working from both sides? Seventy-two hours."

"But not full-scale operations, Bill, right?" Keeler protested. "I mean, we'd have to weight limit the bridge. Sort out which kinds of trains could cross it."

The engineer nodded. "Yep, but the man was asking about service restoration. That's my guesstimate."

Hush nodded. "We're going to hold a meeting over in our Memphis office at three this afternoon," he said. "But as the head of the federal task force on these bridge bombings, I would like to request that the railroads gear up now to restore this bridge. We need some positive news here, people. Getting this one back would be a positive development, which was not possible at Thebes or St. Louis. Will you guys agree to try?"

The railroad people looked at Keeler and then at one another. The senior engineer said he would call corporate headquarters and see how much help they could get from the other companies and what they could get going. Hush thanked them and then pulled Keeler and Powers aside.

"I think, Mr. Keeler, that you should go on down the river to Vicksburg. I'd like you to make a personal inspection of that bridge from the point of view of someone having planted something on it. Exclude no possibilities. Pipes, wires, conduits, utility lines, dynamite stuffed in handrails, nuclear carrier pigeons—anything you can think of. You follow?"

Keeler nodded. He said he would have to come back to Memphis to review the structural safety of the Frisco Bridge once repairs began. Hush asked Keeler to stay for the afternoon conference, after which he was to get downriver the fastest way possible. Then he turned to Powers.

"Let's you and me and this cast of thousands go back over to that water-treatment plant and see if we can put this thing together. And let's not forget motive."

"You mean go do some police work?"

"I mean just that," Hush said. "This was pretty elaborate. Thomas is right. There ought to be some evidence."

Hush finally got to talk to Lang at one o'clock from the Memphis office. She sounded harried. He first asked how she was feeling.

"The antibiotics caused me some plumbing problems," she said. "But the infection is flat. Physically, I'm okay. Mentally, I'm questionable."

"Qualifies you for headquarters," he said, laughing. "No illusions that way. How's the head shed behaving?"

"The director is pretty disturbed, which of course means Wellesley is snapping at low-lying branches all over the building. Carswell is pressing hard to take over the case. Will you, in fact, have something to report later this afternoon?"

He explained what he had set in motion in Memphis, with both the state police forces and the railroads. Then he told her his thoughts on the Trainman's real target.

"The railroads," she said. "Okay, but why?"

"That's what you're going to find out. I want you to go to Information Resources. Tell 'em we need a database scan for individuals who may have a reason to hate trains or railroads."

"You mean like someone who's been injured in a train wreck? Or has had property condemned by a railroad? Our system's not likely to have anything like that."

"I know. But IR will know who does have that kind of data. As in the railroads. Have the IR people liaise with the railroads' security people. Get them to generate a list of individuals who have reason to hate them, or who have threatened them or sued them."

"Hates railroad companies? God. That could be a very big list."

"Yeah, but then we cull the list by adding technical knowledge of railroad operations and chemical- or gas-based explosives, for starters. You know, a database drill: Start wide and then focus, focus, focus. In the meantime, I'm hoping the state police will come up with some physical evidence here. Our guy needed some stuff to do what he did."

"Got it," she said. "A political observation: Shouldn't *you* be telling the director this? I mean, as a matter of visibility?"

He hesitated. "Yes," he said finally. "But you do it. Give him enough to take to the NSC meeting so he doesn't look bad over there. That might also deflect Carswell."

"Okay," she said. "Although I still think—"

"Yeah, I know, and your instincts are correct. But right now I'm more useful out here getting all these folks to work together. Besides, our bad guy is out here, along this river."

"But you know how things work here at headquarters," she said. "Face time is important."

"I can't be bothered with that right now, Carolyn. This is all a campaign of some kind. We need to disrupt his plan, his timing, but we've got to think further out of the box." He paused and sighed. " 'Out of the box.' Listen to me."

It was her turn to laugh. "You'd fit right in with some of our newer helper bees from down Pennsylvania Avenue. Okay, I'll go to the mountain. Anyone else I should back-brief?"

"The team in Sit-Four, and Tyler Redford. I'll be in with something this evening, I sincerely hope."

Matthew fished in his briefcase for an Advil, which he washed down with some cold coffee. Hill saw him do it and bummed one for himself. It was late Tuesday afternoon, and they were back in the CO's conference room, waiting for a secure teleconference connection with Washington. Through the open door of the conference room, Matthews could see Mehle talking urgently on the phone in Colonel Anderson's office. The two lieutenant colonels were standing next to Mehle's desk, their arms full of three-ring binders. There were military police stationed in the hallway, and Matthews had even seen the depot's provost marshal in the building. Military police seemed to be everywhere since Mehle had taken virtual command of the depot, now that he thought about it. Like storm troopers.

"We should have tried for Vicksburg right from the start," Matthews said softly. "We could have been across the river by now."

The engine parts had arrived that morning, and engine two was now scheduled to be fully up and ready to roll by 10:00 P.M. With the Memphis bridge out, Colonel Mehle had sent in a high-precedence message proposing to take 2713 via the Vicksburg bridge.

"Yeah," Hill said. "Hindsight is wonderful. The problem is that the Vicksburg bridge is normally restricted for weight. That sucker's old."

"That's the reason?"

"I suggested Vicksburg to Mehle when we first did the new route, but we would have needed to get a weight waiver. That might have required specifying what's on the train, in advance. Mehle said, 'No, file for Memphis.'"

Matthews nodded. That explained Memphis. One of the lieutenant colonels noticed Matthews and Hill watching them through the open door and kicked it shut with his toe. Matthews gave the closed door the finger.

"Tom," Hill said, lowering his voice. "I'm not going to go through with this."

Matthews froze. He had been afraid of this. "You're the only guy qualified to be train master," he began, but Hill cut him off.

"I tried to find out the technical details on the specials last night," he said. "What the safety systems were, what monitoring they required. What to do if those lights started changing colors. I basically got a security door slammed in my face by one of those Special Ops goons in there."

"Maybe they're doing you a favor, Carl," Matthews said. "Maybe you don't want to know too much about those weapons. If I were the train master, I wouldn't want to know *anything* about them. That way, if it turns to shit, I could lay it right down on Mehle and his crowd, where it goddamn belongs."

Hill shook his head. "That's barracks lawyer talk, Tom," he said. "The train master is responsible for the safety of the operation from gate to gate. I'm comfortable with the CW part of this: I know what is and what isn't in those old casings. But this nuke stuff . . ." He shook his head. "I think they're in worse shape than we know, and Mehle and his SS in there are covering it up."

Matthews sighed. He had known Carl Hill for three years. Hill had a stubborn streak in him a mile wide, especially when it came to safety issues, which was precisely what made him a good train master. The fact that Carl was probably right as rain didn't help matters.

"Okay, if that's how you feel about it," he said. "We need to inform Mehle, then."

Hill laughed. "You mean *I* need to inform Mehle, don't you? Look, Tom, I understand the box you're in. You're right at your twenty. I've got seven years to go. I can survive Mehle."

Matthews was about to reply to that when Mehle's door opened and he and the two lieutenant colonels came into the conference room.

"The teleconference is no longer required," Mehle announced. "I have new instructions to route twenty-seven thirteen through Baton Rouge."

"Through yet *another* city?" Hill asked, his anger visible.

"That's right, Major. You got a problem with that?"

Before Matthews could say anything, Hill stood up and threw his empty ceramic coffee mug across the room, where it shattered against the wall over the trash can in the corner. There was a sudden stunned silence in the room.

"First Memphis, now Baton Rouge?" Hill shouted. "You bet your ass I have a problem with that. The answer is, No way in hell. I refuse to be a part of this. It's against all the rules, Army and otherwise. Plus, it's stupid. If there's an accident—"

"Accepted," Mehle said quietly. Matthews saw an expression of cold triumph on Mehle's face. He suddenly realized Hill had walked into an ambush. Which is when he saw the tiny red light on the conference call box in the middle of the table. The bastards had been listening to them!

"What?" Hill said.

"Your resignation is accepted, Major. Wait here, please."

Mehle nodded to one of the lieutenant colonels, who got up before the shocked Hill could say anything and went out of the conference room, closing the door behind him. Hill just stood there, his face turning beet red. A minute later, the lieutenant colonel came back into the room, accompanied by Lieutenant Colonel VanSandt, the depot's provost marshal. Behind VanSandt were two large military policemen. Mehle stood up.

"Colonel VanSandt, take Major Hill into protective custody for violation of depot security regulations concerning special weapons," he ordered. "I will file the charges and specifications personally. Hold him at the stockade at Fort McClellan in protective isolation. He is to talk to no one, is that understood?"

"Including his family, Colonel?" VanSandt asked.

"No one," Mehle repeated. "Major Hill? Go with the provost marshal, please."

Hill set his jaw. "This is a travesty. I don't work for you, Colonel. I work for Colonel Anderson. And I insist on notifying my wife of this—"

"I'll have you held in an Area Twenty-six bunker if you prefer, Major."

Hill blinked. Matthews almost stopped breathing. Area Twenty-six was the storage area for the known leakers in the CW tombs.

Mehle leaned forward. "You should understand that I now consider you to be a grave threat to national security. Colonel VanSandt, deadly force is authorized to prevent this officer from communicating with anyone, do you understand?"

VanSandt's eyebrows rose. "I'll need that in writing, Colonel," he said.

Matthews could tell that the two MPs in the doorway were trying not to show their alarm at what was being said in the conference room. Mehle bent down and scribbled something on the legal pad at his place at the conference table. He ripped off the sheet and handed it to VanSandt, who glanced at it, blinked once, and then nodded. "Let's go, Major."

Hill was led out of the room.

"Close the door, Major Matthews," Mehle ordered. Matthews got up and closed the door; then he sat back down at the conference table. His knees felt a little weak. Deadly force authorized?

"All right," Mehle said. "I've given orders to seal the entire depot until twenty-seven thirteen is under way and safely across the Mississippi. No one in or out, and all phone service will be cut off until further notice. Major Matthews, you are now the train master for twenty-seven thirteen."

Matthews's jaw dropped. Train master? He was speechless. First of all, he wasn't qualified. Second, he did not want to be the officer in charge of this thing. But if he refused, what would happen? Would he join Hill in the stockade with a gag in his mouth? And be kicked out of the Army at nineteen years with no pension? Mehle watched him work it out.

"Look, Tom," Mehle said, changing his tone of voice, "there is a real emergency in the country right now. These bridge bombings have disrupted the entire national transportation system. I've been on the phone all morning with Washington, and it's much worse than the news is letting on."

Matthews wasn't fooled by the sudden use of his first name. He found his voice. "So why not hold the train, Colonel? Or at least hold out the specials? The remaining bridges are going to be terribly congested. The chances for an accident en route are going up, not down."

"You're forgetting the stay-time problem, Tom. The specials aside, you have to roll that CW stuff west by Thursday."

"Like you just said, there's a national emergency, Colonel. If we're going to screw around with the route, why worry about EPA rules at this point?"

One of the lieutenant colonels spoke up. "The main reason we cannot delay is that, as of last night, our instruments have detected an increase in the temperatures on the specials."

Matthews was appalled. "Whoa," he said. "You mean as in they're getting ready to cook off on their own?"

"Not exactly," Mehle said carefully. "But nevertheless, there is a discernible change. The problem is not the fissile material, of course."

Matthews had to think for a moment, but then he got it. Temperature, not radiation. A chemical reaction, not a nuclear one. The high-explosive components in the sealed plutonium pits had become unstable. "Wonderful," he said to no one in particular. "Just goddamn wonderful."

"We must move this train, Tom," Mehle said earnestly. "We *must* move this train. Now. Get it out west. And above all, get it over the Mississippi. Think about it: You have a family living here. You have a personal interest in getting this train out of Anniston, don't you?"

Matthews understood where Mehle was going with this. The colonel was worried about something happening right here on the depot. That revelation scared him more than anything else he had heard this morning. He thought of Ellie and all the rest of the families living on or near the depot. If the HE in one of those weapons went off, there would not be a nuclear blast, but there would be a very dirty and highly radioactive mess right on the depot. And if the others went off in a sympathetic detonation . . .

"You have the technical knowledge of the chemical weapons casings," Mehle said. "And you've been to nuclear weapons safety and handling school. Engineer Godowski can handle all the route operations with the various rail lines. The routing will be directed from the ops center here at Anniston, under my command."

"But through Baton Rouge?" Matthews said.

"That's not something we *want* to do, Tom," Mehle said. "We know the best route would be Vicksburg, but that bridge is getting clobbered right now with all the diverted traffic from the three bridges north of it; plus it's weight-limited. Washington has authorized the bridge at Baton Rouge; there's less traffic, and it's also cleared for heavy trains."

Matthews shook his head. He needed time to think, but Mehle wasn't giving him much maneuvering room.

"Look, Tom, these weapons are of crucial importance to our anti-terrorism intelligence program. You've heard all the experts: Russian nukes are disappearing out of the old Soviet arsenal. Getting our hands on some was a godsend. Now we can redesign our nuclear-detection equipment and our NEST teams to find these things when and if they show up here in the States. But first we *must* get them to Idaho."

"Two officers have already died in that effort, Major," one of the lieutenant colonels said. "When the plane hit your improperly positioned fire truck."

Matthews got up and walked to the wall map, trying to still his pounding heart. Mehle hadn't threatened him—yet, anyway. Maybe the choleric colonel was right. And the situation was bad enough, especially if they had a HE instability problem building in the Russian weapons. If one of those things let go, those big pressurized tank cars *should* be able to contain it, unless of course there was a chain reaction with the other warheads. He didn't want to think it past that point.

"Okay, Colonel, I'm not really qualified, but I'll do it," he said, turning around to face Mehle. "But I want orders in writing that make it clear I objected to taking unstable nuclear ordnance out on the civilian rail lines and through an American city. And you have to promise me to do nothing to Carl Hill other than hold him, *and* remove that deadly force authorization."

Mehle nodded slowly. "It was never issued. I just said that to scare Hill. What was on my note was that deadly force was specifically *not* authorized. That was all for effect. You can check with VanSandt. But otherwise, I agree."

"I also want permission to tell Carl's wife that there is, in fact, nothing wrong. I won't say anything more than that, but you can't just let her find out Carl's in the stockade and leave her hanging."

Mehle glanced at his staff officers but then nodded again. "Agreed," he said. "Now, plan out a route from the Birmingham junction to Baton Rouge. Once across, I need a divert contingency route to Pine Bluff, Arkansas, in addition to the main run to Idaho."

"Pine Bluff, sir?"

"Yes. In case the specials start to go out of limits. The Pine Bluff Arsenal has a small-scale incinerator there."

Matthews nodded. The Pine Bluff Arsenal was another chemical weapons depot. It was a hell of a lot closer than Idaho, although he wasn't sure if their CW incinerator could separate the high explosive from a plutonium core, if it ever came to that.

"As soon as you have the route calculated," Mehle continued, "I'll transmit it to Washington for operational approval. They're going to have to apply some pressure at the national level to get priority for this train and to facilitate the state EPA clearances."

"I shouldn't think that would be hard," Matthews said.

"Harder than you think, Tom. This train isn't carrying oil, coal, chemical feedstocks, perishable food, or medical supplies. Those are the commodities getting priority right now. That's how bad it's getting out there."

"Launch when, Colonel?"

"Shoot for Wednesday night. That's the other thing: Our security people are recommending we run twenty-seven thirteen during hours of darkness only. Do the route planning ASAP. Launch at sundown tomorrow."

"If we run only at night, it will double the time, Colonel."

"I have pointed that out. I suspect once we get moving, the temperature problem might change Washington's priorities. But first and foremost we have to get that train across the goddamned Mississippi River."

At 7:00 P.M. Tuesday, Washington time, Hush initiated a secure conference call back to the situation room at FBI headquarters. With him in the Memphis office conference room were ASAC Thomas, Powers, Keeler, and a stenographer. On the Washington end were the deputy director, Tyler Redford, Carolyn Lang, AD Carswell, and two agents from the Sit-Four watch team.

Hush began by briefing the Washington group on the Trainman meeting he had just concluded with all the police agencies. The level of cooperation was 100 percent, he reported, thanks to the leadership of Capt. Mike Powers of the Missouri Highway Patrol CIB. He then reviewed their theory that the bridge bombings were the work of a single perpetrator. It looked like their man was working a master plan for which he had evidently made detailed and extensive preparations. Whoever he was, he knew a lot about railroad operations, the vulnerabilities presented by the Mississippi River bridges, and explosives.

"Senior Agent Lang has already briefed all that, Mr. Hanson," Wellesley interrupted. "What do you have that's new?"

Hush saw some eye rolling in the faces around him, but he pressed on. "What's new is that the railroads have confirmed they can get the Frisco Bridge back in operation in seventy-two to ninety-six hours. I have Mr. Morgan Keeler here from the Army Corps of Engineers and he can amplify that."

Keeler leaned toward the pyramid-shaped speakerphone in the middle of the table and explained the extent of the damages and how the bridge could be put back in operation. He seconded the theory that they could be dealing with a single perpetrator.

"Are you an expert, Mr. Keeler?" Wellesley asked, his tone of voice clearly dismissive. "Do you have some evidence we don't know about?"

Hush knew that the deputy director was aiming that skepticism at him and not Keeler, but Keeler was not intimidated.

"Based on the fact that the explosives used on these bridges could have been carried in by one person."

"All right, that's all well and good, but I say again, is there any definitive physical evidence one way or the other?"

Hush took this one. "From the Thebes bombing, we have the Pyrodex residue and residue from the Detcord blast. We also have three pieces of cloth that were retrieved from the scene; they retained some traces of dynamite. They may have been used to wrap the initiators. We also have evidence of someone climbing the ladder from the river. Some*one*. Not a crowd. From St. Louis, we have minute traces of Detcord residue that are identical to the stuff used at Thebes. We have the chemical remains of the booby-trap bomb, plus one fragment that Agent Lang, um, recovered."

"Very well. And from the Memphis bridge?"

"Nothing from the bridge. But from the waterworks, we have tool marks on the gate chain and the valve chains; brass residue from the relief valve of the propane tank, which indicates he used the aperture on the relief valve to attach something that pressurized the tank; some pickup truck–size tire tracks from behind the fence, and evidence of intrusion at a gravel mine not far from the bridge and some more of those same truck tracks nearby. The state people are focusing hard on that truck evidence; it may be nothing, but if we can get any leads on a similar truck at St. Louis or Thebes, we might have something."

"A single pickup truck in all the great Midwest," Wellesley said. "Wow."

"I know, Deputy Director. But unfortunately, that's how it's done. One lead at a time." Wellesley's Air Force background is showing, Hush thought.

"Okay, okay, but what are *we* doing?" As in, what are *you* doing?

"*We* are making the best possible use of the considerable cooperation being afforded by state and local law enforcement. On-scene forensics, detailed knowledge of the local terrain, the ability to talk to local people without the out-of-town federal agent in mirrored sunglasses routine, which tends to make civilians just clam up. Our people are involved, of course. Think of it as not having to start from scratch, Deputy Director."

Powers handed him a piece of paper, which Hush scanned and then relayed to Wellesley. "We've just got a report in that the Dallas police have recovered the missing Union Pacific security guard, the one on the MacArthur Bridge, remember? Found him unconscious on a tank car. Single blow to the side of the head. They've got him in a hospital."

"Is he talking?"

"Not conscious yet."

That brought a pause. Then Carswell chimed in. "A single blow to the head. Maybe it's not just one guy."

"Why do you say that?" Wellesley asked.

"Because if it had been a gang up there and the guard surprised one guy, that guy would try to hold the guard's attention while one of the other humps took care of business."

"There've been other personnel casualties?" Wellesley asked. "At Memphis?"

"Yes," Powers said, consulting another report. "Five railroad security people were injured when the pipe exploded. Burns cases. Two critical."

"So this bomber, if your assumptions are correct, is not shy about hurting or even killing people if he has to."

"So it would appear," Hush said. "Don't forget the Army officer on the MacArthur. While the local cops are gathering evidence, I asked Agent Lang to check on something. Carolyn, anything to report?"

"I've begun the queries in NCIC," Lang replied, "And I've forwarded parallel queries to the Secret Service, BATF and DEA, and also to the military authorities. I'm meeting with the general counsels and chiefs of security of the three largest railroads first thing in the morning to see how best to frame a database query. Although, when I asked them the 'Who doesn't love you?' question, they just laughed."

"This isn't a laughing matter," Wellesley protested. "I'll have the director call their CEOs."

"They didn't think it was funny, Mr. Wellesley," Lang said. "Just hopeless."

"Because it's a wrong theory," Carswell said. That produced a moment of silence.

"Well, we've got to disabuse them of that notion," Hush said, deciding to ignore Carswell. "This is what *we* do best, Deputy Director—use our considerable data resources to find needles in haystacks. Carolyn, take some NCIC people with you to that meeting. Have them explain how we winnow multiple databases."

"Maybe we should call in the profilers," Carswell suggested, his voice heavy with sarcasm.

"Great idea," Hush said immediately.

They kicked around other possible courses of action for another half hour, after which Wellesley told Hush to wait fifteen minutes and then call him back secure on his private line. That ended the teleconference. Keeler said Powers was giving him a police escort down to the Vicksburg bridge that evening to coordinate the next morning's inspection. They wrapped up some more details, and then Thomas and his people left to complete setting up the Trainman situation room. Hush reached for the phone.

"Now for the real scoop, right?" Powers said.

"Yeah, well, this is the Bureau," Hush said. "At my level, the back-channel discussions are a lot more important than what gets said in open meetings. Not like that in the state police world, I presume."

Powers kept a perfectly straight face. "Absolutely not. Everything we do is totally aboveboard, out in the open, with honesty and fair play for all. Amen."

Both men laughed out loud, and then Powers left, shutting the door behind him. Hush placed a call to Tyler Redford, hoping to catch either him or Lang before he had to talk to Wellesley. Instead, he got one of the senior agents from IITF, who had been on leave for the past ten days. The agent said that he wasn't sure what was going on but that Redford had been called to a special meeting up on the seventh floor with the assistant director for National Security affairs, Mr. Carswell.

"Oh yeah? What is that all about?"

"I just got back from leave, so I'm not sure, Mr. Hanson," the agent said. "But supposedly there's a new task force."

"Say again?"

"What I heard was that the director has decided to reorganize the whole Trainman lash-up. Some woman named Lang is going to head the thing up here at headquarters."

Hush was speechless for a moment. He thanked the man and hung up. He sat there in the empty conference room digesting this little bombshell. This must be the news that Wellesley wanted to share with him. Had he been relieved of the command of Trainman? By his erstwhile deputy? Something didn't make sense here: She had supposedly been assigned to this operation almost on probation, a get-well assignment after her disastrous ASAC tour in St. Louis. If Trainman had been moved to the National Security division, then where did that leave him? An assistant director in the field on his own? Supposedly doing what?

He refilled his coffee cup with some of the asphaltlike goop remaining in the brewer, looked at his watch, and punched up the secure drop for the deputy director. Wellesley's executive assistant put him on hold for a few minutes. At just about the moment Hush was going to hang up, Wellesley came on the line.

"Hush Hanson. Thank you for calling back."

As if I had a choice, Hush thought. "I understand there's been a change made in the task force alignment," he said.

"Your network is alive and well, I see," Wellesley said. "Yes. That happened late this afternoon. The director came back from the White House and told me to up the ante, organizationwise. Trainman is getting much too big. This has nothing to do with you, Hush, nor should you consider it any sort of reflection on your performance. We simply need to feed the public perception that—"

"Excuse me, Deputy Director," Hush interrupted. "But that's not how it's going to look, especially out here in the field. This is going to look like an assistant director got fired."

"No, it won't, because we want you to continue to honcho Trainman in the field. Carolyn Lang is going to head the Washington end of things, but the director himself is now heading up the interagency task force."

"The *director?*"

"Himself. The interagency group is now almost at cabinet level."

"That's unheard of."

"Hush, I really don't think you appreciate the scale of what's been happening since those bridges started going down. The country is beginning to experience major commercial disruptions in the movement of critical commodities. We're talking coal for power plants, food, every kind of petroleum product that doesn't go through one of the major pipelines, chemicals for the manufacturing of goddamn everything. And that doesn't include trucks."

Hush was still trying to get his mental arms around what he was being told. "Trucks?" he said.

"That's right. I didn't know this, either, but a hell of a lot of transcontinental semitrailers actually ride the rails for the cross-country segment, and then they go by tractor-trailer locally."

Wellesley was trying to distract him. "And what exactly am I supposed to be doing, then?" Hush asked.

"Just what you've been doing: You are to be the on-scene federal prime mover. You are to organize and synergize all the local law-enforcement agencies along the Mississippi River to make sure all their people are leaning forward."

Organize and synergize? Leaning forward? "They already are."

"Which is why it's vital you remain in the field, right? So, you'll report to the director, through Carswell."

Wait a minute, he thought. *Through Carswell?* "I don't understand. I thought you just said—"

"I know. But Lang isn't an assistant director. Carswell is. The two of you will report to the director through his office. Keeps the wiring diagram cleaner."

"And her job is what, exactly?"

"Her job will be to act as point person here in Washington. She's the one who'll have to go on television, do the dance up on the Hill, and absorb the howls and uproar from the railroads. Think about it, Hush: Who's got the better deal?"

Wellesley was trying to smother him in distractions. What was clear was Carswell had maneuvered himself into taking over Trainman. Wellesley kept it coming.

"You're going to be at the sharp end of the spear, Hush. The rest of us back here in Washington will do everything in our power to support you. You are working for the director, not Carswell. He's is just there to pull it all together; we can't have the director dealing with raw field information, now, can we?"

"I suppose not," Hush said, still bewildered.

"Good," Wellesley said. "Now, there's one caveat: You issue no public statements. Everything related to Trainman will be coordinated out of Washington. The longer this thing drags on, the more the Bureau will have to defend itself. That's best done here at headquarters."

Hush found himself nodding, almost against his will. Carolyn Lang. He had definitely been asleep at the switch here. And then he wondered: Had *he* been the victim of a setup? He decided it was worth a probe.

"And what about our little nonconversation in the director's office when this whole thing started, Deputy Director?" he asked.

"From a Washington perspective, Hush, who's going to be the goat here if another bridge drops? You or Ms. Lang?"

Hush sensed a hole in Wellesley's logic, but he couldn't think of what to say. "Very well," he said. "I assume the director will promulgate all this by Teletype?"

"Coming out tonight to all SACs. You just get back to work. We'll make it clear that you're the Man. Trust us on this one, Hush."

Hush hung up the phone with that infamous phrase ringing in his ears. Trust George Wellesley. Sure, snake. He placed a quick call back to IITF and instructed the agent who answered to have Tyler Redford call him the moment he got back in. Then he hung up and sat there, trying to digest this turn of events. He was pretty sure he had just been had. And somehow, Carolyn Lang was involved.

10

AT 8:30 P.M. WEDNESDAY, Major Matthews waited in the command car at the end of the train for word on the special tank cars. The entire train was ready to go, with all the cars carrying CW casings inspected and cleared for main-line operations. The engines were fueled, and the route detachment embarked, both in the command car and up forward in the communications cab. The seventy-eight cars and three engines stretched almost a mile ahead of them on the siding, putting the command car way back in the woods from the switching area. The train needed only the two specials cars to be complete. The depot's stubby switch engine was parked on a parallel siding behind the command car, waiting for the call from Assembly 9.

The command car was an oversized caboose painted out in Army olive drab. It contained a bunk room forward, a bathroom-shower area and small kitchen in the middle, and a lounge area in the back. The lounge had been converted into an ops center. On one side was a rack of radio equipment, two communications consoles, a GPS navigation console, and a monitoring panel showing the security and pressurization status of every car on the train. On the front bulkhead was a small-arms locker, which contained twenty M16s and four military 12-gauge riot guns. There was a center table and chairs out in the middle, and lockers for chemical warfare suits and breathing apparatus mounted on the other side. There was a tiny railed porch on the back of the car, and a single window on each side. On the roof were five whip antennas and a GPS radome. The MPs' car, next forward, was similar to the command car, but without all the operations equipment. It also had a larger bunk room.

Matthews shivered in the air conditioning, which seemed to run on only one setting: full blast. Thankfully, there were blankets on the bunks in the bunk room. The MPs were out along the tracks, maintaining a security perimeter. Once the train was under way, there would be two MPs riding in the engine security pod to provide armed security for the engine set itself. There was no internal connection between the engine security node and the engineer's cab: To get from one to the other would require the men to climb along a railed catwalk on the right side of the engine. The pod contained backup communications equipment, a rack for the MPs' weapons and ammunition, and external hard points for two M60 machine guns. There was also night-vision equipment and space to store two protective CW suits.

Matthews had inspected the command car, the MPs' car, and its forward pod two hours ago and found everything in place. They had tested communications links between the command car and the pod, and between the main consoles and the depot's operations center. Both nodes could monitor voice communications between the engineer and the various railroad traffic-control centers, and there were also frequencies on which they could contact both local and federal law-enforcement agencies en route. He was resisting the impulse to go inspect them all again.

He fixed himself another cup of coffee and watched out the window as the last bands of sunset silhouetted the pines. He had finally told his wife what was going on, and he had given her the official letter, signed by Mehle, ordering him to take the train out to Tooele. The letter contained his objections. This was their insurance policy should it all go terribly wrong, he had said, and then he had sworn her to secrecy. If the depot had not been sealed, he would have had her get the hell out of there and take Marsha Hill and her kids with her. As it was, they were all just going to have to hunker down and play the Army's game.

Matthews kept telling himself that as long as they did not experience a major rail accident, the specials ought to be reasonably safe. Those 200,000-pound pressurized tank cars were massive containments in and of themselves, and the initiator charge was not a huge bomb but, rather, a segmented sphere of high explosive designed to implode the core. As long as there was no nuclear reaction, he kept telling himself, those big tank cars could probably handle one of those things cooking off.

He looked at his watch. Almost 9:00 P.M. He wondered what in the hell was holding them up. He tried not to think about Carl Hill, and whether or not Mehle would keep his word. The phone from the depot's operations center rang.

"Major Matthews," he said.

"This is depot operations. From Colonel Mehle: Washington has put a hold on twenty-seven thirteen. Stand down the train until further notice. Maintain all personnel on station. ETD is now twenty hundred tomorrow. Acknowledge, please, Major."

"Will comply," Matthews said.

He hung up the phone. So it will be Thursday after all, he thought. Goddamn Army: Hurry up and wait. He stepped out onto the back platform of the command car and yelled for the sergeant.

11

HE PARKED THE TRUCK in the only available parking space next to the Baton Rouge City Park at the foot of Battery Street. It was 5:30 on Thursday afternoon, and the sun was almost directly in his eyes, its dying light amplified by the shimmering glare off the river. The black rhomboidal web of steel trusses holding up the railroad bridge two miles downstream to his left was etched in high definition against a metallic bronze sky. The park was small, sandwiched in between a warehouse complex and a barge-repair yard. It was also nearly empty, which made him wonder why all the parking spaces were taken, until he realized the shipyard workers had all parked there.

He got out and looked around. There were two elderly black women sitting on a bench, chatting and admiring the big river. A decrepit-looking dog was snuffling through the few bushes that grew along a wobbly wrought-iron fence. Bedraggled pigeons roosted on the bronze hat of the obligatory mounted general. Out on the river, a tug exchanged passing signals with another tug, both of them pushing big barge strings in opposite directions. The upstream tug was running at full power against the current and seemingly getting nowhere as it strained upstream. A light breeze came off the river, suffused with the oily smell of the petroleum-cracking plant just upriver.

His attention was drawn to the white ship moored across the river at the Jameson wharves. With a full-load displacement of eight thousand tons and at 510 feet long, the SS *Cairo* was just exactly right for what he had in mind. She was a relatively new ship, which meant that she needed only thirteen officers and ratings to run her. The ship was loading bulk grain, probably rice, into her forward holds, whose hatch covers were opened upright like giant *M*'s along her deck. According to the harbormaster's schedule, she was bound downriver at 11:00 P.M. for the 150-mile run to the Gulf. She was typical of the shallow-draft freighters that ran the river, with a six-level-high superstructure all the way aft, but flush-decked from there to her bows.

He lit up a cigarette, put his foot up on the lower rung of the old iron railing along the seawall, and looked downriver toward the bridge. It was too far away to see any signs of the security forces, but he knew they were there. The network news had been filled with the story of the railroad bridges, complete with vivid footage of the damage done so far. The National Guard was now patrolling bridge approaches and Coast Guard boats were making determined patrols along the river. They had shown city and state cops, railroad cops, the Army Corps, and several flavors of feds crawling like ants all over the remaining bridges, looking for bombs and wires.

It's all working, he thought, blowing out a long plume of smoke. The railroads were searching, inspecting, sanitizing, and guarding the remaining bridges. And no doubt their legions of lawyers were busy looking for someone to sue, some individual or entity they could flatten and bankrupt. Like they had flattened and bankrupted him, *after* annihilating his family. He shut out any thoughts of the Army officer who had been killed, or the burned railroad policemen fighting for breath through seared lungs in a Memphis hospital. This is a war, he kept telling himself. War involves casualties. If those railroad cops caught him on one of the bridges now, they would shoot him and throw his bleeding body to the channel catfish. Fair enough, he thought. Death was not something he feared anymore. He'd treat them just like those locomotives had treated his family: like a machine, without compunction, without mercy. All he had to do was to close his eyes, summon the scene at the crossing, and all sense of fair play and responsibility drained right out of him. He was determined. He was implacable. And he was winning.

He took another long drag on his cigarette and blew the smoke out slowly, savoring the perfumed cloud in his face as it dispersed the gnats. There was a fair chance he might not survive tonight's operation. If he didn't, four out of six wasn't bad. If he did, well, there were two more bridges. They were undoubtedly expecting Vicksburg to be hit next. He had been coming down the river, knocking the bridges down one by one.

On any federal situation map, Vicksburg was the obvious next target. Actually, he was saving Vicksburg, but after tonight, they would sure as hell know he'd been there, too.

He took a last drag, pitched the cigarette into the river, and headed back to his truck. The women and the dog had gone. Looking around to see if anyone was watching, he went to the back of his truck, which now had a windowless cap bolted on over the bed. He opened the back of the cap and checked the bulky rubber-covered block that took up one side of the bed. The business end of a small outboard stuck out of one end of the block. A coil of dark nylon line was attached to the other end. A small overnight bag was jammed in between the block and the tailgate. Next to the block was tied down a rusty-looking, stripped-down dirt bike. Despite its decrepit looks, it was fully functional, and came complete with a stolen Louisiana motorbike license plate and a superefficient muffler.

He would have to wait until full dark to preposition the inflatable boat, and the only loose end was whether or not the gates to the fuel pier downstream of the interstate bridge would be locked. He had a cure for that, of course, but it would be better if he could just get out there without leaving signs of intrusion. He got back into his truck and went to find someplace for dinner. All this plotting and scheming had stimulated his appetite.

Hush stood in the Civil War gun pits overlooking the Mississippi and watched a long train pull out onto the Vicksburg bridge, its three locomotives pumping hot columns of blue diesel exhaust into the Thursday-evening air as it headed west. A National Guard mobile command post, bristling with antennas, had been pulled up into the little parking area just below the gun pits. There were several Guardsmen standing around outside the CP, looking somewhat incongruous in their uniforms and with their civilian haircuts, and more patrolling the bridge decks. Below and to their left was the Mississippi State Welcome Center, which offered stunning views of the river and excellent maps of all the nearby Civil War sites. The building and its parking lot had been commandeered by the state police and National Guard, and there were more people and vehicles down there. The approach streets to the bridge had been cordoned off by military police. All the commotion had produced a great deal of gawking by the local populace.

Hush thought it marvelously ironic that, once again, the heights of Vicksburg were occupied by military forces. The contrast between the huge Civil War cannon and the satellite dishes on the mobile CP was sublime. Because of the height of the bluffs on the Mississippi side, this bridge stretched level across the river, not descending to ground-grade level until well past the far banks. It was a trussed bridge with a single track running down the left side and a very narrow two-lane roadbed carrying old U.S. Route 80 alongside the tracks on the upstream side. There was an abandoned tollbooth and plaza at the Vicksburg end of the roadbed ramp, but most automobile traffic crossed the river about a half mile downstream on the much newer Interstate 20 highway bridge. There was a boarded-up bridge keeper's booth in the toll plaza, with signs limiting the size and weight of vehicles crossing the old roadbed. Tourists could drive their cars across to the other side, but there was nothing over there but a Corps of Engineers sand and gravel depot and a twenty-foot-long remnant of General Grant's ill-fated canal.

The woods and bayous on the Louisiana side were slipping into deep shadows now as the sun settled over the western banks. The western sky had been filling with cumulonimbus clouds for an hour or so before sunset, and the troops were all sporting rolled-up rain gear. Directly below them on the river itself was a brightly lighted casino complex, which Hush, a devotee of Civil War history, considered a perfect desecration. Where Admiral Porter's squat black gunboats had once traded twelve-inch shells with Confederate gun emplacements up here on the high bluffs, a faux steamboat now squatted. Draped with strings of flashing red and blue and white lights, it was embraced by a multilevel parking lot filled with pickup trucks.

Hush had spent the entire morning with Morgan Keeler going over every inch of the Vicksburg bridge, accompanied by some junior Army engineers and railroad security people. It had been difficult to do because of the procession of big trains going across the bridge, with only five-minute intervals between them as the railroads stuffed as much traffic as they could across the remaining river bridges. A river patrol had been set up below the bridge, extending a few miles up and downstream, to ensure no one could approach the bridge from the water. A radar-equipped Navy patrol boat was moored to the center pier tower to provide nighttime surveillance. On the other side, National Guard Humvees patrolled the high levees, their slitted yellow headlights starting to show through the dense line of scraggly trees that lined the river. Heat lightning was flickering over the Louisiana delta country to the south.

They had inspected the rail and the road track beds, the truss structure's pin boxes, and every one of the main girders, looking for evidence of tampering, new wires, or any suspicious modifications. They had climbed up into the high truss steel, disturbing hosts of pigeons and getting covered in rust and flaking black paint, while a procession of trains below rattled the old structure. They climbed down the concrete face of the pier towers on rusty, creaking ladders, which did nothing to alleviate Hush's acrophobia. Throughout the day, Keeler treated Hush to an exhaustingly detailed tutorial on how the bridge had been constructed, how old the steel and its fittings were, what all the pipes and wires slung under the track bed carried, how communications were maintained along the tracks, what the maintenance problems were and how hard it was sometimes to get the railroads to maintain the aging structure properly. While it was more than Hush had wanted to know, it was clear that Keeler held the huge old bridges in great affection. Powers had showed up from Memphis at midday, at which point Keeler had gone south to conduct similar inspections of the railroad bridges at Baton Rouge and New Orleans.

Over the past two days, Powers had spearheaded the effort to accumulate and make sense of the physical evidence that had been collected by both local and federal forensic teams at all three bombing sites. Of the three, the Memphis incident offered the most promising leads. Assuming they were right about the Trainman operating on his own, they were pretty sure he was driving a pickup truck. Powers had instructed the state police in Missouri to compile a list of all the drivers of trucks and cars from whom they had taken statements on the night of the MacArthur Bridge bombing. It was confirmed there had been one pickup truck in the middle of interstate bridge at the moment the MacArthur had been dropped. One long-haul trucker's statement mentioned a tan pickup truck with a single passenger maneuvering erratically in front of him in the fast lane just as the bridge went down. That was all he had: no further identification, pretty sure it was a Ford, either a 150 or 250, not sure which. The tire tracks from the water plant's perimeter had been matched to a size that would fit an F-150 truck, which, as Powers pointed out wearily, narrowed the search to a few hundred thousand vehicles operating in the six states along the southern Mississippi.

The water-treatment plant had produced a few more clues. Brass traces on the relief valve of the propane tank were similar to the metal found in the fittings of oxygen-acetylene welding rings, which indicated that maybe he had pressurized the propane tank with welding oxygen. The chains on the gates and the big valves had been cut with a large bolt cutter, of the kind available at major hardware stores; the shape of the cuts indicated that it was relatively new. The ignition source for the explosive mixture that pushed down the pipe had not yet been determined, but there was tungsten residue.

The FBI laboratories, with the assistance of the Bureau of Alcohol, Tobacco, and Firearms, had begun to shape a profile on the explosives used so far. The Thebes bridge had been blown with black powder and not Pyrodex, as originally thought, along with a military variant of detonating cord to shatter the main girder of the next span segment. The black powder had been initiated by a small dynamite charge, which in turn had been fired by a blasting cap, probably remotely fired. Traces of wire had been found in the pin cavities.

The black powder was of a type available nationally for sport hunters, but the Detacord and the dynamite might prove more useful, especially the military Detacord, since the armed forces bought this type from a single manufacturer. The same cord explosive had been used to drop the St. Louis span, and the booby-trap bomb had also been a military explosive. The one-inch fragment that had hit Lang in the chest was a piece of steel that had originally been the end cap on a pipe bomb. The pages of the thick notebook that had taken most of the energy out of the fragment had given up traces of an identifiable thread lubricant. All of it was fragmentary, and nothing seemed to point anywhere conclusively.

On Wednesday afternoon, Hush received an update indirectly from Carolyn Lang through Tyler Redford on the database searches. The railroad companies had come in with a hodgepodge of records, some computerized, but most on paper. There was no consistency in the format of the records, and also no consistency in the time lines. Lang was reportedly disheartened at the sheer scale of the effort that would be needed to sort through it all to find possible profiles. The technical director in Information Resources was suggesting the creation of their own temporary database using the railroad companies' information and the FBI's database structure, which could then be accessed by law enforcement all over the country via the NCIC.

There was one significant problem: FBI general counsel was warning that there were Privacy Act problems with that approach, and the railroad lawyers were also leery of having the government assemble such a database. Some of the cases had been settled under gag orders; others contained information that the railroad lawyers thought might expose the railroads to further liability. On the other hand, the director and the Attorney General were pushing hard to expand the investigation, so Lang was using that as the hammer to keep IR's efforts going. Carswell still considered the whole thing useless and was loudly seconding the general counsel's warnings.

Hush told Redford about his conversation with the deputy director, repeating Wellesley's assertion that he had the better part of this dual-command deal. Redford had not been so sure about that, but there was too much going on at the moment to do much more than cope with the hourly crises. Hush was still anxious to talk directly Carolyn Lang, but so far, they had not connected, leaving Hush very uneasy.

The end of the train finally came abreast of his position on the hill and he walked down the grassy hill to meet Powers, who was waiting on a pedestrian overpass that went over the railroad track to the Center.

"So now what? We wait?" Powers said, talking around a cigarette.

"We wait," Hush agreed. "There's no guarantee that this is the next target, though."

"Got that right," Powers said. "Hell, he could see all this security and simply sit back and wait, like Saddam Hussein, for us to stand down."

Hush nodded and stopped on the footbridge. The red taillights of the westbound freight were disappearing into the twilight over on the Louisiana side. "We've still got next to nothing in the way of leads. Some bits of evidence, two competing theories, but that's about it."

"Journey of a thousand miles and all that shit," Powers said, flicking the cigarette down onto the tracks below.

"The ultimate answer is going to come from Washington, you know," Hush said. "If they can ever get all the frigging lawyers out of the soup, there's gonna be a name or ten that will suggest a possible motive for all this. *If* Carolyn can keep IR going on the project."

"People with a hate-on for railroads?" Powers said. "What're we talking here—ten thousand names?"

Hush acknowledged the scale of the problem, but his own political antennae still told him that, the case aside, the real action was in Washington right now. And here he was, climbing around railroad bridges out here on the Mississippi River. Powers seemed to read his thoughts.

"Any more information on your new command arrangements?"

Hush shook his head.

"You don't mind my asking," Powers said, "How do you read this new setup of your task force? One day that lady was your deputy, and now she's in charge back at the zoo?"

Hush smiled. "Word do travel," he said. "Actually, the director himself is in titular charge. Lang's job is to face all the irate citizens. Carswell is supposedly 'coordinating' field inputs. The deputy director tells me I'm better off out here. You figure it out."

"Well," Powers said.

"Yeah. Well," Hush said, "I think I'm in the middle of a lateral arabesque, careerwise. Ty Redford said she wants to talk to me off-line. Maybe she can explain why I'm getting this nonstick sensation on the bottom of my shoes."

Powers laughed out loud, which caused some soldiers to look over at them. The Guardsmen had been activated for the emergency, jerked out of their homes and jobs, and none of this seemed all that funny to them. Down the tracks a single white light appeared in the distance as the next eastbound train got its turn on the bridge. They could hear the engines of the next westbound train idling upriver on the Mississippi side.

"There's a captain I know in the Mississippi state cops; lives here in Vicksburg," Powers said. "He invited me to meet him for a drink when we were done. Why don't you come along? Let all these military types do their job."

"At least they know what their job is right now," Hush said, following Powers down the steps to the cruiser, where Little Hill stood waiting. Hush waved at the Jackson office agents standing around the open door of the commandeered Welcome Center. They did not wave back.

At 9:30, he parked the truck in the shadows of a darkened warehouse on the Louisiana side and shut off the engine. He waited for fifteen minutes, just watching out the window to see what might be shaking along the levee. The warehouse was across the street from the levee, so he

190

couldn't see the river from where he sat. He looked left, upriver, where he could see the tops of the railroad bridge about a mile upstream. The city of Baton Rouge itself appeared only as a loom of light over the tops of the levee. He had long since memorized the lay of the land along the nearby banks: a barge-repair shipyard, complete with floating dry dock, a long seawall to which barge tugs often tied up, an operational fuel pier, and then his immediate objective, the abandoned Esso fuel pier. About three hundred yards downstream from his truck was a slanting access ramp that ran up one side of the levee from the street. Signs declared that private vehicles were not allowed to drive on the levees. There was a similar access road to his left for the shipyard workers to use.

He had seen signs of thunderstorms out to the west at sunset, but the night along the river was just humid and dark. That was fortunate: He was going to need good visibility and calm winds. He waited five more minutes before starting up again and heading for the nearer access ramp. When he reached it, he cut his lights and turned diagonally left up the steep gravel road to the top of the levee. He paused there for just a second to make sure there were no cars or trucks below; then he drove over the hump and down to the riverbank. He turned left, went a hundred feet or so, and then shut down next to a grove of trees. He checked his watch—plenty of time.

He watched some more, rolling the windows down so he could hear the sounds of the river. There was some night-shift work going on in the shipyard, where the crackling blue-white glow from a welder's arc illuminated openings in the sides of a grain barge under repair. A large rail crane that operated along the shipyard pier was idling in place, its boom lights swinging gently in a breeze that did not reach the river. Its diesel engine pumped a bluish cloud of smoke across the water. Out in the channel, a tug was breasting the current on the way upriver to pick up a barge load, and another one was coming downriver, pushing a string of hopper barges. The city of Baton Rouge was mostly to his right front as he looked across the river; to his far right, the interstate highway bridge crossed the river on a flattened arc. He could make out to his far left the red lights atop the railroad bridge, and beyond those shone a white and amber glow from the lights of the port around the big bend. The water flashed a thousand oily reflections at him as waves, churned up by the barge and tug traffic, slapped the bulkhead piers. Across the half-mile-wide channel a small Coast Guard cutter was patrolling, its white hull and running lights distinctive in the darkness. He had expected the river patrols, but they weren't going to save this bridge.

A small gravel road meandered through the trees right next to his truck. The road ended at the rusting chain-link gates of the abandoned fuel pier, whose plank and steel-mat decking had long since fallen into the river, leaving only two rows of stumpy, rotting pilings. He would inflate the boat, throw it down into the water, and then tie it off to one of the pilings. The boat was only about six feet long and made of black synthetic rubber. The engine was a compact twenty-two-horse outboard, which he had sprayed with flat black paint. The combination should be next to invisible.

Then he would return to the truck, go back over the levee, and drive south along the levee road, then west to the state highway about a mile west of the river and parallel to it. He would take the state road farther downstream to the place where he was going to hide the truck. That would end the first phase, the reasonably safe phase. Once he left the truck, things were going to get a lot more interesting. He checked his watch. He was approaching endgame now. After tonight, they'd have a much better chance of finding him, because people were going to see him. He checked to make sure that he had taken his beeper off and that his cell phone was charged up. He patted the butt of a government-model Colt .45. Old but serviceable, he thought. Just like me.

At 10:05 P.M. on Thursday, Matthews heard the cars ahead of him jerking into motion in a series of thumps and bangs that worked their way back to the command car. The bulk of the two pressurized tank cars dead ahead prohibited him from seeing the rest of the train, but they were definitely under way. He and the MP sergeant stepped out onto the back platform of the command car and watched the pines begin to move astern of them as the train gathered speed in the darkness.

It had been a long day of waiting, especially since they had all had to sit there baby-sitting the train. He had talked to Mehle twice about the route clearance, and both times the colonel had seemed almost solicitous about the people locked inside the security perimeter on the siding. Even the two civilian engineers had remained aboard, camping out with the MPs in their crew car. The guards had been divided into two teams of six for the perimeter patrols, and they had gone on four-hour watches throughout the night and the next day. Two extra comms specialists had been assigned to stand six on, six off communications watches. Departure clearance had finally come in at 8:30 P.M. The two special tank cars had been brought out and coupled up an hour later, just ahead of the two military cars.

The lights of Anniston's main entrance loomed over the train as they approached the depot's lockout gates. With a mile-long train moving through them, both inner and outer gates were open, an unavoidable breach of security. The train continued to pick up speed as it switched onto the westbound main line. Matthews half-expected there to be a small send-off crowd at the gates, but there were only the usual guards, reduced to black silhouettes by the sodium-vapor lights shining from the towers flanking the gates. The inner gates began to swing closed as the command car cleared the base perimeter.

"Why'd them big tank cars come out last?" the sergeant asked. He was a large black man who chain-smoked evil-smelling cigars.

"Because they contain the most dangerous cargo," Matthews said. He was curious to see what the sergeant might have heard.

"Oh, yeah. The mustard. That shit gets loose, we'll be the first to know, won't we, Major?"

"You saw those tank cars. I think we've got more to worry about from those ten-year-old MREs than from any leaking mustard gas."

The sergeant laughed. The Army's MREs or meals ready to eat, were often the butt of jokes. Matthews had already heard the MPs discussing how they would send someone to hit the local burger joints if they were held on sidings for any length of time. But at least the mustard gas cover story seemed to have leaked out according to plan.

The train continued to accelerate in the darkness. The smell of diesel exhaust began to make it all the way back to the command car as the train's velocity increased. Matthews saw the first signal tower fly by in the darkness, and he tried but failed to read the lights. He had spent some of the long hours attempting to learn something about rail route operations. The engineers had introduced him to a whole new language in the process. He had learned about blocks, divisions, strings, about a dozen kinds of engines, that this train was called a "unit train" because it would not change its composition during the trip to Utah, that its designation number was odd because it was a westbound train, and that, in train language, the composition of a train was called "the consist." Carl Hill would probably be at home in this milieu, he thought, but Carl Hill was languishing in the stockade at Fort McClellan.

The radio operator called him into the command car. Colonel Mehle was on the net and wanted to speak to him personally. Now what? he thought as he sat down at the comms console.

"This is Major Matthews," he said.

"This is Colonel Mehle. Switch to secure mode."

Matthews switched the cipher controls, and Mehle came back on. "Some big-deal interagency task force has just released an intelligence warning to the effect that there is a level-three terrorist threat to all of the Mississippi River bridges," he said. "The DOD's estimate memo says that the Bureau is split on the matter, that one theory is there is one guy doing it, while the other theory is that it's a group doing it. Either way, they're pretty sure that it's not over."

"Understood, Colonel," Matthews said. "Is there a change to train orders?"

"Not at this time. I've informed headquarters that twenty-seven thirteen has launched. Your ETA to Birmingham is still twenty-three-thirty."

"That's what the engineer is telling us."

"Okay. Norfolk Southern is telling us that there'll be a hold at Birmingham. East-west traffic is pretty screwed up, as you might imagine. Full security perimeter at all stops, okay?"

"Yes, sir. Understood."

Mehle signed off, and Matthews went to fill in the sergeant. They could forget any midnight runs to the local burger joints.

Hush and Mike Powers returned to the Vicksburg bridge just after 10:00 P.M. They had met Powers's friend at a restaurant downtown, where they enjoyed some drinks and dinner in a private room. The people running the restaurant had been exceptionally friendly. During dinner, the three of them had talked of nothing but the bridge bombings. The Mississippi captain was openly impressed at the degree of cooperation going on between the state cops and all the federal authorities. He also described a jump in the number of railroad crossing incidents now that train traffic through Mississippi had quadrupled during the past few days. For

Hush, it was a nice break to talk to real cop stuff and to forget about his own bureaucratic problems.

There was heat lightning flashing over Louisiana when they went in to the Welcome Center to check on developments, but there was nothing more to report. The bridges in Baton Rouge and New Orleans were under heavy security, including a watch on all the utility lines and pipes. The railroads themselves had doubled and then tripled their own security forces in the switching yards, and they had initiated physical inspections of all their trains destined for a Mississippi River bridge crossing.

There was a Teletype for Hush from Carolyn Lang, indicating that IR was getting closer to negotiating release of the litigation records from three of the four major rail carriers. The bad news was that Carswell's office was putting a lot of pressure on to turn IR to other avenues of investigation. There was a second message from Tyler Redford, indicating that the Bureau was rethinking the public-relations approach to the case, again because of the internal disagreement on who was attacking the bridges. The federal intelligence world continued to come up empty with respect to terrorist groups.

"Wonder what the hell that means," Powers said after Hush let him read the Teletype. "I should think that intel report reinforces our theory of a lone bandit."

"If he is alone, he's been preparing for a long damn time," Hush replied. "We'll have to make sure that database search goes back far enough."

Hush suggested a walk to work off the lengthy dinner. The night air was heavy and humid as they left the air-conditioned center, crossed over the railroad cut, and walked down the path to the darkened toll plaza. The bridge had been closed to all vehicular traffic since the extra security measures had been put in place. They showed their credentials and walked past the National Guard sentries as they made their way out onto the narrow roadway that paralleled the tracks. The single track glinted in the glare of the temporary floodlights put up to illuminate the bridge's deck area. A westbound train came out onto the bridge as they were walking. It was close enough to the roadway that they could have reached out and touched the boxcars with a broom handle. Hush felt the old bridge tremble with the weight of the train, and the noise made conversation impossible. Hush took off his suit jacket because of the mugginess.

He gazed out over the river, whose surface reflected the thousands of multicolored lights strung over the fake riverboat upstream. The bluffs above the river were dark, and there were not that many lights on in the city itself.

The train finally ground past about the time they reached the middle of the bridge. A soft wind was stirring through the old steel trusses, almost drowning out the noise of truck traffic on the interstate highway bridge just downriver. Hush thought he heard the distant rumble of thunder, but as he listened, the sound of an eastbound train slowly filled the river, accompanied by a blaze of white light in their faces as the train began the climb out onto the bridge structure from the bottomland on the Louisiana side. They continued walking across the bridge, checked in with the guards on the western end, and turned back towards Vicksburg. The banks behind them were in total darkness. It wasn't hard to imagine that the ghosts of Grant's army were still sweating back there in the bayous somewhere, searching for a way around the guns of Vicksburg.

He pulled off the road into a minimart parking lot and drove the bike around to the back side, shutting down and then stashing it between two large Dumpsters. The front aprons and the gas lanes were brightly lighted, but back here there was only a single security light, and it was focused on the back door of the minimart. A hundred yards up the road was the entrance road to the Baton Rouge marine terminal. As he watched, two large semis rumbled past the minimart and turned into the terminal complex in a noisy cloud of dust and air brakes. The terminal yard was fenced, but there were no guards at the main entrance, and the big rigs just sailed through. Inside the fence, there were two lines of large warehouses paralleling the river. He could see the high booms of pier cranes rising above the warehouse roofs, their white floodlights illuminating the raised superstructure of the SS *Cairo*.

He checked his watch. One hour and a bit until sailing time. The *Cairo* sailed from this terminal once every ten days, regular as clockwork, carrying bulk cargoes down the river and out across the Gulf to Mexico. She was one of six medium-size shallow-draft freighters that were based in Baton Rouge. Her departure time varied as a function of the loading schedule pierside and the traffic-control requirements down at the larger port of New Orleans. But to get the sailing time, all anyone had to do was call the tape at the terminal control office, where an automated voice announced all significant sailings, much like a movie theater listed show times. And show time, he thought, wasn't a bad phrase for what he was about to do.

He reviewed the plan: Drive the bike into the terminal complex and go directly to the general parking area for ships' crewmen, which was located at the remote end of the piers. He would wait and watch for a few minutes, then dump the bike in the river and walk directly to the ship. He would be carrying a small seabag and wearing nondescript working clothes when he went up the gangway. He had actually been aboard *Cairo* and three of her sister ships at the terminal in the hour before a night sailing, and he had never seen a soul on deck. The engineers were always below, making ready for sea, and the deckhands had long since secured for the night once the cargo hatches had been latched down. The only people who would be up would be the master, the river pilot, one mate, and one helmsman in the pilothouse. The routine of sailing from the terminal was just that: absolutely routine, so any 'night owls would be watching late-night TV in the crew's lounge. In his trial runs, he had roamed freely through the entire after superstructure, just as long as it was a late-night sailing. Like tonight. He had mapped out where the officers' cabins were, as well as the areas to avoid, such as the lounge.

He would simply go on board, go directly to the engineer's cabin, and let himself in. Once there, he would put on the black wet suit, which included pants, top, head hood, and diver's boots. He would then put on a shirt and some khaki pants over the wet suit, oversized cowboy boots over the diver's boots, and an oversized yellow Caterpillar ball cap. After that, he would check out the rest of his gear, and then he would wait. Once the ship got under way, he would put on a Bill Clinton rubber face mask and then leave the cabin and climb to the bridge, carrying the small bag that contained his tube breather, face mask, floatation vest, and a set of flippers. He would have the .45 in his hand. Just before he left the cabin, he would make the first of two phone calls on his cell phone. He needed to time everything so that the ship was pointed downstream in the channel just before he made his move. Then Brother Bill was going to take them for the ride of their routine lives, straight down to the Baton Rouge railroad bridge.

•   •   •

They were walking back into the parking lot of the Welcome Center as the end of a very long eastbound train cleared by them in a rattle of clicking and clacking. It was Hush who first heard the phone ringing over in the shadows of the toll plaza. It sounded like it was coming from the roadway behind the tollbooth. He looked at Powers, who nodded, yes, he had heard it, too, and then a couple of the sentries apparently heard it. Hush walked over toward the toll plaza, where he could make out a bank of pay phones mounted along the concrete wall. They did not look very modern, but one of them was definitely ringing. A Guardsman up on the visitors center's veranda came over with a flashlight and shone it down the line. Hush and Powers walked into the plaza and went down the line of phones until they could pick out which one was ringing. Hush looked at Powers, who shrugged. Hush picked up the phone.

"FBI," he said.

"*Stop the trains,*" a rasping voice said, sounding like it was coming through some kind of breathing apparatus. "*There's a bomb on the bridge. You've got fifteen minutes. Stop the trains!*"

Then silence. Hush looked over at Powers, then hung up the phone.

"What?" Powers said.

"Some guy said there's a bomb on the bridge. He said, 'Stop the trains. . . . You've got fifteen minutes.' "

"You think it's real?"

Hush thought fast. The next westbound train was audibly approaching from the cut to their left. Now that it was in motion, there was probably no time to stop it. But if they really had fifteen minutes, it should get clear in time.

"Have to treat it that way," Hush said, heading for the command center. Powers hurried after him, yelling up to the Guardsmen to get their people off the bridge. By the time they got up to the parking lot, the military officers were converging, having already been alerted by their sentries down near the toll plaza. Hush explained what had happened and confirmed that they needed to get their people off the bridge. The senior National Guard officer issued some quick commands on his radio, then said he'd call for an EOD go team, which had been prepositioned at the Air Force base near Meridian. There was a flurry of further radio communications, which were made difficult by the noise of the passing train. The CP operators informed the railroad operations center in Jackson to hold up all traffic once this train got clear of the bridge. The radar patrol boat was warned to get away from directly under the bridge. A minute later, they heard the two-engine set pulling the passing train spool up to maximum power as instructions to get clear came down the track circuits.

Hush rejoined Powers outside of the command post. The troops and the cops were milling about and casting anxious looks at the dark bulk of the bridge. Everyone was looking at their watches. Hush looked at his: about ten minutes to go. Two large searchlights mounted in the Civil War gun pits came on and began to play along the length of the bridge. The string of cars seemed interminable, one after another, with no end in sight. Nine minutes.

He had made the phone call the moment he heard and felt the ship's main engine change from low idle to operating rpm, a steady vibration as the propeller bit in to move the ship off the bulkhead pier. He watched through a window and finally saw the lights on the far shore appear to move. The ship didn't need a tugboat because she had a bow thruster, so she came off the pier in a steady sideways motion and was then captured by the river's current. When he saw the lights of Baton Rouge begin to slide to the left in the window, he put on the rubber mask, chambered the .45, lowered the hammer, put the cell phone under his left armpit, and stepped out the door. Turn left; go forward. No one in the passageway. Good.

Climb two sets of interior stairs to the pilothouse level. Small vestibule, chart room to the right, communications room to the left. Both doors closed. Pilothouse door closed. He adjusted the rubber mask, which was beginning to make his face sweat, checked the .45, and stepped through the pilothouse door.

The pilothouse was an expansive area extending the full width of the ship and covering about twenty feet from back bulkhead to the front windows. There was a doorway hatch on either side leading out onto the bridge wings. The lighting was a subdued red, to facilitate the officers' night vision. Between him and the front windows was the helmsman's console, behind which an Hispanic-looking man stood with both hands on the trick wheel. Mounted on the back bulkhead to his left was a chart table, but there was no one there. Standing at the windows on either side of the centerline gyro pelorus were two middle-aged men dressed in civilian clothes. He knew one had to be the master, the other the pilot.

Where was the mate? There was usually a mate doing the navigation. The helmsman finally saw him.

"¿*Qué*—" he began, and then saw the gun.

He waved the helmsman down to the deck with the gun, motioning for him to get flat. The man obeyed instantly, shutting his eyes. The master and the pilot were oblivious to what was happening behind them as they talked softly, looking forward out the windows. He stepped forward, looking around again for the mate. No one else appeared to be on the bridge or the bridge wings. Through the front windows, he could see the rest of the ship, all the way to the bow, beyond which he could see the railroad bridge. The ship's head was pointed between the two main channel pier towers. There was a small Coast Guard cutter broad on the port bow, hovering around the bridge. Downriver, there was a tug and barge string coming their way. One of the men standing by the windows pointed the barge string out to the other, who raised binoculars to examine its lights.

He stepped up onto the small wooden platform behind the wheel, put one foot on the helmsman's neck, and quietly turned the wheel slightly to the right. Then he reached over to the one-armed engine-order telegraph and shoved the brass handle all the way forward and down to the full-ahead position. Both men at the window whirled around at the sound of that, and he leveled the gun at them.

"Down," he said. "On the deck. Now."

There was a jangle of bells as the engine room responded to the full-bell order, and a moment later he could feel the deck start to shiver as the ship's main engine spooled up. The two men at the windows were still gaping at him, but they hadn't moved. A telephone right next to a captain's chair on the starboard side began to ring. The ship had finally begun to respond to the rudder, and her head was starting to swing very slowly to the right. He pointed the .45 at one of the men and pulled back the hammer. "Down, now, or die."

Both men dropped to their knees, their hands raised.

"On your knees, crawl over there; then get flat," he ordered, pointing with the gun to the port side of the pilothouse. He looked back through the windows and saw the ship's head swinging faster now. Too fast. He spun the wheel back over to port, and she steadied. The two men were knee-walking over to the port side. The bridge was coming up faster now as the ship accelerated. It was maybe a thousand yards away and starting to fill the windows.

"Get flat!" he yelled to the two men, and they obliged. The phone was still ringing next to the captain's chair, but he ignored it. He stepped backward, keeping the gun trained on the flattened men, and locked the pilothouse door. Then he stepped back to the helm and once again corrected her head. There was some interaction going on with the river current, because he felt rather than saw that her stern was swinging out, that she was getting slightly cocked across the current. It didn't matter; as her speed came up, he would be able to steer her right back on track to the target.

Eight hundred yards. He gripped the .45 harder.

At the Vicksburg bridge, everyone watched with bated breath as the clock ticked off the allotted fifteen minutes. The westbound train got clear at the four-minute point, and then there had been nothing to do but wait. There was a crowd of Guardsmen milling around the CP, and more troops were out on the overlook of the Welcome Center. Some, Hush noted, were sporting video cameras, hoping to get the shot of a lifetime even though it was full dark. Hush and Powers had climbed to the top of the hill where the Civil War guns were, and the operators in the mobile CP were all standing around the brightly lighted doorway, staring at the empty bridge.

"Maybe I should turn my back," Hush said. "Then it'll go off."

Another minute passed. Still nothing. They had been over that bridge for an entire morning, Hush thought. He, Keeler, and Keeler's whole team, and they had found absolutely nothing. There had been a Kansas City Southern bridge engineering team going over every square inch behind them, and two sergeants from Army EOD behind *them.* Every wire, every conduit, every steel truss beam had obviously been long encrusted in dirt, grease, and grime. The only shiny metal on the whole bridge was on the rails themselves. Even the pigeon droppings looked aged.

"I can't believe there is a bomb on that bridge," he said finally, after another minute had passed. "Too many people went over it today, and the day before that."

"Maybe it's in the damn water," Powers said. "Maybe the sumbitch mined it."

Hush shook his head in exasperation. He raised his portable radio. "This is Hanson. How long until the EOD team gets here?"

"Estimating twenty minutes. The Army's clearing a landing zone for a chopper out on the street."

Hush acknowledged. "I guess all we can do now is send out the explosive ordnance guys and see what they can find."

"I'm intrigued by that phone call," Powers said. "He knew the number of that pay phone, and that someone would answer it. If we get lucky, maybe we can trace it."

"You know it'll be a damn digital cell phone."

"Yeah, but did anybody check those phones this morning?"

"I didn't," Hush said. "I just assumed they were all long dead. Some of them had rotary dials, as I remember."

"Why don't we go down there and have a look-see?"

Hush looked down into the empty toll plaza. A scrap of white paper was blowing around the base of the boarded-up toll booth, but otherwise, the whole area was still.

"Maybe we should let the EOD guys do that," Hush said. "They like playing with bombs."

"If there's a bomb that supposed to get this bridge, it won't be down there," Powers said. "What the hell else do we have to do?"

Reluctantly, Hush agreed, and they walked slowly down into the toll plaza after informing the CP that they were going to check out the phone booths.

Five hundred yards. The lights along the shore were definitely accelerating now. Keeping one eye on the terrified men flattened on the deck, he pulled out the cell phone, fingered in a number, and then pressed the send button. When the dial displayed CALLING, he pitched the phone through the pilothouse door and over the side. That will keep them busy up at the Vicksburg bridge, he thought.

They were twenty feet from the bank of pay phones when a blinding white flash exploded with a small thunderclap to their left. Both Powers and Hush hit the deck as fragments of metal and wood whined around the toll plaza, followed by a cloud of acrid white smoke. Hush was just picking his head up and trying to clear his ringing ears when there was a second flash, this time from the direction of the toll booth, and another shower of debris rained against the concrete walls of the toll plaza. He got a photoflash glimpse of Powers, who appeared to be trying to reach China through the cement of the roadway. Then came a third blast, and then a fourth from right in front of them, each of them eye-searing pulses of unholy light punching out wave fronts of heat and ear-lancing pressure. Hush flattened down beside Powers and tried to make himself small as the barrage continued, blast after blast, enveloping them in a cloud of concrete dust, shattered plastic, and metal fragments of the pay phones as each of them detonated down the line into pulverized bits. Hush felt like a piece of meat going through a food processor.

When at last the explosions stopped, Hush opened one eye and promptly sneezed in the cloud of cement dust. He thought he could hear shouts, but they seemed to be very far away. He realized he had been holding his breath. He gasped in some more air, then immediately erupted into a coughing fit that hurt his chest. Powers was getting up on his hands and knees beside Hush, his eyes dark and round in a mimelike mask of cement dust. Small circles of light from several flashlights above them were bobbing around the ground.

"Got any more goddamned good ideas?" Hush rasped at him, spitting out bits of cement.

The pitometer log reading on the console displayed the ship's speed in red octal numbers in a quivering digital display. The *Cairo* passed through twelve knots, then thirteen. He adjusted the wheel again, using less rudder now. She was definitely getting cocked across the current, but it still didn't matter. He looked up as he heard a series of urgent whistle blasts coming from downriver. The distant tug's captain was indicating a danger signal as he saw the big ship accelerating diagonally across the channel. He found the brass handle for the ship's whistle. He pulled it several times. The phone stopped ringing.

Four hundred yards. Dead on for the pier tower. The tops of the bridge began to disappear in the upper parts of the bridge windows.

There was an excited hammering behind him as someone tried to get out onto the pilothouse. He checked the wheel one more time and then settled it amidships. Still dead on, with the grayish white concrete pier tower clearly centered in the bridge windows. The digital readout showed 13.5 knots. He jerked out several more blasts on the ship's whistle, then stepped back, all the way back to the pilothouse door, anticipating what would happen next.

Three hundred yards. Nine hundred feet, and closing fast. The bottoms of the bridge decks were no longer visible. Just the swelling image of the pier tower.

He saw a blur of movement by the door leading out to the port bridge wing. He didn't hesitate, pointing the .45 to his left and firing two rounds. All the glass exploded out of the door's window. A man yelled outside.

Two hundred yards, and still dead on. Fifteen knots. Full-load displacement of eight thousand tons. With the current, they would hit at seventeen, maybe eighteen knots. The pier tower was filling all the windows now, and then she hit, sooner than he had expected. He had forgotten that most of the ship, over one hundred yards of it, was in front of him. He just barely had time to grab the door handle as the ship thundered into the pier tower in a prolonged, earsplitting crash of rending steel and exploding concrete. He saw two of the forward hatch cranes tumble down onto the deck in a tangle of cables even as he fought to stay upright. The helmsman on the deck cried out as he rolled sharply up against the base of the console. The other two men slid rapidly across the waxed tiles of the deck, fetching up against the forward bulkhead. Lighting fixtures and ceiling tiles crashed down out of the overhead and the pilothouse was suddenly filled with dust. The front end of the ship dissolved in slow motion as the pier tower tore into her bow and crunched aft for nearly a hundred feet before forward motion finally ceased. He could feel that her engine was still going full ahead, so her stern began to swing rapidly to his left, causing a horrible grinding noise as the wrecked bow began to pivot around the pier tower embedded in the ship's guts.

The center span of the bridge came down as he started to move away from the door toward the starboard side. An enormous avalanche of crashing steel thundered down onto the ship just forward of amidships, knocking him completely off his feet as the ship heeled hard down to starboard and then reeled back the other way. All of the windows along the front of the pilothouse imploded at once as the superstructure deformed. The span broke its back across the ship's fore decks, and then the two segments slid off on either side in a maelstrom of wreckage that arrested the ship's swing. Overhead, the ship's whistle bellowed out a continuous howl of protest, like some mortally wounded prehistoric beast.

When the ship stopped rocking, he climbed back to his feet, grabbed the small bag wedged by the chart table, and ran through the door on the starboard bridge wing, careening off the bulkhead and then the cat-walk railing as the ship lurched over to starboard again. Even from this height, he could feel her movements getting heavy, and he sensed he was running slightly uphill as he scrambled aft and down the outside ladders.

By the time he made it to the main deck, the ship was truly dead in the water, wedged diagonally across the center channel by the tangle of the wrecked center span on either side, and going down by the bow as her forward holds filled. The pier tower was off to starboard now, a great black notch cut twenty feet into its base. The ship's main deck forward was almost awash. He heard shouts from inside the ship's superstructure, and then there was a whoosh of white smoke out of the single stack as the main engine was shut down by an emergency shutoff system. The ship's whistle continued to sound, drowning out the rumble of sounds coming from inside the dying ship.

He ran forward along the main deck through a cloud of mist and dust, hugging the starboard lifelines, clambering over the wreckage of the cargo cranes, whose thick grease-covered black cables were tangled all over the deck like monstrous snakes, until he made it to the platform of the pilot's accommodation ladder. There he scrambled through the lifeline chains, then ran down the steep steps as fast as he could. The ladder swayed dangerously, as it was no longer married to the sheer steel sides of the ship. When he reached the waterline, he heard shouts above him, looked over his shoulder, and saw three or four white faces up by the platform. He snapped off three more rounds and heard the sounds of ricochets spanging away into the night at the top of the ladder. The faces disap-peared.

At the bottom of the ladder, there should have been another platform, but it was already submerged as the ship listed to starboard and settled by the bow. The river pilot's ladder, which normally sloped backward at a forty-five-degree angle on the ship's starboard side, was becoming more and more horizontal. There was a strong stink of diesel fuel in the water, and he could hear the huge tangle of steel piled up around the bow cracking and settling.

He threw the pistol into the river. Using a knife, he quickly cut off his pants and shirt and threw them away. Then he pulled off the rubber Clinton mask, put on the diver's face mask and flippers, clamped his teeth down on the breathing cartridge's mouthpiece, and jumped into the oily black water. He took a final bearing on the pier tower, then submerged, holding his two hands straight out before him like a diver and kicking hard with his flippers to get away from the ship. He could hear through his rubber headgear the rumbling and banging sounds as the forward bulkheads in the ship began to collapse behind him. He kicked hard, desperate not to get entangled in the bridge wreckage.

Hush got to his feet, but none too steadily. Powers sat back on his haunches for a moment as he batted debris out of his face and hair. Hush looked through the lingering dust cloud at the opposite wall. Where the bank of pay phones had been were now only black blotches of gouged concrete all in a line. He shook his clothes out and nearly fell down. He still couldn't hear anything very well. Then there was a crowd of men around him, holding him up by his arms, telling him to sit back down. A couple of medics arrived to work them over, but he was pretty sure he was not really injured. Powers was staring at his left hand, which was bleeding copiously. Hush tried to figure out how he'd missed seeing that, but then a medic was dabbing at his own face and he felt stings and could see black smears on the gauze. He felt a trickle of blood coming from his right ear and running down his shirt collar. Inanely, he wondered if it was going to show. Then one of the FBI men pushed through the crowd.

"Director Hanson, we have an emergency transmission!"

Hush could barely hear the man, even though he was visibly excited and standing two feet in front of him.

"Go ahead," he said. His own voice sounded far away. Powers was staring at him, looking like a panda, with a "Now what?" expression on his face.

"Baton Rouge, sir. They got the bridge in Baton Rouge. With a god-damned ship!"

The current almost got the better of him. He was swimming hard but nearly blind, aiming to get well downstream of the pier tower and over into the calmer water closer to the Louisiana banks. All he had to do was get out of the main channel and then let the current carry him down to the abandoned fuel pier and the boat. The river patrols should all be converging on the sinking ship.

The breathing tube gave him ten, maybe fifteen minutes of air so he could remain almost entirely submerged. But he had forgotten about the eddies that formed around large objects in a current, and he felt himself being captured by some powerful underwater force. He was pulled first one way, then another, and he realized he was probably being sucked into a small whirlpool behind the pier tower on the downstream side. Determined not to panic, he surfaced and stopped struggling. He cleared his mask and looked around. He'd gone the wrong way. The gray mass of the concrete pier tower was right alongside, lined with telephone pole–size wooden pilings as buffers against minor collisions. The pilings on the upstream side had been snapped and swept away by the ship collision, and there was a great gouge torn out of the concrete face about thirty feet up. There were bits of shattered steel plates and some girders from the ship's bow still impaled on the stumps of the wooden pilings. The ship itself was about two hundred feet away now, its head almost submerged in the channel, its whistle still blowing into the night. The small Coast Guard cutter had gone alongside to get people off, just as he had anticipated. The ship had settled sufficiently into the river that the crew was able to step off the main deck onto the cutter. The wreckage of the center span was no longer visible, at least not from his very low vantage point.

He felt himself being swept down the channel side of the pier tower, where he could see a visible bow wave rising on the upstream face from the current. Instead of trying to get out of the current, he swam across and into it, toward the nearest wooden pole, which he grabbed just in time to keep from being swept around to the back side of the tower, where a nasty whirlpool was sucking air with a vicious sound. He then pulled himself hand over hand back upstream, working steadily but conserving his energy, until he reached the first of the snapped pilings. He rested for a moment, actually feeling a little bit too warm in his wet suit, and looked back out at the ship.

Details were difficult in the darkness, but he could see the white hull of the cutter backing away frantically as the ship heeled farther to starboard and settled on down to the bottom of the river. Her entire main deck went out of sight in a boil of trapped air, but the white superstructure remained visible, tilting out of the water from about one deck above the main deck. All her lights surged briefly and then went out, and the whistle finally subsided. As he watched, he could see the cutter close back in toward the leaning superstructure, where there were probably some more of the crew stranded. One of the big river tugs came around her stern and nosed in to assist with the pickup. He heard a succession of whistle signals downstream as another tug with a full barge string pushing ahead began to maneuver to stop now that the channel was blocked.

He spat out the expended breathing tube and took several breaths of air in preparation for what he had to do next. He would launch from the base of the pier tower and swim hard upstream and then out to the left, hopefully getting out of the eddy system around the tower and into the calmer waters closer to the Louisiana banks. All he would have to do then would be to drift down, swimming as little or as much as he wanted to, until he came abeam of the abandoned fuel piers. After that, he would have the boat and could make his escape downriver.

A wave of cool air swept over the river, followed by a flash of lightning and a quick crack of thunder. Perfect, he thought. Once it started raining, he and his rubber boat would be invisible out here. He looked straight up to see if there was anyone out on the bridge above him, but he could not see that well in the darkness. The shock of the collision had apparently just completely dismounted the center span, because there was no wreckage dangling over the edge a hundred or so feet above him. He had also managed to catch the bridge without a train. Oh, well. They'd have enough problems with that freighter sunk in the main shipping channel.

Thebes, St. Louis, Memphis, and now Baton Rouge. One, two, three, four, in not quite military order. That left Vicksburg and New Orleans. But first, he had to get to the boat. He took a deep breath and pushed off into the surging current.

12

IT TOOK THEM just under two hours to run the 150 miles from Vicksburg to Baton Rouge in Powers's cruiser. Little Hill had turned his blue lights on and gone flying down the Delta's Route 61 like the proverbial bat out of hell, chased by the lightning flashes of an approaching front all the way. Hush had been on a secure radio most of the time, keeping in touch with the CP at Vicksburg, which, in turn, was in contact with the Coast Guard Marine Safety Center at Baton Rouge. The focus there was to get all the crew off the stricken ship and then to deal with the immediate snarl in barge traffic, not to mention two seagoing ships that had been ordered to anchor south of Baton Rogue.

Their own injuries were painful but superficial, with the possible exception of Hush's hearing. Powers was sporting a bulky bandage over his left hand, and Hush had several sticking plasters on his face and head. He had given urgent orders to the FBI team at the bridge to trace the call to the pay phone via the Vicksburg telephone company's central office. Powers was still sure it was going to be a cell phone, but Hush thought they might be able to find out *whose* cell phone. The Columbus EOD team had arrived as they were leaving. Their leader, a burly, red-faced captain, wanted to know what the hell the two of them had been doing down there, and Hush had invited an embarrassed Powers to please tell the man.

They arrived in Baton Rouge at 2:00 A.M. and went directly to the city end of the railroad bridge, from which they were able to get a clear view of the disaster out on the river. The bridge had what was by now a sickeningly familiar look: a great gap out in the middle where the center span had been. The superstructure of a sunken ship lay just upstream of the bridge, square in the center of the channel, surrounded by Coast Guard boom boats that were trying to contain her leaking fuel oil. Hush had been told that the ship was the eight-thousand-ton SS *Cairo,* but it looked much diminished out there in the river. There was the usual crowd of state police and military vehicles at the base of the bridge. The Resident Agent of the Baton Rouge office, one Charles Rafael LeBourgoise, met their car. LeBourgoise appeared to be close to retirement age. His tanned face was deeply lined and he was completely bald. He and Hush had run across each other before, but Hush had not seen him for several years.

"Look at this mess," Hush said, staring out over the river. "How the hell did he get control of a *ship?*"

"Apparently, he just walked aboard at the terminal," LeBourgoise said wearily. He had been up since the initial report came through the Bureau's communications system, and he was bleary-eyed. "The first anyone saw of him on the ship was when he showed up in the pilothouse in a funny face mask with a forty-five in his hand."

"And then?" Powers asked.

"Well, we've had only a quick interview with the master and the river pilot. But apparently he made the pilothouse crew—that's just three people—get down on the deck. Then rang up full speed and steered her into the far pier tower over there. Hit it hard enough to dislodge the center span."

"Son of a bitch," Hush said, shaking his head. "Anyone killed or injured?"

"On the ship, there were some engineers hurt in the collision; a couple of burns cases and some broken limbs. But no one was killed, and they're pretty sure they got everybody off before she went down. Those small freighters don't carry a big crew. The master said the bow was smashed in all the way back to the second hold. No way to save her."

"And on the bridge?"

"Security people saw her coming; everybody scrambled. They said someone was laying on the ship's whistle before she hit. There was no train this time, fortunately."

"And what happened to our bad guy?"

"He was seen going down the river pilot's boarding ladder. Two deckhands saw him, but then he popped three rounds up the ladder and they lost interest."

"And then what? A waiting boat?"

"We don't know. No one saw a boat. The river pilot thought he saw the guy in the water, but by then the ship was going down and they had bigger problems on their hands. It was dark, the ship's whistle was going full blast, and nobody could shut it off. Then a compressed-air line let go on the main deck and deafened everybody out there. By that time, nobody gave a shit what had happened to the bad guy. They were lucky to get the people off."

"And just one guy, right?" Powers asked. "No helpers?"

LeBourgoise wiped his gleaming head with his hand. "Listening to them," he replied, "the whole deal went down pretty quick. They only *saw* one guy. Pilot said he had what looked like a wet suit hood on under his ball cap. But mostly what they were looking at was that 1911 M one A one government-model forty-five."

"Those do tend to get your attention," Powers said.

"One guy," Hush said. "Full speed ahead and then hang on, Sloopy."

"You're dating yourself," Powers said with a grin.

"Like I said, good news is that there wasn't a train," LeBourgoise said. "Bad news is that there aren't going to be any trains for a while, not on this bridge."

Another flash of lightning turned night into black-and-white day out over the river, revealing a great wall of rain coming toward them. Everyone scattered to their vehicles. Powers, LeBourgoise, and Hush piled into Powers's cruiser just as the squall line hit. For a few moments, no one could hear anything because of the pounding rain, but then the noise began to subside. LeBourgoise, looking at their bandages, asked Hush what had happened up at Vicksburg, and Hush filled him in. He said the people on the scene in Vicksburg were still trying to figure out how the string of small bombs had been set off; the bridge had not been damaged, though.

"You guys were pretty damn lucky," LeBourgoise said. "But what was the point of all that?"

"I think it was supposed to be a distraction. As soon as the word got down here that the Vicksburg bridge had been hit, it would have been natural for the security forces at this bridge to relax a bit."

"We did get that word," LeBourgoise said. "But by then, the guys on the bridge saw the ship coming. He screwed up his timing."

The bulk of the squall passed and they could see the lights out across the river again. "Tracing that call will probably get us nowhere," Hush said. "But now we know something we only suspected: We're after a lone ranger."

"He still could have had help," LeBourgoise said. "Getting on the ship and then, later, getting off."

"What, with a submarine? I don't think so, Rafe. But for now, let's start with how he got aboard that ship, and where."

"Probably right where she ties up, at the Baton Rouge marine terminal," LeBourgoise said. He pointed through the front window. "Over there, around that bend where all those quartz lights are. That's the main ship terminal. That's where the *Cairo* sails from."

"All right, let's get that place sealed. Then canvass the whole world up there—what they saw, when, where. Check all the vehicles. Then the surrounding neighborhood, if there is one." He looked over at the older man, who was listening patiently. "Hell, Rafe, what am I saying? You know the drill."

The RA nodded politely. Hush realized he was being somewhat formal around Hush because Powers was there. Powers said he would contact Louisiana authorities and coordinate state police assistance.

"And then I'd like to interview the people who were in the pilothouse of that ship myself," Hush said. "They're the first witnesses we've had who've actually seen this guy."

"They took them downtown to the city hospital for observation," LeBourgoise said. "We'll get 'em over to the office in the morning. And I can show you the initial interviews. You really think this is just one guy?"

"Well, people saw him tonight, right?"

"Yeah, but simultaneous bombs up where you were? A getaway into the river at night? That sounds like more than one guy to me." He reached into his coat pocket. "Oh. Almost forgot. This came for you."

He handed over a Teletype, which Hush opened. He sighed audibly.

"What?" asked Powers.

"Hate mail. The deputy director's coming out tomorrow morning." He looked at his watch. "Today, I guess. Gets in at around noon."

"Lucky you," Powers said with a wry smile. LeBourgoise was studying the back of the seat in front of him. His relief that Hanson would be there to entertain the visiting firemen from Washington was palpable.

"Yeah," Hush said. "Lucky me."

"Mr. Hanson," LeBourgoise said, "we've made arrangements at the

Holiday Inn downtown. Might I suggest that you guys get some sleep? If you'll forgive my saying so, you both look like hell."

"Yeah, buddy," Powers said. "I feel worse than I look."

Hush thought he saw Little Hill break a tiny smile. "I suppose," he said absently. There really was nothing more that he could do here. The Baton Rouge squad had their work cut out for them. Right now an assistant director would definitely just be in the way. He glanced in the car's mirror. Powers was right: He looked bad and felt worse.

Major Matthews was sound asleep in the command car's bunk room when the duty corporal shook him awake. He had a flashlight in his hand and Matthews was blinded by the sudden white light.

"Sir. Sir? We got high-precedence message traffic. Sir?"

"Okay, okay. What time is it?"

"Zero two hundred, Friday morning, sir."

"Okay, I'm coming," Matthews said, rolling out of his covers. The car's air conditioning, especially at night, kept the bunk room at a steady fifty degrees. He shivered as he pulled on his uniform trousers and boots, and then he went out to the communications console. Half the MPs were out on detail, walking the perimeter around the train, which was sidelined in north Birmingham on a double spur line. The corporal was on watch at the communications module, while the rest of the security detail slept in the next car's bunk room.

Matthews sat down at the console and focused his eyes on the screen. It displayed an operational-immediate precedence message from the operations center at Anniston. He keyed in his personal code and the message was displayed. It reported the destruction of the Baton Rouge railroad bridge.

"Whoa," he muttered. He read on. Train 2713SP was ordered to return to Anniston Depot at first light. Dispatch orders had been sent through the Norfolk Southern rail network to ensure route clearance back to Anniston. The window for eastbound dispatch was estimated between 0745 and 0915 this morning, although with the new traffic disruption, their exact departure time was unknown. He sat back and did the math. It was only about sixty miles back to Anniston, so if they made their window of opportunity for the line switch, they should be back before noon. The message said that revised route planning was in progress at the depot, with an estimated relaunch date Friday evening and the river crossing now slated for Vicksburg. He was directed to acknowledge the message personally. He typed in "Will comply" and his personal authentication code, then hit the send button.

"We goin' back, sir?" the corporal asked.

"Looks like it," Matthews said with a yawn. "For one day, anyway. Then we try again, this time via Vicksburg instead of Baton Rouge. Not too many bridges left out there, it seems."

He walked out to the back platform and looked around. It was considerably warmer outside. The lights of Brimingham twinkled over the trees to the south. They had been routed originally to the Boyles switchyard in east Birmingham, but at the last minute, traffic control had diverted the train to the northwest part of the city. It was now parked among the ruins of an abandoned steel mill, whose remains consisted of two parallel rows of twenty rusting chimneys, spaced on either side of a football field–size expanse of weed-covered concrete. The rusted-out shell of a diesel locomotive was parked nearby on the inboard track, and there were mounds of building rubble piled on top of concrete slabs whose rusting rebar stuck out like old bones. Behind the ruins was a small mountain of slag. He had watched with some concern as the train had been backed down the weed-choked siding, the ties rocking visibly under the weight and the rails protesting continuously. The gentle breeze blowing through the ruins smelled faintly of sulfur and rust.

Someone had put the train about as far out into the boonies as they could, which in a way, given its declared cargo, made sense. Looking forward, he could see the silhouettes of the patrolling MPs along the length of the train and hear their boots crunching in the oil-soaked gravel. The big engines up front were shut down except for one, which was idling to provide head-end electrical power to the containment systems and the two manned cars at the rear of the train. As he stepped back inside and headed for the bunk room, he thought about going out to take readings on the Russian weapons, then decided he almost did not want to know. Returning to Anniston, he decided, might be going backward in more ways than one.

Once out of the vortices around the pier tower, he had let the river do the work, carrying him downstream at a leisurely four knots and away from all the commotion up by the bridge. Two harbor police boats that he had *not* seen also went to the ship instead of scouring the surface of the water for him. He made it downstream to the fuel pier and retrieved the inflatable boat without incident. Now he was purring down the river below Baton Rouge at twenty knots, holding right out in the center of the channel to avoid being seen by night fishermen along the banks. His knew his rubber boat ought not to show up on radar, and that seemed to be the case when he zipped right by an upstream-bound river tug and its barge string. A big rain squall had obliterated the scene upriver.

Ten miles south of the interstate highway bridge, he turned the boat in toward the Baton Rouge side, aiming at a row of wooden pilings set into the river bottom along the east bank, where barge strings could be parked awaiting clearance to proceed upriver. There were eight darkened grain barges tied up to the pilings, in two lines of four. Their slab sides rose fifteen feet out of the water, indicating they were empty. He nosed the rubber boat into the shadows between the bluff, sloping bow of one and the flat stern of another. The engine made a suddenly loud racket as he entered the steel tunnel. He shut it down and coasted in to the inner line of barges, then out from under them to bump up against the pilings. The riverbank was ten feet away. Beyond the muddy banks and brush along the river, there was a county road, and a half a mile up that road was his pickup truck. Hopefully no one had stolen it.

He would sink the boat and the engine in the mud along the piers, wade ashore, and get to his truck. After a quick change into dry clothes, he would sleep in his truck until dawn. Then he would figure out where to go next. He was well out of the city and should also be beyond any highway cordons the police might have set up around Baton Rouge. If he did get stopped, he had a pretty good cover. I'll bet the FBI is going right the hell out of its mind about now, he thought as he slipped down into the water and then opened the boat's air valves.

Hush awoke to the sound of knocking on his door. He sat bolt upright in the bed and immediately regretted it. His body was hurting all over, and the bandages on his face felt like dead insects clamped to his skin.

"Just a minute," he croaked. He untangled himself from the sheets, got up, steadied himself for a moment, and then found his bathrobe. He slipped it on as he went to the door and looked through the peephole. To his surprise, he saw Carolyn Lang. He unlocked and opened the door.

"Jesus!" she gasped when she saw his face.

"Nope, just me," he said, squinting in the light. He had taken his watch off. From the light penetrating the closed drapes, he had clearly overslept. "What time is it?"

"Ten o'clock," she replied, still staring at his face, her hand at her mouth.

He swore. He had planned to be down at the Baton Rouge office by now, interviewing those ship's officers. "Come in," he said. His voice still sounded somewhat distant in his ears.

She entered the room, averting her eyes from his battered face. He limped over to the single chair in the room and dropped carefully into it. She sat down on the end of the bed.

"I guess I overslept," he said. "Aren't you early? I was told Heinrich was coming in at noon."

She pulled her skirt down over her legs. Despite his misgivings about what was going on in Washington, he still found her desirable. He thought briefly about the sexual harassment connotations of her sitting on his bed in his hotel room and tried to smile. It hurt his face. She saw him wince.

"What?" she asked.

"Nothing," he said. "I hurt. So where's the great man? And what the hell is going on back there?"

She hesitated. "Wellesley's not coming," she said finally. "There's been a change of plans since the bridge here was destroyed."

His head was beginning to throb and his mouth felt dry and slightly contaminated. She, on the other hand, looked perfectly delectable sitting on that bed. What had she just said? He tried to clear his ears to stop the ringing. It didn't work.

"I can't hear very well," he said. "Change of plans?"

"Yes. That's why I came to see you. The director has decided to turn full operational control of Trainman over to Carswell and the National Security Division. The director will remain in nominal command. Wellesley informed me late last night. I flew out first thing this morning."

He was wide awake now. "Let me get this straight: NS is in, IITF is out?"

"Yes. Carswell lodged a formal nonconcurrence with the thesis that a

216

lone individual is doing these bombings at the executive conference. They insist this has to be a new terrorist cell. The director now agrees."

"But that's nuts. Several people on that ship saw the one guy—"

"This all happened before the bridge here was knocked down," she interrupted. "But they've read the initial reports of the bombing here. They feel he may have been the only perp on that ship but that he had to have had help getting aboard, and even more help getting away."

"Based on what evidence, may I ask?"

She sighed. "I'm not sure; Heinrich was not in an explaining mode last night. Except—"

"Except what?"

"I have my own theory: It looks better if the Bureau is being whipped by a terrorist gang than by a single individual."

"Wellesley *said* that?"

"No, of course not. Not in so many words, anyway. Look, it was very late, and he was being deliberately ambiguous. Maybe they're hoping if they say that, the guy will finally claim. Truly, I just don't know."

He considered the ramifications of what she had just told him. If NS had the case, J. Kenneth Carswell would surely not be asking for his help. He and IITF were now officially out in the cold.

"This isn't the way Heinrich laid it out for me," Hush said. His ears were ringing harder now, and his head was beginning to throb.

"I did ask him if there were any administrative reasons why they were doing this," she said. She looked away for a moment, and then back at him. "I think this goes back to that question I asked you back in my house. Do you remember?"

He thought back. Yes, of course he did. She had asked about any underlying maneuvers affecting her. Something that might have come out of his meeting with the director. And he had ducked it. He nodded carefully.

She cocked her head. "Wellesley said they were making the changeover for two reasons, both having to do with *you*. He said first and foremost it was for lack of results, and second, because you did not 'take care of business.' He said you could explain that last bit to me."

"Did he really," Hush said.

"He's giving you a fig leaf: the fact that you were injured last night in Vicksburg. The initial reports about what happened at Vicksburg were . . . very alarming. As is your face."

"I appreciate your collective concern."

She sighed again and leaned back on the bed, her hands behind her. Her posture did interesting things to her figure, but Hush had other things on his mind.

"I'd like to ask that question again," Carolyn said. "About your meeting with the director. I want to know what Heinrich meant by your not 'taking care of business.'"

Suddenly, Hush was tired of all this. Last night, he had been damn near killed at the toll plaza, and now his head was pounding, his body ached, and he'd just been told that he had, for all practical purposes, been fired off the most important case the Bureau had had in years. He didn't know if Carolyn was involved in all this, but, if not, she had a right to know what had been going on.

"Okay," he said wearily. "But please remember, you did ask." He stopped to take a breath and gather his thoughts. There she sat in all her splendor, and here he was, looking like someone who had been in a bad bar fight.

"Your instincts were correct," he said. "We did talk about you, and your appointment to the task force. Rather, they talked and I listened. Somewhat in amazement, I should add."

"And?"

"The director began by saying you had been something of a thorn in the Bureau's side."

"That's hardly news."

"Well, the 'business' was that, beyond catching this guy, I was given some additional tasking. I was supposed to create an opportunity for you to fall on your face. In which case, they could say they had given you a chance to shine but you'd blown it. Then they could, in good conscience, invite you to leave the Bureau."

She nodded slowly. "In good conscience. Right. And then let me guess: If this worked, your temporary appointment to AD would become permanent?"

She was everything the director had said she was, he thought. "That's right."

She just stared at him. Her expression was not pleasant. "So you lied to me," she said. "Back there in Alexandria."

"No," he said, shaking his head, and then grunting at the lance of pain that went down his neck. "I simply decided not to tell you. Truth was, after I had met you and worked with you, I considered it a childish conspiracy, and, quite frankly, beneath our mutual contempt. So I decided to ignore it. I guess now that was a mistake."

"How do you mean?"

"I'm out of the Trainman investigation. You're still in."

She looked away and took a deep breath. "There's a deputy from NS, Wilson McFarland, due in at noon. We'll meet with the LeBourgoise and his people here in Baton Rouge, and then we'll go back to Washington."

"Like I said, you're still a player. You won."

"Won what, for Christ sake?" Her eyes were flashing with anger.

He got up slowly, trying not to stagger, and went over to the window. He pulled back the drapes, grunting again as a flood of bright sunlight assaulted his eyes. He realized his hands and his knees were also sore, courtesy no doubt of his efforts to make like a prairie dog in the toll plaza concrete. He found himself holding on to the curtains.

"Well, there was an interesting catch," he said, keeping his back to her. "The director said that, past considerations aside, he felt that you and I were of equal professional value to the Bureau. That, as senior agents, we were probably of equal competence."

"I still don't get it." She was standing now, as well.

"He said that whichever one of us survived this case would get promoted." Hush turned around. "So I guess congratulations are in order."

Her eyes widened and she started to say something, but apparently she couldn't find the words. Then she looked down at her watch. "I . . . I think I'd better go."

"You do that," he said. He felt drained, physically and mentally.

Not giving her a chance to say anything more, he limped past her into the bathroom and tried not to slam the door too hard. He ran water into the sink and bent down to look at his face for the first time. Jesus, he thought. No wonder she hadn't wanted to look at him. He resisted an impulse to bang his forehead against the mirror.

An hour and a long, hot shower later, Hush was dressed and waiting for the room service attendant to lay out his breakfast. He had tried to reach Powers earlier, but they said he had already checked out. He was finishing his breakfast when the phone rang.

"Mr. Hanson, this is Special Agent Mike Carney in St. Louis. We got your number from the Baton Rouge RA. We got a call here this morning from one of our retired guys man named McDougal. Would it be okay if I give him your number there at the hotel? He said he needed to talk to you."

"Sure," Hush said. McDougal. As he hung up, he tried to remember where he had heard that name.

He thought about what to do next. He probably ought to check in with Tyler Redford to see what rumors were circulating around headquarters. He really, really did not want to call into the Baton Rouge office. He could just hear the reaction: Whoever answered the phone would clamp his hand over the mouthpiece and say, Hey, it's Hanson, you know, the AD that just got fired off the Trainman case? He wants to know if we have anything for him to do. Unfortunately, those were the facts. He might as well check out and go back to Washington. The phone rang. This must be McDougal, he thought. But it wasn't.

"Mr. Hanson, this is Rafe LeBourgoise."

"Good morning—I suppose."

"Well, yes. Or maybe no, I guess."

"You've heard."

"Of course. That's why I'm calling. I've received some instructions from Deputy Director Wellesley."

"Give me a minute to get some Vaseline and assume the position."

LeBourgoise laughed. "They want you to take some convalescent leave. The Jackson people apparently painted a pretty dramatic picture of what happened up there at the bridge. Senior Special Agent Lang came in here this morning and said you looked like a walking train wreck. She's apparently passed this on to Washington."

"Rafe, it's not all that bad. I'm up and operating. Dressed even. All by myself."

"Yeah, well, actually, they've *put* you on convalescent leave."

"I was thinking I might just go back to D.C.," Hush said.

LeBourgoise cleared his throat. "I got the distinct impression that they'd prefer you *not* show your face in D.C. just now," he said. "Nothing personal mind you, but the thrust of it was that headquarters would deny any 'he got fired' rumors, but it would be a lot easier to do that if you were elsewhere in the field."

This was the fig leaf Carolyn had been talking about. "Rafe," he said.

"Yeah, Hush, I know. Palace games. Tell me something—I heard Hank McDougal is trying to reach you."

Nothing gets by a good RA, Hush thought to himself. "That's right. I'm expecting his call."

"Listen to him, Hush. I think he can put a spin on all this that might clarify some things."

"Rafe, my head hurts and my ass is dragging. Speak English."

"You've been in D.C. a long time, Hush. Maybe too long. We snuffies out here in the provinces watch what goes on in Fun City and thank our lucky stars we're stuck out here in the field just now. My advice? Listen to Hank McDougal's story. Then go down to Baptist Memorial Hospital—that's our current provider—and get yourself checked out. I'll send a car around. When you're done, call me."

"In other words, put my ugly head down for the moment."

"You're assuming it's still attached, Hush. But, yes, that's the general idea."

"Where's Powers?"

"The Missouri state guy? He went back to Vicksburg."

"Does he know, too?"

LeBourgoise snorted. "You know how word gets out. He said you had the number for his cell phone. The car will be downstairs in a half hour. We've got bigger problems out in the river at the moment."

"What now?"

"That ship was carrying rice. All the holds are flooded."

"And?"

"Water and rice, Hush."

"Oh. Wow."

"Yeah, wow. I'll talk to you later."

Hush hung up and went in to brush his teeth. He did not want to go to any hospital; on the other hand, it might be the wise thing to do. It wasn't as if he had a full dance card this morning. The phone was ringing when he came out.

"Hanson," he growled.

"Mr. Hanson, this is Hank McDougal. You don't know me, sir, but I've been following this case you're honchoing."

So everyone doesn't know, Hanson thought. He sat down on the bed. Carolyn's perfume lingered in the air. "Yes, Mr. McDougal?"

"I used to work for Himself Herlihy in St. Louis. Maybe he mentioned me."

Now Hush remembered the name. "Yes. You were on track for the ASAC job, and then something went wrong."

"What went wrong was a carefully planned operation involving your former task force deputy, Carolyn Lang."

Okay, Hush thought. Time to pay attention. "Former?"

"I've been following the case on the network news. First there was an IITF task force, with you in charge. Then there was a split command, with you in the field, and Lang featured prominently on all the television stations in D.C. The bridges keep dropping, and then the director announces he's assuming direct control over the case, and now, assuming CNN has its facts straight, J. Kenneth Carswell and the NS gang are in charge."

"I guess I can't comment on that, Mr. McDougal."

"I understand, Mr. Hanson. I'm just another retiree now; my current security clearance is for air mail. But let me ask you something: Did anybody warn you about Carolyn Lang?"

"Warn me?"

"Yes, sir. Warn you. As in watch yourself around her?"

Hush tried to think of what to say. His head was still pounding. McDougal interpreted his silence as a yes.

"Well, you should have listened. Just like I should have listened. Because Carolyn Lang is not the problematic little women's libber everybody makes her out to be."

"Meaning?"

"Carolyn Lang is the director's own personal hit *person,* Mr. Hanson. She works directly for him and, indirectly, for Wellesley. You must have wondered why your acting appointment to AD never got confirmed, haven't you?"

"Well—"

"Well, nothing. This director has a list. He doesn't want holdovers from the last regime as his SES people. Just like he doesn't want holdovers getting in as ASACs, from which they might logically go on to become SACs. He wants his *own* people in all those positions of power."

Hush closed his eyes. He did not want to hear the rest of this.

"And if the individuals on his list can't be caught consorting with barnyard animals, he uses indirect means. One of those is Carolyn Lang, who, one way or another, sees to it that obstacles to the director's master personnel plan are removed. Then someone from his private appointments list appears magically as the replacement."

"That's what happened to you in St. Louis?"

"Yes, and that's what's just happened to you."

Hush was stunned. Now he understood what Himself Herlihy had been talking about. But could it be it true?

"You're wondering if I can prove this," McDougal said. "And, of course, I can't. Not directly. But you're still an acting AD, right? Call in some favors. Go check on her assignments record. Then see if anything happened to the senior or second senior guy in her office right after she left."

Hush couldn't think of what to say. McDougal filled in the silence.

"You're known as one of the good guys, Mr. Hanson. Problem is, ever since that thing in Baltimore, you've been a Washington headquarters guy."

"Baltimore," Hush said. Domingo, Herrera, Santos, and Belim. His ghost mantra.

McDougal laughed. "Someone says Hush Hanson, everyone remembers Baltimore. Four bad guys head-shot and two about to-be-dead agents alive and kicking when the smoke cleared. But ever since then, you've been a policy guy, not a field guy. Right?"

"That's correct," Hush whispered.

"The accepted wisdom is that's because you're a decent guy who was afraid he'd get to like gunning bad guys. But this time, it was you in the gun sights. You've been mouse-trapped by a real pro. As someone who's been there, I just thought it was time someone came right out and told you."

Hush was at a complete loss for words. "I don't know what to say, Mr. McDougal," he said.

"You could say thank you."

"Yes, I guess I could. Thank you—I think."

McDougal gave a short, bitter laugh. "Now you know the real reason we called her Razor Pants," he said. "Check it out. And good luck, Mr. Hanson."

• • •

He woke up to the sounds of a chain saw going in the woods nearby. His eyes felt sandy after only five hours of sleep, but apparently no one had spotted him sleeping in the truck. He started up, drove onto the county road, and then headed in toward Baton Rouge. He assumed that any roadblocks would be set up to catch someone coming out of the city, not going in. In the event, there weren't any roadblocks. He crossed the river on the interstate bridge and then drove north up a state highway into Arkansas. By noon, he finally felt safe enough to return to the interstate.

He took some satisfaction in getting through the fourth bridge, but he knew his successes could not last. It was only a matter of time before the FBI figured out the real motive behind the attacks. He toyed with the idea of firing off a quick terrorist letter in the name of some weird group, just to delay the inevitable, but the Bureau would probably see through that at this juncture. As he headed north, he mulled over his next move. After last night, there were only two bridges left: Vicksburg and New Orleans. His freedom of movement had to be narrowing down. He might not ever get to finish it. Based on what he could glean from the radio news, the security efforts were being doubled and redoubled. It was almost time to decide: keep the masquerade going until he knew beyond a shadow of a doubt that they were closing in on him, or go off the grid and try for one more bridge. His escape route was ready.

If he did decide to bolt, there was one niggling little loose end he would like to take care of. They were saying they could have the Frisco Bridge back in operation in three more days. He wondered if they could do it. He'd achieved what he wanted: severe enough damage to render the bridge useless for trains. He had not expected them to mount a herculean effort to put the bridge back in service. Which meant he needed to revisit the Memphis bridge. The question was, How close was the FBI to identifying him? Did he still have another day or so? It was going to be much tougher to finish the job once they'd forced him underground.

Right now, he wanted a shower, a shave, and some decent sleep. But if they hadn't figured it out yet, he might be able to fix the problem at Memphis and still have enough time to get back to his river place to prepare for the final phase. Or should he just quit?

Going round and round here, he thought. He rubbed his eyes to get the road back in focus. He was definitely getting tired. The familiar image of all those smug railroad lawyers smiling condescendingly at him that last day in court stiffened his resolve. Hell with it, he thought. I've already hurt them. Go finish off the Frisco Bridge, and then attack the one at Vicksburg. New Orleans would probably be too hard if he was on the run. But Vicksburg, remote Vicksburg, that would still be feasible, especially the way he planned to do it. He picked up the car phone and placed a call to the Corps of Engineers office in St. Louis. The main operator answered. He asked for his secretary, June Wheeler.

"Right away, Colonel Keeler," the operator replied.

Hush let himself back into his hotel room at 4:30 Friday afternoon after spending some tedious hours at the hospital. For all their efforts, he felt little better, although he was now sporting fewer bandages. He also had some pain pills, about which the pharmacist had warned him in no uncertain terms: "Don't drink, don't drive, and don't try to do anything athletic or accountable once you take one." Hush was looking forward to trying one. The good news was that all the damage looked worse than it was.

The hotel message system told him there was a fax waiting for him at the front desk. He sent for it while he took off his suit coat and tie. Before going to the hospital, he had reached Tyler Redford, who had confirmed that there was all sorts of *sturm und drang* whirling about the Trainman case, with lots of rumors flying about senior officers being removed and entire divisions being under the gun. Human Resources had issued leave papers, which indicated that *Senior Agent* W. M Hanson would be on authorized convalescent sick leave for the next ten days, per the direction of the deputy director. Not Assistant Director Hanson, Hush had noted. Redford tried to be polite about that, but there was no getting around Hush's growing radioactivity. He reported that Carolyn Lang was getting a great deal of visibility in the case, still appearing on television and now spending a lot of time with Carswell's division.

Hush had then asked Redford for a huge favor. He asked if Redford's wife could get a list of Carolyn Lang's duty assignments for the past ten years, and then to see if she could find out if there had been any senior people at any of those offices who had been replaced with someone from Washington under any sort of unusual circumstances at or around the time of Lang's departure. He cited the case of Senior Agent Hank McDougal in the St. Louis office. When Redford wanted to know what this was all about, Hush simply told him that the less he knew, the safer he would be. Redford, an experienced Washington hand, had stopped asking questions. Hush had then gone off to the hospital.

Upon return, Hush took one of the capsules and then washed his face very carefully. A bellhop brought up the sealed fax. It was a no-fingerprints report, obviously computer-generated. The first page gave a chronological listing of Senior Agent C. B. Lang's postings with the Bureau for the past ten years, culminating with her assignment to Public and Congressional Affairs at headquarters after the St. Louis posting. The first thing Hush noticed was that there were a lot of places, six postings in ten years, almost three times what the average agent might expect. The second and third pages listed everyone at civil service grade fourteen or higher at each of her duty stations. These typically included the SAC, the ASAC, and one or more supervisory-special agents. The fourth page had what he was looking for: At each of Lang's duty stations before the PCA posting, one of the senior people had retired within sixty days prior to or immediately after her departure. The fifth page was even more interesting: Of those retirees, only one had apparently retired at end of career; the others were all listed as "personal request—unprogrammed."

He put the report down for a moment. "Personal request—unprogrammed" was the headquarters personnel division code for someone being allowed to retire in lieu of some other, more unpleasant alternative. Five out of six. He looked at the report again. The last five out of the six, in fact. McDougal was the last name on the list. The final page had a list of transfer assignments as people were moved to fill in behind the unexpected retirements. As McDougal had predicted, all the replacements had come from FBI headquarters.

He put the report down, rubbed his eyes, and listened to the ringing in his ears. He could still feel those pulsing explosions at the toll plaza, and relive the sense of utter helplessness he had felt during that short but intense barrage. Redford had surely figured out exactly what Hush was after once he'd seen the pattern of Lang's assignments. Now Hush had some more questions, but, given the superheated atmosphere back at headquarters over the Trainman case, he couldn't ask Tyler to go out on a long limb again.

He looked through the report again. However circumstantial, the bare statistics were pretty interesting. He wondered if she always used a sexual gambit or whether she had a larger bag of tricks. He thought back to that

Sunday afternoon on the chaise. He wondered what might have happened if he'd gone further. The image of a snapping trap came to mind.

But the basic mistake had been his. She and her handlers had seized on the opportunity created by his flight out to Memphis, an opportunity enhanced by his decision to leave her at headquarters. A decision, he remembered now, approved by the director. Then all it would have taken would have been a steady low-key drumbeat of handwringing criticism pointing out the obvious: The investigation was getting nowhere and the bridges were still dropping. Couple that with some casually poisonous chumming within earshot of the other assistant directors—in the hallway after task force meetings, say—and the sharks would gather quickly. And he had walked right into it. What had she called him "a consummate Washington operator"? Oh, right—*that* consummate Washington operator, the one flopping on the cleaning board just now.

He felt a sudden wave of drowsiness, then remembered the pill. He got undressed and went to bed for some of that convalescent leave. Tomorrow would be Saturday. He was weighing the idea of just going home to his place in the valley. Let the Trainman firestorm sort itself out. It certainly had enough high-priced help working on it.

Relaxing on his back on the cool, clean sheets, he watched as massive bronze thunderheads began to extinguish the afternoon sunlight coming through the window. He flushed again with the embarrassment of not having seen this coming, of having taken Wellesley at his word that their target was Lang. "Trust me." Sure, Snake, I'll trust you. They had played him like a true fish: offered him command of a field investigation, planted their long-legged career assassin on his staff, told him that if he could orchestrate her taking a fall, they'd approve his permanent appointment as an assistant director. And now here he was, flat on his doped-to-the-gills ass in a Holiday Inn in beautiful downtown Baton Rouge, while the rest of his world went frothing and baying after the Trainman. Actually, he realized, they weren't. Helped along by the drone of the air conditioner, his eyelids gained sudden weight. Just before he submerged into a mercifully dreamless sleep, he remembered that he had not called LeBourgoise.

Late Friday afternoon, Morgan Keeler stood in the middle of the track bed of the Frisco Bridge. He was about a third of the way up the approach incline and watching as a Union Pacific engine crane set carefully maneuvered a seventy-ton car back onto solid track. It was hot and extremely humid out on the bridge, and the rail crews were sweating mightily to make progress. He was wearing one-piece Army green overalls and his Corps of Engineers hard hat. Farther up the bridge, a whole block of railcars still rested at various angles along the damaged track bed, awaiting their turn as the UP on the west bank and the Norfolk Southern on the eastern side worked frantically to restore service on the bridge. Construction workers on the nearby Harahan Bridge watched with interest.

He had arrived in Memphis a little before noon and had gone directly to the daily status briefing at the FBI office, where he was readily admitted. As he listened to descriptions of the growing pandemonium throughout the national rail networks, he had to restrain himself from showing any signs of satisfaction. The entire southern tier of the railroad system was on the verge of breaking down, and the northern tier was in danger of being overwhelmed by all the rerouted traffic requirements. The loss of the river bridges had also overloaded another of the system's postNAFTA weak points: the north-south track routes, which were, for the most part, regional low-traffic-density lines. The bastards were losing untold millions every hour and clearly going out of their corporate minds. And he wasn't finished with them.

He had listened impassively as the two rail companies working the Frisco Bridge repairs laid out their timetable to get the bridge opened again. Preliminary surface inspections indicated that the bridge structure remained sound. The propane's explosive wave front had essentially unzipped the track bed, shattering ties and derailing dozens of cars, but the steel trusses and cross members were mostly just scorched. It would take a comprehensive strain-gauge analysis to ensure that the main beams and girders were safe. Keeler had announced that he had a strain-gauge analyzer with him. The senior engineer from the UP deferred to Keeler in his capacity as the Corps of Engineers' senior bridge inspector, and Keeler said he would be on the bridge for as long as it took to confirm their preliminary findings. The senior FBI man had asked how long his inspection would take, but Keeler had been noncommittal. He pointed out that there were now several hundred tons of railcars resting on truss elements of the bridge that were not designed for such sustained deadweight loads. That comment had produced a lot of tight jaws around the table.

The FBI man had stressed again the urgency of getting the bridge repaired, saying that there was enormous pressure coming from Washington to produce even the tiniest bit of good news during this dreadful week. Keeler replied simply that his inspection would be, as always, driven by best engineering practices. From the expression on the FBI man's face, he knew there would be some phone calls made to Corps headquarters to see if they might not be able to recalibrate their bridge inspector. He also knew that the Corps, no matter how exercised the Washington scene was becoming, would never directly try to influence a field engineer making a damage assessment like this.

As he stood out on the bridge now, he could see the raw red trench that had been ripped through the ground in the direction of the water-treatment plant. The warm evening air lifting through the repaired ties still smelled faintly of propane. In contrast to the frenetic repair activities, the river slid beneath the bridge in an indifferent wide silver ribbon, its surface carved into a washboard of intersecting V-shaped patterns by the virtual parade of slow-moving barge strings passing under the damaged bridge. He noted with satisfaction that the rail sidings and switchyards leading to the bridge were jam packed with stalled trains on both sides.

It was slow going, however. The engine crane would get one car righted, then have to pull it down the bridge and into a yard to get it clear. Then a separate engine set would hook up the rail train, crawl back up to where that car had been, clear debris, and then lay down replacement track and new ties. It would then back off the bridge to allow the engine crane to go back up and snatch the next derailed car. The same process was going on at the other end of the bridge, but the two repair teams were having to coordinate their efforts to make sure that only one of the very heavy engine cranes was out on the bridge at a time. They were also having to bolt, instead of weld, the rail segments because these were only temporary repairs. He could see above him on the truss sections high steel-walkers repositioning floodlights to illuminate the advancing work area on the track deck below.

He had inspected only about a quarter of the bridge, and he had told the repair superintendents he would probably be out there all night. He wasn't just going through the motions, either. He had his portable computer and a small instrument case that could read out directly the strain gauges embedded throughout the structure. The steel he had inspected so far seemed to be all right, but the pattern of readings from the gauges were telling him an interesting tale, and the germ of a plan was beginning to form in his mind. But first he had to get out onto that crucial center span, where he suspected that a key point of vulnerability might be lurking. Right now, there were too many people and heavy machines working between him and the center span. That was all right with him, though: He would prefer the wee hours of the morning for what he had planned. His main problem was that the manhunt clock was running; the Bureau investigation had to be getting a lot closer.

Major Matthews kicked a piece of granite along the track bed as the sun went down over Anniston Friday evening. It was just after 6:00 P.M., and the MPs were once again on foot patrol along the length of the train. Matthews sensed that everyone was being careful to stay out of his way. He had spent the first two hours after returning to the depot over at the operations center, learning about the growing pandemonium throughout the nation's rail networks from a dispatch manager at Norfolk Southern. The civilian had been summoned up to the Anniston Depot from Birmingham by an increasingly perturbed Colonel Mehle, who was at war with Norfolk Southern. The major issue was the Army's insistence that 2713SP had to get route priority, and the railroad's equally insistent demand to know precisely why, something Mehle declined to share with them. The Army's request to use the bridge at Vicksburg was making matters worse, because there was already an enormous traffic backlog building up now at the two westbound rail junctions leading to Vicksburg, Meridian, and Jackson. Listening to the heated discussion, Matthews was pretty sure the railroad manager knew the train carried chemical ordnance, but nothing about the what was in those last two tank cars.

When he slipped back into the meeting, the railroad manager was just leaving. From the look on Mehle's face, things had not gone his way. Then the two lieutenant colonels had appeared and given Mehle an update on the temperature problem in the Russian weapon containments. The senior of the two, named Marsden, appeared to be the technical expert. He recommended that a cryogenic unit be brought up and attached to the environmental containment system of the two cars to supercool the interiors. Mehle told him to take care of it, and then he had sent Matthews back to the train with orders to ensure that it was fueled and ready to go at a moment's notice. He reiterated the order to keep himself and all his people on board; there were to be no stragglers.

That afternoon, the depot switch engine had come up and detached the two personnel cars and the two special tank cars. The string was reassembled on a siding track to insert a flatbed car between the two special tank cars. On the flatbed were two huge gas chiller compressors, their receiver and accumulator cylinders, a three-hundred-gallon insulated liquid nitrogen tank, and a single truck-mounted two-hundred-kilowatt diesel-powered generator set. Long, heavily insulated hoses went from the nitrogen tank to the containment control boxes on the special tank cars. The depot's laboratory crew worked for about four hours through sunset to get the system up and running. Lieutenant Colonel Marsden informed Matthews that the temps were stabilizing once the nitrogen bath began to circulate. Then the five-car string had been set back out onto the end of the train.

Now they were all doing what all armies seemed to do best: waiting.

Hush struggled to rouse himself out of a drugged sleep. His eyelids felt stuck together, even as his hand was patting the bedside table, searching for the ringing telephone. His mouth felt incredibly dry.

"Hanson," he croaked.

"Hush? This is Mike Powers. You okay?"

"No," Hush said, finally getting one eye open. "Took some damn pain pill and now I'm semidoped up."

"Only 'semi,' huh? Drugs ain't what they used to be."

He opened the other eye. "What time is it?"

"It's ten-thirty, Friday night. Listen, I'm up in Memphis. I just talked to Thomas about what they did to you. What kinda shit is that?"

"Vintage Bureau shit," Hush said, sitting up and turning on the bedside light. His eyelids kept drooping. "The director's cleaning out the holdovers from the last regime. Apparently, he saw a shot and took it. I failed to see it coming."

"Damn, and I thought we were all chasing the bad guy here."

Hush started to laugh but coughed instead. "This is the Bureau we're talking about, Mike. Think J. Edgar and the games he played. Hell, he mouse-trapped Presidents. For some of these guys, the cops and robbers stuff is just a necessary backdrop to their real interest."

Powers laughed. "That kind of stuff never goes on at the state level."

"Right."

"So, you're out in the cold. Now what?"

"Technically, I'm on a ten-day convalescent leave. What I have to decide now is whether or not I can slink back to headquarters. I'm still technically head of the IITF division. But after this . . ."

"Sounds pretty simple to me," Powers said. "I'd go back, pretend to be really contrite and medium devastated, and then find some way to stab the appropriate bastards in the liver."

It was Hush's turn to laugh. "You'd fit right in, Mikey," he said. "So, any developments?"

"Well, your former ace assistant's theory about it being one guy is now in firm federal disrepute. Some anal-oriented dude named J. something Carswell is telling all your guys that we're back to looking for a band of Communists, rabid-ass ragheads, or other undesirables."

"What are the Bureau field people saying to that?"

"Publicly? They say, Yes, sir, yes, sir, three bags full, sir. They're field people: They just want to catch the bad guy and stop all this shit. That shipwreck caper convinced me that it probably *is* one guy. But I gotta tell you, there is a one *hell* of a lot of political heat coming down, both in my channels and in yours, so most guys are playing it safe, you know what I mean?"

"Indeed I do."

"In fact, rumor has it—this is from Himself Herlihy—that your honey-blond deputy might find that fine bottom of hers on the skids, too."

"No shit? But I thought—" He stopped. What the hell *was* going on? She was the one who had served him up. He cursed the fog in his head.

"Thought what?"

Hush sighed. "Hell, I'm too doped up right now to think clearly. That's probably just Himself indulging in wishful thinking. I shouldn't have taken that damn pill."

"Well, look, Hush, here's why I was calling: My counterparts in the state level task force have been kicking around the proposition that we might go our own way on this, especially since Washington is getting all wrapped around the axle. Looks to us snuffies out here that everybody's mostly just trying to cover their asses."

Hush found himself nodding. "First order of business," he mumbled.

"So, I was thinking: Maybe you enjoy your dope for a night, get some rest, and take them up on that snivel leave. Then tomorrow, grab a puddle jumper up here to Memphis. Maybe you and I can get something useful going while all the big shots back east are foaming at the mouth for the TV cameras."

Hush nodded again, and then he realized he hadn't said anything. "Right."

Powers gave Hush his pager and his private cruiser's phone numbers. "Those numbers will get Little Hill, and he can always find me."

Powers was proposing that Hush work behind the Bureau's back with the state police people. It would be very, very difficult to do. If one of Carswell's people got wind of it, somebody very senior would step on Hush's neck. Powers seemed to sense what Hush was thinking.

"Hey, Hush? I understand what I'm proposing here. But I've talked to my chief, who's talked to the governor. The big dogs at the state level are getting antsy about what they're seeing in Washington. For the Bureau, this is turning into a PR problem; for us locals, this guy is killing us economically. Like in crops not getting to market, fuels and fertilizers not getting to the farm, and maybe a whole lot of people going bust. We can muster up plenty of people to chase his ass, but what we might need is access to those big computers of yours. You remember the lawyers' list? That kind of stuff."

Hush took a deep breath, trying to clear his head. "I know, Mike," he said. "And I'm willing to try. It's not like I have a promising career at risk here—anymore. And besides—"

"Yeah. That liver stab."

"Exactly."

"Hold that thought, Hush," Powers said, and then he made Hush repeat back Little Hill's phone numbers before hanging up. Hush wrote them down and then collapsed back on the bed. He looked at his watch: 10:40. Some light from the street below shone through his window, but the sky out to the west of Baton Rouge was mostly dark. The glow of a refinery gas flare across the river sent orange reflections dancing on his ceiling.

In the context of the Bureau's closed-ranks culture, what Powers was proposing went beyond career suicide. Wellesley had given him a face-saving "out" for the next ten days, but Carswell would brook no interference in the Trainman case, or the glory of solving it, from Hush Hanson. But if by some chance IR had completed that database of people with serious grudges against the railroads, and if Tyler Redford could get it for him, and if— He groaned aloud. If, if, if—this was a pipe dream. William Morrow Hanson was rapidly becoming a nonperson at headquarters. Nobody who hoped to keep his own career alive would give him the time of day.

The other problem was personal. If he went freelancing with Powers and the state people, it would put him back in the field. Doing things he wasn't sure he should be doing. Maybe ending up in a situation where they got the bad guy or guys cornered and the guns came out. He would have to walk away from it: Hey, Mike, you and your people go get him— I'll just wait here in the car. I'm not to be trusted with a gun in my hand, remember? The inner me would prefer to slaughter the bastard rather than prosecute him.

He smiled painfully in the darkness. Mike Powers would probably hand him a gun. Hush realized he'd been in Washington too damn long. He gave up trying to think as he slipped back off to sleep.

At 11:30 that evening, Morgan Keeler crouched under the main girder structure of the center span and stared at the portable's green screen, which glowed portentously in the shadows under the track bed. Directly above his head, the bogeys of a gondola car projected three feet through the splintered remains of the ties. The scorched and broken ties stank of propane. Beneath him, the shiny flat surface of the river reflected the glow of a dozen large floodlights mounted high in the center arch. Two hundred feet back along the track, the crane set was banging another car upright, surrounded by sweating crewmen who were lodging steel support rods under its bent axles.

His skin felt tight across his face, and physical fatigue made his eyes sting a little. But he was right where he needed to be. He focused on what he was seeing. The strain-gauge reader's sensing wires were clipped on to four jacks positioned along the main girder. The jacks were attached to flat metal foils that had been soldered onto the steel surface of the massive girders at the time the bridge was built. Changes in strain in the girder were proportional to the amount of deformation in the foils. Normal or unloaded design strain gave a zero reading. Compression strain gave a negative number, and tension yielded a positive reading. The screen told the tale: With several hundred tons of derailed, stationary rolling stock wedged along the girder, the slightly arched steel girder should have been in deep compression. But it wasn't; it was in *tension.*

Keeler knew what this had to mean: The 150-foot-long side girder had flattened out completely under the unusual deadweight of the cars, and then it had sagged through the perfectly horizontal into a negative, downward bowed arch. The sag would not have been visible to the naked eye. The strain gauges, however, did not lie. The girder was right at the edge of the metallurgic failure range.

He sat back on his haunches and wiped his face. The air was close and hot along the catwalk under the girders. He imagined he could hear the billions of ferrous crystals in the steel sliding and grinding imperceptibly against one another. If he wanted to bring the bridge down, here was the opportunity. The recovery engineers were waiting for his assessment of the center span. All he had to do was tell them that the girders had enough load reserve to allow *both* recovery engines out onto the span, and then these massive girders would fail, dropping the entire center span straight down into the river. It was that simple.

He climbed carefully across the underslung catwalk, very conscious now of the ominous creaking and groaning noises coming from the track bed above, and set up his instrument to measure the other main side girder. The readings came in just about the same, with maybe a little less magnitude showing on the dancing, spidery green lines. But still in tension, no doubt about it. He disconnected the wire clips and shut off his machine. Hell, the thing might let go even before any extra weight hit it. He looked back over his shoulder to see where the western recovery crew was. The crew on the eastern side was farther back down their side of the bridge. In another ten hours or so, the first of the massive engine cranes would be ready to stick its nose out onto the center span.

He thought hard. It might not work. They would be able to pick up several cars before the engines actually came out onto the bridge. That might unload the calculations to the point where it would become progressively safer for the engine to advance out onto the overloaded span. He climbed back up onto the track bed, momentarily blinded by all the white lights above. The individual cars were jacked over at odd angles, some still on the rails, others crashed all the way through the steel cross-supports of the track bed. He found what he was looking for: The cars nearest the western end were relative lightweights, compared to the hundred tonners out in the middle of the span. So it shouldn't make any difference if they lifted one or two of them.

He swallowed to lubricate his suddenly parched throat. The real problem was the recovery crew. He didn't want to kill fifty or so trainmen gratuitously. But he did want to drop that center span. He would have to figure out a way to get them to advance the crane engines out onto the center span while holding the people back until they were sure the span would hold. Right. He would set it up that way: He would report that the span's side girders were dangerously close to deformation limits. They could hook up a second engine behind the crane set, thereby controlling the entire set's movement from the rear cab without getting a manned engine out onto the dangerous span. If one of those side girders let go, everyone in Memphis would hear it, and the engineer ought to have time to jump clear before the crane was pulled over into the river. Once it happened, the railroad people would immediately finger him for the miscalculation. For now, though, all that pressure from Washington would predispose them to take his word for it that the center span was marginally safe, especially if he couched it in sufficiently cautious language. He looked at his watch again and then back at the crews. Ten, maybe twelve hours. Daylight. Early to midafternoon tomorrow. That would give him time to get some rest after his long night drive, and drop back by that FBI office to see what he could find out about their investigation. He had two more bridges to take care of, and he needed as much warning as possible before they developed a workable profile of who might be doing this to them.

13

AT NOON ON SATURDAY, Hush was tapping his fingers impatiently on the cruiser's center console as he waited for the traffic jam ahead to clear. Little Hill had offered to run the berm with sound and lights, but there really was nowhere to go until the jackknifed tractor-trailer sprawled across the interstate had been moved. Mike Powers had considerately dispatched Hill to pick Hush up at the Memphis airport, since Hush was now operating outside of FBI channels. Hush had been able to contact Tyler Redford at the office just before he checked out of his hotel in Baton Rouge. He had decided to take Redford into his confidence about working the Trainman case off-line with Powers and the state police. Redford's reaction had been entirely predictable: "Carswell's people in the field will find out," he warned. "He'll get the director to cut off your hands and feet." Hush tried to pacify him by pointing out that the state people were going to work only the now officially discredited one-man theory. Redford wasn't fooled: "You're technically on convalescent leave," he reminded Hush. "The deputy director will be watching you like a hawk for any chance to issue a retirement invitation. Don't give the bastards an opening."

There was finally movement ahead, and Little Hill pushed the cruiser onto the berm. He drove up past the wreck scene, slowing down long enough to let the Tennessee cops see who he was. They waved him through and then they were free again. Little Hill said it would take them about twenty minutes to get downtown to the bridge. Hush had pressed Redford to see if he could find out whatever had happened to that list of names IR was supposed to be developing based on the railroad counsels' information. Redford initially balked, going off again on the point that the Trainman case was simply too hot for anybody, especially Hush, to start screwing around with from the outside. "The President is involved," he said, "and there's a pack of congressmen from the big farm states along the river raising absolute hell because of what's been happening to agricultural-commodity shipments." TV talking heads were accusing the FBI of fumbling the case, and the director was firing someone each time another accusation of Bureau incompetence was made on the evening network news programs. So far, one deputy AD and two section chiefs had been relieved of their duties and put "on staff." The spectacle of the ruptured ship lying under the wreckage of the Baton Rouge bridge was keeping the story very much alive. The only bright spot was that the Frisco Bridge was predicted to be back in service this afternoon. In the end, however, Redford relented and promised to see what he could find out.

Hush had also asked about Carolyn Lang. Redford reported that she was still the principal spokesperson for the interagency task force, although there were now hallway rumors circulating to the effect that she was walking a real tightrope because Carswell either didn't trust her or didn't like her, or possibly both. There was also the problem of her being the author of the one-man theory. Hush told Redford that he agreed with her theory, despite her apparent role in what Wellesley had just done to him. Redford said that word of that little caper was also working its way around headquarters, and, for what it was worth, a lot of people who knew and liked Hush were upset with what had happened.

Little Hill checked in on his radio and reported that Captain Powers was over on the Arkansas side, where there was less city traffic and the approach to the damaged bridge more accessible. As they went over the interstate highway bridge, Hush could see a small army of railroad repair people gathered on the bridge as one of the giant engine cranes was being positioned to retrieve the first car on the center span. Actual access to the railroad bridge approaches took another half hour of checking in with railroad security people, followed by clearance through the National Guard roadblocks.

Hush let Little Hill do the talking, not wanting to call attention to himself. Little Hill said only that this gentleman had been summoned by Captain Powers, the interstate coordinator for all the state police forces working the bridge cases. This explanation, plus Little Hill's imposing bulk, seemed to be sufficient for the roadblock cops. Hush was relieved; the last thing he needed right now was for word to reach the Memphis FBI people that AD Hanson was on the scene. Ex-AD, he reminded himself. He was also counting on the fact that most of the FBI effort right now would be down in Baton Rouge, where agents would be scurrying around like ants after their mound has been kicked over.

The cruiser bumped its way through a long line of emergency vehicles before finally heaving to a stop at the interior security perimeter, past which no vehicles were allowed. Above them, the lofty approach ramp of the railroad bridge rose into the hulking steel arches over the river. To the left three huge diesels were idling on separate tracks. A strange-looking contraption sprouting bundles of rails slung under an II-frame was positioned at the base of the bridge. Powers was waiting for them near one of the rumbling locomotives, and Hush climbed the bank to join him. He left his suit jacket in the cruiser, as it was very warm out on the gravel roadbed under the bridge approaches. Powers was in a short-sleeved uniform and wearing mirrored sunglasses under a wide-brimmed felt hat. He looked every inch the state trooper that he had been for years. The bandage on his left hand had been reworked, and there were still some smaller bandages on his face. He grinned when Hush walked up.

"We need to get you a hat," he said, shouting to be heard over the big diesel. "Your bandages are going to get sunburned."

"In more ways than one," Hush said. "I've been thinking about your little proposition."

Powers took Hush's arm and steered him away from the noisy diesel. A few seconds later, the engine spooled up and backed away from the approach switch so that the repair train could ascend the bridge. Up at the center span, the engine crane was beginning to back down the line with another battered grain-hopperr in its grip. Hush back-briefed Powers on what Tyler Redford had passed on.

"So he's going to try to get his hands on that list?"

"Yeah, but he has to watch his ass, like everybody else in the headquarters right now. It probably doesn't help that he was my deputy at IITF."

"I know how that goes. How about that Lang woman? Could she get it?"

"I don't think I want to do business with her just now," Hush said, setting his jaw. He explained what McDougal had told him and what he'd found out on his own.

"Goddamn," Powers said. "So that's why those St. Louis guys called her what they did."

"Yup. I should have paid a lot more attention. What's going on here?"

Powers explained the process as the engine crane inched its way back down the approach tracks. "Morgan Keeler is honchoing this thing right now. He gave a briefing this morning. Says the center span is touch and go, stress wise. They're being real careful with that big crane set. Only letting one crane at a time out on that center span."

"That must slow things down a lot."

"Yeah, but he said if the first couple of extractions go okay, the weight would be reduced and then he'd let both engines go out. The railroad people are doing whatever he says."

"Yeah, well, why not? If he's wrong, it'll be on his head and not theirs."

Powers shook his head. "You Washington guys. Don't you ever think about anything but blame?"

Hush smiled, but Powers was right. They had to stop talking as the big engine crane drew near and the rail train's diesel prepared to go up the bridge. They watched as several railroad superintendents conducted a quick radio conference, and then one of them gave a hand signal and the rail train started up. There were now two diesels pushing the rig up the bridge; the second one had all the people on board. It looked to Hush like an engine crane was also starting up the Memphis side, although it was difficult to see through the steel maze of the bridge structure. High-rise office buildings shimmered in the Memphis heat behind the bridge.

He felt absolutely useless in the midst of all the activity around the bridges, where dozens of workers were moving railcars, servicing the engines, positioning materials for the rail train, removing damaged ties and bent rails, and talking incessantly into handheld radios. There was a great deal of diesel smoke, noise, and dust, and Hush was about to go back to the cruiser when he saw everyone stop and look up at the bridge. The rail train was approaching the center span, creeping slowly now, with the workmen dropping off onto the bridge structure before the crane actually went out onto the center span. Hush thought he could see Keeler in his white hard hat up there, standing on the parapet of the western pier tower, a radio pressed to his mouth. On the other side, engine crane with another, smaller engine married to it from behind appeared at the pier tower on the Tennessee side and stopped. The center span still had about twenty railcars sitting out on the damaged track bed. As Hush and Powers watched, there was some more radio conferencing, a lot of hand signals up on the bridge, and then both engines advanced very slowly out onto the center span. Hush could see that the locomotive engineers on the western side were standing just outside the door to the engine compartment.

The rail train went first, because the working end of its frame extended some eighty feet out in front of the actual engine. The crew riding the second engine hung back for a few minutes, then eased gingerly out to the first damaged section of track and began unbolting the deformed rails. Over on the Tennessee side, an engine crane was advancing, aiming for an eighty-ton gondola car that was listing badly to port out on the track bed just beyond the pier tower.

Hush was turning to go back to the cruiser when there was a sound like a cannon shot, a huge, punishing boom, from up on the bridge. He whirled around and saw a small cloud of dust puff out from the middle of the center span on the left side, and then came another enormous boom as the main girder on the right side broke. He saw a mad scramble of workmen on the center span as they raced the twenty yards to the safety of the pier towers just before the entire center span folded into a steel-crunching slow-motion V of crumpling trusses and girders, then collapsed straight down into the river, taking the engine crane and the rail train with it as the drivers jumped off, accompanied by a roar of grinding and fracturing steel that seemed to go on forever. The wreckage hit the river with an impressive splash, sending up a huge wall of water hurtling out in all directions. Hush joined everyone else in a mad dash farther up the banks of the river as the small tidal wave came ashore in a brown rush, sweeping water all the way back to where the damaged railcars were waiting on the tracks. They beat the water by only a few feet, jumping up onto the platform of a tank car to avoid being doused. The river area around the bridge was obscured for a moment by a large, dense cloud of dust. When it cleared, they could see a couple of track workmen hanging on to the stubs of the main girders over on the Tennessee side. Hush looked at Powers.

"Think maybe Keeler screwed up?" Powers asked.

Hush pointed over to where some railroad engineers were standing.

One of them had taken his hard hat off and was stomping it into pieces, while the others were all talking into their radios at the same time.

"They seem to think so," Hush said, shaking his head. "Washington is going to go snakeshit over this."

They walked back through the mud toward the concrete ramp of the bridge approach. Hundreds of small fish were flapping desperately on the ground. A crowd of railroad men was streaming down the tracks from the western pier tower. They could see Morgan Keeler in the middle, gesticulating frantically while the men around him kept pointing back toward the missing center span. Out on the river, three Corps of Engineers tugboats were milling around the wreckage area, looking for anyone who might have gone into the river when the span fell. When Keeler reached the approach ramp, he tried to bull his way through the crowd to where Hush and Powers were standing.

"He needs protection," Powers shouted to Hush while reaching for his radio. "Those guys are ready to string him up."

While Powers called for Little Hill, Hush elbowed his way through the crowd of angry men to reach Keeler's side. He identified himself to the nearest men as FBI and announced in a loud voice that they were taking Keeler into custody for questioning in connection with what had just happened. This seemed to mollify the nearest men long enough for Hush to pull Keeler away to Power's cruiser, which the ever-watchful Little Hill had managed to bring closer to the approach ramp. Hush told Keeler under his breath to get in the backseat and look like a prisoner. Once in the car, Keeler stared, white-faced, out the window. Hush got in the back with him, and Powers jumped into the front seat. Powers instructed Little Hill to get them the hell out of there. The big trooper turned on his lights and siren and blasted his way through the angry crowd of railroad people converging on the bridge head. Once out from under the interstate highway complex near the river, Little Hill turned right on the nearest state road, extinguished the sound and light show, and sped due west, away from the bridges and the prospective lynch mob.

"Am I really under arrest?" Keeler asked finally. His normally lean and drawn face was almost cadaverous.

"No," Hush said. "That was just to get your ass out of there before those people strung you up. They seemed to think you were personally responsible for that."

Keeler took a deep breath. "In a way, I guess I was," he said.

"So what did happen?" Powers asked.

"They were going by my calculations. They needed to get both ends of the center span worked to get the bridge clear. Everyone was pressing to get the thing done. I gave them clearance to take two engines out on the center span. The main side girders let go."

"Did you make some tests or measurements before you let them out there?"

"Yes, of course. I had a strain analyzer connected to my computer. I've been working the bridge since last night. Took readings from every strain gauge out there. Those girders should not have failed." He shook his head.

"Do you have that data? Can you back yourself up?"

Keeler shook his head again. "Lost it all when the bridge failed. You saw it, I assume. It was pandemonium out there when that girder fractured. Those of us on the parapet were busy hauling in the rail train's crew."

This admission brought a moment of silence. The cruiser continued to bore a straight line west on Highway 64. Then Powers's radio sounded off. It was the Arkansas Highway Patrol lieutenant in charge of scene security at the Frisco Bridge. He was reporting that the ASAC of the Memphis office of the FBI was on the scene and asking which FBI agent had taken Keeler into custody.

"Oops," Hush said.

"I got it," Powers said. He responded to the lieutenant that he, not anybody from the FBI, had Keeler in protective custody and was taking him to the Corps of Engineer district office in St. Louis. Keeler would make a full report to his superiors there, and that report would be made available to the pertinent railroad authorities. The lieutenant said he would pass that on. Little Hill pointed out that northbound Interstate 55 was coming up. Powers told him to take it, and then to boogie.

"Can't let them know I was even there," Hush said. "Supposedly I'm still convalescing down in Baton Rouge."

Keeler nodded toward Hush's battered face and Powers's hand. "What happened to you two?" he asked.

Hush told him what had happened at Vicksburg. Hush did not elaborate on the change in the FBI's command arrangements. Then the lieutenant was back on the radio. The ASAC Memphis wanted to talk to Powers. Powers shot Hush a look and picked up the microphone.

"This is Captain Powers."

"This is Larry Thomas. I need to get something clarified here. Several people are telling us that a really tall guy who identified himself as FBI was with you when Keeler was taken in protective custody."

"Don't know anything about that," Powers said promptly. "My driver was with me, though. Really big guy, black hair, kinda ugly?"

Hush saw the ghost of a smile cross Little Hill's face. Thomas told Powers to wait one, and then he was back. "Your driver in uniform? 'Cause this guy was in civvies."

"Look, Mr. Thomas," Powers replied, ignoring the question. "There was pandemonium going on there at that bridge. Those trainmen were ready to string Mr. Keeler up to the nearest bridge beam. My driver and I moved in, told everybody we were arresting Keeler, and got him the hell out of there. You check around, you'll probably find someone who saw Batman and Robin in that crowd."

There was a pause. "Where are you taking Keeler again?" Thomas asked.

"To St. Louis. That's where his district headquarters is. He's going to have to make a report, and probably get himself a good lawyer, knowing the railroads. But we couldn't just leave him there at that bridge."

There was a pause, as if Thomas was talking to someone else. "Yeah, okay," Thomas said. "If you don't mind, I'm going to have some of our people from the St. Louis Office meet you there. We're already getting a lot of heat from Washington to explain what the hell just happened here."

"Roger that," Powers said. "We'll call Herlihy's office when we get in and he can send some folks over. That okay?"

Thomas said that would be fine and signed off. Powers hung up the mike. "I'll call our ops center in Jefferson City and get a car to meet us at Cape Girardeau. They'll take you two into town separately. We don't want to show up at our headquarters in St. Louis and find a car full of feds who want to look in the window."

"Got that right," Hush said. He saw that Keeler appeared to be bewildered. "Just some bureaucratic maneuvers, Mr. Keeler. This has nothing to do with you."

"When will we get there?" Keeler asked.

"Two hundred and fifty miles or so. Eighty-five miles an hour. Three hours."

"Two and a half," said Little Hill as he laid into it.

• • •

By 6:00 P.M. on Saturday evening, train 2713SP was still stuck at the Anniston Depot. Matthews had had his hands full all day with special requests from some of the enlisted guards to either go home or call home, or call their girlfriends, all of which he had had to deny. The only consolation he could offer his unhappy troops was that he, too, was stuck on the damned train. The depot phone system was still sealed, as was any access, in or out. There were rumors of trucker problems out by the main gate, where the parking lanes were filling up with semis and their irate drivers. The two original train engineers had asked to be replaced, citing union time on station rules, but their requests had been summarily denied by Colonel Mehle. The sound of passing trains out on the main line had been continuous since they had returned.

At 6:30, Mehle showed up at the special tank cars with Lieutenant Colonel Marsden and two enlisted technicians from Fort McClellan. They climbed up on the cryogenics car, and then there was some heated discussion, which Matthews watched as inconspicuously as he could from the railed platform of the bunk-room car. Some of it seemed to be about the reliability of the cryogenics plant. Mehle finally saw Matthews and signaled for him to join them. Marsden was tight-lipped, and he dismissed the techs when Matthews walked up to the flat car. Mehle cut right to the chase.

"Marsden here is having second thoughts about the safety of the specials," Mehle said, with an "I could happily kill him" expression on his face.

Matthews said nothing, just took a deep breath. If one of Mehle's own people was saying that, now was a great time to shut his own yap.

"I'd be a lot happier if you hadn't raised the safety issue, Major," Mehle snapped. "But now that you have, Lieutenant Colonel Marsden here wants to put some distance between himself and this shipment."

"All I've said is that the cryogenics should have brought the temperatures inside the four containments down; the fact that they have not is significant. I can no longer—"

"Yeah, yeah, I've got all that," Mehle said, glaring at Marsden. Matthews recognized that this might be a good time to get on the side of the angels, especially with a like-minded witness right there.

"Colonel," he said, "this shipment is dangerous enough without the

245

Russian weapons. Why don't we disconnect these tank cars and put them back in Assembly Nine until this railroad crisis is over? We shouldn't take these things through municipal areas."

Mehle's face became redder than usual. "Because, Major Matthews, I have been ordered to get 'these things,' as you call them, out of here and out to Utah. As you well know."

Matthews had to wait until one of the sentries walked by and got out of earshot of the officers. "Yes, sir," he said, "I understand that. But we have changed circumstances. We don't know what's going on within those warheads. This isn't a CW problem; it's a conventional explosives problem with the potential for a radioactive release."

"Maybe," Mehle said. "Or it might be something else. We've removed the tritium booster plugs, and there are no neutron sources in the weapons, of course." He patted the thick steel sides of the tank car. "Look at this thing: Even if one of the implosion spheres let go, it's a shaped charge, directed inward. The blast wouldn't even be audible outside."

"Unless it sets off a sympathetic detonation with the other weapon," Matthews said. Marsden was beginning to nod his head. Mission accomplished, Matthews thought. "If you got a sympathetic detonation," he continued, "there might be enough overpressure to pop a main seal on the tank car, or blow back down the cryogenic lines. You could have plutonium fragments in there, Colonel, radioactive metal dust. That's some bad shit."

"*I don't give a good goddamn. Do you understand me?*" Mehle screamed at him. Then he lowered his voice, aware of the nearby MPs staring. "We're not putting it back and we're not sitting here beyond twenty-three hundred tonight."

This was news, Matthews thought. "We have route clearance?" he asked

"That's right, Major," Mehle said through clenched teeth. "We have clearance to Birmingham Junction. At twenty-three hundred. I've ordered my stuff put into my command car." He smiled when he saw Matthews's reaction to that bit of news. "That's right, *I'm* going to command this train. Personally. No more retrograde movements, Major Matthews. But don't unpack. You get to come, too."

He ordered Marsden to recheck his cryogenics system and to inform him when the Texans arrived. Ignoring Matthews, he left the train. What Texans? Matthews wondered.

Hush checked in with Tyler Redford at 6:00 P.M. from the Holcomb Bluffs Hotel, where Powers had stashed him once they split up in middle Missouri. Redford had taken Hush's phone number and asked him to stay by the phone. He called back in fifteen minutes.

"You would not believe this place," he said. "You heard about what happened in Memphis?"

"Yes. Got to watch, even."

"Holy shit! That *was* you, then?"

"Me, what?" Hush asked innocently.

"Don't start with me, Hush. The Memphis office came in with their hair on fire after that bridge went down. There was word from the scene of an FBI agent taking that bridge inspector, Keeler, into custody right after the bridge collapsed. Said they talked with Powers, who said *he* had Keeler and that there was no FBI involved. The ASAC out there in Memphis, guy named Thomas, said he thought you were supposed to be in Baton Rouge. Said he thought Powers was blowing smoke."

"Well, actually he was. Look, as far as the scene was concerned, we just did what we had to do. Those railroad people were ready to lynch Keeler. He was the one who made the calculations letting two engines out on the bridge, and everybody knew it."

"Shit," Redford said. "Well, as you might imagine, Carswell is on the warpath. Right now, they're trying to deal with the loss of another bridge. But as soon as they get that fire under control—"

"Yeah, I know. They'll come looking for me. Well, I'm on leave. That's all you know. Last time you heard from me, I was doing prescription dope in Baton Rouge. That I was pissed off at being sidelined, and now I'm out in the countryside somewhere, sulking."

Redford laughed. "I'll tell 'em, but you know that won't wash for very long. Thomas is reporting that the state cops are trying to grab a piece of the action here, maybe run off with the case. Carswell and his people, not to mention Heinrich, will be looking for a human sacrifice if they hear that."

"By any chance is anybody looking for the bad guy?"

Redford lowered his voice. "Differing opinions going around on that. As long as the entire Washington establishment is targeting the Bureau, the first order of business is political survival. Some of the copy-room sages are saying that, if we were really clever, we'd let the state guys take the lead and some of the heat for a while. Where is Keeler, by the way?"

"Taking sanctuary in his district headquarters here in St. Louis. Probably looking for a good lawyer. That was a major mistake, especially since all his inspection data went into the river when the bridge collapsed."

"Wouldn't want to be that sumbitch right about now," Redford said. He was silent for a moment. "You going to work this thing off-line with the state guys?"

"Why not? Can't dance. And I still think this is one guy doing this shit. Any luck on that list?"

"I talked to my counterpart in IR, but he says they've been ordered to knock off any further work on said list."

"But the railroads came through? They turned over names?"

"Apparently. Trouble is, no one in IR is willing to talk to me or anyone else about it. You have to understand, everyone not directly involved in Trainman is getting in his hole and pulling it in after him."

"But the list exists?"

"I believe it does."

"I owe you, Ty," Hush said.

"I've still got a mortgage and one in college. You and I never talked, Hush."

"Understood."

There was another one of those awkward pauses, during which Redford was talking to someone else in the office. Then he was back on. "Look," he said, "there's going to be a director's press conference in five minutes. I'll get back to you with what comes out of that. Meanwhile—"

"Meanwhile, I'll lie low."

"You do that, Hush. Lower than whale shit."

Hush decided to take a shower and clean up while he waited for Redford to call him back. He thought about seeing if he could watch the director's press conference, but he was starting to hurt again and beginning to hunger for another one of those magic bullets. The trip up the Arkansas-Missouri interstate had been nerve racking as Little Hill threaded the police cruiser at very high speed in and out of endless lines of semis on I-55. Powers had made good on his promise to get Hush and Keeler separated. Two state police cruisers had rendezvoused with them at the Missouri state line. One took Keeler into St. Louis, while the other took Hush to the hotel north of the city. Powers had gone to his headquarters and had promised to call him at the hotel around 8:00 so they could plan out their next moves. Hush flopped on the bed and closed his eyes. At 6:40, Redford called back.

"Man, you're gonna love this," he said excitedly.

"Lay it on me."

"He had Carswell by his side, and they did the best dance they could about the Memphis Bridge. Tipped the bedpan all over the Corps of Engineers."

"They name Keeler?"

"No, but there's a media posse headed over to Corps of Engineers national headquarters in Arlington even as we speak. But he had Carswell by his side."

"Yeah, you said that. So?"

"Carswell, Hush, but not Lang. It's official: Lang's been canned."

Hush whistled softly. Well, well, well, he thought. Fly too close to the sun, get your pretty wings singed. Hush was about to say something when Redford asked him to hold on for second. The phone was muted, and then he was back.

"I have someone who wishes to speak to you, Mr. Hanson," Redford said, his voice suddenly changing over to formal Bureauspeak.

Mr. Hanson? Hush was fully awake now. Then Carolyn Lang's voice came on the line. "Good evening," she said pleasantly, as if nothing had ever happened. "I've become the latest Trainman casualty. I've heard a rumor that you're going solo. Want some help?"

"You shouldn't listen to rumors," Hanson replied in as civil a tone as he could muster. "And besides, *good* help is hard to find."

"Good as in reliable?"

"Good as in honest. Truthful. Professional. Trustworthy. Focused on the bad guy. That kind of good."

There was pause on the line. Hush was working very hard to control himself, to appear totally dispassionate and unconcerned. He wanted very much to yell at her, but he would not give her that satisfaction.

"You may change your mind," she said. "I have something that might interest you."

"I doubt it very much, Carolyn. Other than your body, I suppose."

He had let that slip without even thinking about it, and he could actually hear her hiss of breath. But she was obviously in control of herself, too.

"I was thinking more along the lines of a list," she said. Her voice was perfectly emotionless. He could just imagine the expression on Redford's face right about now. But then he realized what she had just said.

"The railroads' list?"

He heard her ask Redford to give them some privacy. "That very one. And there's a name on it that is going to ring some bells. Really ring some bells. You're in Baton Rouge?"

"I guess I'm not really ready to tell you where I am, Carolyn, until I know whom you're working for these days."

"I've been 'detached'—that's the operative word these days—and supposedly I'll be going back to PCA. Just like you will supposedly be coming back to IITF."

"Unless of course I decide that I've been sufficiently humiliated in the field as to want to retire. And then the director can put his own guy in at IITF. That was the plan, wasn't it, Carolyn? That was *your* mission, right?"

"Whatever gave you that idea?"

"A guy named McDougal, for starters."

There was another pause. He said nothing, letting the silence build.

"All right," she said. "Yes, that was my mission. That's what I do here. Or, rather, that's what I *did* here. It seems we were both taken for a ride this time. At that little meeting you had with the director and Heinrich."

This damned woman was always surprising him. "The one you wanted to know about? That meeting?"

"Yes, that meeting."

He couldn't help himself. "So how's it feel to be the sandbagee for a change, Carolyn?"

"It makes me feel the same way you're probably feeling right now—sucker punched. I thought I was the player, the one in control. That I had earned some loyalty-down from the director's office. That I was a senior insider in the Bureau. Part of the real executive team, the inner circle. And now I want some payback. That how you feel?"

"Absolutely. But why in the hell should I trust you? Why should anyone trust you?"

She lowered her voice to just above a whisper. "For the most traditional bureaucratic reason in the world, Hush. Because I have some information you need. I know who the Trainman is."

• • •

At 7:10 P.M., Morgan Keeler paid off the taxi driver, walked two blocks down Smith Street to the Van and Auto Storage office. The garage advertised that they could roust a vehicle up out of storage with one hour's notice, twenty-four hours a day, seven days a week, and he hoped they were good for it. His other truck was still down in Memphis, but that was all right, because he wouldn't be able to use it anymore after tonight. He produced the false driver's license in the name of Thomas Brown, gave it to the clerk, and paid up the balance of the storage fee in cash. The clerk told him the vehicle would be right up. He went to the window and stared out at the night.

Endgame, he thought. He had planned meticulously for this stage, but it was still going to be a big step to disappear and actually become a fugitive. The past few hours in the district office had been extremely unpleasant. Even though it was a Saturday, word of what had happened down in Memphis had brought all the supervisors, plus the district engineer himself, into the office. All of them had questioned him intensely. The railroads were already making lawsuit noises, and the Washington media were besieging the Corps of Engineers Washington headquarters to find out officially who was the engineer who had the Frisco Bridge on his hands. The railroads already knew, but they were waiting for the Corps to come out and officially name Keeler. Fortunately, all the railroad crews had been able to get clear, so there had been only two minor injuries when the engine crane set was pulled over the edge. The loss of the bridge, however, was trouble enough.

According to the district engineer, a burly brigadier general, the loss of Keeler's computer was even more damaging from the Corps' perspective. Keeler had made sure that both the strain-gauge test set and the computer went over the side in the general rush to escape the collapsing center span. He had altered the strain-gauge summary data that morning to indicate that the girders were minimally safe before showing his results to the railroad repair superintendents. Afterward, he had removed the hard drive and pitched it into the river.

But none of this mattered anymore. He was running out of time. He had pretended not to listen in the car, but he was pretty sure that the state police forces were going to work the case outside of Bureau channels. That meant two investigations would be running. His chances for evading both were pretty slim, especially if either one of them went back to research railroad accidents. He remembered the FBI man's mention of motive. He'd seen some of the press conferences emanating from FBI headquarters, and yet no one there had mentioned motive, probably because they were all still hung up on finding a terrorist cell. But somewhere, somehow, somebody had to be looking for a motive. He figured he could get one more bridge, and that would have to be Vicksburg.

"Vehicle's up, Mr. Brown," the clerk called form the side door.

Keeler thanked him and went outside. Waiting for him alongside the building was a dark green Ford Econoline G-20 van, which had been modified to become a camper. He had bought it at a bank auction three years ago and never registered it. He had deposited the van here in the warehouse with the temporary plates still on it. In the meantime, he had stolen four license plates from vehicles in Missouri, Illinois, Tennessee, and Arkansas. He had also managed to lift the registration from the truck his landlord drove, which allowed him to create a set of registration papers for the van using the farmer's name.

He drove the van out of the lot and headed for his cabin on the river. The world was obviously about to fall in on Morgan Keeler, senior bridge inspector, on Monday morning, so he had decided to wrap things up at the cabin, then head south for Mississippi. Tomorrow being Sunday, the district office ought not to discover his absence until he failed to check in for work, although, given the current media interest, that might not work. Even the Bureau, preoccupied with terrorists, might make a connection to the Trainman case when he disappeared. Either way, it would take only a day to get into Mississippi, whereas getting down to New Orleans would take much longer.

After that, he didn't much give a damn what happened. If he got away after destroying the Vicksburg bridge, he might even try for New Orleans. He turned the van up onto the southbound interstate ramp and headed downstate. He felt a mix of emotions as he drove south: fear, excitement, and even anticipation. Endgame, he thought again. The word had a nice ring to it.

Colonel Mehle came aboard the command car at 10:40 P.M. Saturday night. He was wearing Desert Storm cammies and a military-issue side arm and carried a small suitcase. Accompanying Mehle were two Army warrant officers whom Matthews had never seen before. They kept to themselves and did not volunteer any information as to who they were or why they were coming along. Matthews, who had his own hands full resetting the security details aboard the train in preparation for their 11:00 P.M. departure, did not have time to find out who they were. The locomotives up front were running, and Marsden's technical people were making last-minute checks on the cryogenics plant. The good news was that the temperature in the two tank cars had come down two degrees each, which was at least progress in the right direction. Mehle had promptly commandeered one of the cryogenics techs to ride the train to Idaho.

At exactly 10:55, the depot's main gates were opened and the train got under way for Birmingham Junction. It switched onto the main Norfolk Southern line and began a slow acceleration to road speed. The command car, with Matthews, Mehle, the two warrants, a comms specialist, and one MP, was the last car to bang through the points onto the main line. Matthews watched the security light towers at the depot fade into the Alabama night as the train gathered speed. Then Mehle was calling, so he went back inside the command car to review the route to Idaho Falls and the INEL.

Carolyn Lang called Hush from the front desk just before midnight Saturday. She told him she had taken a commercial flight out of Washington direct to St. Louis. He agreed to meet her in the bar downstairs after she had had a chance to drop her things in her room.

Carolyn came in and walked directly to his booth. She was dressed in a dark business suit and was carrying a small leather briefcase. There were strain lines in her face that hadn't been there the last time he had seen her. She slipped into the booth and signaled the bartender that she, too, would have coffee. He raised his eyebrows at her expectantly but did not say anything. She waited for her coffee to arrive before opening the briefcase. Then she produced an unbound inch thick document and put it on the table in front of him.

"This is the condensed list. IR compiled a database from the material the railroad companies provided. They were in the process of reorganizing the names into categories of incident when Carswell called them off."

"So Carswell and company are still chasing terrorists?"

"Yes. They simply can't bring themselves to admit that one guy might have done this much damage. Plus, it makes the Bureau look better if—"

"Yeah, I know that theory," Hush said. He looked down at the document, but, much as he wanted to, he did not pick it up. "I was serious about my question as to whom you're working for now."

"I understand," she said, avoiding his stare. "But the price of looking at this list is that I get to play." She looked back up at him. Her bright eyes held his own gaze in a grip that surprised him. "I'm not especially proud of what I've been doing, but there's more to that story than you know."

"I guess I'll just have to take your word for that," he said. "Such as it is."

She blinked at the insult and then looked down at her coffee. "I suppose I have that coming. I would have thought—well, never mind."

"Thought what? That I'd sympathize because I liked the insider game, too? Trouble with that, Carolyn, is that I fancied myself a player in the great game of cops and robbers. You know, going after bad guys and protecting the good guys. But you, you betrayed people. Bureau people. The good guys."

She nodded, her lips set in a thin line, and looked away. There was no one else in the bar. The bartender was polishing her already-glistening glassware while pretending not to watch them.

Hush leaned forward across the table. "Look at me," he ordered, keeping his voice low. What he really wanted to do was slam his fist on the table and really yell at this woman. She faced him again. "Why on earth do you think I would want you on *my* team?" he asked. "Even supposing there is a team."

"They weren't good guys, Hush. The people I set up were problems, every one of them. They were too senior to fire outright without embarrassing the Bureau, and they were all retirement-eligible."

"This is something you *know*, Carolyn? You were privy to their personnel files, their performance records? You were briefed by *their* superiors, who were requesting that the director send in a *Judas* to get these guys?"

She flinched when he said the name Judas, but she did not back down. "Yes. These were men who were more than willing to go astray. It wasn't like it was hard to do."

"I guess I know something about that. I've had some hands-on experience with your principal weapon, remember? Of course you do. What was that, phase one?"

"No!" she said, coloring. She took a deep breath. "You were different. You were the first one I'd been sent to, to—"

"To entrap," he suggested. "Learn to say the word."

"All *right*," she said. "To entrap. But you were a purely political play. Not like the others. There were substantive grounds for the others. Identifiable, documented performance problems, and yes, I was briefed. My job was to leverage whatever the problem was to the point where management could act effectively, and not just issue another performance counseling letter."

He leaned back in the booth. "So what was my 'performance' problem, Carolyn?"

She shook her head. "It wasn't performance of duty," she said carefully. "Your problem was your integrity. Basically, they wanted to replace you with someone who was a lot more . . . compliant."

"And that didn't give you pause, huh?"

She nodded again. "Like I said, there's history. I'm not entirely a free agent."

"Bullshit. I've checked the files. You've been doing this for ten years. In my case, you just rolled with it. Hell, what was one more victim for the Bureau's very own black widow? St. Louis gave you the wrong name."

She had the grace to blush. "No," she said softly. She raised her coffee cup. He saw that her hand was trembling a little. "No. I don't expect you to believe me, but no. That's why I was so relieved when you left town and had me stay back in Washington. I knew what was coming, what you would think."

He shook his head slowly. "Wow, Carolyn Lang. You are a piece of work."

"And you, Hush? When the big boys told you that you could have SES if you knocked *me* off? You tell them to get lost?"

"Nobody in the Bureau tells the director to get lost and survives the hour. The difference is that when I realized you weren't what they described, I elected *not* to slip you the knife. You, on the other hand, had no such scruples."

She started to respond to that, but then she looked away again. Hush decided that he'd had enough. He touched the document that lay on the table between them. "So, let's get on with it here—what's in this thing that I would give a shit about?"

She lifted her chin. "It's sorted alphabetically by name. There's a person's name, a two or three line incident description, such as a car getting hit by a train at a crossing, a date, and the disposition of the case."

"And what? I get to go through this whole thing?"

She put a protective hand on the document. "I want in. The Bureau is going the wrong way."

He stared at her.

"Look, we're in the same boat, Hush. We've both been squeezed out. You don't have to like me, but you will absolutely want to know what's in this."

He thought about it. There was no way to tell in advance if she really had something. If she didn't, he decided, he would simply renege. "All right," he said. "But only if Powers agrees. And he knows about you."

"I'll take my chances with Powers. Open it. Look at it."

He pulled the document over and started through it. There were hundreds of names and incidents. Pedestrian accidents. Crossing accidents. Derailments. Toxic chemical exposures. More crossing accidents—lots of crossing accidents. He thumbed through it page by page while she sipped her coffee and watched him. He was trying to concentrate, but he wasn't satisfied with where they'd left the other problem. He got as far as the *F*'s and looked up at her. He started to speak, but she waved him off.

"Keep going," she said.

He read some more, then stopped again, this time at the *J*'s.

"Keep going. Read the names carefully now."

"C'mon, Carolyn, what the hell am I—"

"Just keep reading. I want you to find it just like I did."

On the fifty-seventh page, he stopped at the name: Keeler, Morgan J. "My God," he whispered. "This is *our* Keeler?"

She nodded. "*Col.* Morgan J. Keeler, U.S. Army Corps of Engineers. 1986. At-grade crossing incident. His entire family, wife and two little kids, smashed to a pulp by a Union Pacific fast freight. As soon as I saw the name, I asked the UP counsel's office to send me the entire case file. Just to be safe, I asked for five other files, as well."

His thoughts were whirling. *Keeler?* God, it fit. Technical knowledge. Access. And now motive. In spades. "Whose fault?"

"His wife's fault, according to the police reports, the Railroad Safety

Board investigation, and the court cases. It usually is the car driver's fault. The train engineer said they misjudged how fast the train was coming and drove through the lights."

"And they were all killed."

"Yes. Again, that's usually what happens. Keeler sued, claiming the lights weren't working. He lost. Then he sued again on a legal technicality, and lost. Then they sued *him*. They won. Damages, lost revenues, legal fees. Two-and-a-half-million-dollar judgment against him. He's still paying. His government pay is garnisheed."

"They sued *him?* After his family was wiped out? Damn. Has he ever made threats?"

"Oh yes! In open court, no less. It's in the record. Shouted that he would get the bastards if it was the last thing he ever did."

Man, has he ever, Hush thought as he sat back in the booth and rubbed his lower jaw. "He's a bridge engineer—where does the explosive knowledge come from?"

"Vietnam. He led a sapper company. They blew up Vietcong tunnel complexes. Look, I have his current address. I got directions from the Corps district office. It's twenty miles south of a town called Festus, Missouri. That's about forty miles south of St. Louis."

"I'm surprised the Corps people told you," Hush said.

"I told them we'd needed to interview him, and that his home might be better than doing it in the St. Louis Field Division Office. Less bad publicity for the Army Corps. Hinted that there had been some threats. Made it sound like we were doing him and them a favor. They were actually grateful."

Hush let out a long breath. "Have you brought this to Carswell and company?"

She gave a short laugh. "I tried, actually. When I first got my hands on the list, but before I found Keeler's name. J. Kenneth went off on me; told me to stop coming around with wild-ass theories, and to tend to what I do best—namely, show my legs to the television crews."

"He sounds like a candidate for your real competence," Hush said.

She sighed and he told himself to stop it. "Look," she said, "I know you're angry with me. But right now, no one involved with Trainman at headquarters except IR knows about this list, and even they don't know about Keeler. This sounds like an opportunity to me."

"But for whom, Carolyn? I've been put on convalescent leave. If I work

Trainman off-line and Heinrich finds out about it, I'll be up on disciplinary proceedings. So will you."

"Not if *we* bring in the Trainman," she said.

"That gets back to my real problem, Carolyn. How do I know this isn't phase three of your professional setup job? You entice me into going solo after Keeler as a suspect, and then tell Carswell? Or the director?"

"Because I've been shunted aside, too."

"So say you."

Hush realized that they were at an impasse; Carolyn seemed to recognize the same thing. She stared off into space for a minute, drumming her fingers on the table. Then she seemed to make a decision.

"Okay, Hush, you can play it that way," she said. "What I hear you saying is that you're much more worried about getting in career trouble than in nailing this lunatic."

"Wrong," he said. "Your condition for handing this over is that you get to play. To tell the truth, I'm worried about being in the field with you. About having to watch my back. I haven't been in the field for a very long damn time, so *if* I do something about this, I don't need that. I may not be too bright, but I sure as hell learn. My career was just fine until they threw you into the game."

"Was it? Then why did you become a target? Because you're a lone ranger, that's why. Because you do not cultivate allies in high places. What were you thinking—that you could just do an excellent job and that would be enough? In this day and age? Are you truly that naïve?"

"Perhaps," he said. "But at least I don't go around the Bureau stabbing other agents in the back."

"Listen to me," she said. "Keeler has systemic knowledge and an overwhelming competence to destroy the bridges. He's had practically unlimited access since this thing began, and a first-class, declared motive. If you won't go after him, I will."

"Go after him? By whose authorization? With what warrant? And what would you do with him—arrest him? And take him where? Turn him over to whom? On what charges?"

"I'd bring him in for questioning and make my case to Herlihy right here in St. Louis. I'll tell you what: I think he'd confess. A guy who does what he's done is going to be proud of it. This wasn't for personal gain—this was for revenge."

Hush laughed. "Take him to Himself Herlihy? Your good friend? Whose handpicked successor you drove into retirement?"

"Hank McDougal is a serious drunk. A full-time lush."

"That's what you say. You know what? I'm tempted to let you head out there. Then I'm tempted to drop a dime on *you* for a change."

"That would make you feel better?" she said. Her eyes were bright with anger.

"Yeah, it would. Because if they jerked you back to Washington, then and only then would I know you weren't working for them anymore."

"And what would you do then?"

Hush hesitated. He didn't want to admit this. "I'd go after Keeler."

It was her turn to laugh. It was not a pretty sound. Then she reached inside her purse, withdrew her weapon, and put it on the table. The bartender's eyes grew round when the Sig appeared. Carolyn noticed her reaction across the room and told her they were FBI. Then she pulled out a cell phone and handed it to Hush. "Here," she said, the challenge bright in her eyes. "Go ahead. Tell them I'm here. You know the number."

Hush, his jaw set, didn't hesitate. He took the phone and turned it on. When it beeped, he began dialing the number for the main operations center in Washington. Carolyn put the weapon back in her purse and passed her hand through her hair. Her face was bright with color.

"Operations," a voice said.

"Stand by, one," he said, looking across the table at Carolyn. He put his thumb over the phone's microphone. "You sure you know where he lives?"

Her eyebrows came up and then she nodded emphatically. He removed his thumb. "This is Assistant Director Hanson," he said, and gave his validation code. "I want to get a message to Senior Agent Carolyn Lang."

There was a pause on the other end. "You're on her cell phone, Mr. Hanson," the voice said dryly. "Why don't you just tell her yourself? And by the way, where are you, Mr. Hanson?"

Hush thought fast. The operator had told him half of what he wanted to know, but he had screwed up by using her phone. "I'm on her phone because *my* department issued it to her. In the meantime, answer my goddamn question."

"Yes, sir. Sorry, sir. But—"

"Be quiet. I'm on convalescent leave in Baton Rouge. I want to know if Lang's still in the building."

Carolyn was listening with interest. The operator's tone was definitely more respectful. "It's just past one in the morning, D.C. time, Mr. Hanson," he said. "We can page her or call her at home, if you'd like. Oh, and Assistant Director Carswell has asked that we report any contact from you. Is there a number there in Baton Rouge where we can reach you?"

"The number that's displayed on your console, smart ass," Hush said curtly. "Leave a message on her office voice mail to contact me on this phone, please. I need to close out my case file on the Trainman case."

"Yes, sir. Uh, sir? You should send that file in to the NS situation room, Mr. Hanson. Senior Agent Lang is no longer assigned to Trainman."

The other half of what he wanted to know. "Really. Well, I guess that makes two of us, doesn't it," Hush said. "I'll turn the case file into the RA here in Baton Rouge. They can transmit it to NS. Disregard my message to Agent Lang."

He ended the transmission and gave Carolyn back the phone. He stared at her for a long moment. "How do I know I won't regret this, Carolyn?"

"I guess you don't," Carolyn said. "But we both know that Keeler might rabbit after what happened in Memphis."

Hush nodded. "Which was a disaster he probably engineered," he said. "But you're right. We need to move, and move fast. We should also tell Powers. He can provide backup."

"The state cop? And he will say, Based on whose authority? On what warrant? On what charges? No, we do it. Take him and hand him over to Powers, if you want to."

Hush pursed his lips. She was proposing that they go pick up Keeler. Right now. On their own. With no backup and no arrest authority. They'd be breaking every rule in the *FBI Manual*. She sat there watching him.

"What more do we have to lose?" she asked.

"Now there's the question of the hour," Hush said.

14

KEELER FINISHED loading the van just after midnight. He had supplies for two weeks, plus everything he'd need for the Vicksburg bridge. He closed the back doors, got in, and backed the van across the yard to where the boat on its trailer was waiting. He hooked up the trailer and then took one last look around. The night was clear, with a partial moon. It had cooled down noticeably from the day's heat. The air smelled of freshly plowed dirt overlaid with a faint whiff of chemical fertilizers. The cabin was dark, but everything was in place there, and in the woods, too. He was going to leave nothing behind, not a trace, as anyone who came looking was going to discover. He pulled the van and trailer over in front of the cabin and went back inside one last time.

He went directly to the picture room. He stood in the doorway and looked, for the last time, at the pictures of his lost family. He did not go in and sit down. He just looked, passing over the grotesque pictures and concentrating on the other ones, the happy scenes. Before the train. He thought about taking some of the pictures with him, then decided against it. His quest for revenge was enough. He shut the door and went back outside.

He drove out the long dirt road to the county road and then went south on U.S. 61 for twenty miles to Bloomsdale. There he picked up a dirt road that headed back east toward the river and a fishing camp, which was nestled at the junction of a creek and the main river. As he drove in with just parking lights, he could see four darkened campers and one fair-size RV scattered among the trees. The ramshackle office was dark, but there were envelopes and a slot to make a night's payment. He put the cash in an envelope, and marked down the van's license plate number, and slipped it through the slot. He drove the van down to the boat ramp in the small cove below the bluff.

It was full dark now, but there was enough moonlight. He backed the trailer carefully, watching in his mirror until he saw the boat's stern lift, and then got out to tie the bow line off to one of the steel stanchions set in the ramp's concrete. He backed some more until the boat came free, then pulled the van back up to the campground and parked in a spot farthest from the other campers. He went into the back, where he grabbed a dark windbreaker, a black watch cap, a flashlight, and a cut-down double barreled 12-gauge shotgun. He loaded the coach gun and his windbreaker pockets with shells, stepped out of the van, closed and locked the doors, and then just stood there in the shadows for five minutes, smoking a cigarette and watching the campground.

After making sure no one was out and about, he went down to where the boat was bobbing lightly against the mud banks next to the ramp, clambered aboard, and cast off. He let the boat drift downstream away from the camp before firing up the outboard. Keeping the engine at low speed, he moved out into and all the way across the main channel. There was more light out here on the main river, but there did not appear to be any shipping or barges coming. He wanted to make sure there weren't any other nocturnal fishermen out here before he headed north. Now that he had the van safely away from the cabin, he needed to go back there to finish up. When he was satisfied that he was alone, he lit up another cigarette, pointed the boat upstream, and slowly advanced the throttle to full power.

They drove out in her rental car, crossing the city from north to south on I-70 before picking up I-55 headed down toward Arkansas. They could see the recovery effort still going on out under the MacArthur Bridge as they left St. Louis. A maze of bright white and yellow lights illuminated the cluster of tugs, barges, and floating cranes. It took forty minutes to get down to Crystal City, where they got some high-octane coffee at a truck stop, and then backtracked up U.S. 61 to get to Festus. They missed the turnoff into the farm road and lost fifteen minutes looking for it until Hush got out and started reading mailbox numbers. Carolyn turned off the main headlights once they found it and started down the long dirt road, keeping the car in low gear.

They had agreed to approach Keeler's place quietly but not covertly. The car would have its parking lights on, and they would drive directly to the house. When they got close, Hush would call Keeler's home phone number and tell him they had come down at this unusual hour because threats had been made against his life after the Memphis bridge disaster. Once they had the opportunity to take him into custody, they would take him back to St. Louis. Where in St. Louis, they had not yet decided: There was still the problem of Herlihy, and the small matter of warrants.

"I still don't like doing this without backup," Hush said as the car bumped cautiously along the dirt road. The fields on either side had been freshly plowed, and the deep furrows stretched out in the moonlight in what looked like an infinite series of parallel lines. Carolyn slowed to a stop.

"Maybe we should call Powers, then," she said.

"If we reveal who the prime suspect is, and the state people get their hands on Keeler, the Bureau is left out in the cold."

She banged her hand on the steering wheel. "You never quit, do you? Always the goddamned bureaucrat. Who *gives* a shit who gets credit? The Bureau had you and me and the right theory and threw us all away. *Let the state people break it. I don't care!* If we're right, we've stopped a one-man disaster machine."

Hush felt himself redden in the darkness of the car. She was absolutely right. But his instincts about backup were also right. It was the one advantage the cops always had over the bad guys: They could bring a crowd. And suppose Carswell and company were correct and Keeler *was* the leader of a posse of terrorists? The problem was that they were both so far off the reservation now that calling in Bureau help was out of the question. He rubbed his eyes. It had been a long day.

"Okay," he said. "I'll call Powers." He stopped. He didn't have a phone number for Powers—it was in his briefcase. He told Carolyn the good news. She put the car in park and shut it down.

"Dial star seven seven," she said with a sigh. "That will get you the state police. I saw the signs out on the interstate."

The Highway Patrol operator said she could not place a call to Captain Powers, even when Hush identified himself as FBI. She was willing to place a call to headquarters, and they might be able to reach him. Hush patiently gave her the number of Carolyn's mobile, and then they waited. Carolyn slid the windows down and shut off the parking lights. Crickets and peepers serenaded them from the line of brush and grass on either side of the dirt lane.

"I'm amazed at how Keeler's name just popped up," he said.

"It didn't just 'pop up,' " he said. "A couple of dozen IR people have been working around the clock, sorting through ten feet of legal documents and court records. Manually. The file with Keeler's name in it was originally seven hundred pages. That was just one."

"That's what the Bureau does best, though—collect, sift, comb, and pick out all the pieces, one by one, until suddenly there's a picture and you wonder why the hell you never saw it."

"If we could lose all the office politics, it'd be a dramatically effective outfit," she said.

"Office politics?" Hush said ruefully. "Isn't that just another word for people like you and me?" Then the mobile chirped. It was Powers.

"My wife is not pleased," he began. "So this had better be an ax murderer in the orphanage."

"Better," Hush said. "We're pretty sure we know who the Trainman is." He went on to tell him what they had discovered. Powers listened in surprised silence.

"That's pretty damned disturbing. And you're with Lang? Isn't she the one who torpedoed you?"

"Yep," Hush said, looking across the darkened front seat. "That Lang. It's a long story."

"Well, look, I'm glad it's you guys and not me, because your people are going to go apeshit if you two bring in the Trainman. I'll get you backup, but how's about you make sure he's there before I roust out a squadron of cavalry?"

"Right. We'll call you from the house as soon as we know. He may have already skipped."

"After Memphis, *I* would have skipped. There is an avalanche of heat coming down on him right now: the media, railroad lawyers, and even your guys. Herlihy called me, said the Memphis bridge had been Washington's only hope of a 'positive development,' as he put it."

"Well, we might bring in a real positive development. Carolyn thinks he'll admit everything, that he's probably proud of what he's done."

"You got any paper for this? Warrants? Court orders? Proof of purchase?"

"Got squat," Hush said.

"You're brave, Hush. Not very smart, maybe, but really brave. Think spontaneous confession, or he'll walk." He was silent for a long moment. "Okay. Call me if you step on a snake. Better yet, call this number." He spelled it out. "It's our special operations center in Jefferson City. I'll alert the duty CIB lieutenant. And remember the toll plaza in Vicksburg, okay?"

"How could I forget?" Hush said touching his scalp.

There was another pause, as if Powers was trying to think of what to say. "You guys are way out of bounds with this move," he said finally.

"We know," Hush said again. "We never had this conversation."

"Got that right. Okay, we'll wait to hear from you."

"Let's do it," Hush said, and Carolyn started up the car.

"You told him about what I did?" she asked.

"I think the St. Louis people told him. Probably Herlihy. Watching feds stick one another in the back with dull knives is a popular pastime for local law."

She did not reply as the car bumped slowly over the rutted road. They could see a grove of trees and what looked like a small one-story cabin and some outbuildings in the distance. The structures were pale gray in the dim moonlight. There were no lights showing. Hush made the call to Keeler's listed number, but there was no answer.

"Pray for no dogs," he said. Carolyn nodded.

There were no dogs, nor anything else stirring at the cabin. They parked right out in front of the house, waited for lights, and then they went up and knocked on the door. No answer. Hush knocked again while Carolyn stepped back out into the front yard to examine the windows. She had her weapon out but was holding it down by her side. Hush called out Keeler's name, but they both sensed that the cabin was empty. Hush tried the front door. It was not locked.

"I'm going in," he whispered, drawing his own weapon. "You want to watch the perimeter in case I get in trouble, or come in?"

"I'll come in. Shouldn't we call Powers now?"

"We don't know what we've got here, Carolyn. He could have skipped, or he could be in here with a twelve-gauge."

"That's a cheery thought. So I should call the ops center, tell them what we *think* we have, and that we're going into the house."

"Right," he said, stepping back from the door. Carolyn went back to the car to make the call. Hush called out Keeler's name again, but his voice echoed off the empty outbuildings. A soft wind skirted the corners of the porch, bringing a muddy scent of the big river. There was still no reply, nor any sign that anyone was in the house. Carolyn came back to the door. They got their weapons set and went through the door. Once inside, Hush called out again. There was still no reply.

"We'll go room to room," Hush whispered. "Watch windows."

She nodded. The cabin had a front and a back porch. The front door opened into a central living room that had a fireplace to their right at one end and the kitchen at the back in an L configuration. To the left was a hallway, with what appeared to be two bedrooms on the left side, and a bathroom at the end of the hallway. The floors were wood. The bathroom door was open, and they could see moonlight through the lower half of the partially opened bathroom window. A roll-down shade was flapping gently in the night breeze.

The bedroom doors were both closed. The house smelled faintly of fireplace ashes, but it appeared to be neat and clean otherwise. Hush decided not to turn on any lights; the moonlight coming through the windows was sufficient. They walked together, covering each other, far enough into the living room area to be able to see into the tiny kitchen. There appeared to be some dishes in the sink. There was one small pot on the stove. A door led from the side of the kitchen back into the central hallway, and another door led out to the back porch. Hush opened the back door and looked out. There was nothing to be seen but a grove of trees, behind which appeared to be the river. It was time to check the bedrooms. He indicated for Carolyn to stand in the entrance to the hall-way, while he went through the kitchen door into the hallway near the bathroom. He called again and then knocked on the back bedroom's door. Then he opened it while Carolyn watched the windows and the other bedroom door, her weapon pointed down the hallway.

The back bedroom was small, perhaps twelve feet square. A single bed lay against the back wall of the house, flanked by two small night tables. There was a dresser to his right and a single closet door to his left. The room looked almost unused. There were no clothes strewn about, no shoes under the bed, no magazines or books on the night tables. Hush stepped into the room and went over to the closet door as Carolyn covered him from the doorway. The closet was partially filled with clothes, both hanging and stuffed up on top of a shelf. He closed the door and they went down the hall to examine the second room. This time, Hush covered while Carolyn opened the door. He heard her gasp in surprise.

"Get a load of this," she said softly as she stopped in the doorway.

Inside the room, the walls were literally plastered with pictures of Keeler's family. There were happy pictures of two little children and a smiling young wife. There were school class pictures, church picnics, Christmas scenes, an Easter egg hunt, camping trips, playgrounds. There were also some grotesque pictures of the wreck at the railroad crossing. Every square inch of the walls had been covered. Moonlight coming through the front and side windows glinted off the glass and plastic panels of the picture frames as they looked around. There was no bed or other furniture in the room except for a single chair and a small wooden table. On the table were several candles in holders. The candles were in various states of burn-down, and some of them had melted into a waxy heap on the table itself. The room smelled of dust and candle wax.

"It's a shrine," Hush muttered. "Keeler is definitely our guy."

Carolyn moved into the room to study the pictures by flashlight while Hush stepped over to the closet. Inside, he found a large file cabinet, which appeared to be filled with legal documents. Hush closed the door.

"Okay," he said. "We missed him. I don't think there's an attic, and I didn't see a trapdoor. We need to check the outbuildings, then call off Powers's alert team."

Carolyn nodded absently while she looked around. She studied the pictures of the train wreck and shook her head. The images were thankfully in black and white, but the only thing recognizable in most of them was the huge diesel locomotive emblazoned with the railroad's logo. There were *things* in the rain ditch alongside the rails, and several gray-looking tarps scattered here and there. In one picture, the frame of a car, blackened and twisted almost beyond recognition, its tires reduced to blobs of burned rubber, lay smashed under a boxcar whose front wheel trucks had crimped the frame neatly into three pieces. There was a tiny tarp covering something up in the boxcar's springs.

"Carolyn?"

"Yes, I'm coming. This is . . . terrible. These pictures . . ."

"You ever get called to a train wreck, don't go," he said. "They're always meat grinders. You want to make the call while I check the out-buildings?"

She nodded and, after checking again to see if there was an attic or crawl-space access, they went back out of the house. The moonlight seemed brighter after the shadowy interior of the house. Carolyn opened the driver's side door and got in to use the cell phone. Hush went around the side of the house and through some trees to the largest outbuilding. It was a wooden shed, with open doors at each end. It was big enough to hold a pickup truck and maybe a tool room on one side. There were assorted garden tools and a riding lawn mower under an overhang roof, and two smaller sheds could be seen through the larger doors. He first checked the little sheds, no more than outhouse-size tool storage, and then went back to the main shed. Hush heard Carolyn close the car door in the distance, and he assumed she would come over. He could hear marine diesels straining through the night from the direction of the river.

Standing in the entrance, he examined the larger shed. Inside were shadowy objects that looked like workbenches and some stands for power tools. He stepped into the aisleway, his weapon pointed down at his side, and wished for a flashlight. There were two side walls and the overhanging roofs outside, so it did not look like anyone could be hiding in here. He thought he heard a sound behind him and spun around, but there was no one there. He opened a wooden cabinet and found tools of all kinds stacked on shelves. In the cabinet beneath the workbench were more tools, some of them electronic test equipment. He went through all the drawers. He closed up the cabinets and stepped back to the entrance of the toolshed. Damn, damn, damn, he thought. We flat-assed missed him. The press of a cold steel gun barrel against the back of his neck convinced him otherwise.

Matthews awoke as the familiar whiplash banged its way through the string of cars, jerking the tail-end car into forward motion. He sat up in the darkened bunk room and rubbed his eyes. Mehle's bunk was empty. The two warrants had taken racks in the front of the bunk room, away from the dayroom door. One of them was snoring heavily.

Matthews looked at his watch: 2:10 A.M. None of the other bunks had been slept in, which meant that the colonel was still out there in *his* command center, probably driving the comms operator nuts with his pacing back and forth and constant haranguing of the engineers to go faster: "Why are we stopping now, goddamn it? Let's go! Let's go!" When he wasn't yelling at the engineers, he had been on the secure radio, talking to the ops center at Anniston, and occasionally to some office in the Pentagon. Matthews had stayed up until midnight before finally telling his choleric boss that he was going to get some sleep. Mehle had waved his hand at him dismissively and then, sensing that the train was slowing again, grabbed the intercom phone to yell at the engineers again.

Mehle was a man possessed, Matthews decided. The train had been sidelined repeatedly en route to Birmingham, and each time it slowed to rumble over switches onto a parallel track, Mehle had become angrier. At one point, while they were stopped on a siding, one of the engineers had walked all the way back to the command car to explain how the railroad's traffic-control system worked, that trains moved across the system into and out of geographical blocks of space along the main line, and that diversions to let other traffic pass by were *routine*. The fact that the entire southern-tier system had been disrupted by the loss of the bridges meant that the traffic-control system was in overload. Stop and go was the way it was going to be until they cleared Oklahoma. Mehle wouldn't hear of it.

"We need to get this bastard across that river," he shouted. "And we need to do that right goddamn now. Do you understand? You tell those goddamn traffic people that we have an extremely dangerous cargo on board and the sooner they get us out of their system and good to go on the other side, the better off everybody'll be. Got it?"

The engineer walked back up the tracks, shaking his head and muttering to himself. Matthews wondered at the time if the engineers might just walk off at the next junction and refuse to run the train anymore until the crazy colonel was taken off. He again rubbed his eyes and looked at his watch. They were moving, but they should have been in Birmingham by now. From Anniston, it was only a couple of hours. He had gone to sleep in his Skivvies; his cammie trousers and shirt hung on a hook at the head of his bunk.

Underneath his clothes hung a holster rig and a military-issue 9-mm semiautomatic, which Mehle had insisted he and the sergeant in charge of the MPs wear for the duration of the trip. Mehle had come aboard armed, and he had posted an M16-armed MP in the forward diesel control cabin with a separate handheld radio, somewhat to the annoyance of the two engineers. Another armed MP had been posted in the secondary communications pod mounted on the back of the lead engine. The MPs at the front of the train were to stand four-hour watches and check on each other, which meant that they had to climb back over the engine's side catwalk periodically to see if the other guy was still awake. Mehle had also insisted the MPs deploy up and down the entire length of the eighty-car train every time it sidelined, and Mehle himself had walked it each time they were stopped for opposing traffic. Matthews finally talked him into setting a watch routine so that all the guards would not be rousted out for every stop and thereby be exhausted by daylight.

He decided to get up. They had to be nearing Birmingham by now, and he knew they would probably be shunted off to that siding at the abandoned steel works again to take their turn in the long queue awaiting clearance to the south and west. Mehle would undoubtedly spin up again. Better to be up and in uniform than asleep in his tree when Mehle hit the fan.

The colonel did not disappoint him. The train entered Birmingham from the east and turned immediately north and then west, rumbling over several switch points as it left the lights of the city and its interstate highways to their left-hand side. As soon as he could see the two lines of the rusting chimneys, Matthews told the colonel that this was the same remote siding they had been sent to before. Mehle swore, called the front engine, and told them to stop the train where it was. The engineer protested: The front half was already onto the siding spur, but there were still forty or so cars out on the main line. They would have to get the whole thing clear before they could stop it. Mehle told them again, this time in a cold and deliberate voice, to stop the train. The engineer obliged by putting on the brakes, but he said he could no longer be responsible for this train and that he would be back to the command car as soon as they had it stopped. He asked if the colonel understood that they were creating an extremely unsafe condition on the main line and that all traffic on it would now be halted as soon as his stop signal got back through the system. The colonel did know, Mehle replied, and then, to Matthews's surprise, Mehle broke into military formalese: He told the engineer to inform traffic control that they had a possible fire on board and to keep all other traffic clear of 2713 until such time as the problem could be properly investigated by the embarked military detachment. The engineer was to remind the control center that 2713 carried military ordnance. Mehle hung up the intercom and turned to Matthews.

"Wake up those two warrant officers in there and tell them to go forward and do their thing."

"Their 'thing,' Colonel?"

"Those warrants are Army railroad engineers. We're about to take over both ends of this bastard. In the meantime, I'm going to deploy the guard force and have everyone inspect for 'possible' smoke. I need time to get those union pukes out of the engines."

Matthews was thunderstruck. Mehle was going to kick the civilian engineers off the train? The colonel's face was flushed with anger and fatigue, and Matthews thought his eyes were unnaturally bright. He wondered if Mehle was on something. "Sir, can I know what your intentions are?" he asked.

"My intentions," he said, "are to get this sucker back out on the main line and headed west for Meridian, Jackson, and Vicksburg. We're not going to get anywhere if we allow the railroad to stick us back here in east bumfuck Egypt for the rest of the night. Go roust those warrants."

Matthews hurried into the bunk room as Mehle called out the entire guard force.

It felt like a shotgun, which meant that Keeler was probably standing far enough away to avoid a turn and kick maneuver.

"Twelve-gauge, double barrel, single trigger," Keeler said quietly. "So put your weapon on the workbench there, please."

Hush exaggerated his lean forward to put his weapon the bench. The barrel did not stay with him; Keeler apparently knew better.

"Now let's go back to the house. Keep your hands out at your sides, palms out, please. Your partner, by the way, is in the trunk of that car."

"Did you hurt her?" Hush asked as he walked back out of the work shed.

"Only her pride, I suspect. I did listen to her tell someone that there was no one here, for which I'm obliged."

Keeler's voice was behind him and slightly offset. Hush tried to figure a move, but it would be tough against a shotgun that was out of kick range. Keeler read his thoughts.

"You don't have a move, so why don't you relax. I'm not going to kill you, or her, unless you make me. I only kill bridges."

"That Army officer's widow would argue with you," Hush said.

"That was an accident; he got to the wire before I did. I was going to trip it from a safe position. You know, slow things down a little. I just need to set some things up here and then I'll be on my way. Now move. To the house."

He prodded Hush in the back with the shotgun. Hush started forward.

"Your bridge-dropping days are over, you know," Hush said as they cleared the edge of the trees. The car was still where she had parked it. He was speaking loudly so she could hear him.

"Not quite," Keeler said. "Two to go. *Then* I'm done." They were approaching the front steps.

"You'll never get near either one of them," Hush said. "Not now. We know who you are."

Keeler snorted. "That's what they were probably saying at Baton Rouge. *I* didn't get near that bridge. That ship did, though. Wasn't that something?"

"I'll give you that," Hush said. There were no sounds coming from the car, but unless Keeler had tied her up, she would be out of that car very soon. Every FBI agent had been trained how to get out of a locked automobile trunk.

"So which one's next, then?" Hush asked as he neared the steps.

Keeler said, "Whichever one will do the most damage, I guess. Inside."

Hush stepped up onto the porch, and Keeler instructed him to open the door, go in three steps, and then kneel down on the floor and put his hands on his head. Hush did as he was told, still trying to think of a move. He felt like an idiot: This was the price of not having backup. And now he was on his knees, just like the agents had been in Baltimore.

Keeler stepped in behind him and closed the front door. Good, Hush thought; he won't hear her efforts to get out of that trunk. Somehow, he had to keep Keeler talking, to reinforce what he had said about not hurting them. He also needed to buy Carolyn some time. He heard Keeler walk up behind him and then he saw stars and fell sideways onto the plank floor, trying to break his fall, but his hands weren't working that well. Then Keeler stepped in and hit him with the gun's steel barrel on the right shin, so hard that Hush almost passed out from the white-hot lance of pain that shot up his leg. His eyes watered so badly, he could not see, and his head was still ringing. Then Keeler tapped him again at the same point and he did pass out.

When he came to, he was in the back bedroom. He was lying on his side and he had a splitting headache. There was a rope around his neck. His hands were bound behind his back, and his feet were jerked up behind his back. The rope came between his legs. When he tried to straighten his legs, the rope around his neck tightened. His right leg throbbed with such pain that he assumed it had been broken. He thought he could hear Keeler moving around the house, but the pain and the nausea were so bad, he could hardly concentrate. He realized he was lying on the bed. He tried to shift his position again, but he had been on the edge of the bed and succeeded only in rolling off, directly onto his injured leg, triggering a new lance of pain. He fainted at once.

Keeler heard the thump from the bedroom, picked up the shotgun, and walked back down the hall to see what was going on. The tall man was down on the floor, his right leg partially pinned under him, the rope stretching tight against his throat. He was obviously out cold. He went in and adjusted Hanson's inert form so he wouldn't choke to death, then closed the door. Almost as an afterthought, he opened it again and set the knob latch, and then he pulled the door closed again. He went back to the front windows to check the car, but there was nothing going on there. He gathered up the pictures he had come back for, slipping them out of their frames and rolling them into his coat pocket. Then he set the three timers, picked up the shotgun, and stepped out through the front door. There was a blur of white over by the car as a blast of gunfire blew the doorjamb into splinters right next to his face. He dropped to the porch floor and let go both barrels of the shotgun in the direction of the car. He heard the car's windshield blow out and a yell. He quickly reloaded the shotgun as he bellied backward into the open doorway, kicking the screen door away from him. When it closed again, he fired two more blasts right through the screen, again in the general direction of the car, blowing out a front tire and shattering more glass. He quickly reloaded and did it again, removing some more of the car's glass and settling its front end down onto the ground. He reloaded and then listened. Then he checked his watch. Three minutes, maybe only two. Shit!

Still down on the floor, he pushed the screen door back open with the barrel of the shotgun. The spring creaked audibly and the woman behind the car put two more rounds through the doorway, blowing chips of wood out of the ceiling behind him before ducking back out of sight. He crawled out through the door, keeping flat, and rolled twice to the right, ending up behind a corner post, with the shotgun leveled at the car. For a moment, the only thing he could hear was the sound of his own breathing.

"Lang," he called.

"You better be inside," she called back. "Because here I come."

"I'm right here, Lang. Right out on the front porch. With the shotgun and a whole pocket full of shells. Come on, let's see who can hit what."

He thought he saw movement at the car's right rear, and sure enough, two rounds came banging up at the porch from *under* the car. The bullets whacked audibly into the front of the house. He didn't hesitate: He fired one round into the dirt in the center of the car's body. A shower of sparks and a cloud of dust puffed out from under the car. He held back on the second round, knowing she was waiting for him to fire the other round, and then she'd stand up while he was reloading and take him on. Gutsy damn broad.

"I don't want to shoot you, Lang," he called. "But if we keep this up, I'm bound to get the gas tank."

There was a moment of silence.

"Listen to me, Lang," he called. "Hanson's tied up inside. In about a minute, this house is going to catch fire, big-time. And then I'm leaving."

"You can try," she said.

He did not reply. He moved to the right some more, until he was right on the edge of the porch. He didn't think she could see him in the shadows behind the railing. The car, on the other hand, was in full moonlight. Both front tires were down and something was leaking out from under the grill. He carefully opened the well-oiled breech, pulled the dead shell out, and replaced it. Then he covered the gun with his upper body and closed it noiselessly. He lifted the gun over the railing and fired another blast into the car, back by the quarter panel. He saw her head come up from behind the car and he fired again, off to one side, just enough to make her eat dirt again. He reloaded and then sat back on his haunches.

"Face it," he called. "Handgun against a scattergun. No chance." He waited for her to reply, but nothing came back. Had he hit her? "I don't want to kill either one of you," he said. "I just need to get down the river and gone."

"So go to it," she said. She was still behind the car, keeping the most steel between her and his shotgun.

There was whumping sound behind him in the house as the first incendiary let go in the kitchen. Then a second one. He vaulted over the porch railing and rolled out into the yard, ending up in a prone position behind a nearby tree, the shotgun still pointed at the car. The third device let go under the living room floorboards, throwing a blaze of hot light out onto the porch.

"Decision time, Lang. You can come after me, or you can get your partner out. You hear me?"

She did not reply. The sounds of the fire grew, and the walls of the cabin began to shake.

"What's it going to be, Lang?" he called. "You throw out your gun and go into the house, I'll let you do it. You don't, he's toast, and there's no telling how you, me, and baby here are going to come out."

The crackle of flames behind him was becoming louder. Somewhere a window shattered.

"He's in the back bedroom, Lang," he called, beginning to inch backward in the dirt toward the river. "Hear that fire? What's it going to be?"

"All right," she said. She threw out the gun. "All right."

He kept himself down on the ground and scuttled backward even faster. He had reached the grove of trees by the time she finally stood up, her hands showing. She looked briefly in his direction, but he was already into the deep grass between the trees. She bolted for the house. He got up and ran for the boat.

Hush felt the whole cabin shaking as he came to again, and then he recognized the sound of fire. His first instinct was to try to get up, but the rope around his neck tightened immediately. Wrong move. He thought he could feel heat through the door. Then he heard someone rattle the door handle and swear. Carolyn!

"In here," he yelled, although it came out more like a croak. "I can't move."

"Hang on!" she shouted. The rumble of the fire was definitely getting louder, and smoke was beginning to sift through the crack around the door. His right leg throbbed unmercifully, and he wondered what she was doing out there. Then there was a mighty crash against the door, and then another one, and another one, until the door began to splinter inward. A final crash and her hand was through the hole and she was releasing the latch. She kicked the door open and a wall of smoke and heat tumbled into the room behind her. She quickly pulled the noose off his neck and unwrapped his wrists, then helped him stand up. His feet were still tied, and neither of them had a knife. There was no time for the ropes, however, as the flames began to roar in the hallway, palpably sucking the air out of their lungs. She lunged over toward the back bedroom window, picked up one of the night tables, and knocked out the frame and all the glass. He bunny-hopped on one leg over toward the window and she shoved him right through it. He fell heavily onto the back porch and thought he would faint again when he bumped his shin. She came scrambling out behind him with a yell as the bed inside erupted into flames, and together they rolled off the porch onto the mercifully cool dirt. She got up immediately and dragged him by his armpits away from the house, which was fully engaged by now. When they were a good hundred feet away, she collapsed onto the grass beside him, puffing hard.

"Where's Keeler?" he wheezed.

"It was you or him," she said. "And he had a shotgun."

"Help me get this damned rope off my feet."

They clawed at the ropes together for a minute before the ends came loose. He fell back onto the grass as a wave of pain shot up his leg. Then he rolled onto his side and struggled to his feet. She looked up at him from the grass.

"And where the hell do you think you're going?" she asked, staring at his dangling, useless right leg.

"After him. He's got a boat."

By 3:15 A.M., 2713 was rolling again, this time headed southwest through Tuscaloosa on the Norfolk Southern group seven track toward Meridian, Mississippi. Matthews was having a cup of coffee on the back platform of the command car with the MP sergeant as the Alabama night went whistling past. Mehle was inside, berating someone in Washington, filling the air with invective.

Matthews was still absorbing what had happened up in Birmingham. The report of a possible fire on an Army ammunition train caused the night to erupt in fire trucks and police. The two railroad engineers had come huffing back to the command car, passing the two Army warrant officers walking forward, whereupon Mehle summarily dismissed the two civilians and told them to get the hell off *his* train. He then informed the local FEMA office in Birmingham that there was no fire but that there was the possibility that some of the ordnance on the train had become unstable. He recommended that FEMA order the railroad to clear the train out of town to the southwest as soon as possible to preclude an absolutely catastrophic ammunition explosion within the outskirts of Birmingham. Five minutes later, the senior warrant officer in the front engine notified Mehle they were cleared to back out of the siding. Matthews had been dispatched to round up all the MPs, who barely had time to jump on board before the train jolted into motion. The two civilian engineers had been left standing in the grass alongside the switchyard with the bewildered fire companies, all of them wondering what the hell was going on.

Mehle had apparently planned this entire little drama, Matthews discovered, when the comms operator told him that Mehle had rigged it with the Army Chemical Corps officials at the Pentagon to alert all of the Federal Emergency Management Centers along the route to stand by in case there was a problem with the train or its cargo. Which explained how FEMA had gotten into the problem so fast, and why the railroads had given 2713 its sudden route priority out of Birmingham. Matthews asked Mehle what he intended to do the next time they were held up for traffic. "There isn't going to be any next time, not until we're over that goddamned river," Mehle declared. "We're going to run this thing straight through to goddamned Vicksburg."

The sergeant knew nothing about railroad route and traffic control, but he had the sense to ask how they were just going to run straight through with all those trains out there on the main lines. Matthews had been thinking the same question, but he did not want to admit that he thought he knew the answer. He was pretty sure that Mehle, with Army engineers at the controls, was simply going to ignore traffic control and run the train straight through, ultimately forcing the railroads to treat 2713 like a runaway train.

He also realized that Mehle must be getting some help from high places in Washington, and then he understood why the train had waited until late Saturday night to roll: Washington did not work on Sundays, so the regular authorities at the Department of Transportation were not available to challenge Mehle's unorthodox maneuvers. The colonel had a plan all right, and Matthews was suddenly glad he was on the last car in the train. The sergeant was staring down at the shiny rails as they were extruded out from under his feet into the darkness behind him. He looked worried.

"You know that chiller setup ahead?" he asked.

Matthews threw the remains of his coffee out onto the blur of ties under his feet. He was pretty sure he didn't want to hear this. "Yeah?"

"Those temps? According to the readings log, they're back up to where we started, back at Anniston."

"Wonderful," Matthews said. He thought briefly about jumping off the train as an alternative to going inside and breaking this bit of news to Mehle. It was tempting.

Hush lurched down the path toward the grove of trees and the river. Lang followed, until she realized they had no weapons.

"Wait," she called, "My weapon's out by the car."

He stopped, nodded soundlessly, and held on to a tree to keep himself upright while she ran back past the burning house. His head was spinning just a little, and the pain from the knot on his shin was making him feel nauseous again. He tried to recall where his Sig was. She was back in two minutes with her weapon in her hand.

"I put another call into Jefferson City," she said. "Look, you're out of it. You wait here. I'll see if I can find him."

He started to remind her about the shotgun, but she just pushed past him. The house collapsed in a roar of burning timbers behind them, sending a great wall of glowing smoke mushrooming out into the yard. He realized he couldn't just let her go by herself, so he hobbled down the path after her, bouncing from tree to tree to keep himself upright. When the path began to steepen, he wrestled down a tree branch to support himself. He was staggering back to the path when there was a familiar flare of red light, followed by a thundering blast that weirdly enough seemed to explode *up* in the trees ahead. He thought he heard Lang scream, and then there were fragments buzzing all around his face. He dropped instinctively, avoiding hitting his leg for change, and hugged a tree trunk until the dust settled.

"Carolyn!" he called.

"Down here," she called back. "What the hell was that?"

"He leaves bombs behind," he called. "Like on the MacArthur. Stay put. I'm coming down."

He pushed ahead, using his stick as a crutch, moving from tree to tree through the lingering smoke. The undergrowth was about knee-high, but the path was just visible. The MacArthur Bridge and the toll plaza at Vicksburg, he reminded himself. Bastard knew how to slow down a pursuit. He still couldn't see her, but he assumed she was taking cover ahead of him. He would try to find a clear path and lead her back.

"Hush, be careful," she called. "I think I see wires on the path. I think they're trip wires."

Hush slowed down as he advanced on the path, watching for wires. Most of the smoke was behind him now, and he could smell the riverbanks. Then his stick snagged on a vine, even as part of his brain realized it wasn't a vine. He dropped flat this time, no longer worrying about the leg, as another tree bomb hammered the night, this time *behind* him. Then a second one went off, and then a third, and then a fourth, a punishing constellation of hot, ear-squeezing blasts that threatened to jelly his brain. Each explosion pumped another humming, slashing cloud of wood fragments and choking smoke through the woods. He felt his fingers clawing involuntarily into the soft dirt as he tried to become one with the earth. At least it's dirt this time, he thought, not concrete.

Finally it was over. His ears rang from the explosions, and he began to sneeze from all the smoke and dust in his face. He opened his eyes and saw only blades of grass. When he realized he was sneezing, he started to laugh. At last he sat up, and he saw Carolyn rising from a crouch about fifty feet away, staring at him in amazement through all the smoke.

15

POWERS AND HIS response team showed up two hours later, about one hour after the country sheriff and three deputies arrived at the remains of the house. For purposes of talking to the county law, Hush and Carolyn decided to stay with their cover story about Keeler, namely that they had come out to warn him that people were making threats against him after the Memphis bridge disaster. Keeler had apparently panicked, thought they were coming to arrest him, shot up their car, set the house on fire, and bolted. He had had explosives stored in the house, which accounted for Hush's injuries and the series of loud booms heard halfway across the county. All that remained of the house were blackened concrete pilings nested in a glowing ash heap, overseen by the blackened remains of the chimney. The deputies were poking around the sheds when Powers and company arrived, at which point the Missouri Highway Patrol investigators took over.

The county sheriff reported that Keeler had been a bit of an enigma in this county of large cotton farms. They knew he worked for the Corps of Engineers and that his main office was up in St. Louis, but beyond that, he stuck to himself and was seen in town only infrequently when he came to purchase supplies and groceries. His landlord had told people that the river cabin seemed to be more of a weekend home for his solitary tenant, because he was usually gone all during the week. In any event, the sheriff was only too grateful to back out of what looked like a complicated mess and let the state cops handle it. One of the deputies returned Hush's weapon to him before they left; Hush was grateful that the sheriff did not press for an explanation of how it had ended up in the shed.

A state police forensics team arrived at daybreak and began to check out the sheds. By then, Hush was able to hobble around a bit with the help of makeshift cane. He had a purple knot on his shin the size of a squashed golf ball, and a smaller one behind his right ear. Carolyn Lang had some road rash on her knees and elbows, courtesy of her own efforts to reach China when the tree bombs began exploding all around them. Powers was fascinated by the explosives in the trees.

"Why the trees?" he asked.

"Because I think he mostly wanted to disrupt pursuit. I think the bomb on the MacArthur was a screwup, because what happened out here to-night was just like that and the toll plaza at Vicksburg—a lot of noise, fire, smoke, but all done in such a way as to flatten us, not kill us."

"I remember the flatten part," Powers said. "Vividly."

"Same thing when he was shooting at me," Carolyn said, "When I was behind the car. He could have gone for the gas tank."

"Did he admit he was the Trainman?" Powers asked. "That he had blown the bridges?"

"Yes," Hush said. "Bragged about it, even. He's the guy."

"Does he have help?"

"We don't think so," Hush said, looking at Carolyn for confirmation. Her face was smudged with soot, and there were some scratches on her cheek. "This is personal revenge. I don't think he's finished, either."

Powers kicked at a rock, knocking it into the pile of ashes that had been the cabin, raising a puff of sparks. "So," he said finally. "Tell me. How you guys want to play this?"

"Let's take a little walk," Hush said. "Slowly, if you please."

They went back through the ruins of the grove crunching carefully over the shattered limbs and piles of scorched leaves in case there was yet one more wire. They came out on the banks of the river, which was turning the color of polished bronze as the sun rose. An incredibly long string of barges was gliding swiftly downriver with the current, its tug seemingly running at idle. The banks smelled of mud, fish, and rotten wood. The notch in the banks where Keeler had pulled up his boat was visible to their left.

Hush rested his throbbing leg on a log and explained to Powers where he and Carolyn stood with respect to the FBI's investigation. "I assume the Bureau doesn't know anything about what happened here last night?" he asked when he was finished.

"Not from us, they don't. And I don't think the sheriff back there is going to tell anybody but his buddies down at the general store. Not that he believed your story, by the way."

"Figured as much," Hush said, remembering the business with his weapon.

"But there'll be a federal inquiry under way after what happened in Memphis," Carolyn pointed out. "The Corps will report Keeler's missing."

"But not that he's the Trainman, right?" Powers said. "That's something only us chickens know for a fact."

Hush looked at Carolyn again. They had a decision to make, which was what Powers was trying to tell them. What, if anything, were *they* going to report to the Bureau? The tugboat sounded a long blast on its whistle as another tug and barge string appeared around a bend about a mile downriver. The upstream-bound tug answered in kind. The noise provoked a wedge of ducks to launch themselves across the river from a nearby bed of reeds.

"What I want to do is what you and I talked about, Mike," Hush said. "We know who this guy is. Let's go after him, state by state, road by road, whatever it takes to find him."

Powers raised his eyebrows at Carolyn Lang. "Personally?" she said. "I concur. Screw those people." She started to go on but then stopped.

"You're both stumbling over a *but*," Powers said. "You've both been in the Bureau too damn long to start playing games with a major case just because the outfit decided to shit on you."

Hush and Carolyn nodded at the same time. "Our duty," Hush said, "is to report what we were doing out here, and why, and what happened."

"We can still do that," Carolyn said, "As long as we exercise some discretion in our choice of who gets our report. And how."

The two men stared at her. She tossed her head and put on that crooked smile. "I mean, *I* could source the report. In writing, of course. I'd even mark it 'Urgent.' Then I'd submit it to the nearest field office, which happens to belong to one Mr. Herlihy. I could put it in an interoffice-mail envelope and just . . . turn it in. It is Sunday, isn't it?"

Powers didn't get it, but Hush did. "Herlihy would be told by his secretary on Monday morning that some kind of report had been sent to him by Carolyn Lang, marked 'Urgent' Since he hates Carolyn, he is just as likely to put the damn thing in his too-hard box."

Powers was grinning now. "In the meantime—" he began.

"In the meantime, you could mobilize the assets of your state police task force to find Keeler. If he's running in the South, it's probably going to be local law that catches up with him, anyway."

They kicked it around some more, looking for holes and assessing the urgency of action. Powers clearly wanted a shot at catching Keeler, knowing what he now knew. Keeler had vowed he was going to try for one or the other of the two remaining bridges, which gave them an advantage: They knew where to focus the search. And while the federal effort could probably develop a lot of information about Keeler, it would indeed be the legions of local cops who could do the best job of combing the back roads and highways of the Mississippi Delta to find him. Keeler had been planning this thing for years, so it wasn't likely that he would be going anyplace to which credit cards, utility bills, phone numbers, or vehicle registrations could point. He would be on the run in the rural South, possibly even using the river. If he was really smart, Powers pointed out, he would go to ground somewhere until the government and the railroads began to relax their vigilance.

"It's like the IRA says," Powers observed. "The guys guarding the bridges have to be lucky every time; Keeler has to get lucky only once. Hell, he could stretch this thing out for another year."

"I don't think so," Carolyn said. "He's working down a plan, and everything's in place. He was confident enough to tell Hush that. Hell, in a year, they'll have some of the bridges repaired. No. He's out to stick an ice pick in the railroads' eye, and now he *wants* them to know it's him. He's got momentum, and he knows his targets. He won't stop now."

"And suppose Herlihy reads your report right away?" Powers asked. The sun was fully up now and they had started back to where their people were still examining the area around the burned-out cabin.

"That's not likely," she said. "Although I'll generate it right away. I've got my portable at the hotel in St. Louis. Then I'll drive downtown and put it into the admin system. Like I said, it's Sunday. That should give your people a twenty-four-hour head start, Captain. Maybe even more."

Powers shook his head and whistled. "Aren't you a piece of work, Senior Agent Carolyn Lang."

"You guys sound like a broken record," she said. "Let's get to it."

. . .

Keeler got back to the fish camp at just after three in the morning. He had run the boat at full speed down the river, whipping by some tug and barge strings, trying hard to beat whatever manhunt the two FBI agents might have called out after they picked themselves up from his grenade serenade in the willow grove. He had learned that little technique from the North Vietnamese, who always seeded a battlefield with some lethal distractions before disappearing back into the jungle. He went downriver as fast as he could, in case they got a helicopter up. Once he reached the fish camp, he pulled the boat into the cove and then went up the ramp to get the van. He retrieved the boat and got it onto the trailer and then towed it back to his parking place. The campgrounds were still dark, although the night was turning gray at the edges as morning twilight approached.

He parked the van, drew the shades on the back windows, and flopped down on the bunk in back. He should have been exhausted, but his nerves were thrumming and he was wide awake. Definitely endgame. He knew it and so did the FBI—now. He would be lucky to get one more bridge, and now that he had been identified, there really wasn't any choice in the matter: It would have to be Vicksburg. New Orleans was too large a metropolitan area, with far too many police of every variety. And too far from here. The Vicksburg bridge was a simpler proposition, with only a small town nearby and a relatively easy setup for what he had in mind. Given what he'd done before, they would be focused intently on the physical security of the two remaining bridges. Even if they guessed right on which bridge would be attacked, they'd never see him coming.

He would be willing to bet that it had been that hotshot blond agent who'd figured it out, because the other one, the quiet one, seemed to be more bureaucrat than field agent. A committee guy—task forces, multiple meetings, cover your ass with paper. He'd met plenty of those in the Army Corps of Engineers, of course, but he'd expected better from the FBI. He had been surprised when just the two of them showed up: The Bureau usually operated in squads. But it didn't matter. After tonight, they'd alert the whole damn law-enforcement world.

He stared at the ceiling of the van. So, if he was going to get one more, it would have to be soon. Like in the next twenty-four hours. They couldn't know about the van, at least not for a couple of days or so, and the boat would improve his disguise. Drive down into Mississippi in a few hours looking like any other retiree fisherman. Dark glasses, a slouch hat, maybe stop by a Wal-Mart somewhere and get some hair coloring. Just enough to get him through the roadblocks and checkpoints, although he didn't think they'd extend those tactics to Mississippi for another day or so. The next step was to get himself into position between Jackson and Vicksburg. He knew right where to go.

He jumped when he heard a door slam somewhere in the campground. He forced himself to relax. He needed to get some sleep. He had at least an eight-hour run through Kentucky and Tennessee to get into position by nightfall. He wished he had a television in the van, because it might be interesting to know what the FBI was doing in reaction to discovering his identity. On the other hand, ignorance just now might indeed be bliss.

Colonel Mehle's grand plan to drive straight through to Vicksburg came undone at Meridian, where they ran into a full-stop and hold signal for the first time since Birmingham. They had passed a dozen other trains sidelined on either side of the main line during their all-night drive down through Alabama. On each of them, the crew of the sidelined train had been standing in engine doorways, staring at their passing as if some kind of circus was going by. Matthews had even seen some blue flashing lights at road crossings as they approached Meridian near dawn.

He had told Mehle about how the log readings showed rising temps, but, surprisingly, Mehle waved it off. He'd deal with that problem on the other side, he said. They'd divert the train to the Pine Bluff Arsenal should the temps head dangerously out of limits. But first and foremost, he intended to get this train through all the traffic to Vicksburg and across the river. Matthews, his eyes stinging from fatigue, had gone back into the bunk room and dropped into his bunk without even taking his boots off.

He was awakened by the squeal and juddering vibrations as the engineers brought the train to a harder than usual stop. He heard Mehle fulminating on the intercom in the next room. Now what? he thought, trying to focus on his watch. It was 7:15. Morning. They had to be in Meridian by now. He tumbled off the bunk and went into the bathroom to splash some water on his face. Mehle's imprecations were even louder through the single connecting door. He dried his face, took a deep breath, and went into the command room.

"I don't care how many trains there are out there. We cannot stop this train. Do you understand me?" Mehle appeared to be bleary-eyed but definitely not sleepy. He listened for a moment, swore again, and slammed down the intercom phone. "Post the goddamned guard," he shouted to Matthews. "Apparently, now all the sidings ahead of us are full, and we have to wait for them to empty out before they'll let us go forward."

"But how—"

"Goddamned incompetent civilians," Mehle said in disgust. "Obviously no one shut off the *east*bound traffic on the bridge at Vicksburg. They've been letting eastbound trains come over the whole time we were approaching. Now all the main line *and* all the sidings between here and Vicksburg are literally full of trains. We'll just have to wait. Get the goddamn guard posted and get someone to make some goddamn coffee."

Mehle disappeared into the goddamn bathroom. Matthews went in and shook the sergeant awake and told him to post the guard. Then he went out to the back platform.

They were stopped on what appeared to be the main line. There was a dense green forest on one side and what looked like a public golf course on the other, with huge sprinklers going as the sun came up. Right next to them on a siding was a long freight pointed in the opposite direction. Its engines were idling right across from where Matthews stood. The engineers were out on the catwalk, gawking at the MPs as they deployed down the train with its slab-sided armored engines. Up about a mile ahead, there was a white headlight aimed right at them, he hoped it was mounted on the front of a *stopped* train. If this was Meridian, Mehle hadn't done too badly.

Within twenty minutes, the sergeant was back to report that the security perimeter had been set. Matthews had found the makings for coffee and handed a cup over to the sergeant. A replacement came into the command car to relieve the comms operator, who had been stuck on watch all night because they had not stopped since Birmingham. There being no sign of Mehle, Matthews took his coffee and went outside to inspect the flatcar containing the cryogenics unit. As he climbed the small ladder leading up to the equipment deck, the train's whistle sounded and then the train jerked into motion again. Matthews had to grab a railing to keep from falling. He wondered what they doing now, until the train stopped again, leaving enough clearance behind them for the nearby freight to enter the main line. As soon as that train had cleared, 2713 backed down to the switch points, then went ahead to turn off onto the siding. A crew of three track walkers using walkie-talkies had come from somewhere to supervise the switching operation. Matthews saw Mehle come to the back platform of the bunk-room car in his cammie trousers and a green T-shirt. He had shaving cream on his face, and he was shaking his head in disgust as he realized his train had been sidelined again.

Matthews walked over to the instrument panel of the chiller unit, putting his fingers in his ears to block out the noise of the diesel generator set, and studied the dials. All the needles of the chiller unit seemed to be operating in the green wedge, indicating a normal range. There was a board where a record was being kept of internal temperatures within each of the special tank cars. The last reading had been taken when they left Birmingham, presumably by the sergeant. Now, hours later, the most recent readings for the forward tank car were one degree above where they'd been at the Anniston siding. The rear tank car showed a two-degree rise.

Damn, not good, Matthews thought. It isn't even full daylight yet. Even more reason not to be stuck here on a siding in the Mississippi heat. As he walked back toward the ladder, the distant eastbound freight came by, moving faster than Matthews would have thought prudent in a siding and switch area, and throwing off enough of a shock wave to buffet the cars parked on the siding. He went to report the good news to Mehle. As the fast freight cleared by, he could see yet another headlight twinkling in the shimmering morning haze to their west. He had a premonition that they might be here awhile, no matter what Mehle did. He was going to suggest they get another chiller unit.

Their state police charter flight landed at the Jackson airport at 3:30 P.M. where a Mississippi Highway Patrol car picked them up to take them to Vicksburg. They had flown to Jackson and not Vicksburg to avoid encountering any FBI people who might be working the Vicksburg airport. Hush was still limping, but a hospital cane was helping a lot. He had had the leg x-rayed in St. Louis. Thankfully, it had not been broken, although it surely felt like it every time he bumped something with his shin. Powers had returned to his Jefferson City headquarters to coordinate the five-state manhunt for Keeler, after which he, too, would fly to Mississippi, aiming to get there by sundown.

Everyone agreed that the next target had to be the Vicksburg bridge. Hush reported what Keeler had said about going after the most valuable bridge, which obviously was a reference to the giant one at New Orleans. On the other hand, time was the one commodity Keeler did not have. Facing a massive FBI and state police manhunt, he would certainly avoid public transportation. Since his truck was still in Memphis, they assumed he had a second vehicle, although the DMV files had no record of one. The closest rail bridge in terms of driving time was at Vicksburg, where Keeler had spent a lot of time going over the bridge. Hush had been with him for most of it, but Keeler might still have had a chance to plant something. And, finally, Keeler had very likely been trying to mislead Hush when he inferred he would go after the bridge in New Orleans. Every way they looked at it, they kept coming back to Vicksburg. The big question, of course, was *how* he would do it.

The security forces along the entire river were on full alert. Each river state had called out National Guard troops, and the Coast Guard had mobilized reserves to patrol the river approaches for each bridge and even to set up waterborne roadblocks along the Mississippi. Powers reported that the Bureau was strangely silent for the moment, although it was a Sunday. That made perfect sense to Hush: If Carswell and his people still really thought they were dealing with foreign or domestic terrorists, they were necessarily chasing their tails. They weren't saying anything because they didn't have anything.

As they drove west through the Mississippi countryside on I-20, Hush still felt very uneasy about what they were doing. He had been a federal agent for over twenty years. Operating solo like this went totally against the grain of all his training and experience. The FBI was effective because it overwhelmed criminals by sheer weight of numbers, effective intelligence, and dogged adherence to proven law-enforcement techniques. Time and again, the Bureau had triumphed because of excellent teamwork, despite all the palace games that went on in the background as senior people promoted their careers and protected their bureaucratic turf. Carolyn Lang had surprised him: She was showing herself to be a real hunter, focused on catching this elusive bastard, and if her superiors in the Bureau weren't willing to listen to the right answer, she'd bring this guy to them in a bloody bag if that's what it took. Powers, of course, had to be delighted at developments: Because he was providing all the assets, he was assured of playing a preeminent role in the final wrap-up.

Assuming, Hush had to keep telling himself, that they could stop Keeler. So far, the man had been ten steps ahead of them at every turn. Those tree bombs were still ringing in his ears.

"I sure as hell hope we're doing the right thing here," he mused out loud. Carolyn was in the right-front seat; he was sitting sideways in the back with his right leg cocked up on the seat. The trooper driving them was concentrating on not hitting anything big as he bulleted west down I-20. She turned around to speak directly to him.

"*We* figured out who the Trainman is," she said. "And I have made a full report."

"*We* went to apprehend him on our own, and he was waiting for us. That was a mistake. If we'd brought a squad—"

"He would have never shown himself. He was coming back for something and to destroy that house, but he could have just turned around."

Hush thought about that.

"I'm betting he stashed a vehicle somewhere up or down the river," she continued. "He came back by boat, and then he returned to that vehicle by boat. The good news is that we don't have to know where he *is* as long as we know where he's going."

"We think we know where he's going," Hush said. "But that's not what's bugging me. We should have reported what we've been doing. Really reported it. This subterfuge of a Sunday morning drop-off isn't going to fool anyone, Carolyn."

She shook her head. "I disagree. If we'd raised a bunch of hell and called for a five-state manhunt, what do you think headquarters would have done? They'd have done nothing until they could get *their* story straight, and Carswell would have been focused on punishing us, not pursuing Keeler. He doesn't believe it's one man."

Hush nodded again despite himself. They would have wasted an entire day broiling in the outrage of an infuriated senior assistant director. At least this way, someone was actively pursuing the correct bad guy. Time was critical.

Ten miles out of Vicksburg, they hit the first roadblock. The Highway Patrol had funneled all the traffic down into one lane with flares, where they were inspecting driver's licenses, insurance papers, and, most importantly, faces. Their driver asked if they wanted to fly by, but Hush said no. He wanted to see what the cops were doing. When they got up to the inspection point, both Hush and Carolyn showed their FBI credentials, and the surprised trooper waved them through without a word. The trooper had been holding a black-and-white fax copy of Keeler's picture.

"That's the interstate," Carolyn said. "How about the back roads?"

"They got 'em covered," the trooper said, accelerating back up to eighty-five. "County guys are all in it. Drew 'em a circle ten miles round the bridge, both sides of the river."

"Are there lots of back roads?"

"Not that many," the trooper drawled. "Lots of bayou country round Vicksburg. That's what took Gin'ral Grant so long."

Hush shot Carolyn a look. He'd forgotten that southerners were still keeping score.

" 'Sides," the trooper continued, "local law, they know all the folks in their patch. Some stranger comes through, somebody'll holler. We get to Vicksburg, where y'all want to go, exactly?"

Good question, Hush thought. They could not just show up at the National Guard command center above the bridge. They had no legal standing in the current crisis. Hush also didn't want to encounter FBI officials from the Jackson office at the command center, or in motels along the interstate.

"Any decent hotels in the city?"

"There's a coupla pretty nice bed-and-breakfast places, down on the river. My wife works at one—called The Corners. Want me to call?"

"Yes, please."

The trooper got on the car phone. Rooms were available, and Hush told him to go there. They would be without a car, so they would just have to wait for Powers to get in. Hush looked at his watch. It would be dark in just a few hours. He was certain that Keeler would either strike quickly or turn the thing into a siege. And once Herlihy got to his office on Monday morning, he was also pretty sure their own brief foray into independent operations would be swiftly curtailed. Assuming, he reminded himself, that Herlihy could find them. He reminded Carolyn to turn her cell phone off.

She did and then leaned back in the front seat, massaging her temples. Hush found himself wanting to do that for her. He was confused by how he felt about Carolyn. He thought he had been pretty attentive to the currents of power within Bureau headquarters, but obviously he had become complacent. It had never occurred to him that he might be on the director's hit list, and it had certainly never occurred to him that the director might use someone like Carolyn Lang to knock him off his perch. And yet, for all of that, she was the most interesting and attractive woman he had met in many years. She had admitted that there was more to the story. Maybe later he could find out what she meant by that.

Colonel Mehle called a council of war in the command car at 5:30 P.M. on Sunday afternoon. Both of the Army warrants came back from the front engine, as well as the sergeant and Matthews. Mehle had dark circles under his eyes. His mouth and hands were twitching like a smoker in bad need of a cigarette. Three irate officials from the Kansas City Southern and Norfolk Southern Railroads had just left. They had made it abundantly clear that there would be no more stunts like the one Mehle had pulled the night before. They didn't care who he had going for him in Washington. Last night, there had been sidings available to clear the line in front of 2713. Now there were none. It was that simple. They would clear the backlog *he* had created, and then they might—*might*—let him run to Jackson, right along with the other westbound traffic that was piling up all over Alabama. And if he got to Jackson, there was the bridge bottleneck to be dealt with. Mehle had actually smiled at that last, to Matthew's utter confusion.

Matthews had grabbed three hours sleep earlier. According to the sergeant, Mehle had spent the entire day at the communications console haranguing anyone who would listen to him that he needed to "get this goddamn train off this goddamn siding pretty goddamn quick." The troops were all starting to call him Colonel Goddamn. The comms operator said that the railroad operations and traffic centers had stopped taking his calls, and the Pentagon had not been able to budge the duty officials at Transportation.

Nor had their efforts to get a second chiller delivered been successful. Matthews had been given this task, but after several phone calls to Sunday duty officers, the nearest chiller set compatible with the one already installed on the flatbed was in San Antonio. With the rail bridges down across the Mississippi, every truck in the southern tier had been pressed into interstate service. Nothing that had not been slated for transportation a week ago was going to move anytime soon. The temps had come up again, the forward car by two degrees, the rear car by one. Lieutenant Colonel Marsden back in Anniston had recommended cooling the black metal sides of the special tank cars, but they were stuck out on the northern outskirts of Meridian, and while there was a watering system on the nearby golf course, there was no way to get the water over to the rail line. Mehle's fulminations had come perilously close to attracting media attention, and only some quick talking by Matthews had deflected a couple of nosy reporters who had become curious about the odd-looking engines.

"What are the temps right now?" Mehle asked.

The sergeant reported the current readings. "Sun's going down," he added.

"What the hell is in those two cars, anyway?" asked Taggart, the taller of the two warrants. The other warrant was called Jenks. They were both crusty-looking Texans, in their forties.

"Same as what's in this whole train," Mehle said. "A load of fifty-year-old CW munitions casings that very badly need to find a home at our destruction site in Tooele. Okay. Major Matthews, I want you to start monitoring the frequency and direction of all the trains running this main line. Specifically, I want to know the time interval between trains."

"Yes, sir," Matthews said. It being apparent that Mehle was at the end of his string, he was not about to ask why the colonel wanted this information.

"Warrant Officer Taggart, I want you to estimate the speed of the trains coming by this position. Particularly westbound trains. There's a line switch up at the head of the siding, right?"

"Yes, sir," Taggart said, shifting a chaw of tobacco in his cheek. "But it's a remote; this district is under centralized control. It's locked against us right now."

"Can it be overridden locally?"

Taggart's eyebrows rose. He was beginning to get an inkling of what Mehle had in mind. "Yes, sir, physically it can, but if you're thinking of us goin' out on the main line without dispatch clearance, there's no way."

Mehle stared at Taggart for a moment. "Tell me something, Taggart: Is there surveillance on the line? I mean, can the central control station tell if there's a train moving down a particular segment of track?"

"Absolutely, Colonel. The whole system is set up to avoid collisions. The tracks constitute an electrical circuit. You can't run her through a stop signal, and there'd be red lights all the way down the line soon's we tried it. And red lights would be the least of our worries."

"What would be the worst of our worries?"

"*Head*lights," Jenks said.

Mehle absorbed that. Then he smiled. It wasn't a pretty sight, Matthews decided. "Right," Mehle said. "That's not feasible, then. Okay, I still want to know the interval timing and average speed of passing traffic, east and west. That's all. Dismissed."

Matthews waited for the other men to leave the command car. He had not been fooled by Mehle's quick shunting aside of the warrant's concerns. Mehle got up and went into the bathroom to wash his face. He came back out and sat down again. He lifted his coffee cup, found it empty, frowned, and put it back down again.

"You know what the real problem is?" he said.

"Yes, sir. We don't know what's going on in those warheads. And if we guess wrong . . ."

"Yeah. And it's a goddamned Sunday. Even with a national rail crisis going on, everybody in Washington's home reading the goddamned papers. I had some help last night. But if we don't get this train across that goddamn river and out into all those wide-open spaces on the other side, the world might end."

"Colonel, we shouldn't have brought those things out in the first place. Not goddamned nukes."

Mehle glared at him. "Well, *Major*, we did. And now that we're loose, there is no one in Washington or anywhere else who's gonna admit it. They keep telling *me* to solve the problem. So I'm going to solve the problem."

Matthews stared down at the table. He did not know what to say.

"There's some personal and professional history here, Major," Mehle said. The bite had gone out of his voice. "Last year, I was given an important mission at the NSC. It went off the tracks. Correction: *I* screwed it up." He looked across the table at Matthews. "I'm not going to screw this one up, understand? We're going to get across that goddamned river, and then we're going to get these things to a safe place in Idaho."

"Not if we have a head-on collision, Colonel."

"There won't be any goddamned collisions. Once I figure out the traffic interval, I'm going to force that switch, take this train out, and go head to head with the next eastbound train. Soon as they figure out we're out there and that we're going too fast for some joker to throw a switch and divert us off the main line, they'll have to let us come through. I only have to get to Vicksburg."

"But that's where the bridge is," Matthews said. "The bridge is the real bottleneck now."

"Yeah, but the *Army* controls that bridge right now, doesn't it, Major? Make sure they're watching those intervals. I'm going to sleep. Call me in two hours."

Keeler came off the southbound I-55 at 5:30 P.M., just west of Canton, Mississippi, tired, stiff, but alert. He had altered his appearance significantly. He had turned his hair and eyebrows an ugly gray-white and changed into some seriously raunchy fisherman's clothes. He had painted two of his front teeth dark brown with some nail polish, and the rest were badly stained after a few hours of sucking on a tea bag. He melted down a candle and shaped a fake hearing aid for both ears, and he had ready some thick reading glasses to complete the image of a tottering geezer. Keeler, who in reality was fifty-five, now looked a raggedy-ass seventy-five, just another old coot out on a cross-country fishing trip along the Delta but otherwise minding his own business. Even if the cops stopped and searched the van, they would find mostly fishing and camping gear, stale food in the fridge, and cigarette butts and clothes strewn all over the interior. He had set the scene to make any cop who stuck his nose in there want to get it over with in a hurry, thereby missing the three hundred feet of Detacord and the detonator can that were rolled into a coil of shrink-wrapped plastic inside the spare tire. His driver's license, insurance ID card, Missouri registration, and license plates all matched to his former landlord. Only the picture was his, although it bore a not very good resemblance to his new, old-man face.

He knew his disguise would not stand up to a thorough search with explosive-sniffing dogs and a detailed cross-check with the Missouri police, but the van, boat, and fisherman disguise should do for a state highway roadblock, where the road cops would be mostly interested in getting the traffic jam moving along after the first half hour of their shift had gone by. The really tough roadblocks, where there might even be FBI, would begin within some as-yet-unknown radius of Vicksburg. He did not intend to challenge those.

He took Mississippi State Highway 22 west-southwest into the evening twilight, keeping right at the speed limit, much to the annoyance of the Mississippi farm boys in their huge pickup trucks, who would come up behind the boat, huff and puff a few inches from the trailer, and then roar around him at eighty miles an hour, only to brake hard and turn off the road a mile or so ahead. He hit his first roadblock just west of Flora, where U.S. 49 crossed the state highway. He put the thick glasses halfway down his nose when he saw the line of road flares, and then the three state police cruisers, one for each lane and one for pursuit. They all had their blue lights going, and the cops were shunting what traffic there was on a Sunday night into a brief flashlight interview. A burly cop glanced at his face. Keeler went slack-jawed, peering up at the cop through the Coke-bottle glasses, and hawked up something in his throat. The cop recoiled and waved him through immediately. He pushed the glasses down as soon as he was clear. He wasn't positive, but he thought he had seen what looked like a wanted poster in the cop's hand.

His immediate objective was access to the Big Black River, which he intended to reach by following Highway 22 almost down to Interstate 20, then turning back northwest up a country road called Askew Ferry Road. If he could get onto the Big Black in his boat, he'd be well on his way to the target. He was surprised to find himself increasingly relaxed about what he was planning to do that night, emboldened by the fact that he had taken down four bridges in just under two weeks and evaded discovery until the wee hours of this morning. They had probably figured out that he was aiming at Vicksburg. If he wanted to achieve a real surprise, he should turn south and go on down to New Orleans, but he also knew that the longer the highway dragnet was out, the more likely that they'd pick him up. He flipped the high beams on to catch any lurking roadside deer and took it up to sixty. Twenty-five miles to Askew Ferry Road. And, more than likely, the next roadblock.

The trooper pulled off the interstate at the Clay Street exit and drove past the national battlefield park into Vicksburg. He told them it would have been shorter to go to Washington Street, which paralleled the river, but the entire area around the bridge was blocked off to vehicular traffic. Hush asked where the railroad ran through the town; the trooper, who mostly worked the Jackson area, wasn't sure. They drove down toward the riverboat district on Clay and turned left onto Oak Street, which paralleled the river. From there, it was only six blocks down to The Corners. They crossed a set of railroad tracks two blocks north of the hotel. The crossing was being supervised by a city policeman, who waved the cruiser through without getting out of his squad car.

The Corners was a complex of two brick buildings. One was the original Whitney home, built in 1878, and the other was a contemporary two-story annex, constructed to resemble the original building closely, and connected by brick walks and gardens to the main house. The establishment was located on the corner of Oak and Klein streets, right across the street from the more grandiose Cedar Grove Mansion Inn. The trooper delivered them to the main entrance, which fronted on a lovely garden courtyard that was actually the back of the original building. The bluffs of Vicksburg continued to rise above the garden in a tangle of sagging brick walls and huge old trees. A congenial hostess checked them into adjoining rooms on the second floor of the Annex. They used their personal credit cards, since they did not want their government cards showing up in a Bureau search system.

The sun was down by the time they carried their bags through the back garden and over to the Annex. The riverfront of the Annex consisted of a side staircase that led up to a large galleried front porch. A second set of stairs took them up to the second-story porch, from which they could just see the wide sweep of the Mississippi River as it rounded the big bend, joined from the north by the Yazoo channel. There were rocking chairs and wicker side tables out on the porch, and fans turned lazily overhead. The rooms, which were adjoining but not connected, were decorated sumptuously in period Victorian furniture, with fourteen-foot ceilings, canopied beds, large armoires, and operable fireplaces. The only touch of modernity were the humming air conditioners. Hush's room even had an oversized whirlpool tub in the bathroom.

Hush put a call into the Jefferson City operations center to leave the inn's phone number for Powers. Then he took off his jacket, tie, and shoulder rig, started the tub filling, and went back out onto the porch, setting the dead bolt in the door so he wouldn't lock himself out. He sat in one of the rockers to watch the remains of the day subside into the Louisiana bayous across the river. Carolyn came back out and joined him. To his surprise, she brought a bottle of scotch and two glasses. She had removed her own suit jacket and was dressed in a straight skirt and sleeveless blouse.

"Anticipation is everything," she said, pouring them each an inch of the whiskey. "I figured I'd need at least one drink on this little trip."

There was no ice machine nearby, so they sipped their whiskey neat. It was a balmy evening. Hush stretched his injured leg out in front of him, tipped his glass in a *salud* to her, and closed his eyes. He reminded himself not to forget that the Jacuzzi was filling inside. A train whistle sounded in the distance behind the building, and soon a long freight came rumbling around the corner at the Oak Street crossing to their right. They could not see it because of all the trees across the street, but they listened to its labored progress as it passed a few blocks in front of the inn, sounding its whistle continuously as it crossed a succession of streets on its way to the bridge. The woman at the desk had apologized for all the extra trains, but the bridge bombings had trains coming to Vicksburg all day and night now. Hush went in to check the tub, which was almost full. He came back out and told Carolyn he had put a call into Powers, and now he was going to go soak his battered body for a while. She poured him another hit of scotch and said she's probably do the same thing. There was little more to do until Powers showed up.

He went into the room, shucked the rest of his clothes, and lowered himself carefully into the steaming water. The tub was built for two, which meant he just about fit in it if kept his knees up. The bruise on his leg was multicolored by now but was slightly less painful. He turned on the jets and lay back, drink in hand, wondering again what the hell he was doing here. The combined state police forces had a pretty good dragnet out. But then what? How could Keeler attack this bridge? The whole world had to be guarding this and the bridge at New Orleans by now. If it was anyone but Keeler, he thought. He felt the air stir, and then the bathroom door opened. Carolyn stood in the doorway.

"My room doesn't have a Jacuzzi," she said. She stood hip-shot in the doorway, one hand on the door, the other holding her scotch. Hush was too surprised and too tired to do much about maintaining his modesty. He just blinked at her for a moment, trying to think of something clever to say. But mostly, he just looked straight at her as a range of conflicting emotions swept over him. "By all means," he said, trying to keep his voice steady.

Keeping her eyes on his, she stepped into the bathroom, put down her drink, and began to take her clothes off. Blouse, bra, then skirt and panty hose. Not a tease, but not quickly, either, and he watched in fascination as her body was revealed to him. Keeping her panties on, she came over to the tub and sat down on the rim. She did something with her hair, first letting it fall and then pinning it up again into a golden ball to keep it out of the water. The red welt between her breasts was at eye level as she fixed her hair, and he found himself aching to move, but he held himself very still, wanting to see what she would do. Finally, she reached across him and put her fingers lightly on the ugly lump on his shin. Then she stood up, turned around, and stepped across him. The back of her panties were wet from the sides of the tub. She sat slowly down in the steaming water, ending up sitting shoulder to shoulder with him, their hips pressed hard against each other. She reached forward for a washcloth and some soap, then handed them to Hush. She leaned back in the tub, her head level with his, and closed her eyes.

Hush started at her neck, using his hands and the cloth to cleanse her skin. He turned slightly to reach her, working his way down her front, caressing her large breasts more with his hands than with the cloth, until she put her left hand on his thigh and then slid it down to curl her fingers around his penis, holding him as he hardened, while his own hands explored the rest of her, slipping carefully over the wet nylon to feel once again softness between her legs. She turned to him and they kissed hungrily, their hands working almost independently as he pressed his tongue into her eager mouth. Finally, she rolled toward him, coming up on her hands and knees, and then she stood up to step across and straddle him. She lowered herself just far enough to press the front of her transparent panties into his face, letting him kiss her there while he held her buttocks in both hands until she began to buck anxiously, at which point, he pulled her panties partially down her thighs and let her subside onto his full length. She groaned from somewhere deep down in her throat and then her breath caught and he could feel the velvet pulsing of her climax. After a minute, she leaned forward, her breasts arching to meet his lips, and then he started to move, trying for control, trying hard to extend the pleasure, but he could not, and he finally gave up, pumping harder and faster, his hands tight around her buttocks, the flesh of her chest hard against his cheek until he came deep inside her, his own breath catching and then exhaling in a shuddering burst of pent-up air. He opened his eyes and kissed the red welt between her breasts and then leaned back so that he could kiss her again and again, still inside her, until he realized that she was weeping. He pulled her close and just held her as they subsided. He wanted to ask her what was wrong, then decided instead to say nothing.

298

"I'm sorry," she whispered after a few minutes. "I'm truly sorry."

He stroked her back for a few moments. "I think it might have been worth it, actually," he said. She pulled her head back and looked at him; he tried to keep a straight face but couldn't. The crooked smile came back and her eyes shone. She slipped sideways, extracted her underwear, and settled back down in the water. Her expression grew serious.

"I told you there was history."

"I'm curious, but if you don't—"

"No, I want to tell you. Eleven years ago, I had an affair with another agent. He was pretty senior, and he was also married. The present director was the AD over the Inspection Division then, and he found out. He held off the Office of Professional Responsibility in return for my helping him help the previous director to force my lover into retirement."

"Ah," Hush said. "And after you did that, you got to do it some more."

"That was the price of my not taking a hit for my part in the affair. After I had a chance to work with you, I went back to Heinrich and told him I didn't want to go through with it," she said. "He reminded me that I had been doing this for a long time, and I could always stop."

"But if you did, he'd expose you to OPR."

"He would indeed. That's also when he first dangled the possibility of promotion. He said the director had the right to appoint his own SES people. That they'd tried to send you polite messages that it was time to go, but you weren't listening. That this administration was really interested in promoting women."

Hush found himself nodding.

"I'm ashamed to say that I went for it. Not that it took all that much. Like I said, I enjoyed being an insider. But you didn't deserve what I did."

"What exactly did you do, Carolyn?"

She sighed. "Agreed with Carswell. About the bridges being the work of a group and not an individual. That put you out on point with no support at headquarters. That also gave the director the fig leaf he needed. Given the internal consensus, he could legitimately cave to pressure from downtown and remove you."

He nodded again. He wondered what he might have done in her situation. "The games we play," he murmured. He looked at his watch.

She got out of the tub and began to towel off. He watched with pleasure: She was a sight to see. She saw him watching and smiled. "Don't tell me," she said.

"Well," he began, peering down into the water, but then the phone rang. He reluctantly got out of the tub and walked, dripping, to the bathroom door, from which he could reach the phone. It was Powers.

"I'm inbound to Vicksburg," Power said. "ETA about forty minutes. We need to meet."

"We're at a B and B called The Corners, but we don't have wheels," Hush said. "Your call."

"They have a bar?"

"Don't think so. It's a B and B. But Lang brought some scotch."

"So she's good for something," Powers said. Hush put his hand over the mouthpiece and told Carolyn what Powers had just said. She laughed and resumed drying off.

"Okay," Hush said. "We're in the second building, second floor."

"What'd he say?" she asked after he hung up the phone.

"He said we have forty minutes," he said, reaching for her towel.

At 8:00 P.M., the train was still shut down on the siding. Colonel Mehle had slept for the last two hours, and everyone in the detachment, from Matthews down to the lowest private in the guard force, had made goddamn sure that none of them woke him. Matthews finally went into the bunk room to check on him. Mehle, who had just awakened, looked at his watch, asked for the report on the passing trains. Matthews and the warrants had constructed a profile that showed with some exception the frequency settling at one train every ten minutes, with an even division between east and westbound traffic. The passing speed appeared to be about twenty miles per hour: the eastbound trains slowing as they came into the Meridian junction, and the westbound trains gaining speed as they left it.

Mehle and Matthews studied the route map for the segments between Meridian and Vicksburg. From Meridian to Jackson was about eighty miles. From Jackson to Vicksburg, it was an additional thirty-five. Under normal circumstances, they could have been at the bridge in about two and half hours, allowing for a slowdown at the Jackson junction. Mehle asked about the temperature readings on the special tank cars, and he wasn't pleased with the answer. The temps had not come down now that it was dark. Matthews finally mustered courage to ask the colonel what he intended to do, but Mehle did not answer. He asked for some fresh coffee and went back to studying the route maps.

Matthews walked forward to have a little chat with the two Texans, who, he had discovered, were Army reservists. They were a phlegmatic pair, much given to western mannerisms and a natural circumspection. The older of the two, Taggart, had been a river tug skipper with the Corps of Engineers Southwestern Division before leaving active duty and switching over to railroading with the Southern Pacific. That was before all the big mergers, and now he worked for the Union Pacific. The other one, Jenks, had spent a long hitch in the Army as a tank mechanic in the Armor. Once out, he had worked his way up with the Burlington Northern Santa Fe to line engineer. For this trip, Taggart was the driver, who, in the absence of a conductor, was technically responsible for the operation of the train. Jenks was aboard as the engineer, responsible for the operation of the diesel locomotives of the three-engine multiple unit, as the railroad men called it. After the previous night's run, both were getting concerned about Mehle. Matthews speculated that the colonel planned to jump the switch.

Their relaxed attitude vanished. "No way, José," Taggart said, with Jenks nodding agreement. Taggart slitted some chaw out the window of the front engine's cab and then explained. "This is a main-line track we're talkin' about," he said. "Single track. Don't use dual tracks anymore, most places. Which means they got centralized traffic control, the whole point of which is to push as much traffic up and down the line as the line can safely hold."

That made sense to Matthews, although he had seen occasional segments of dual track.

"Key word there is *safely, comprende?* Someone local throws that switch up there and there'll be hell's bells ringing at the control center, not to mention some seriously hostile communications coming over that phone right there."

"I understand," Matthews said. "But what would happen if you moved the train out onto the line and just headed west?"

Taggart shook his head and spat again. "If we was *real* unlucky, we'd come around the first bend and run head-on into an eastbound. Just plain unlucky, we'd run up the ass of some westbound that was stopped for traffic ahead."

Matthews nodded. He did not know what to tell them.

"That old boy contemplatin' anything like that," Taggart declared, "he better come up here and get himself a lesson on how to drive an MU, 'cause J-Bird'n me, we gonna be *long* gone. We gonna go get ourselves a video camera, follow your sorry asses up the line, and make us some money on that tape. You follow?"

Without being openly disloyal to the colonel, Matthews tried to convey that he felt the same way about the proposition; then he left the engine cab with as much dignity as he could muster. As he trudged back past the sentries, he wondered what he would do if the colonel attempted such a stunt. Order the MPs off the train and refuse to go along? What would the troops do? Would they understand what was happening? Then he remembered the colonel was packing a side arm. He touched his own hip and realized he'd left his holster rig on his bunk. Maybe being the only guy on the train without a weapon wasn't such a good idea just now. And then he realized that the two warrants weren't armed, either.

It was just after 9:00 P.M. when Keeler rounded the bend upstream of the Kansas City Southern Railroad bridge over the Big Black. For most of the run, he had had only fitful moonlight by which to navigate along the river. He thought that *river* was too grand a word for the Big Black: Big black ditch was more like it. So far, the river had been only about thirty feet across, with high, sloping muddy banks littered with snags and the exposed roots of trees. It was obvious that the river occasionally justified its name, based on the deep banks, but now it was not very deep and not very wide. He'd made good time coming down from the campground until he'd run the boat smack aground on a sandbar within distant sight of the I-20 highway bridge. He'd been going just fast enough that the boat slid entirely out of the water, and he only was barely able to tip up the outboard, shut it off before the prop grounded in the hard-packed sand, and keep himself upright at the same time. The sandbar rose nearly a foot out of the water. He had wondered how the hell he missed it.

It had taken him fifteen minutes of grunting effort to refloat the boat, interrupted by the sight of a flashing blue lights up on the interstate highway bridge a third of a mile away. He froze when he saw the lights, watching to see if there were police up on the bridge, but then the lights had disappeared to the right of his line of sight. Once he had the boat refloated, he'd let it drift down toward the bridge with the engine off, just in case there were watchers. He didn't think that anyone up on the flat highway bridge would be able to see much in the darkness below with all those headlights flashing by, but he had not wanted to take unnecessary chances. After that, he had slowed it down on his run south, which had saved him when he ran over a submerged tree about a mile below the highway bridge.

With the railroad bridge in sight, he killed the engine and let the boat coast quietly toward a clump of willows on the western bank near the top of a dogleg turn. He studied the trestle. It was a single-track affair, with solid steel sides crossing flat on large concrete pylons about fifty feet over the river. The west bank came down in a steep angle to the river, while the eastern bank stretched back two hundred yards in a gentle rise to the railroad grade. The banks of the river around the bridge appeared to be covered in a solid dark mass of greenery, which he finally recognized as the notorious kudzu plant. There appeared to be some big white rocks in the river under or just below the bridge, and there was a white patch of concrete indicating a parking and fishing area downstream of the bridge on the west bank.

He landed the boat about two hundred yards upstream of the bridge, its stubby bow thumping into the mud as willow branches squeaked down its metal sides. As he watched, a train came out of the east, going much faster than he had hoped they would be going tonight. It chased its headlight out onto the bridge and sundered the night with the roar of its locomotives. The clatter of the cars echoed along the banks of the river, drowning out all the night sounds until the train had passed. He got out of the boat, his boots squishing into stinking mud, and pulled it up on the bank. He walked out from under the branches and hunkered down to scout that fishing area under the western abutment. He wanted to make sure there were no late-night catfish hunters out there, or sex-crazed teenagers parking in the shadows, for that matter.

A whine of mosquitoes in his ears had him quickly fumbling for his cigarettes. He turned away from the bridge, bent over, cupped his hands, and fired one up. Then he squatted down at the margins of the bank, checked to make sure there wasn't a dozing cottonmouth within striking range, and studied the trestle again in the dim moonlight. He exhaled a large cloud of fragrant smoke into the air around his head, grateful for the surge of nicotine that was helping to keep his eyes open. He knew he was very tired, and he had been hard-pressed to stay awake for the last few miles of his river trip. Underneath his weariness, though, he felt a strong current of elemental readiness, of final anticipation. This one was probably going to be the last one he could get. Probably, hell. They knew who he was, and the Mississippi night was humming with cops. He knew what was waiting for him at the Vicksburg bridge, but he was counting on his unorthodox approach to get him physically out onto the bridge. After that, he'd have to play it by ear. You don't have to drop it to wreck it, he kept telling himself. But you do have to get there.

A white light flared to the east, preceded by the long dissonance of a diesel whistle, its tone rising in obedience to Doppler's principle. He checked his watch. Five minutes since the eastbound train had gone through, which meant there must be a siding east of here. He knew that was pretty much standard track layout for bridges, so that a train could be shunted off the main line to allow repair equipment to get to the bridge in case of a problem. This train was moving much slower. That was good. Probably still getting up to speed from the siding. He'd be willing to bet that every siding between here and Jackson had a train parked on it, and ditto for the other side of the river.

Some night creature lunged through the carpet of kudzu up the bank and he cocked an ear to track it. But then the train was on the bridge and its noise overcame all of his situational awareness until it had passed. The huge diesels had been straining as they came into view, with pulsing plumes of hot exhaust just visible in the penumbra of the headlights. The train appeared to be going only about twenty miles per hour, and the red-lighted windows of the control cabin gave the lead engine a malevolent aspect, as if it were some powerful beast, intent on prey. He took advantage of that big headlight to scan the upper works of the bridge for security forces, but there was no one visible. He would have to go check for cops guarding any crossings nearby, and then he needed to get up to grade level to examine the tracks. The trestle was perfect for what he had to do; the problem was going to be the train's speed. He was going to need one that was just creeping. As the long line of boxcars clicked and clacked across the river, he stubbed out his cigarette, checked to make sure the boat was secure, and then began a careful climb through the kudzu to the trestle abutments.

·   ·   ·

They were both dressed for field work when Powers came up the steps in the semidarkness. Hush had turned on the porch lights on Carolyn's side to attract the bugs, but he had left them off on his side to keep from being too visible from the street below. Another train was rumbling by through the trees down the hill, its whistle blaring away and its headlight silhouetting the trees. Powers arrived bearing a bag of grease burgers. Conversation was impossible with all the train noise, so they pitched into their takeout until the train and its noisy whistle went farther down the tracks.

"How's the leg?" Powers asked. He was in uniform, with an enormous side arm bobbling on his hip. He accepted a small inch of scotch in his coffee.

"Wishing Keeler hadn't done that," Hush said. "Any word?"

"As a matter of fact, there is," Powers said, crumpling up the hamburger bag. "We think, anyway. A county mountie reported a van with a boat trailer stuck back in the woods on some campground west of Jackson. It has access to the Big Black River. About twenty miles east of here."

"And?"

"Well, the way the Mississippi state guys tell it, some old geezer in a van pulling a boat shows up at the campground and asks if he could have a spot for the night. The lady signs him up, he pays cash money, and then he asks how to get down to the Big Black from the campground."

"Where was this?"

"Place called the Askew Landing Campground; it's just north of Interstate Twenty. The campground lady thought it was a little peculiar, him wanting to drive back into the woods to get to the river that late in the day. But fishermen, you know? So anyhow, an hour or so later, a deputy comes around, checking for out-of-state vehicles. This is a pretty well-run place, so the lady mentions the guy. Seems they thought there was something not quite right with him. How he looked. That was enough for the deputy."

"He went to see."

"Right. Found the van and trailer at a put-in, but no boat. Missouri plates on the vehicles. He calls them in. When the inquiry comes in over the Missouri computer net, our center picks it up because it's a Mississippi inquiry, and we'd coded any tag queries coming from Mississippi for intercept. Seems the van and the trailer are registered to the farmer who rented one Morgan Keeler his cabin. Our guys call the farmer, but he knows squat about any van or boat trailer."

"This has to be Keeler," Carolyn said.

"Doesn't *have* to be, but I'd be willing to make that assumption. And now he's loose on the Big Black, which comes down out of middle Mississippi and eventually joins the big river, down below Vicksburg. It's a feasible route to the bridge. Guy just won't let go, will he?"

"You didn't see those pictures," Carolyn said, and Powers nodded over his coffee.

"He's got something with him, too, it looks like," Powers said. "They found the van's spare tire out on the ground, dismounted off its hub. Like he'd had something stuffed in there. The tire's on its way to the local state lab for a residue check."

"Or he's running to New Orleans," Hush said.

Powers shook his head. "Why drive to within twenty miles of Vicksburg if you're running for the Big Easy? Besides, you're talking more'n two hundred miles downriver to New Orleans. No, I think he's gonna try us on here."

"So what happens next?" Carolyn asked.

"We've alerted the security people in and around the bridge, especially the Coast Guard and state marine safety patrols out on the river. The Navy has set up a coastal surveillance radar on the town-side bluff to look down on the river. The Guard and the local cops are all at on high alert, and no vehicles are being allowed anywhere near that bridge, from either side. I guess now we all just wait."

"And how much of this has leaked back out to the Bureau, or to Washington?" Hush asked.

"Well, the Jackson people know something's up," Powers said. "But funny you should ask." He pulled out a Xerox copy of a Teletype from his jacket pocket and handed it to Hush, who unfolded it as if it were contagious. The message was from Herlihy in St. Louis to the deputy director in Washington, demanding to know the whereabouts and official status of Senior Agent Carolyn Lane. Hush handed it to Carolyn, who grimaced.

"It's showing today's date-time group," Hush said. "Looks like Himself came in and read his mail after all."

"Damn," Carolyn said as she crumpled up the message. "Okay, but he still has a problem—what to tell Washington on a Sunday night."

"If it were me, I'd send in a red rocket," Hush said.

She smiled at him. "You're not Herlihy. See, the way I wrote it up, it's all uncorroborated information. I also neglected to name the agent who went with me to question Keeler. Herlihy is fully aware of what the current 'right answer' at headquarters is."

"So?" Powers said.

"So the last thing Herlihy wants to be is the guy who tells headquarters that they're all wrong—'they' being the director, the deputy director, and specifically our AD over National Security, Mr. Carswell."

"Who does not tolerate rejection well, I take it," said Powers. He was shaking his head. Hush realized that the big cop was vastly enjoying this little federal sideshow.

"And in the meantime," Carolyn said, "The Jackson Office will have reported what's going on with you guys, and that will have gone on the net to everyone involved, including Herlihy in St. Louis."

"Which puts Herlihy between a rock and a hard place," Hush said. "He's scared to approach the throne with bad news, but he's also scared that the state cop task force is gonna run with this thing, and, maybe worse, even catch the Trainman."

Powers shook his head again and grinned. "You guys . . ." he said.

"Our responsibility," Hush reminded them, "is to protect the bridge. Catching Keeler is important, but not as important as stopping him."

Powers grin disappeared and he hunched forward. "Nobody's putting that notion in writing," he said quietly, "But you better believe that these Mississippi boys have some long-gun shooters up on those bluffs. If Keeler's coming, he better be coming in a goddamned submarine."

Hush looked at his watch. It was 9:30. "How long would it take him to get to the big river?" he asked.

"We've looked at that," Powers said. "It's about twenty-two miles down to the Mississippi from the camp, then about twenty or so back up to Vicksburg, depending on whether he comes up the main channel or through the bayous."

"And when did he put in at that campground?"

"Seven, seven-thirty. Local cops say he could run twenty miles an hour down most of that river at night, long as he didn't hit a snag. He could make it to the big river in an hour, hour and a half."

Another train was approaching, its whistle ripping through the quiet of the evening. "Eight-thirty to nine o'clock to the Mississippi," Hush said. "So if he made that, he could be on his way north right now."

"Yup. That's why I'm in field gear."

"And they're obviously still running trains across this bridge."

"One every five, ten minutes. It's wall-to-wall trains out there along the Jackson-Vicksburg line. There's no switchyard here, so they're staging them out of Jackson."

Hush nodded. Then they had to wait while the train blared its way past them, creeping through the town crossings at five miles an hour.

"Question is," Powers said, "What do we do with you two? You show up at the command post, your parents have left instructions."

"So we don't go there," Hush said. He was beginning to formulate an idea, but first he wanted to talk to Carolyn—alone.

Carolyn looked at him in surprise. "What? Of course we do. At least go to the bridge. I want to be there when Keeler shows up."

Hush set his jaw. "No. We go there, we'll get all wrapped around the axle as soon as someone from the Jackson office spots us. No, we wait here."

She stared at him in consternation.

"You've done the important bit, Carolyn," Hush said. "The state people have the appropriate assets in the field right now. The military controls the bridge, and everyone knows who and what they're looking for. They know he's probably coming by boat. We have nothing more to contribute, so we should just stay out of the way." He looked right at her, willing her to acquiesce and wait for Powers to leave.

Powers looked at his watch. "I'm going down to the CP. The Mississippi cops are setting up a net behind where they think he is in the bayous. They're going to get some bloodhound teams out from the state prison, start working the area. If he's out on the river, they won't find anything, but they'll make noise, maybe slow him down, especially if he he's creeping through the swamps."

"We don't have a vehicle," Hush said. "Can the Mississippi people scare us up something? If you trap him, I might be able to talk him out."

Powers nodded. "Long as he doesn't start shooting. These Mississippi boys don't screw around. They'll shoot his ass and let those dogs eat him. I'll get you a car; I'll tell them to leave the keys at the front desk. Meanwhile, I think you'all are doing the right thing. Sit tight. Keep your cell phone on. I'll call if we get something."

Carolyn tossed her head and looked angrily off across the porch. Powers gave Hush a sympathetic wink as Hush thanked him for bringing dinner. When Powers was out of earshot, Carolyn leaned forward. "Why?" she said.

Hush smiled. "Now who's getting all territorial? You want in on the kill, right?"

"Damned straight. That son of a bitch shot at me and locked me in the trunk of a car. I want to be there."

"But where's 'there'? Out on the river? In some bayou with the bloodhounds? Scaling the ramparts of Vicksburg? C'mon, Carolyn, we'd be *in the way*. And you know we can't go waltzing down to the CP. Our people would probably take *us* into custody."

"I don't care," she said, but he sensed that she was weakening.

"You know what?" he said, getting up. "They may be wrong about what Keeler's planning. Go get your jacket. Let's take a walk."

She sighed and went to get her FBI jacket.

Matthews was up on the chiller flatbed, fingers in his ears to deaden the racket of the generator, when he thought he heard the second and third locomotives start up at the head of the train. It was full dark now, and he had been helping the sergeant take readings by flashlight. The temps had remained steady over the past hour. The frequency of trains past their siding had shortened significantly. They got down from the flatcar and walked past the rear special tank car toward the command car.

"Want me to get the troops back on board?" the sergeant asked.

"Let me make sure," Matthews said. It was a cloudy night, with only intermittent patches of moonlight. The lights of downtown Meridian were visible to the southeast of their siding. He could hear a television playing in the MPs' crew room as he went past it to reach the command car. The comms operator was copying a track dispatch order as Matthews came in.

"Got clearance to move," the operator said, handing him the dispatch order. "I called the colonel a coupla minutes ago, when it first started to come in."

"He still up there in the engine?" Matthews asked, scanning the dispatch order. It gave them clearance as far as Newton. "Yes, sir," the operator said.

Matthews checked his watch. They had about six minutes. He went back outside to the platform and shouted for the sergeant to remount the MPs. The guards, who had heard the engines start up, had already been slowly migrating toward the back of the train. They came double-timing down the gravel to their crew car. Matthews watched as the sergeant counted heads, then gave a thumbs-up signal to Matthews. He went back inside and told the operator to inform the colonel that everyone was back on board. Newton, he thought. He checked the route map. Newton was only about thirty miles from Meridian. A train came rushing by out on the main line, going the other way, and Matthews thought briefly about what Taggart had said about red lights and headlights. He looked at his watch again. Two minutes.

They left the B and B at 9:45. The day's heat was still rising from the bricks and the buildings, but Hush had put his jacket on to cover his shoulder rig. Carolyn carried her jacket over her hip, concealing her own weapon. Heat lightning illuminated the thunderheads that were building out over Louisiana. The lights of the port terminals below them sent amber reflections out on the big river. Hush could see people having dinner inside the Cedar Grove Mansion Inn's restaurant, but otherwise, there was no traffic. The neighborhood was a curious mixture of shotgun cottages, bricked terraces studded with ancient trees, and a few isolated stately mansions. There were lights on in some of the cottages, but there was no one on the streets.

"I remember reading about the siege of 'Fortress Vicksburg' during the Civil War," she said. "They made it sound like a big city, but this is barely a town."

"My guess is Vicksburg never recovered from the war. The people seem to be very hospitable, though."

They reached the Klein Street crossing, to find the tail end of an east-bound train rolling through the red-lighted crossing. Another city cop car was parked sideways across the street, the door on the driver's side open. A rotund municipal cop was resting ponderous haunches half in, half out of the car, giving Hush's FBI jacket the eye as they walked up. The tail end of the train went by in a prolonged screech of steel wheels against the crossing channels. There was a single brakeman dangling off the last car, looking intently back down the rail line. Hush flashed his FBI credentials.

"Why's the road blocked off?" he asked the cop.

The large policeman spat indifferently onto the street. "Highway Patrol's orders," he said with a thick Mississippi accent. "They gonna run trains all night. Y'all cin cross, you want to, but Ah'm s'posed to check out any ve-hic-les that come by."

Hush was staring at that lone brakeman hanging off the back of the train as it banged and clanged around a curve. His hunch was taking form.

"Is this the only railroad in town?" he asked. "And is this the one that crosses that big bridge over the Mississippi?"

The cop nodded, as if these were dumb questions.

"Where does it come from?" Hush asked.

"Jackson," the cop said, spitting again to relieve the lump in his cheek. "They's a spur, comes down from the fertilizer plant up the Yazoo River, and another spur from the docks down yonder, but this here's the main line. KCS. Comes in from Jackson, out east a here. Runs a cut through the town."

"Tell me," Hush said as casually as he could, "does this railroad parallel I-Twenty coming out from Jackson?"

The cop reckoned, yes, it did.

"Does it cross the Big Black River?"

The cop nodded again. "I-Twenty does, so, yeah, the railroad'd have to cross the Big Black," he said. "Big Black, she runs north-south."

Another train appeared in the distance to their left, its bright, yellow headlight wobbling through the trees along the river bottom, illuminating the piers and warehouses down on the river itself. It treated them to a long bast on its air horn as it approached the first street crossing a few blocks away. Hush thanked the cop, took Carolyn by the arm, and steered her back toward the bed-and-breakfast and out of earshot of the cop.

"What?" she said with a look of confusion on her face.

"Keeler had a boat, right?" he said. He had to raise his voice over the noise of the locomotives as they approached the crossing behind them.

She nodded.

"Okay. He puts the boat in north of the interstate and heads south down that Big Black River. Which is a tributary of the Mississippi. Everybody's assuming he's trying to get to the big river, and then to the bridge."

She nodded again.

"But does that make sense? That he'd go right toward a heavily defended bridge, which he has to approach up a heavily patrolled river? He has to know what he'd be up against. He's seen the security arrangements around that bridge."

"And your point is?"

"This rail line. It comes to Vicksburg from Jackson, which is east of here. The cop said it crosses that Big Black River somewhere."

"I'm still not—"

"He's not coming up the river to get to that bridge," Hush said urgently, interrupting her. "He's going to hop a train, ride the *train* to the bridge, and then do something. The bridge security forces are looking at everything but the trains."

"Like that brakeman we just saw?"

"Just like that. Only maybe not so overt. I'll bet he took that boat down the Big Black until he got to this rail line at a trestle or a bridge. Then he can come to the Vicksburg bridge whenever he chooses. Not on a boat. On a goddamned *train!*"

She was nodding thoughtfully. "And the whole world is watching the river," she said. "We need to call Powers."

"Right. Get him to stop all the westbound trains until they can be inspected. Or, if we're wrong, until they nail Keeler. Where's that phone?"

"Back at the hotel, of course," she said. "Use that cop's radio."

Hush went back down to the city cop and explained what he needed. The cop obliged by getting on the radio. The city central station had a frequency into the CP down by the bridge. They finally got a patch established, and the cop gave Hush the mike. Hush identified himself by name only and asked for Powers. The CP communications operator asked him to wait. He was back in a minute with the report that Powers had gone downriver where the prison dog teams thought they had a possible locator on Keeler, down near Hennesey's Bayou. Hush asked if they could establish radio contact with Powers for an urgent message, and the operator said he would try.

Hush started back to tell Lang what he had learned, but the cop was waving him back. There was someone else on the circuit, wanted to speak to Mr. Hanson. Hush hesitated. There were Jackson Office agents at the CP. He picked up the mike.

"This is Hanson," he said.

"Hey, Hush. This is Rafe LeBourgoise."

Aw shit, Hush thought. "Yes, Rafe?"

"The CP operator said you are calling in on a Vicksburg police frequency? You here, in the area?"

Hush couldn't think of any way to evade the question. "That's right," he said.

"Well, that's good. That's very good, in fact. Headquarters is looking for you. The director's office, in fact. They kept telling me you were in Baton Rouge, on medical leave. I have told them you are not in Baton Rouge. They seemed very insistent that you were."

"I was; then I left," Hush said. There was a moment of silence, during which the radio speaker hissed some static at him. The city cop was listening with interest. Carolyn was walking back over toward the car.

"Is Senior Agent Lang with you? I think they *really* want you both to check in, Hush."

"Okay, I'll do that," Hush said, avoiding LeBourgoise's question about Carolyn. "But in the meantime, why are you here instead of in Baton Rouge?" Carolyn joined him in time to hear Hush's question. She mouthed "Who?" at him. He mouthed back LeBourgoise's name.

"Because of a report Senior Agent Lang sent into the St. Louis office. That the Trainman may be Colonel Keeler of the Corps of Engineers. Assistant Director Carswell doesn't think this is true, but when they found out that the state police task force was mounting an operation against Keeler, they ordered me and some of my people up to Vicksburg to augment the Jackson Violent Crimes Squad. Where are you now, exactly, Hush?"

"Actually, I'm just on my way into Vicksburg. We're coming into the town from Jackson." The cop's eyebrows went up at that.

" 'We' meaning you and Senior Agent Lang?"

Hush thought he heard LeBourgoise say something to someone near the radio. "That's right," Hush said. "Listen, I'd like to clear this circuit, if we can. I'm expecting a call from Captain Powers."

"But, Hush—"

Hush leaned into the cop car and set the mike back on its hanger. He gave Carolyn the high sign that they needed to get out of there. LeBourgoise's voice was still audible on the speaker, so Hush punched off the radio's power button.

"Hey, now," protested the cop.

Hush leaned into the car's window. "That guy is not who he says he is, Officer," Hush said hurriedly. "In fact, I think he's the guy everybody's trying to find. Can you leave that radio off the air for about five minutes? And then turn it back on and you can tell anybody who asks anything they want to know. But we need five minutes to get down there and nail this bastard."

The cop's eyes widened. "Well, hell, yes. This that bastid doin' the bridges?"

"We think so. Just give us five minutes, okay?"

The cop nodded and got out of the car, pulling himself together and looking around for bad guys. Hush limped up the street with Carolyn, trying to ignore his sore leg. As they walked, Hush explained what Le-Bourgoise had said and what he'd just done.

"Good Lord!" she exclaimed. "You think LeBourgoise's been told to pick us up?"

"If not, he soon will be," Hush said. He looked back at the train, whose engines had now reached the Oak Street crossing down the street from The Corners and was beginning the long right turn to the east, which would take it out through the Vicksburg cut and on to Jackson. East, Hush thought. The next train ought to be westbound. Keeler could come at any time. And then he remembered that he hadn't gotten his message through to Powers.

"C'mon," he said, heading for the B and B. "We need that damn phone."

Keeler found what he was looking for after forty minutes of scouting the area around the trestle. He had first checked the tracks to the west, skulking through the weeds along the line, but all he found was a dirt path crossing about two hundred yards west of the bridge. Then he had re-checked the dirt road that ran underneath the bridge on the west bank for fishermen or other vehicles. The whole area stank of urine, old beer, and fish scraps. The concrete pylons were covered in graffiti of all kinds. In the moonlight, he could see broken bags of trash, some rusting old lawn chairs, and quart-size plastic motor-oil jugs littering the banks in both directions. The concrete along the banks was uneven and rough, as if several trucks had simply emptied their loads of concrete along the banks and left it at that. The white objects in the river he had thought were stones turned out to be segments of the concrete columns that had originally held up the bridge. Evidently, they had been broken up in some long-ago disaster. He was glad he had not tried to run the boat any farther south. Below the bridge, the river widened somewhat, then disappeared around a bend to the right.

Another train came westbound while he was under the bridge, and its headlight, shining down between the railroad ties on the bridge, revealed the hiding spot for which he had been searching. At the top of western bridge abutment, where the steel girders on either side of the bridge deck were pinned to saddle joints, there was a ledge in the concrete that was directly under the track bed. He wanted to shine his flashlight up there, but he was afraid to show a light. As the train rumbled overhead, he walked back upstream, initially on the dirt road and then down through the dense kudzu vines, to retrieve his equipment from the boat. He hauled out the coil of Detacord, a small black canvas tarp, and a flat backpack. He debated whether or not to sink the boat, then decided against it. He wasn't sure how tonight would turn out. He knew what he was going to do to the train with the Detacord, but after that, there was a blank. Now that the manhunt is up, he thought, there is no point in planning too far ahead.

16

MATTHEWS HAD BEEN watching for signs of Newton to see where they would be sidelined. When they blew through the town at fifty miles an hour, Matthews understood why Mehle had elected to ride in the engine. The track telephone line began ringing about one second after they rumbled over the KCS cross-tracks that came down from the north. The comms operator picked it up, listened for a moment, winced, and handed it over to Matthews without a word. Matthews identified himself and then listened to an extremely angry traffic controller ordering them to stop at once. Matthews acknowledged the order and said he would communicate it to the engineer.

"I already called the engineer," the man protested. "What the hell is going on with that train?"

"I have no idea," Matthews said. "I'm at the back of the train. I'll try the intercom."

"You better do more than that, mister. I've got two heavy freights comin' right at you; one's just west of Forest. Stop that son of a bitch right now and back her down to the Newton siding, you hear me?"

"I hear," Matthews said, knowing full well that it wasn't going to happen. The comms operator was asking what was going on, but Matthews ignored him and got on the intercom circuit to the engine. As he expected, it was Mehle who answered.

"We got problems?" he asked in a deceptively calm voice. It seemed to Matthews that the train was going faster now, plunging into the darkness of the Mississippi countryside.

"Yes, sir. We were supposed to stop and sideline at Newton. Traffic control is going apeshit. There are two eastbound trains coming at us; one's only about ten miles ahead."

"Very well. Call them back; tell them they better stop that pogue. We're keeping on."

"Colonel, what the hell are you doing?!"

"Mind your mouth, Major. We're not stopping anymore until we're across that goddamn bridge. Tell them whatever you'd like to; tell 'em we're carrying eight thousand tons of nerve gas on this son of a bitch and we're taking it through. That's all."

Mehle hung up. Matthews stared incredulously at the humming intercom. "Get the traffic center back on the horn."

The comms operator dialed frantically, screwed it up, and tried again. The train was definitely accelerating; Matthews was sure of it. He tried to calculate relative velocities as he waited for the operator. Ten minutes, maybe less. The operator handed him the phone.

"Control?" Matthews said. "We are unable to stop this train."

"Throw the goddamn emergency brakes, then. I've got the lead freight stopping now, but there's another one behind him."

"Sir, I'm telling you one last time: We cannot stop this train. Be advised, this is a U.S. Army train. We are carrying eight thousand tons of toxic munitions and we intend to keep going until we're across the bridge at Vicksburg. I cannot stop this train. Do you hear me? I cannot stop this train!"

"Goddamn it, you can't do that! You—"

"Listen to me," Matthews shouted into the phone. "You better back all your traffic off this line, Control. And don't even think about trying to divert-switch us—we're going fifty miles an hour. You copy? I *cannot* stop this train!"

He reached forward and hung up the phone, silencing the controller's continuing protests. Then he reached for the intercom, thought better of it, and headed through the command car's bunk room to the forward door. He checked to make sure he still had his side arm, then let himself through the door. A blast of air hit him the in the face. The back platform of the MPs' car was just across the coupling from him. He waited for the swaying cars to line up and then jumped across the space between them, trying to ignore the roar of the wheels below. He was dimly aware of some white buildings flying by in the moonlight as he climbed over the railing and let himself into the dayroom.

The sergeant, dressed in only his uniform trousers and Skivvies shirt, was playing cards with three of the MPs while a television droned on at the other end of the room. Most of the troops were in their racks. The smell of popcorn and cigarette smoke filled the room. The sergeant stood up when he saw the expression on Matthews's face.

"Get your people up and dressed out in full gear," Matthews ordered. "Mehle's going to try to run this thing through the system all the way to Louisiana, and we've got at least two trains coming at us right now."

The sergeant didn't stop for questions. He began shouting orders, and one instant later it was assholes and elbows flying everywhere. Matthews waited for some semblance of order to form while he considered his options. Mehle probably had the two warrants at gunpoint. He was just nuts enough to ram the damn train west until he hit something or got across that bridge. The rush of the train's slipstream through the open back door was audible above the confusion in the crew car. He saw an intercom connection at the back wall of the car. He called up to the engines again.

"What now?" Mehle answered.

"Colonel, I think they're going to try to clear the line. I told them we couldn't stop until we were across the bridge at Vicksburg. If you slow her down a little, they'll have more time to get the other trains clear."

"Nice try, Major Matthews, but no dice. I slow down and they'll throw a switch somewhere and take their chances. You tell 'em what I told you to?"

"I told then we had toxic munitions on board, not nerve gas. They know we originated in Anniston."

"You should have obeyed my orders, Major Matthews. But either way, I'm not slowing. You better alert your guard force."

"I already have," Matthews said as the sergeant and his squad leaders gathered around him. "I told them to prepare for a crash."

"Good thinking. But assuming we don't crash, have them prepared to deploy the entire force, at my command. Understood?"

"Yes, sir," Matthews replied. "But Colonel—"

Mehle had already hung up. Matthews did the same. The sergeant raised his eyebrows at him.

"We're screwed, I think," Matthews said. "Just be glad we're all the way at the back."

"Yeah, right," said the sergeant. "With a hundred and sixty tons of

318

leaking mustard ordnance next door. Shee-it. You were right the first time, Major."

Keeler crouched on the ledge and positioned the black tarp half under and half over his body, with the open end pointed at the back of the ledge cavity like a black plastic taco. There was about a foot of clearance between his head and the ties above when he was in a sitting position, but to anyone glancing up at the ledge from the fishing area below, there would only be a black shadow in a black hole where the bridge met the abutment. Or so he hoped. More importantly, there were two feet of clearance between the ties, which, without the normal gravel ballast, lay open to the air. If he stood up on the ledge, his head, arms, and shoulders would be poking out right next to or even directly under the tracks, with more than enough room to allow him to handstand his way through the ties and onto a car. He had already checked to make sure there was enough room between the channel walls of the trestle and the tracks to allow a man to crouch next to a passing train. Not a lot of room, he told himself, but enough that he would not be struck by the edges of a boxcar. His plan was to wait for a slow-enough train, then pitch the backpack with the Detcord up through the ties, hoist himself up to the track-bed level alongside the tracks, and hop aboard. Once on the train, he would have to find a hiding place in case they were giving the trains a visual inspection before letting them out on the Mississippi bridge.

He tried to relax as he waited. The concrete around him stank of pigeon droppings and railroad grease; he was grateful for the tarp. He could see pretty well out either end of the loosely wrapped tarp now that his eyes were fully night-adapted. The Big Black was still as glass to the north, although he could hear some water noises as the current meandered around the fallen bridge columns just below the bridge. There was no wind; somewhere in the distance, a yapping dog was worrying the night. He patted the backpack to make sure he hadn't left it behind.

Endgame, he thought again. If he got away tonight, he would end up on foot over on the Louisiana side, with no vehicle or boat. Hell, if he managed this right, he might just ride the front end of the train on out west like any hobo and see what homelessness was all about. Or he might just get off and walk back down the tracks and introduce himself to the cops. A trial might be pretty interesting; give him a chance to tell his side of this thing, to show how heartless the railroad had been after his family had been immolated at that crossing. If it ever came to a trial, that is. He recalled what that pig-faced railroad security officer had said up in St. Louis: We find them before you do, they're gonna get dead. Then the ties above his head began to vibrate.

Hush finally raised Powers by going back through the state police operations center in Jefferson City and asking them to contact Little Hill. Carolyn sat nervously on the bed as he explained to Powers his theory that Keeler wasn't going directly to the river.

"But what if he is?" Powers asked.

"So keep your people looking," Hush said. "But I strongly recommend you stop and carefully inspect every westbound train before you let it out on that bridge."

"Don't think we can get that," Powers said. "We already tried to get them to stop all the trains after we found that van. It wasn't five minutes later and we were being overruled by the goddamn Secretary of Transportation back in your hometown. There's a real panic on, Hush."

Hush looked over at Carolyn, trying to think. "Okay, so try this: Tell 'em you have to stop and inspect all westbound trains—say somewhere between that Big Black trestle and Jackson, wherever the sidings are. In the meantime, let the *east*bound trains run; clear out that backlog entirely. That way, they don't lose everything."

"I can try, I guess, but I don't know. These railroad people have some serious political muscle."

"I don't know anything about the ground between here and Jackson," Hush said. "Would it be worth it to send some people down that rail line on foot or on some kind of work vehicle? Like if he's waiting to jump a train, maybe flush his ass out?"

"Yeah, we can maybe get the railroad cops to help with that, although most of our people are down here in the bayous right now. It's all pretty much boonies out there, from what the state guys say."

"Well, then, concentrate: Send some teams to crossing points, and maybe one down to that bridge over the Big Black. Work back toward Vicksburg."

"What I need is some more people," Powers said. "How about Bureau assets?"

"If *we* were still in the game, we could turn on lots of people." Then he remembered LeBourgoise. He told Powers, who said he would call the CP. That suited Hush: Powers would get some more people, and LeBourgoise would have something to do besides hunt for them.

"What are you guys going to do?" Powers asked.

"We're going to go out and scout the rail line here in Vicksburg. I have this bad feeling he's ahead of us."

The train came much too fast, telegraphing its approach first with its incredibly bright headlight and then by a rumbling vibration that shook the abutment for a full minute before the huge diesels flashed overhead, four feet above him, showering the tarp with bits of dust and sand. A soon as the engines had passed, he sat up, pushed aside the tarp, and looked up. He had to close his eyes immediately to protect them from the rain of fine debris. Blinking furiously, he crouched and then stood up, hugging the edge of the concrete ledge. He cautiously raised his head and shoulders up through the ties. The thundering thirty-six-inch wheels flew by two feet away at eye level. He was conscious of a suction of sorts, a deadly invitation to lean under the flashing wheels. The heavily creosoted ties massaged his shoulders each time a wheel pair went over, sagging and then popping back up in tune with the five-ton wheel bogeys. An occasional hiss of compressed air washed over his face from leaking brake couplings. It took all his nerve to stand there as the eighty-ton cars whipped by, inches from his face. He backed away some more and then tried it: Hunching his shoulders, grasping the rough, splintery ties with gloved hands, he lifted himself off the ledge, through the space between the ties, and up onto the track bed to crouch, teetering for an instant in the slipstream and then flattening against the trestle's side wall, the train's wheels now four feet away. The suction effect was even more pronounced up here, and he had to hold on to the end of a railroad tie to keep himself from tipping forward. The train appeared to be accelerating now that it was getting across the bridge.

Much too fast, this one, and, of course, going the wrong way—east, toward Jackson. There was no clickety-clacking here, as this was all welded rail. Just the bumping noise of aging ties and a heavy jolting as each car came out on to the bridge structure, compressing the huge I beams supporting the track bed. He realized it was the truss pins that were making the jolting noise, not the train. He also realized he had not brought up the Detacord or the backpack. He looked to the left, but the edge of the abutment blocked his view of how close the end of the train was. The rush of air past his face made his eyes water.

Okay, he thought. I need to practice this. Should have brought goggles. He steeled himself to lean forward, his face coming uncomfortably closer to the rushing wheels, and then he wedged his lower body back down between the ties. He hung there like a tired gymnast for a moment, then settled through the ties onto his tarp. The rain of small particles continued as he rolled himself under the tarp and waited. After about two minutes, there was an abrupt silence as the end car came by, dragging the rumble and roar eastward across the bridge. The rails above his head ticked and hummed for about thirty seconds after the train had gone.

He slowly pushed away the tarp and shook the dust and sand out of his hair. He checked his watch. He had to do something soon. Once someone found his van and boat trailer at that campground, the police forces would know he'd gone down the Big Black, which, in turn, meant that someone might figure out he would be trying for a train. What he needed now was a slow *west*bound train. He would watch the next couple of trains; if they didn't go slowly enough, he might force one of them to. He had seen the loom of yellow lights from a signal tower over on the other side of the bridge. If he had to, he would go over there, climb the tower, and force the signal disk to rotate into a diagonal position, meaning, Proceed, but slow down and be prepared to stop. He looked at his watch again and wondered what the FBI might be doing right now. He had meant to bring along his battery-powered police scanner, but the hasty departure from the river cabin had upset those plans. He sighed and sat back to wait some more. He wished he had some way to listen in on the railroad traffic-control circuits.

Matthews had the entire guard force hop the gap and crowd into the tail-end car with him, each man jumping the coupling while the man behind him held his chemical defense gear and M16 rifle. Once inside, he told them to stand easy, crap out in the bunk room if they wanted to, but to keep their gear handy. Separately, he told the sergeant that he thought the traffic people would probably clear the main line until they literally had nowhere to put the trains that had been coming east, at which point they would announce how far ahead the next immovable object waited. Hopefully, Mehle wouldn't think they were bluffing.

He and the sergeant studied the route map. They had been running at pretty high sped for almost thirty minutes, so they ought to be coming into the Jackson junction pretty soon. The map showed a group seven Illinois Central line running north-south through Jackson, as well as a group five IC line coming up from Hattiesburg to the southeast. The bad news was that this meant lots of trains; the good news was that there should also be lots of sidings. The sergeant said he hoped the major was right. Matthews said he hoped the major was right, too.

Matthews toyed with the idea of coming up on the secure Army command circuit, and maybe calling the main Army Operation Center at the Pentagon. Tell them what Mehle was doing, and that they had a train full of dangerous ordnance roaring through the night, risking head-on collisions with every train strung out through Mississippi. But whom would he call, especially on a Sunday night? And maybe Mehle was operating under secret orders from the Pentagon to do what he was doing. Mehle was taking a terrible chance, which might mean he indeed had been told to do whatever it took to get over the Mississippi River. It was the age-old problem when a military subordinate questioned his superior's orders: The superior officer might know something the subordinate didn't. The intercom buzzer sounded. Matthews picked it up.

"Yes, sir?"

"Call the KCS traffic center. Tell them I am slowing to thirty miles an hour. I want a clear shot right through Jackson to Vicksburg."

"Yes, sir, I'll try."

"No, no, you call them and tell 'em what I said. Tell them I'm going to take her back up to fifty as soon as I clear Jackson."

"And if they have nowhere to sideline the rest of the traffic out there?"

"Then tell 'em we're gonna play Casey Jones." Mehle hung up.

Matthews told the sergeant what the colonel had said. Some of the troops who were waiting in the command room were shaking their heads. One suggested they go forward and uncouple the two end cars and let Colonel Goddamn go take his chances. The sergeant told the man to shut his yap while Matthews placed the call to the Kansas City Southern control center. Their reaction was predictable. First, the maximum safe speed through the Jackson junction was twenty miles per hour, and, second, they had six trains coming into Jackson from Vicksburg.

"How many can you sideline?" Matthews asked, bending down to look out the windows at the increasing number of streetlights he was seeing through the back window. "I think we're coming into Jackson right now."

"We know where you are, mister," the dispatcher said. "And if he doesn't slow that thing down, you'll have a head-on in about four minutes."

"He's not going to slow her down because he thinks you're going to try to switch him off the main line," Matthews said. "Look, I'm not a part of this, okay? I don't have a vote. I'm eighty cars back from the engines. I do know the guy in charge, and I'm telling you he's going to drive on through. That's all I can tell you, all right? Back those guys up if you have to, but fucking do something!"

He hung up the phone before the dispatcher could argue with him any more. He tried to think of what to do next. Matthews was almost positive that if Mehle saw a train coming at him, he would hit the brakes. He decided to try one more time; he called the front engine on the intercom.

"What?"

"Dispatch says there are six eastbound trains ahead coming into Jackson."

Mehle laughed. "They're just trying to bluff me into stopping, and I'm not stopping. Got it?"

"Yes, sir, that's what I told them. But how do you know they're bluffing?"

"Just look out the window, Major. Left side. Tell me what you see."

"Lights—lots more lights."

"Look down, Major," Mehle said, and hung up.

Matthews went to the window and looked down. He saw tracks. Two sets of tracks, not one. Son of a bitch, he thought. And then he felt the train begin to accelerate again.

They crept down a secluded back street in Vicksburg in the unmarked car that Powers had commandeered from the Mississippi Highway Patrol. Carolyn drove while Hush consulted a map he had torn out of the hotel room's chamber of commerce brochure. The railroad line was not shown, so they were reduced to hunting it street by street. The neighborhood that backed up to the rail cut consisted of mainly small cottages and ramshackle houses; what people they did see stared hard and long at the obvious police car until it had gone out of sight. They found few crossings: the at-grade crossing at Oak, a few blocks down from their inn; an over-pass at Washington, another at Mulberry, and a final one at Confederate. For the most part, however, the north-south streets of the town simply ended at the cut, which was sunk down below the level of the surrounding streets and blanketed in a strangling carpet of kudzu vines.

Just about every time they made their way down a street that dead-ended at the cut, there was a train going through. They saw one going westbound, apparently committed before Powers had been able to get the word through to Jackson, but all the rest were coming eastbound from Louisiana side.

"Looks like they're going to play ball," Hush said after they saw their third eastbound train.

"They will until they run out of eastbound trains," she said. "Then they're going to want to unload the backlog at Jackson."

They drove back toward the river side of town, approaching their hotel from the casino district on Oak Street. They had to wait for an eastbound train made up entirely of tank cars to clear the crossing; then they drove across the bumpy tracks. The Corners was just visible up ahead on the left when Carolyn suddenly swung the car into a driveway of a darkened house and cut the lights.

"What?" Hush asked.

"Bu-cars," she said. "At The Corners."

Four trains had gone overhead before Keeler finally thought he might get a shot. He had felt the by-now-familiar vibrations of a train thrumming in the bridge structure, but then they changed. When he could hear the approaching engine, he peeked out of the tarp. The headlight was starting to illuminate the far bank and the stunted trees that grew along the right-of-way. Definitely different—slowing down, he realized. Great, he thought, except the damn thing was going the wrong way. Then he heard the unmistakable sound of the train's brakes clamping down with a stri-dent shriek of steel on steel, and there was a sudden surge of power from the engines. The earth began to shake under the bridge's foundations, and the tracks right over his head started jumping around in the tie plates and rail anchors. For a long moment, he wondered if he should bail out from under the tracks, but then it began to subside. The locomotives were close now. He could hear the difference between the two engines and a roar of compressed air from the tracks above. It sounded like the train was going to come to a halt about a hundred feet behind him. The headlight was right overhead, boring a blue-white column of light through the cloud of dust that was rolling out over the trestle.

He was starting to pull himself out from the tarp when he realized the rails were starting to thrum again. He froze, trying to figure out what the vibration meant, and then he understood. Another train was coming. From the other direction. On the single track.

The transit through Jackson had been a nightmare of frantic radio transmissions from the traffic-control centers of the Illinois Central and KCS lines, with Matthews trying desperately to broker between the irate controllers and the implacable Colonel Mehle. The train had never stopped moving throughout, even at the crucial switch junction between the east-west and north-south main lines, where there had been train headlights coming from both directions, police cars at crossings, and astonished yard dispatchers crowding the doorways in the control towers at the Jackson switchyards. As soon as they were through, Mehle had the engineers gunning 2713 back up to road speed. They ran through the western part of the city with the whistle going full blast, ripping the tranquillity of the normally sedate Sunday night to pieces. They had passed four trains on sidings as they left Jackson, which left, as Matthews remembered it, two unaccounted for. Ten minutes later, they roared through Clinton, where the fifth train was sidelined. Its last car, just barely clear of the main line, passed within an arm's reach of the side of 2713.

Then the rushing night turned dark again and they were finally closing in on Vicksburg, now only thirty-five miles away. The KCS dispatcher had warned Matthews that the speed limit in the town of Vicksburg was five miles an hour due to rail-loading limitations and a very hard west-to-south curve down by the river. Matthews relayed that to Mehle, who said he would see about that. Fifteen minutes later, there came an emergency stop transmission from the KCS center. Before Matthews could relay it forward, the crew cars were jolted as the engineers hit the brakes hard, raising a cacophony of squealing metal from underneath the cars and filling the ventilators with the smell of smoking brake shoes.

Matthews ran outside to the back platform and looked ahead, but the train was going around a curve and he could see nothing but the loom of the headlight through the distant trees, until he realized he was seeing two lights. The intercom came on back inside, with Mehle yelling something about bracing themselves. The sergeant and his troops tried to brace themselves against the walls and desks, but the train was stopping too hard, so all they did was fall around. Matthews looked again and could now definitely see two lights, their own, plus another as the rear end of the snaking train straightened out and finally squealed to a stop.

"Deploy the guard force, on the double," Mehle yelled over the intercom. The control center was also trying to call in, but Matthews couldn't hear them over the pounding of boots as the sergeant and every MP aboard bolted out of the car and began running forward alongside the train, weapons at port arms. Matthews got on the circuit with the center and reported that they had stopped and that there had been no collision. Then, checking his side arm once more, he jumped off the platform and jogged forward along the train.

The night was humid and becoming overcast, with a million insects buzzing in the trees along the right-of-way. The smell of burned brake metal lay heavy on the ground. He jumped up onto the chiller platform to check the temperatures in the special weapons cars but then realized he had forgotten his flashlight. He swore and got back off, then headed for the front of the train. The guards were in position now, scanning the nearby woods, their weapons ready. Not knowing what was going on, their young faces reflected a mixture of fear and excitement, and Matthews made sure he said something to each of them as he trotted up the nearly five-thousand-foot length of the train.

The engines were running at high idle as he approached, and then he stopped short as he realized that he was about to trot out onto a trestle. The front engine of 2713 looked to be stopped a bare hundred feet in front of the other train, with the second engine's rear wheels just beyond the other end of the bridge. As Matthews approached, he saw a tense group of figures standing between the locomotives. He stopped in the shadows about five cars back from the front. Mehle, gun in hand, had both warrant officers out on the tracks. The sergeant and two MPs were pointing rifles at what appeared to be the engineers from the other train. A nearby MP was watching, and when he saw Matthews, he came over, his boots crunching in the gravel.

"This shit's getting pretty weird, Major," he said.

"You're telling me," Matthews replied. Mehle was gesturing angrily with his pistol. The two warrant officers were standing with their backs to the engine, their facial expressions suitable to men facing a firing squad. The engineers from the other train were staring in amazement at the huge black armored engines and the red-faced colonel waving a gun at them. Matthews definitely did not want to go up there, for fear of startling Mehle into shooting someone. He could not hear what anyone up there was saying over the rumble of the multiple diesels. Then the other train's engineers put their hands up defensively and started backing away from Mehle, walking backward toward their own train while trying not to trip over the railroad ties. Mehle nodded to the sergeant, who followed the other engineers to their engine with his two MPs. Then Mehle pointed the warrants back up onto the front engine of 2713 and followed them up the ladder.

Matthews waited for a moment at his end of the bridge, which appeared to cross a medium-size stream in the darkness below, and then, when he heard the other train's engines spool up, he turned around and started jogging back down the train, shouting for the guards to reboard. The crazy bastard faced them down, he thought to himself. He's going to make them back all the way across the damn river, just like he said. The troops were converging on the rear car at just about the time he heard the banging and clanging of 2713 starting forward, jerking the slack out of the train as it began to follow its subdued adversary back down the line toward Vicksburg at five miles an hour. Matthews finally stopped running and let the crew car come to him. He swung on board like an old railroad hand, then turned to pick up the sergeant and his two troops as they came off the other end of the bridge. To his surprise, they weren't there, and then he remembered that Mehle had put them on board the other train like some kind of prize crew.

He went back into the command car and found the comms operator waving the phone at him. Matthews reluctantly sat down to talk to the KCS control center, which had apparently been calling nonstop ever since seeing what no doubt appeared to them like a head-on collision. A senior route supervisor came on the net and told Matthews that police authorities had been notified and that they were issuing orders to the other train to stop at once to prevent any further forward motion by 2713. Matthews, knowing that the other train was probably *not* to going to stop anytime soon, simply acknowledged the man's angry message. Then he reminded the control center of 2713's cargo and repeated his earlier observation that the best thing for everyone to do now was to let this train get across the river, after which it would conform to normal traffic rules. The supervisor began to fulminate again about the hundreds of road violations already ticketed against 2713. Matthews interrupted him, told him to shut up and listen.

"We've got about fifteen miles to go and then we're no longer a problem, right? Think about that, and just get the goddamned road clear. That's the best thing you can do right now. Do you personally want to be the reason we have a major derailment of chemical weapons in the middle of Vicksburg? Do you? Then stop talking, think for a minute, and do what you gotta do."

He hung up the phone and told the comms operator not to answer the goddamned thing anymore. Then he went into the bathroom and washed his face. He stared at his hollow-eyed image in the mirror. Mehle was infecting his judgment. There was going to be unending hell to pay for what they'd done tonight, but right now, he saw his mission as being that of getting this train safely across the bridge while keeping Mehle from going totally around the bend, if that was still an option. He could just imagine the scene on the other train, with armed soldiers standing behind the engineers, and an armored monster following them down the tracks as they went backward, its headlight right in their frightened faces. The real fun, he thought, would begin once they got beyond the bridge.

Keeler held on for dear life underneath the sixth car from the end of the train. It was a covered gondola car, with two bulges on the bottom separated in the middle by an inverted **V** of space. Within the space was a heavy lattice of steel support members, and he was suspended in the lattice with the pack. When he had realized that the train was actually stopped right on top of his hiding place, he had stood up directly underneath the car, only to find himself staring right at a pair of what looked like Army combat boots. In the glare of the headlight from the other train, he was able to make out the legs of other figures standing out along the right-of-way. Army? National Guard troops, maybe? Obviously, something had gone wrong with traffic control out on this line, and there had nearly been a head-on collision. So now military security forces were—what?

He had crouched back down and waited, not knowing what was going to happen next. And then, to his surprise, he heard the rumble of multiple engines from up front, and the sound of men running back down the tracks. He heard an authoritative voice command everyone out there to reboard. He stood up again so he could see out. He got a quick glimpse of a white MP armband as a soldier ran by. Military police? Jesus, was this an *Army* train? At that moment, he heard a second set of engines increase rpm, and he only barely managed to drop below the tracks before the car above him jerked into motion.

He had waited for almost a mile's worth of cars to pass overhead to make his move, lunging upward to get aboard the first car that presented a suitable hiding place. He was just in time, as the end of the train had been visible. The pyramidal space he now occupied was about five feet high and the width of the car. There were two steel plates on either side that prevented anyone at grade level from seeing him. He pulled the backpack over closer to where he was hiding, then extracted some light nylon line. He fashioned a crude harness, looped it around the steel beams, and tied himself in. He checked the Detacord and the initiator can, closed up the bag, and tied it by its straps to another beam.

Something didn't make sense. He wanted to climb over to the side to see what kind of a train he'd jumped, but not if there were soldiers out there. All that mattered was that it was westbound. It would take him to his target. The Vicksburg bridge had a single track. All he had to do was get out there and onto the bridge itself. Drop off the train—they never went fast because the bridge was old and couldn't stand the vibration loads—and get under the track bed. Once there, the bridge was his.

The bottom of the car was covered in a film of dust and grease. He checked his harness, then fished a small bottle of water out of the backpack. He wondered what an Army train was doing out here. He wished he had brought a coat or at least something to cover his face. But then he forced himself to relax in his steel lair. The night was still young. This might actually work out. He lifted the water bottle in a mock *salud* to the memory of his family. The Army was taking him to his target. Perfect. And then he had another thought. There was only one commodity carried on an Army train: ammunition. He thumped his fist on the indifferent steel: perfect squared. This time, he wouldn't blow up the bridge. This time, he'd blow up the goddamned train.

Hush leaned back and tried to see out the left-rear window, but there were bushes in the way. "Damn," he said. "The goon squad."

Carolyn placed a call to Jefferson City. Little Hill called her back in one minute.

"Where's Captain Powers?" she asked.

"We're back at the bridge," the trooper said. "He's in the CP. Some problem with a runaway train east of here."

"Terrific," Carolyn said. "Do you know if he's asked for Bureau help in scouting the rail line coming from Jackson?"

"I'll find out; you need to talk to him?"

"No. Just pass to him that now would be nice."

The trooper said he would get Powers that message, and Carolyn hung up. She looked over toward the hotel. A figure was walking up the street in their direction, looking into driveways.

"What kind of plates does this car have?" she asked

"Mississippi government, I'd guess. Why?"

"One of those inspectors is coming this way. Checking driveways. What do you want to do?"

"How far away?"

"Four houses. No, three. I think it's a woman, actually. She's being casual about it, but she's checking."

"No time to rabbit, then, right?"

"We could, but she'd make us. Tough to outrun a radio."

"Well," Hush said with a grin, moving closer, "we're a man and woman in the front seat of a car. Let's see just how nosy she is."

He reached for her face with both hands and kissed her once, then again. She drew a back for a moment, and then she kissed him and he forgot all about the nosy agent. When they came up for air, the woman was nowhere to be seen, nor were the bureau cars.

"Magic all around," Hush murmured. She smiled and he momentarily lost interest in trains and Keeler. Then her expression changed. She was looking over his shoulder in the direction of the tracks they had just crossed. Hush turned around. The last eastbound train that had come through was visible again at the crossing—going backward.

• • •

Carolyn started up the car and backed it out onto the street, the lights still off. She confirmed that the Bureau cars were gone from in front of The Corners, then turned down the block toward the Oak Street railroad crossing. The gates were down and the lights flashing, and there was no doubt about it: The train they'd seen was definitely going backward. Through the trees to their left they could see a brakeman with a large hand held light perched on the rear coupling of the last tank car, looking anxiously down the tracks.

"What the hell, over?" Hush muttered.

"Must be a traffic problem," Carolyn said. "There must be a westbound train out there that's been given priority, and they're making this train go back across the bridge."

"I hope someone's inspecting them before they let them out onto that bridge," Hush said. "Maybe we better check in with Powers."

Carolyn pulled the car over to one side of the secluded street, parked and fished for the phone. The pulsing red lights from the crossing painted their faces with alternating bands of red and shadow. The huge tank cars bumped through the crossing, their wheels banging on some discontinuity on the river side of the street pavement. She raised Little Hill, who went to find Powers.

"Where are you guys?" Powers asked.

Carolyn told him, then mentioned that there had been Bureau cars at The Corners. She held the phone so that Hush could hear.

"Yeah, well, they're all gainfully employed right now," Powers said. "We've got feds checking that whole rail line between here and Jackson. Actually, there should be a car at that crossing."

Hush looked through the windshield but could not see any cars. Unless they are on the other side of the train, he thought. He took the phone.

"Mike, they going to inspect all westbound trains?"

"Well, we've got something of a problem in that department right now. Seems the Army is running some kind of ammunition train on the KCS line out of Jackson. The control people said there was a near head-on with it out by the Big Black River trestle. They're saying some Army colonel on the train is threatening people at gunpoint and making a train back up all the way into Louisiana to make room for his train. It's kinda crazy out there."

"Is the train that's backing up a tank-car train? We've got one right here."

332

"No idea. Probably not, though. The tank-car train's probably making room for the other one. The KCS control people are freaking out, want us to arrest everyone on the Army train. Problem is that they're traveling with a platoon of military police."

"How the hell did an ammo train get out on the main lines at a time like this?"

"Guy just jumped a siding somewhere and started trucking. Says he'll be good once he gets it across the big river. They're going to Utah or Idaho somewhere. I asked some more questions and one of the National Guard people said this thing came out of Anniston, sort of implying there were things about this train I didn't want to know."

"Anniston, Alabama?"

"I guess. Why?"

"The Army's got a big chemical weapons dump at Anniston. Your Guard friend might be right."

"Yeah, well, we're going to try to stop it just outside of Vicksburg and take a quick look. By the way, LeBourgoise really wants to know where you are; says there's a team of inspectors here from headquarters."

"Wonderful. Okay, we'll lay low for a while. Call us if anything develops."

"Rent-a-goons," Hush said as he handed Carolyn the phone. "Carswell and the director must be really spun up."

The engine set on the tank-car train came backing through the crossing, slowing down perceptibly. As the crossing cleared, Hush suddenly saw two sedans on the other side, parked next to a city police car. There were FBI agents standing around the cars, one of whom pointed at their unmarked car through the gates.

"Rock and roll," Hush said, and Carolyn started up. Because the big diesels had stopped right next to the crossing, the gates remained down. Carolyn turned their car around and drove south down Oak Street. Hush could see headlights coming on behind them, but the gates mercifully stayed down. The train let go a long blast on its air horn, then started to edge out of their sight toward the distant bridge.

"Pedal to the metal," Hush said.

Carolyn complied immediately as they both reached for seat belts. She turned left onto Klein Street, which bounded the other side of The Corners, then climbed the steep hill and went right on Washington. While Hush checked the mirror for signs of pursuit, she took the next left and the one after that, heading back north now through the older part of Vicksburg. They crossed over the rail cut, and Hush automatically looked down to the right to see if there was anything coming.

"Can you find your way back to that crossing?" he asked. "They'll never expect us to go right back there."

"I can try; we're over the tracks."

Hush fished out the map and then looked for a street sign. They came upon Clay Street, and he had Carolyn go left, back toward the river. As they came down a hill near the casino and convention center area, they cut across Oak Mulberry Street.

"That should take us back to the crossing," Hush said. "But right now, let's park in the casino lot. See if we have a tail."

She drove straight down into the crowded parking lot. Even on Sundays, Hush concluded, the games must go on. She swung the car around and parked it among the pickup trucks facing up the hill, so that they could watch the main streets. They waited. There was little traffic along the streets of downtown Vicksburg, which appeared to be a collection of three- and four-story buildings, many with false fronts.

"We can't avoid our own people forever," Hush said, fidgeting in the darkened car. Carolyn's face was a white blur in the shadow.

"What about Keeler?" she said, rolling down the front window. The parking lot was infused with the smell of popcorn.

"Well, what about Keeler? We're on the sidelines. Powers has people inspecting the westbound trains, which should complete the cordon. I think we're done."

"So what are you saying?"

"I think we ought to stop this hide-and-seek shit and drive on down to the CP and find LeBourgoise or the Jackson people. We're going to have to do that sooner or later."

There was still very little traffic visible on the streets above them. An occasional pickup truck came into or left the casino lot, but the streets remained empty. Hush thought he heard a rumble of distant thunder out over the river behind them. A slight breeze was stirring up the hamburger wrappers in the parking lot.

"That'd be one sure way of leaving Vicksburg," she said. "Personally, I'd like to wait, see what the hell happens. I still think he's going to make his play. Tonight. This is the South. Come daylight, all those good ole boys'll find him."

Hush nodded in the darkness. "Yeah, you're probably right," he said. "But the longer we stay out of sight, the more we become fugitives ourselves, as opposed to two agents working a problem from a different angle."

"If I have to leave the Bureau, then so be it," she replied. "But for right now, I want to see how this comes out tonight, and that won't happen if we're in a car going back to Jackson."

"Now I know why you never got married," he said with a smile.

"*What?*"

"Because this is too much fun, isn't it?"

She laughed, but then they both heard a sound they had not expected: the urgent wail of a westbound train, coming from the east side of town. Carolyn started up the car.

As the Army train entered the outskirts of Vicksburg, it slowed down to a crawl to permit the eastbound train to back down into a siding. Matthews came out on the rear platform in time to see the sergeant and his two MPs trotting across the tracks toward the command car. They jumped aboard, grinning like a trio of teenagers who had just outrun the local cops. Before Matthews could question the sergeant, the comms operator was calling for him through the doorway.

"Colonel wants the guard force deployed," he announced. "Out *on* the cars. He isn't going to stop. Says to get 'em out there, spread 'em out along the train, and shoot anyone who tries to mess with us."

Matthews looked at the sergeant, who laughed out loud. "Shee-it, this is getting interesting," he said.

"You clear it with me before anybody starts shooting at civilians or cops. You got that?" Matthews said, handing him a portable radio.

"Hell, I know that, Major. We'll get 'em out there, make it look good. Man! What a ride!"

He stuck his head into the command car and told the troops to stand by to debark, and that they would then reboard every fifth car. He told them to keep their weapons handy, not to let anyone on the train, warning shots authorized, but *not* deadly force unless he said so. There were some questions, but the sergeant ignored them and started yelling for them to move it, move it, move it, and out they came, flying down the steps even before most of them realized the train was still moving. Matthews watched as they jogged up the sides of the train in the semidarkness, their rifles at port arms, their white MP armbands bobbing up and down. The sergeant, carrying a riot gun and the portable radio, followed as tail-end Charlie to make sure they went where they were supposed to. Matthews waited until he thought the farthest forward car had been reached and then called the sergeant on his radio. The sergeant confirmed that everyone was in position, and Matthews informed the front engine. To his surprise, Colonel Mehle came up on the portable radio circuit and declared he was taking direct command of the guard force. Immediately, the train increased speed to a steady five miles an hour, and Matthews went to get some coffee and await developments. He hoped and prayed the traffic-control people were not planning any fun and games—he was pretty sure Mehle would have no compunctions about shooting.

Carolyn gunned the sedan straight up through the parking lot, evoking a protest of horns from some pickup trucks as she cut across lanes and rows. Reaching Oak Street, she turned right and accelerated back toward the at-grade crossing, which was only six blocks away. They skidded to a stop next to a city police car as the crossing lights began to flash and the gates started down. There was no sign of the Bureau cars. They heard the train's whistle again as they got out. The train was definitely coming from the east side of town, but they couldn't see it yet.

"Call Powers," Hush said. "Find out if this is that Army train."

As Carolyn tried to reach Powers, Hush went over to the cop car and showed his credentials to the elderly policeman sitting inside.

"We're working the bridge operation," he said. "We were told all westbound trains were being stopped for inspection. Do you know why this train is coming through?"

The cop shook his head. "They don't tell me jackshit," he said. "Just to stay here for my shift and check out any vehicles for this old boy." He held up a fax picture of Keeler.

The train's whistle sounded again, closer now. Hush watched intently, anxious to know if this was yet another train backing down or a real westbound. Carolyn was walking over, the phone at her ear. She switched it off.

"Little Hill says Powers was off on another possible sighting south of town but is on his way back now. This train is that Army deal they were talking about. It's apparently been cleared through town and over the bridge."

"Has it been inspected?"

"Hill didn't think so. He said there are military police on the train and, apparently it won't stop. He said there's some kind of problem with the engineers, but the word the CP has now is to get it across the river. I didn't know the Army had trains."

Hush could see the train's headlight now, still about a half mile away, but clearly a westbound train was making its way through the cut. The engineer was leaning hard on the whistle.

"Do you have a direct phone number for the CP?"

Carolyn shook her head. Hush asked the cop if he could use his radio. In about thirty seconds, he had a patch through to the command post. He identified himself and asked to speak to someone from the KCS. A voice came on the net. Hush identified himself again and asked if the train now coming down into Vicksburg had been stopped and inspected. The KCS man said no, it had not, but that the National Guard had orders from the Pentagon to let it through, over the objections of the KCS traffic center.

"Did that train cross the Big Black River?" Hush asked. The whistle was louder now, the headlight steadier.

"Those dumb sons a bitches damn near caused a head-on collision right on that bridge. Some crazy Army bastard is running that train, but the military people here are gonna let it through. Right now, this bridge is theirs, not ours."

Hush thanked the man and handed the mike back to the cop. "We've got to stop this train," he said. "It stopped on the bridge. I'll bet my ass Keeler's on it."

"Hush—" she began, but he cut her off.

"Give me the car keys," he ordered. She handed them over to him and he ran for their car. The train sounded its whistle again; it was about two blocks from the crossing, but its headlight was still pointed off to one side as it entered the west-to-south curve. The whistle was loud enough to drown out the clanging crossing bells. The cop had gotten out of his car, obviously wondering what Hush was up to.

Hush jumped into the car, started it up, and drove it past the cop car and between the gates, knocking the tip off of one of them. He stopped when the car was parked directly across the single track, then got out, leaving the headlights on. He pulled the keys and closed the door, hurrying back through the gates. The train's powerful headlight was swinging slowly toward them now as it approached the crossing. The cop started yelling at Hush that he couldn't do that, but Hush pushed past the cop and got into the police car, which he started up, backed up, and pointed directly at the crossing. He put the car's headlights on high beam, then pointed the big chromed spotlight into the crossing area and switched it on, too. The cop was literally jumping up and down, but Hush ignored him, getting out of the car and locking the keys in it.

As he came back toward her, Carolyn grabbed his arm and pointed across the crossing. There were three cars coming fast from the other side. The lead locomotive's whistle blared again. The rumble of the big engines engulfed the crossing area, making speech impossible. The cop was beside himself, shouting into his shoulder mike, but the noise from the train was overwhelming. The black armored engines were now only about fifty yards from the crossing, and the driver was laying hard on the whistle to see if he could move that car parked on the tracks. Hush realized then that the engines were not slowing down.

"He's not going to stop!" Hush shouted into Carolyn's ear. "I *know* Keeler's on this thing. We need to get alongside, see if we can spot him!"

The three cars on the other side screeched to a stop at the gates, and their doors flew open. About a dozen FBI agents swarmed out of the cars, holding up their hands against the blaze of light coming from the two cars and the spotlight pointed at them. Almost simultaneously, the huge black engines, air horns on full blast, pushed into the crossing and slammed into the car in a slow-motion crash, overturning it and then rolling it across the crossing in cloud of dust and shattering glass.

Hush ran up through the gates, drew his weapon, and squatted down, with Carolyn right behind him, looking to see if anyone was hiding underneath the train. He had gotten a quick glimpse of some white faces in the windows of the front engine, but he then concentrated on the first of the covered gondolas, whose undercarriage was fully illuminated in the headlights of the cop car. He never saw the MPs perched on the backs of the cars as the train continued to grind through the curve, shoving the battered car off to one side, upside down, its headlights still on, pointing off into the trees. After a few minutes of looking, Hush realized that he could not really see underneath the train, but the shape of the gondola cars definitely made it possible for someone to hide under there. Then he noticed that there was a slight depression at the right side of the crossing—where the concrete edge of the road ended and the gravel track bed resumed. He yelled for Carolyn to cover him, and then he ran up to the side of a gondola car, grabbed a steel ledge in the middle of the car, and threw himself underneath the car and into the depression, ignoring Carolyn's scream of protest.

He landed on his back, his feet toward the end of the train. Sharp points of gravel dug into the back of his head. There was just under two feet of clearance beneath the train, whose massive bulk was thumping across the rail joint at the crossing and dropping dirt and dust on him every time a wheel hit. The blaze of white light from his left was partially blinding him, but now he could see up into the steel concavities under the car. Carolyn was bending down beside the track, screaming between the wheels for him to get out of there. On the other side, there were some more people yelling at him. He ignored them all and waited, gun pointed up, steeling himself to disregard the awesome mass of metal that was rolling over his head, and adjusting his position closer to the center when a coil of air-brake hose threatened to take his face off. Carolyn was down on her hands and knees alongside the track now, her own gun out, her face a mask of fright at what he was doing.

After five more harrowing minutes of huge glistening wheels banging across the joint, showering his face with dust and dirt repeatedly, the end cars approached. He tried to scrunch deeper into the gravel, but the rocks were the size of plums, all hard-edged and immovable. Suddenly, there was a roar of compressed air rushing through a big pipe inches from his face, followed by a frightful squeal of brakes. The train slowed perceptibly as the back wheels of a car came across his position, followed by the front wheels of the next car. Shit! Hush thought. Someone had told the engineer there was a man under the train. Well, at least they'd get it stopped, and then he'd order the Jackson office people to make a thorough search. And then, just as the train stopped, he found himself looking into the stunned face of Morgan Keeler.

When Matthews got word that there was a man down under the train, he immediately thought it had to be one of his MPs. He ordered the sergeant to get off and investigate, then jumped down off the train himself and ran forward, telling each man that he passed to stand fast. He ran awkwardly because of the gravel and the ties, but the obstacles just made him run harder. The farther up the train he went, the more confused he became, because all of his MPs appeared to be right where they were supposed to be. Because of the curve, he couldn't really see up the front of the train. Then came the sudden squeal of brakes under the cars, and then the sergeant reported that all his people were accounted for, but he said the train had hit a car.

Oh, Jesus, Matthews thought, and ran faster.

Keeler overcame his astonishment about one instant before the FBI man lying down there on the track bed did. He shifted sideways to put the shoulder of the steel bulge between Hanson's rising gun and most of his own body, then swung his own .45 down to point at Hanson's head. At that instant, the whistle sounded, and both Carolyn and the agents on the other side of the train, who could not see Keeler, began yelling at Hanson to get out of there, shouting that the train was going to move again. Carolyn stuck her head under the car, reaching for Hanson, who yelled that Keeler was right there and that she had to back out.

For a split second, Keeler looked right at Hanson, then he swung the .45 to point at the woman's upper body. Carolyn saw where Hush was looking, looked up herself, and froze.

"Stalemate, Hanson," Keeler yelled. "Back out, or I kill her."

The FBI man was pointing a weapon right at his face. Keeler saw something flash in the man's eyes, some decision, some sure knowledge that he could fire and hit him. He looked back at the woman. To his amazement, she was bringing up her own gun. He squeezed his own trigger. The blast from the .45 knocked the back of his hand up into the steel underbody of the car, stunning it, even as a tremendous shock clanged through the car as the train suddenly started forward again. He almost dropped the gun as he scrambled to hold on, feeling but not hearing the shot that Hanson had fired at him, wincing as the bullet ricocheted off the steel and flayed his face with shards of steel. But then the car was moving beyond Hanson, the train going ahead, faster than it had been, and he knew the bridge was next.

• • •

Hush rolled out as soon as he could, barely escaping the crushing wheels as the train accelerated, the cars swaying dangerously in the curve that led toward the bridge. Carolyn lay on her back on the gravel, her gun hand thrown out, fingers splayed, her eyes wide with shock. A massive red stain spread across the front of her blouse and jacket. As Hush dropped to his knees beside her, he saw her eyes roll back into their socket, and then she coughed wetly and stopped breathing. The city cop was there by then, and Hush shouted at him to get an ambulance.

He pulled her inert form away from the track and put her on her side, wound side down. Tears in his eyes, he checked for a pulse and then began to give her mouth-to-mouth resuscitation, tasting the salt of blood on her lips and hearing the dreadful sound of his own breath bubbling out of the hole high in her chest every time he pushed air into her lungs. He heard someone come running by but did not look up to see who it was. He worked frantically as the final cars went banging by on the tracks, their wheels shrieking with the strain of the curve. He wanted to do chest compression, but he could not bring himself to touch the blood-soaked blouse, for he fear of doing more damage. Then the cop was back, something green in his hands. He pushed Hush aside and got to work on Carolyn. Hush sat back on his haunches, overwhelmed by a feeling of utter helplessness.

Matthews was horrified to see the woman lying by the side of the tracks, her FBI jacket a sodden mass of blood. Had Mehle done this? Or, worse, one of his MPs? He slowed for just a second but kept going, determined to get up to that engine and end this madness, specials or no specials. He raced down the right-of-way as fast as he could go and finally caught up with the rear engine. A single MP who had seen him chasing the train was running behind him, trying to regain his post on the train. Matthews swung aboard, caught his breath, and then began to climb across the catwalk toward the front engine. The engine noise was stunning, the huge cylinders pounding his eardrums and giving him an instant headache, but he pressed on, jumping across the couplings and then going crabwise down the right side of the middle engine. He jumped again, and the noise became slightly more bearable as he got closer to the front cab. When he could see into the cab, he stopped and was immediately sucked up against the air intakes. Then he nearly fell off when the engine leaned away from the curve on some uneven track. When he recovered his balance, there was Mehle, standing in the cab's rear doorway, pointing a 9-mm pistol at him.

"What the goddamned hell are you doing here?" Mehle screamed. "Get back to your post! On the goddamned double!"

Matthews put his right hand out, palm up, while holding on to the railing with his left, and began to creep forward slowly. He had to get closer to the purple-faced colonel.

"Colonel, you've got to stop this," he shouted. "An FBI agent's been shot. Something's going on we don't know about."

"I don't give a good goddamn about anything but getting this goddamned train across that goddamned bridge, understand?" Mehle yelled, and then whirled around as one of the warrant officers stood up behind him. The man quickly sat back down. Matthews used the moment to get closer to that steel door. Mehle whipped back around and pointed the pistol right at Matthews's face. They were now only about four feet apart.

"The specials temps are stable," Matthews lied. "There aren't any other trains in front of us." He inched forward again, but then Mehle fired two warning shots. Matthews felt the heat of both bullets passing his face and recoiled against the steel side of the engine. At that instant, one of the warrants came flying low through the door, tackling Mehle from behind. They fought viciously on the catwalk and then the other warrant came through the door and grabbed Mehle around the neck. Matthews stepped quickly past the struggling men to give the warrants some working room, but then there was a shot, followed by another, and all three men rolled off the catwalk and down onto the embankment, disappearing into a stand of tall weeds alongside the track. Matthews stared into the engine cab at all the controls as the train continued to rumble toward the great black bridge. He realized he had not the first idea of how to stop Mehle's goddamned train.

Hush stood up, knees shaking, unwilling to look down at Carolyn. Something evil in his brain rephrased that: Carolyn's body. He patted his holster; his gun was gone. But hers was right there. He scooped it up and saw the train disappearing down the bridge line. When he saw several FBI agents starting across the tracks in his direction, he took off after the train, his vision locking down to the taillights up ahead. Keeler was at the

342

back end of the train, about six or seven cars from the end. He ran faster, tripping awkwardly over the gravel ballast, trying to stay on the ties. He was vaguely aware of people shouting behind him, but he didn't care. The train was going faster than it had been, but he *would* catch it. His lungs started to burn and his heart pounded as he loped along the tracks, intent on the huge black cars with all their gobbledygook military nomenclature stenciled on the sides. His injured leg sent a stab of pain up into his thigh each time his right foot hit the ground, but he squeezed the pain right out of his head. Then he remembered what all the Army nomenclature was about: This train was from the chemical weapons depot at Anniston. Great God, he thought, Keeler is going to drop a load of chemical weapons into the Mississippi River.

He ran faster, finally overtaking the command car, the bunk-room car, and then an oversized gondola car. The huge wheels crept by as if in a nightmare. His feet and legs, especially the right one, were now beyond feeling. There were percussive whimpering sounds coming out of his throat in time with each stride as he raced forward, gaining on his target, the sixth or seventh car from the end—not sure which, but he swore he'd find the right one, by Christ.

His brain remained totally connected to his gun hand, which was alive and communicating eagerly, knurled steel reassuring straining flesh, his fingers sentient as they gripped the Sig like steel coils. A gun-sight image of Keeler's face superimposed itself like some ghostly hologram in his vision against the backdrop of Carolyn's eyes rolling back, and then he was there. No, too far, he thought. In his rage, he had run right past the sixth car, so he slowed and dropped back, staggering as he fought for breath. It was much darker here without the headlights, and it had begun to rain.

It took him a moment to comprehend that there was a young soldier in battle gear standing on the back platform of the seventh car from the end, his M16 held awkwardly across his chest, gawking at Hush. The soldier yelled something, pointing back toward the other end of the train, but Hush ignored him. He grabbed a handrail along the round-down of the car and swung aboard, then immediately lowered himself down to almost wheel level, looking under the car. The soldier was still yelling, and now the guy was pointing his rifle at him. Hush pointed to the FBI initials emblazoned on his windbreaker, and the kid lowered his weapon fractionally, unsure of what to do. The train was straightening out now, going faster down the last straightaway before the big right turn out onto the bridge.

Then Hush had an idea. He climbed back along the car toward the front platform of the sixth car and motioned for the soldier to come close enough for Hush to tell him something. The kid complied, leaning down, allowing Hush to snatch the M16 out of the MPs hands. The soldier tried to grab for it, but he lost his balance, his arms windmilling as he attempted to stay upright. By then, Hush was pointing for him to get back, to go back to the other end of the car. The soldier complied, a sick look on his face, which changed to wild alarm when he saw what Hush was going to do. Hush had wedged his legs under the lower rung of the platform ladder and was now leaning way over to one side, the M16 cradled almost upside down in his hands, and then he was firing down into the ballasted railroad ties in short bursts of full automatic, firing lengthwise under the sixth car and then the seventh, sending a stream of ricocheting rounds up into the bottom. The noise was deafening, and the rifle was hard to hold on to, but most of the bullets were whacking and spanging against the bottom plates of the gondola cars. When the magazine was empty, he simply dropped the weapon under the wheels, which promptly sliced it into two pieces. Then he was in motion again, jumping the coupling and crawling along the side of the sixth car until he came to the start of the inverted-V plates in the middle. Making sure the Sig was ready for business, he jammed it in his shoulder holster and swung under, crawling across steel ridges, using the underbody's support girders as handholds, looking for Keeler. From underneath the car, he thought he caught a glimpse of the big searchlights at the Welcome Center.

Matthews sat down in what he figured to be the engineer's seat on the right side and stared at all the controls. The huge headlight was boring a conical white hole into a blowing mist of rain, but the windows were obscured. He felt absolutely helpless, unable even to find the controls for the windshield wipers. There was no throttle like in the movies, and certainly no brake pedal. There was a pedestal-mounted control stand next to the seat on the left-hand side, which is when he realized he was on the wrong side. He shifted over into the other seat. He looked behind and was able to see the train behind him through a slanted window. Looking back at the control stand, he saw a couple of interlocked levers, one over the other, one of which had eight positions notched into the handle. There were instrument dials recording main engine amps, pressure in the air-brake system, ground speed, as well as warning lights marked WHEEL SLIP and REMOTE BRAKING AIR. There was an auxiliary panel on the right-hand side, where he finally found the wiper controls. He turned the switch, and the big wipers first smeared and then cleared the windows, allowing him to see that a turn was coming. Beyond that was the big bridge. He was desperately looking around for a control that would apply the brakes when he heard an M16 stuttering in automatic fire somewhere behind him.

Keeler was terrified by the sudden barrage of gunfire and all the ricochets, but he had not been hit, not once. His right eyelid was bleeding from a stone fragment, and he was pretty sure the backpack had a tear or two in it, but he was otherwise unhurt. The only light coming under the car now was from passing streetlights and an occasional car's headlights, but where he was wedged up in the V, it was in full darkness. He could not imagine who had turned loose the M16, and he had reflexively pulled the .45 before putting it back into the waistband of his pants.

There was no more time: The bridge was coming. He pressed his feet and his back against the sloping side of the gondola's underbody to free his hands, then pulled the backpack toward him. Leaving the bulk of the coil in the pack, he pulled out one end. There were gusts of wind blowing under the car now, smelling like rain, and the end of the Detacord whipped back and forth like an anxious snake. He fished again in the pack for the initiator can, probing for it with his fingers, slipping the plastic cap off the bottom, and then the pack came off its attachment in the lattice. He lunged for it, barely grabbing it before it fell onto the tracks below, and then nearly slipped off his own perch. After a moment of scrambling, he got himself and the pack stabilized. He exhaled and tried again, going back into the pack with his fingers. Careful now, he told himself, can't drop this. He fished the soup can–size initiator out, batting his eyelids to clear the blood from his right eye, and inserted the end of the Detacord firmly into the hole in the bottom of the initiator can— which was slippery with his own sweat—until it seated.

Almost there, he thought. The train seemed to be going a bit faster, the wind beginning to whip a dirty spray along under the car. He wouldn't be able to see the bridge until the train and his car went out onto the structure, and then, even in the darkness, he wouldn't be sure until he saw the river through the ties. His plan was simple: This was an Army ammunition train—he was certain of it now. Soldiers on board, an M16 letting go like that, unmistakable sound, probably by accident, some boot-camp recruit getting scared. Once they were on the bridge, he would unreel the Detcord along the track underneath the train, keeping the detonator can in his hands. When all three hundred feet were out, drag-ging along the track bed under the train, he would turn the timer dial to ten seconds, slip down the side of his steel cavity, and, as gently as he could, drop the can onto the top of the rear wheel bogies. The cord would be whipping up along the bottom of all those cars, those *ammu-nition* cars, when it went off. The cord was three hundred feet long; the cars averaged about seventy feet long, so he would cover the bottoms of the last three, maybe four cars. He had to get only one car to sustain a sympathetic detonation, and he'd wreck the bridge. His car should sur-vive, since the cord would probably blow the coupling. Then he'd ride the remains of the train across the bridge. After that, well, he'd have to play that by ear.

The noise of the wheels began to change. He slid partially down the V and poked his head down, craning his neck to see forward. He realized that the train was making a right turn now. There was a fine mist blowing up from the wheels. It must have really started raining. Good. The ground on either side of the train was rising, which hopefully meant they were entering that cut that went under Washington Street, past the CP, and out onto the bridge. He crawled back up and began to undo the plastic ties that held the Detacord in a coil.

Hush was struggling underneath the front end of the car, his strength flagging after that long run. He locked his stomach muscles to hold his body up away from the rushing ties. He was spread-eagled upside down against the underbody, his hands gripping the center I beam, his feet wedged into the secondary beam ledges running parallel to the center beam. He held his belly tight up against the bottom of the car, with Carolyn's Sig stuck hard into his shoulder rig. He was trying to crawl back along the bottom toward that dark cavity in the middle where he knew Keeler had to be lurking, some twenty feet back. The center beam's flanges were plenty big enough, but they were greasy and his hands kept slipping.

As he inched back toward the center, he kept seeing Carolyn on the ground, the graceful way her hand had relaxed, almost casually letting go of the gun, her whole body seeming to puddle on the embankment. I will kill him, he thought. As soon as I see him, I will kill him. I'm not going to yell "FBI," tell him to freeze, or to drop it, or to put his hands up. I will just shoot his goddamned eyes out. I can do it. I have done it before. I *will* do it. He ground his teeth with the effort of holding on.

He got within about eight feet of the center when the car began to lean into a right turn, and he had to change position to get a better grip. A flash of lightning outside startled him, but he concentrated on getting into a cavity right alongside the center beam. He rolled sideways and backed into it, spreading his legs wide to catch steel ledges and hunching his back up against the steel so that he faced across the width of the car's bottom. It was a much more secure position, and he took a moment to catch his breath. The ties were becoming a blur underneath. Was it raining? There seemed to be a mist developing under the car. It was really dark now, as if they had entered a tunnel. No, not a tunnel, but that cut under Washington Street overpass. The toll plaza; then the bridge was next. What was Keeler planning? A suicide bombing, maybe? The train was going too fast for him to drop off onto the bridge. If he crawled out onto the side of the car, those soldiers would see him. He was probably no more than ten feet from Keeler, but there was that enormous void of steel between them. Filled with—what? Chemical weapons?

There was a flare of orange light from the left side of the car. The CP lights, Hush thought. They'd be on the bridge in a few seconds. Whatever Keeler was going to do, he'd be doing it now. He reached for a ledge and then brought his hand back: The metal has become very slippery. The wheel noise under him changed as the car rolled out onto the track bed of the bridge structure. A blast of cold, wet air rose through the ties from the river below, and Hush, suppressing a wave of vertigo, was suddenly glad it was dark. He took another deep breath and forced himself to move across the cavity, trying for hand- and footholds that would keep his right arm free. The lights had disappeared. He got to the bottom of the cavity, craned his neck down, and looked back under the train. There was something there. A rope? A wire? Something that was coming down from the cavity next to his. Being fed down from above, he realized.

Keeler. And that had to be Detcord. The wind was whipping it all over the place, dangerously close to the wheels. A coil of it blew back toward him and he reached for it but missed. His left hand slipped and he almost fell, catching himself at the last instant on the air brake's pipe.

Matthews watched helplessly as the train ground out onto the bridge. This had been Mehle's objective for the entire trip, and suddenly Matthews wondered if he ought to do nothing, let Mehle's goddamned train get across the goddamned river. But there was simply no way: There had been gunfire behind him on the train, Mehle and the warrants had gone overboard along the tracks back in town, and that FBI agent had been shot at the crossing. Something was terribly wrong here, and he had no idea what it was. At that instant, the MP who had lost his M16 burst into the cab from behind him, yelling something about an FBI guy being *under* the train. Matthews stared at him for an instant, then realized he had no choice: He had to stop the train.

And then he saw it: a small red T-shaped handle down on the floor, almost under the control stand. There was a brass plate marked clear as day: EMERGENCY STOP. There were sloping steel trusses flitting past the windows now; the train was definitely out on the bridge. He looked again at the horizontal control lever and saw that it was set one notch past a setting marked IDLE. He grabbed the handle and moved it back to the idle position, and the big engines slowed immediately. "Sorry, Colonel," he said as he reached down for the red handle.

Hush repositioned himself and bent back down. The spray was much stronger now, and he had trouble seeing, but then another hank of the cord blew practically into his face, and he caught it this time. He held it for an instant, felt it stop feeding, and then jerked it with all his strength. He thought he heard a cry from above, and then the remains of an entire reel of the Detacord with some kind of small can attached to it dropped out of the adjacent cavity. The can bounced once on the tracks and then went under one of the wheels. One microsecond later came a red flash and the ripping thunder of an explosion behind them, an explosion that seemed to propagate away from where Hush was scrambling to reposition himself. A second after that came a roar of compressed air in the pipe he was holding and the brakes locked down on the wheels with an incredible screech, jolting the car heavily. The pipe suddenly became intensely cold and his hand let go reflexively, forcing him to scramble again to recover some kind of handhold as the car shuddered to an emergency stop. He grabbed at ledges, angle irons, and even rivets, but everything was wet and greasy and he simply couldn't hang on. He felt himself slipping down the sloping sides of the cavity, his efforts to grip defeated by the heavy shaking coming from the locked wheels, which were now showering sparks up under the car. He grabbed a tie-rod at the last moment, but his feet and lower legs were already bouncing along the ties, battering his heels and knocking one of his shoes right off. Just when he was about to lose his grip, the train finally lurched to a stop in one last jolt that actually kicked his car forward a few feet as a wave of coupling slack came out of the cars behind him. He dropped onto the ties on his back and looked up. There was Morgan Keeler, crouching like a spider up above him, an anguished look on his face even as his hand reached for a large automatic in his waistband.

Time slowed down, but Hush never missed a beat. His vision telescoped to frame Keeler's face. It was just like the range. Draw and shoot. Smooth, unhurried motion: Reach, grip, pull, swing, point, merge, eyes wide, and squeeze. Six rounds this time. Done it a hundred times. A thousand times. It's what I'm famous for. One. Two. Three. Four. Five. Six. The blasts from the Sig echo painfully in his ears, but his concentration never waivers.

Stop.

Refocus.

He rolled to one side as Keeler's body came sliding down the underside, accompanied by the clattering of the .45 he never got to shoot. A practically headless Keeler landed with a sodden thump on the ties, the cocked .45 landing behind him a split second later. Hush winced in anticipation of its going off, but it didn't. He resisted an impulse to grab up the .45 and empty it into Keeler's back. Instead, he lay back under the train and closed his eyes. He tried deep breathing. It was definitely raining outside. He could hear it. Outside. He laughed at himself, as if he were inside a warm, dry house somewhere, and not flat on his back underneath a goddamned ammunition train, with ninety feet of cold air blowing up on his back from the river below. He opened his eyes and caught a gust of smoky, wet air in the face. He shook his head and looked over at

Keeler, at the Trainman. His body lay bent on the ties, his back to Hush. Then there was the sound of boots running along the train, and then more boots, accompanied by shouts. He tried to decide whether or not simply to lie there or to crawl out and face the music. In a perverse way, it was more comfortable right where he was than it was going to be, although suddenly he became aware that his right heel was really hurting.

"Die, Keeler," he intoned to the body's back. "Die for killing Carolyn Lang."

Then he stuck the Sig back in its holster and crawled out on his back, emerging right in front of a startled MP. As the soldier instinctively began to raise his rifle, Hush calmly asked him to please help him up.

Hush was escorted back down the bridge roadway past the end of the stopped train by no fewer than six MPs, one of whom was helping him walk. They passed a small knot of Army people gathered around the third car from the end, examining the grayish blast marks on the bottom of the big gondola. Powers and several Highway Patrol cops ran to meet them at the Vicksburg end. The rain was coming down steadily, cascading in sheets off the high trusses of the bridge, onto and pelting the cars, but it could not remove the acrid chemical smell of high explosive all around the bridge. Powers took over and helped Hush the rest of the way off the bridge and into their favorite toll plaza, where the flickering blue light reflections of several emergency vehicles lit the place up like a disco. Hush finally had to rest, and they sat him down against the concrete wall of the toll plaza. The burned-out holes where the phone booths used to be were right above his head. Powers turned him over to some National Guard medics.

He returned ten minutes later. "Shot at and missed, shit at and hit," he observed, squatting down beside Hush. The rain dripped off his big flat-brimmed hat.

"Was that Detcord?" Hush asked, wiping rain off his face. Powers nodded, took off his hat, and set it on Hush's head to shield him from the rain.

"Yeah, but it was just hanging out in the air. Scared the shit out of everybody, but it didn't do anything but cauterize the bottom of a couple cars. Apparently, they're armored, although some of the Army guys were kind of white-knuckled about it."

"You know what's in those cars?"

"Army major back there said obsolete chemical weapons but that they aren't explosive. Except he seemed real worried about those two big cars near the tail. He says that a crazy colonel and two other guys are somewhere back on the line. Guy's pretty upset."

At that moment, the train out on the bridge sounded its whistle and then banged into motion.

"That was the Army runaway," Powers said. "They've got some KCS engineers on that mother now. They're gonna get it off the bridge so they can inspect it and the bridge, make sure he didn't damage anything. Then it's going to some place called Pine Bluff."

"I got the bastard," Hush said.

"So we noticed," Powers said, "They're gonna need DNA to make an ID."

"He got Carolyn."

Powers's face sobered. "I know."

"She was going to shoot him," Hush said. "He had a forty-five pointed right at her and she drew down on him anyway."

Hush was suddenly overcome by an emotion he couldn't name, but his eyes filled at the thought of losing her. He tried to say something, but all he ended up doing was licking his parched lips like some kind of idiot.

"Hey, hey," Powers said, leaning forward, shielding him from the others. "She's not dead. They have her downtown. It's serious, but the docs say she's got a chance."

Hush looked up at him, confused. "It was a forty-five auto; I saw her stop breathing."

"Yeah, but there was a city cop there. The old guy? His mother's even older, got emphysema. He always keeps an oxygen breather bottle in his squad car. Carolyn had a punctured lung, but he put her on the bottle. C'mon, let's get you downtown to the hospital."

Hush didn't trust himself to say anything; he started to get up. But then he noticed the crowd of FBI agents standing ten feet away, apparently waiting for him. There was a loose cordon of state troopers standing between the agents and him. Powers saw what was shaping up, said something into a small radio he held, and then retrieved his hat from Hush's head. A moment later, as Hush was getting steady on his feet, about a dozen reporters burst down into the toll plaza, and some television camera lights cast a sudden white glare. Hush shielded his eyes as the questions started, but Powers yelled for everybody to shut up.

"Roll tape when I say so," he commanded, and then he waited for everyone to shut up and get ready. "All right? Roll it." Then he turned to include Hush. "This is Assistant Director William Hanson from the Federal Bureau of Investigation, who tonight single-handedly caught and killed the murdering bastard who has been bombing bridges up and down the Mississippi River. His success tonight represents the culmination of an intense five-state cooperative effort between the FBI and local law-enforcement agencies. As you can see, Mr. Hanson has been injured. We are taking him to the city hospital. I see Resident Special Agent LeBourgoise from Baton Rouge standing back there. Since he's the next senior Bureau official here, he and I will be available to answer your questions about this case in fifteen minutes up in the Welcome Center. In the meantime, we need to get Mr. Hanson here out of the rain. That's all."

In Powers's car five minutes later, Hush lay back against the seat and tried to keep his brain in neutral. The mob of reporters and television people had Powers and LeBourgoise surrounded as they walked out of the toll plaza and up the grassy slope to the Welcome Center. It was Little Hill who had taken him to Powers's car, keeping other reporters at bay by simply glaring at them.

"He had that all wired, didn't he?" Hush asked as Little Hill punched the siren impatiently to make some Army trucks get out of the way.

"Cap'n said if you got from under that train alive, the Bureau brass was gonna land on you, but not if you was a hero on the TV."

Hush smiled in the darkness of the backseat. Powers knew his Bureau, and he had executed a preemptive public-relations strike. As far as the anxious public was concerned, the Bureau had gotten its man once again. What the director and his deputy pit bull would have to say in private might be extremely colorful, but in public he was now a hero on the TV. The last of the Untouchables. Mike Powers was a piece of work.

At the hospital, they treated his badly bruised heel and gave him a chance to wash all the undercarriage grime off. Some of the hospital people who had watched the breaking news story congratulated him on apprehending the bridge bomber. Then they gave him a wheelchair, and one of the state cops pushed him into an elevator so he could go upstairs to the surgical recovery area to see Carolyn. The attending physician in recovery actually told him he couldn't see her, but he changed his mind when the gaunt-looking man with the battered face rose out of the chair and looked down at him in a manner that caused everyone else at the desk to stop talking.

There were four Bureau men outside of her room, two sitting and two standing. The two sitting got right up as soon as they saw Hush and the state cops approaching. One of them opened Carolyn's door for him. No one spoke as he rolled in and pushed the door almost closed behind him.

Carolyn was almost lost in the mechanized hospital bed. Her hair was covered up in some kind of surgical cap, and she had two huge black rings under her eyes, which made her look like an underfed panda. Her bloodless lips glistened with Vaseline, and there was an oxygen tube taped under her nose. There were IVs going into both wrists, and another really ugly tube disappeared under the covers near her breastbone. The skin across the top of her chest was black-and-blue. Her eyes were closed, and her breathing was slow and labored. A monitoring system above her bed kept score of her heartbeat and other vital signs with attentive beeps. He could see the top straps of bandages looping up and over her right shoulder. Her face was the color of old ivory.

He pulled his wheelchair as close as he could to the side of her bed and leaned forward. He could hear the agents talking softly outside the door; he thought he heard the word *eyes*. He pushed the memory of what he had done to Keeler out of his mind and just sat there, looking at her, wanting to touch her, but not able to see her hands. Then she opened her eyes, blinked rapidly, focused, and recognized him. She mumbled a question; the only words he could recognize were "get him."

"Yes. On the bridge." He went on to tell her about the Detacord and what Powers had done with the reporters. She appeared to smile and then closed her eyes again. He really wanted to hold her hand, but he was afraid to disturb all those tubes. Suddenly, he was vastly weary. He closed his eyes for a moment and thought about everything that was to come, for both of them: endless debriefs, the mandatory postshooting internal investigation, the recovery effort the railroads were facing, the political machinations that were sure to follow as the director danced his way out of the wreckage of his scheme. Powers, God love him, had done the one thing that would fireproof both of them until they could decide what they wanted to do. He put his head down on the edge of the bed.

The covers moved and he felt her finger tips against his left temple.

"I just slaughtered him," he said. "I didn't warn him. I didn't arrest him. I didn't give him any chance at all. I shot him six times in the face."

He took a deep breath. "I wanted to do it," he whispered. "I *enjoyed* doing it. I'd do it again."

Her hand patted his head gently. "It's okay, Hush. It's okay. It won't ever happen again."

He grasped her hand and held on while she said it again and again.